the dancer

a novel

eric bernat

ISBN-13: 978-1520326504
ISBN-10: 1520326505

Cover Photograph by Greg Weglarski

Cover Design by Paul Wontorek

The unheeded warnings of 1983 and the lost opportunities of 1984 were materializing into the tragic stories of 1985. The future shock of the AIDS epidemic was arriving; the butcher's bill had come due.

Randy Shilts
And the Band Played On

I know he's going to find me, I know it was meant to be. You can change a lot of things in your life, but not your destiny.

Donna Summer

Rumor Has It

One

1985

Mindy woke up for the last time in her young life to discover she was being dragged. In the dim light she could see her own legs, her feet, a toe with pink nail polish, glossy but chipped, poking through a hole in her tights. She could tell she was moving backwards down a hallway, but didn't know why. The hall smelled familiar, a mixture of spices and dust and smoke and age, like a New York apartment was supposed to smell. She knew she'd had good memories there, only now, for some reason, she didn't know and couldn't remember what they were. She knew that she was somewhere familiar and this made her feel safe, as safe as one could while being dragged.

Maybe she had been in an accident and her legs didn't work. Maybe she was being saved. If her legs didn't work that would mean that something was wrong with her spine. If there were something wrong with her spine she wouldn't be able to walk or even stand, let alone dance.

She focused on the toe sticking out of her ripped stockings as if it had been waiting for her to come to. Of her two big toes, this one was her favorite by a wide margin. She took it as a good sign that it was this toe, not the other one, that greeted her. For years she had bent and strained this toe, banged it about, shoved it into pink satin shoes stuffed with cotton and balanced on it, and it had never let her down. Sure, she had put her other toe through the same paces, but it often ached and throbbed, demanding attention and threatening to quit like a bratty employee who required constant validation for his meager contributions to a floundering company. Had it been that toe facing her now, she might not have felt as confident.

She sent a silent message from her brain to her toe: Bend, she told it. It obeyed, curling down and away from her. Before she could feel any relief or celebrate the fact that a working spine meant more

4

dancing, less looking for a sitting-down job, the faithful toe rebelled, curling twice more on its own. Her knee jerked up, a sudden and unexpected jolt she had neither requested nor authorized. Realizing she was not in control of her own leg, Mindy felt strangely detached. She watched the spasms with the same level of concern one might experience after splashing water droplets into a pan of hot oil: first a fleeting interest in what was causing the ruckus, the science behind it, replaced quickly by a question of how long it would last, followed by the survival instinct to step away from it until it stopped. Had it not been her own leg, and if she hadn't been being dragged, she would have done exactly that.

Her mutinous leg knocked into something hard and hollow sounding, wooden. She turned her head slightly to look at the bookcase, sending a jolt of pain from her jaw down her neck to her armpits, where she became reacquainted with the pressure of two hands digging into her, pulling her. On the lowest shelf was a framed picture of him she had never seen before, handsome and smiling in a floppy hiking hat. What was his name? She couldn't find it. She reached out for the picture but her fingers were only able to graze the edge of the frame with enough strength to knock it over, face down onto the floor. Ray. His name is Ray. As quickly as she'd registered her current situation - being dragged - she forgot all about it and tried to sit up to reach the frame. She didn't see who or what knocked into the side of her head, bouncing it against and off the charming, exposed brick wall, one of the many features of Ray's apartment she'd always admired.

Run.

The demand came upon her in an instant without a why or a direction, but complete and non-negotiable, a primal instinct born from neither terror nor elation. Run. Knowledge of where she was and concern for where she was being dragged vanished. Stand. Run. Up, up. Go. Now. No - No - No. Run now Run now Run now. These urgencies screamed from inside her head, sharp staccato needs that puddled into a low, sour groan as they oozed from her lips like an infant's milky spit up.

Run. Mindy no longer knew of Ray or her toes or her spine or dancing, only run. While her broken body began to convulse on the floor, the best part of Mindy obeyed the command. She ran faster than she'd ever run before, toward something far and away. She didn't once look back as the feet she'd so recently effortlessly controlled took turns pounding in place against the hardwood floor. If she had, she might have glimpsed her attacker. But she no longer cared; she only wanted to run. Mindy's strides grew in length like a jackrabbit's, darting from side to side, bounding and soaring effortlessly over whole neighborhoods. By the time her body's back arched up in spasm like a bridge, Mindy was halfway around the world. And less than a second later, when her body's convulsions slammed the back of her head three times against the hardwood floor, Mindy was nowhere to be found.

Two

Joey handed Iris a second glass of Chardonnay. She pretended for a moment that a second glass wasn't necessary, that she didn't really want it, not really, before accepting it with a wink.

"Well all right, if you insist." She reached out her well-moisturized hands to accept the plastic cup.

Joey ran his comb through her ash-blonde hair, slicking it straight back, then all to one side, then back again. Iris took a sip, more than a sip really but less than an outright gulp; it made a louder noise going down than she would have liked. She quickly recovered by voicing her educated opinion that this really was not a bad Chardonnay, as if a less-informed person in the room had been insulting its quality and it was up to her to defend it. "Have you ever been to Napa?" she asked. Her hair was wet from the wash and she was wondering if her ears looked big when Joey tilted her head down, forcing her to focus on something besides her own reflection.

When Joey didn't respond, Iris felt a moment of indignation, resenting the fact that he was making her work so hard to keep the conversation going. Wasn't a certain amount of attention included in the price of the haircut? She quickly calmed and allowed the possibility that she had strayed outside the realm of their common interests.

Joey tilted her head back upright and she caught his eye in the mirror. He looked startled, caught off-guard, like he had forgotten that she was there. He looked down quickly, back to his work. "Your ends are looking good. You've been using that conditioner I gave you?"

"Oh Joey, that conditioner absolutely changed my life. Absolutely. And I do just what you said, a dime-sized amount for the whole head after my bath. Simply exquisite."

The wine was helping Iris relax after her unsettling morning. Before coming to the salon, she had dropped by to visit her oldest and dearest friend, Dorothy, only to find that Dorothy had a houseguest visiting, a very unlikeable woman. Iris was still recovering from their conversation. Next time she'd phone ahead to see if Dorothy had company.

"Simply exquisite," Iris repeated. She decided to try again, "Have you ever been wine tasting in Napa?"

Joey said he had not, giving Iris the chance to reminisce aloud about the trip she and her husband Walt had taken several years before. "While it was still easy for Walter to get away." Iris tried to remember if she'd ever told Joey that her second husband was in politics, working closely with the mayor on the city's waning budget allotment. She couldn't remember if she'd mentioned it before and Joey didn't ask for clarification, so she continued on about the Napa trip, how lovely it was and how much they learned about wine, that it's really an art, wine making. "You simply must go."

After a pause long enough to make Iris think the conversation was over again, Joey said yes, it was on his list and that he had been to California once, to San Francisco, and that he'd even thought of moving there at one point, but then he trailed off without offering any explanation as to why he hadn't.

"Ah, San Francisco," Iris mused before going on to quote a poem or maybe a song, she thought, likening the coldest of winters to a summer in San Francisco. "I may have mangled it," she admitted, "but it really is a clever quote."

Joey smiled as he tilted her head down again. "Oh, yeah," he nodded, "I think it was Mark Twain who said something like that."

"Is it? I was thinking Ezra Pound. Or maybe T.S. Eliot. Someone whose name begins with an E." Then she went on about how T.S. Eliot had provided the poetry that became the lyrics for the musical CATS and had Joey seen it and it was really quite good and all about cats.

Joey said yes, he had seen it a couple of years before when it had first opened on Broadway and he had enjoyed it very, very much. Iris nodded and voiced her agreement with an Mmmm that segued nicely into her humming the melody to "Memory," the finest song, in her opinion, that T.S. Eliot had ever written.

Iris's friend Dorothy Schiff had once been one of the most powerful women in the country. She'd owned and published a newspaper for which she had written a weekly editorial. Now Dorothy was in her eighties; her once sharp mind and agile body were both deteriorating at a rapid and alarming rate, a steep, icy slope of decline. Since Dolly, as her close friends called her, had sold *The Post* for an obscene amount of money a few years ago, a revolving series of once-distant relatives - both in relation and actual distance - had begun a rotation of concerned visits, sometimes staying for days or weeks at a time, hovering around the fragile millionairess, plumping pillows and speaking too cheerfully. Iris didn't know if these visits were a coordinated assault or if it were all a twisted game of musical chairs with each of them vying to be the one present when Dorothy died as if they'd then be most favored in her will.

The current guest was of no blood relation, the daughter of one of Dorothy's ex-husbands and roughly the size of one of those round cars that the Nazis had designed. While Iris had sipped tea and chatted more at than with Dolly, the ex-stepdaughter had sat nearby, blatantly eavesdropping while gobbling scones like they were celery sticks, creating a mess of crumbs which she cleaned up by pressing her index finger into her plate and moving it to her mouth, a ghastly maneuver she repeated long after there was no visible dust left to devour.

What if he's sick? the vulture had interrupted after overhearing Iris telling Dolly her afternoon plans to see her hairdresser.

Gosh, I don't know. Iris had been taken aback by the bluntness of the question as much as by the woman joining their conversation at all. *I don't know that he's* not *sick, I suppose.*

Dorothy's houseguest had used the pause after Iris's response as an opening to unload an unsolicited cautionary tale: how her own hairdresser had passed away only two months before. *So very, very sad,* the woman had lamented as she described how a strapping man who loved hats and glamour had died blind and covered with scabs. She bragged that she had single-handedly filled his hospital room with flowers. *Filled,* she'd embellished while staring off, looking very much like a person trying to work up some tears by drying their eyes out.

They don't know how it spreads, the woman had warned with an air of superiority, as if she might know more than the collective *they* of the medical community.

Well, I thought they were fairly certain it's not air-borne —

Trust me, she'd looked both ways then, as if spies from the Center for Disease Control might have infiltrated Dorothy's living room. *They don't know anything.*

I'm fairly certain that they know it's in... While searching for the proper words, Iris had lost her footing for a moment. *Fluids. Am I right? Blood. Semen.*

Fine. What if he cuts you? Accidentally. The woman had leaned in as much as she could, which wasn't very much. *What if he cuts you and sweats in it?*

Does that happen? Ever? Has that ever happened to you or anyone you've ever known at the hairdresser's? Iris had looked to Dolly for support, but Dolly had been staring off toward something that neither Iris nor the ex-stepdaughter could see, something finite and near, her teacup trembling in its delicate saucer. Iris knew from nature shows on PBS that even animals with no concept of their own mortality instinctively distanced themselves from the pack when their time was coming. She was reminded of a younger version of her dear friend Dorothy, known for her dinner parties, openly entertaining an eclectic array of guests while privately noting that the most uncouth were always the last to leave.

Who knows what could happen? the ex-stepdaughter had countered. *I never would have thought that someone would poison bottles of Tylenol, but they did. And now there's a man in California climbing into gals' windows and doing God knows what, so...* She left it at that, satisfied that her logic was tracking.

Well. Dear. I feel confident that Joey is an upstanding young man and I feel equally confident that if he were in any position to endanger any member of his clientele -

That he would do what? She cut Iris off. *Stop working?* She'd said this the way another person might say Fly to Mars. *No way.* She stabbed her finger repeatedly into her plate, seeing food where there was none. *If he stops working, it's as good as an admission of guilt and then -* she held up her finger as if it illustrated her point. *And then, it's lawsuit city.*

"I like what you're doing," Iris said to Joey. She was tired of thinking about that horrid woman.

"I know what you like," Joey replied, giving a little salute to her reflection. Iris winked back; she liked a bit of sass.

It was a nice touch, the Chardonnay. All the nicest salons were doing it these days, complimentary wine, sometimes fruit and cheese. *Complimentary*, they called it, as if you weren't paying for it, as if it weren't factored into the one hundred and twenty dollars you paid for a cut and color. She chuckled out loud at the notion. Joey hadn't given her the conditioner; she'd paid thirty dollars for it. Of all the big and little lies we collectively accept to participate in civilized society, this one was inconsequential. Most were inconsequential.

For instance, Iris routinely said 'I love you' to her husband, Walt. All the time, she said it, but in the way someone on a CB radio said '10-4'.

Have a good day, dear. Love you.
All right then, I'll see you when you get home. Love you.
I'm going to read in bed, goodnight, love you.

Did she ever say it while gazing into his eyes? No. Had she ever? No. There was genuine fondness there and she was grateful for the lifestyle his job and position afforded them. He was handsome enough and they were able to spend time together in an enjoyable way. She liked him and she knew he felt the same. They were two people who understood the finiteness of a budget. *There's only so much*, Walt would often say about his day at the office allotting funds to a variety of city programs. *The good ones get by with what they're given.* Iris liked her husband and she loved her life.

She liked art and theatre and pretending to watch the ballet. She liked this Chardonnay and she liked toying with the idea of redecorating the living room with mirrors and all-white furniture, a look that was very *au courant.* She loved that, at 54 years old, she could still tell people she was in her forties and get away with it. She liked the warm feeling the wine was giving her and the way it loosened up her thoughts like this. She loved the way Joey was cutting wispy fringe of varied lengths all around her face, very haphazard, as if she were a woman without a care in the world.

Iris studied Joey in the mirror as he worked, his eyes sharp and focused, maybe a little bloodshot. He did look thin, but then again he'd looked thin since she'd known him. He was thin. What else was a thin man supposed to look like? Was he thinner than the last time she'd seen him? Perhaps, perhaps not. He was angular and precise as if his bone structure was something he was doing intentionally.

Iris watched as Joey rubbed his hands together with a product that she'd surely buy on her way out. He pulled his hands through her hair quickly over and over again, pulling pieces together, creating cohesive wisps and curls that weren't there before. She watched closely so she could recreate the look on her own.

Waiting for her credit card to be processed, Iris declined a third refill of chardonnay from the Asian girl with pink hair; two glasses was plenty and she still had a little bit left. She raised her cup toward the girl's hair and said "That's fun" and really meant it. It was 1985, for God's sake! Why not? Young people these days were finding such fun, creative ways to express themselves. She took a twenty-dollar bill from her wallet and folded it in half and then in half again as she walked back to Joey's station.

Joey was sitting at his station as she approached from behind, like he was waiting to get his own hair done. It occurred to Iris that the image would make a compelling photograph: The Stylist Awaits a Makeover From Himself.

He stood and made a face that looked to Iris like that of a person who had nothing to smile about, yet was attempting, nevertheless, to smile. When she slipped the folded bill into his hand he looked first at her shoulder, then her shoes, then her hair and then her eyes. And in that moment she saw the same look that she'd seen in her dear friend's eyes earlier that day, the look of someone done with this world and ready for the next.

It wasn't that Iris didn't care; she did care, on some level. Of course she cared. But she couldn't allow herself to care more than she cared about any of the world's atrocities. And there was so much to care about if you let yourself. There was South America, the Middle East. Crack cocaine and the teenage violent criminal explosion. There were serial killers and world hunger and video games. It was just politics and everyone had a emotional budget; it was self-preservation, actually, to not care too much. She did care, but the fact was that men like Joey were so damned good at finding ways to die. Instead of feeling sad about it, Iris felt unapologetically alive.

She held his hand in both of hers. "I've made another appointment for three weeks from today." She leaned in for his cheek.

Trust me. They don't know anything.

She re-calibrated and kissed the air near his ear instead while patting him on the wrist. Joey thanked her, saying he would see her in three weeks and Iris said yes as if nothing at all was wrong in the world. She knew there was a very real chance that she'd never see Joey again. She preferred the lie, but she also accepted the truth. The necessity of distance was a lesson she'd learned long ago. One could make a career of shaking fists at the sky over the unfairness of life, or accept that fairness was a concept not found in nature. Rainbows and infatuation lasted only long enough to be glimpsed, and even then only from certain angles, while crocodiles and grudges lived on and on and on.

And so would Iris.

Three

GOD HAS A PLAN FOR ME

Joey contemplated the sign that the man on the subway platform wore around his neck. Both of the man's arms were gone, pinched off at two tapered points just above where his elbows would be if they were still there. The message was printed in block letters on a piece of poster board. He was bare-chested beneath the sign, defiant and unapologetic. Heroic.

Joey was caught off guard by the stark display of the perseverance of human spirit in the face of the most brutal atrocities, stopped in his tracks by the man's peaceful acceptance. For someone who'd been spending a lot of time lately wondering if life had any meaning, it felt personal, as if everything in the world had been carefully choreographed to lead Joey to this platform to see this man today. He had an impulse to give the man everything he owned. Instead, he pulled a couple of crumpled singles out of his pocket.

"Hi. Where… where should I put it?" Joey looked around at the man's feet for a box or coffee can.

"Just put it in my pocket." The man seemed more annoyed than appreciative. He shouldn't be required to grovel, but a smile wouldn't have killed him. Joey started for the other man's pocket, then stopped.

"How will you get it out?"

"Don't worry about it, man. Just put it in there." The man's annoyance shifted to confrontation. He didn't seem at all soothed by the balm of his savior's design the way his sign suggested.

But Joey was worried about it. How would he get the money out? How did he get dressed? How did he eat? How did he hand the cashier the money for the poster board? How did he make the sign? Joey started to smile as he returned to his senses. While the jury was still out on whether God had a plan for this man, it was pretty clear that someone among his friends or family did.

Shit, Joey thought. I almost fell for it. The man who only seconds before had looked like a hero suddenly looked like an idiot for allowing himself to be displayed like this.

"I'm sorry. I changed my mind." Joey turned away quickly; he didn't want the man to think he was laughing at him. Joey was laughing at himself, his own gullible sentimentality. Over the rumble of the train approaching the station, Joey heard the armless harbinger yell after him.

"Fuck you, candy-ass faggot."

———

Joey lay sideways in the living room of his darkened east-side apartment, his body draped across the arms of a reclining chair as if he'd been dropped from several stories above. He'd turned the chair to face the window, away from the cardboard boxes behind him, most of them exactly where he'd dropped them a month ago when he'd moved in. A record played on the stereo. Joey had set the needle on the turntable to go back to the beginning on its own so he wouldn't have to get up to do it himself. These were not days of action.

In the previous month, Joey had used surprisingly little of the stuff he'd moved. The need for a specific item had presented maybe three occasions to dig. As a result, several of the boxes had been partially unpacked, their contents spread on the floor beside them, nowhere near properly put away. The overall effect was one of chaos and indecision. From a snapshot it would have been impossible to tell whether Joey was coming or going, moving out or moving in.

He'd stripped down to his underwear in an effort to combat the heat of an un-airconditioned fifth floor apartment in July. A lazy fan oscillated back and forth from the windowsill; a red plastic tumbler half-filled with ice and scotch left a cold circle of condensation on his sternum. The liquor warmed his throat and burned his empty stomach, reminding him of the bag of groceries in the refrigerator. The groceries reminded him that several days ago he'd been invited to a dinner party by a friend he hadn't seen in months. He'd deliberately forgotten to call back to say that he couldn't make it. Joey didn't trust himself lately in social situations and had consequently developed a small clutch of techniques for politely escaping them.

There were other simple tasks that Joey had been having trouble with as of late: remembering to eat, and deciding what, exactly, to eat. Gauging what to chat about politely at work and where to look while a client fished money out of her purse to tip him. Remembering to buy essentials like shampoo when he worked at a place that sold it. Assessing whether to take the subway or walk, when and where to cross the street. Last Sunday he'd stood on a corner for a good ten minutes while the light changed from green to red to green to red, unable to make a decision and finally ending up back in bed for the day.

The problem at the grocery store was that Joey hadn't been hungry. Without any cravings, he'd been unable to picture what might make a lovely meal, like an omelet. Instead of shopping with intention, he'd decided to mimic people who looked like they knew what they were doing. A pretty young mother with a well-behaved child put a dozen chicken legs in her cart, so Joey did the same. It wasn't until the two-block walk home that he'd realized that nothing went together: a two pound bag of rice, a family-sized jar of meat sauce, the chicken legs and two large, hard tomatoes. Bananas, tea, vanilla cookies and Sprite. He'd stuffed the whole bag into the fridge and poured himself a drink.

From where he was draped in the recliner, he could see into the bedroom window of an apartment in the building next door. He could also see into the bedroom window of the apartment directly above the one across from him and, if he stood, the one below it as well. Since moving in, Joey had given each window an appropriate amount of neighborly assessment for a neighbor who had no intention of introducing himself. The lights in the apartment directly across from his were sometimes on and sometimes off, but all behind curtains, all the time. The apartment above the one directly across from him had plants that hung from the ceiling in macramé slings. The apartment below the one directly across from him had always been dark until the night before when Joey had seen a man pacing from room to room, first dressed, then shirtless, then naked. It was this window that he watched now.

As activities went, Joey knew that watching a window below barely qualified. He still had all the unpacking to do, cleaning, organizing. He rationalized that tonight's real activity, as it were, was deliberate chore avoidance rather than window watching. Facing the boxes would have made that avoidance trickier, so facing the window was more about practicality than anything else. He wasn't actually lying around, drinking alone, watching a dark window; that would be ridiculous. After all, he'd seen naked men before, plenty of them. He could go out right now to the baths or even the gym for that matter and see as many naked men as he could stomach. He could see much more than that, see and do much more. In spite of everything there were still, for now at least, plenty of places and plenty of men. So go, Joey told himself. He took a gulp from the tumbler of Scotch and lit a cigarette.

After work, but before the grocery store, Joey had attended a memorial service for his sort-of friend Milton. He and Milt had dated briefly in '77, an affair that ended in mutual ambivalence which allowed them to stay sort-of friends, the kind that have lunch twice a year. At the service, Joey had listened from his seat in the back row while an enraged speaker addressed the captive audience.

These are dark days. Young men are dying, he'd said, *by the thousands. Men like us are dying, and no one is talking about it. No one is doing anything.* Meanwhile, a handful of people had died from eating poisoned headache medicine and the story had been on the front page of every national newspaper for weeks. Joey agreed with the speaker's facts but was surprised by his outrage. When, Joey thought, had the world ever cared whether men like us lived or died? If these were indeed dark days, when had they ever been light? These days were just like all the

17

other days. "What an asshole," Joey said out loud to no one in his apartment, then laughed, wondering if he was talking about the speaker or himself for leaving before the end of the memorial.

Joey glanced at his boxes. He knew from experience that even a small New York apartment, previously lived in by one adult male, like Milt for instance, could take several days to deal with. Books, magazines, video and cassette tapes, could be put out on the sidewalk for strangers to take. Furniture could be claimed by friends or donated to charity. Items of any sentimental or artistic value divvied up among those closest. Families had to be contacted. Sometimes the families didn't call back.

Joey thought of his client that afternoon, casually offering the entire region of Napa like a chocolate truffle held in her palm. *You simply must go,* she'd proclaimed in the way that people with a lot of money often make absurd suggestions to people with less money. As if people with less money didn't travel the world or collect art or experience real cashmere for some secondary reason besides the obvious. As if perhaps Joey found the idea decadent or gauche, or maybe the option might not ever occur to him on his own. The cigarette in his hand burned down to his fingertips. He sat up and brushed the ashes on his stomach onto the floor. He stood up and swallowed the inch of drink left in his cup, thinned by melted ice; it didn't taste like anything. When he bent to pick up the ashtray, he saw that the light was on. Down there. The light was on in the apartment below the one directly across from him.

Joey turned and tripped over a box, almost falling, but turned it into a hop at the last second. It was much darker than he'd thought, only a few steps away from the light of the window and his eyes needed a bit of time to adjust. Joey used his leg like a blind person uses a cane, tapping it around in front of him to find a path for a few steps until he'd cleared the boxes and made it down the hall, past his kitchen and his bathroom. From his bedroom window, Joey looked down and across. There was a light, dim but on, and after a moment the man walked by his living room window then headed down the hall like Joey had just done. Joey waited for several minutes, standing in his underwear with a full ashtray in one hand and an empty tumbler in the other. He felt like a ghost looking down from above only able to observe; his presence, at best, merely suspected by the living. He wondered if it had already happened, if he'd actually already died.

There. Back in the window the man was looking out, half hidden like Joey was. They were practically facing each other. The man ran his hand over his chest and down to his belt where it paused then moved again, undoing the buckle opening his pants. Joey put the ashtray and plastic tumbler on the windowsill and reached his hands into his underwear and pushed them down to his knees. Suddenly, everything about the situation simultaneously aroused and infuriated Joey: the windows, their separation, the man's nearness and distance.

"Come on man," Joey whispered. "Look at me." But the man below did not.

Joey reached his arm along the wall until it knocked into the tall, modern floor lamp. The lamp wobbled on its cheap base when his arm bumped it; it was destined for the trash but Joey hadn't thrown it away. His fingers found the switch and turned it once, then again, and again, making it as bright as it could.

"Look at me," he said a little louder, but the man below did not.

These were not days of eating in and planning for leftovers. They were not days of quitting smoking or vowing not to drink alone.

Joey banged his palm against the windowpane. "Look - " he called out before his jagged breathing cut his voice off. These were days of acceptance that the slightest cough could mean that your lungs were beginning to drown in their own fluid. These were days of fixating on bruises, bug bites and birthmarks. These were days when unpacking into your new apartment just meant more work for someone else in the near future. Joey stood naked in his window, erect and fully exposed, tugging on himself in the same rhythm as the stranger below. "Please." His voice sounded like someone else's. "Please."

It wasn't the boxes that Joey was really avoiding.

I am dying.

"Come on, look at me."

Please, I am dying.

"Fuck fuck fuck fuck - "

Look at me. Touch me.

"Look."

Please.

But the man did not.

———

Someone else did, though Joey couldn't say whom for sure. He could only say that half an hour later there was an urgent pounding on his front door, followed by a demand for him to open up while Joey hurriedly pulled on a pair of jeans.

There were two uniformed policemen on the other side of the door, the pair of them in the doorway itself and somehow then inside his apartment where they took in the state of disarray in silent judgment when he hadn't even invited them in.

A thick book of what looked like blank parking tickets, something about indecent exposure. Joey tried to appear confused and innocent while motioning toward the bathroom, offering the shower as a plausible defense for his behavior. The ticket, torn from the book, was pressed into Joey's chest before it floated to the floor. It looked daunting and garish and, yes, slightly pathetic. But also colorful and rebellious, the way dirty confetti littered around cigarette butts and empty beer cans proved there'd recently been a big, big party. The needle came to the record's end, lifted itself and went back to the beginning as if it were a fresh start, but the preset grooves in the wax played the same songs over again.

Four

"This just in: I'm going crazy."

Joey was sitting across from his best friend Aggie in a coffee shop that smelled of bacon grease and waffles. They hadn't seen each other for two weeks.

"They told me yesterday. I'm going to go crazy and I don't have a say in the matter."

"Crazy?" Joey's voice sounded hoarse.

"Yup. Batshit crazy." As a successful actress on a popular daytime soap opera, Aggie had issues with being seen; she wore large sunglasses indoors that were supposed to act as a disguise but instead made everyone look at her twice. Joey had known her since she worked at Capezio.

"I'm also going to murder someone." Aggie unconsciously rearranged the few items on the small table between them: a small metal creamer, a sticky sugar caddy, and a single daisy wilting in a cheap glass vase like a depressed person who'd been told to liven up a party. She pushed each object closer to Joey then picked up the daisy, smelled it, made a face of disgust and placed it as close to Joey as possible. An orange-haired waitress with a limp refilled the coffees in front of them.

"You kids ready to order?" It was the second time she'd asked.

Aggie smiled and tilted her head as she pushed her sunglasses up onto the top of her head. "Not yet." Aggie knew her angles and showed her face like it was a gift. "Do you have any specials?" Aggie asked as if this would be fun for all of them.

"I think we're just having coffee," Joey clarified, knowing that Aggie wouldn't eat. "Thanks, though."

The waitress ignored Joey and stared at Aggie for a long moment, squinting and slack-jawed as if frozen in the worst picture that had ever been taken of her. Then she grunted and limped away.

Aggie turned back to Joey. "That was a little weird, wasn't it?"

Joey breathed in the burnt smelling coffee. "She calls everyone kid. It's part of her shtick. If she doesn't like you she calls you a ham, but not to your face."

"Who does she call you a ham to?"

"The cashier."

Aggie turned to look at the old Greek man behind the cash register by the door. "How many times have you been here?"

Joey shrugged. "Three."

"Anyway, as I was saying," Aggie re-gathered her steam, "I'm apparently going to murder someone and then have an emotional breakdown. Or the other way around. It hasn't been written yet but I've been given a heads-up." She lightened her coffee with milk.

"Oh. Well that's cool." Joey was unsure whether coffee was helping or hurting his hangover. The creamer was just far enough out of his reach that the effort it would take to reach it felt insurmountable. He wanted to be home in bed but Aggie wouldn't let him beg off their plans. *I'll come to you*, she'd said, making it sound more generous than it was since she only lived over by Lincoln Center.

Aggie shrugged. "Yeah. Maybe cool, but going crazy isn't always as good as it sounds. It could mean they want me off the show. Of course it could also mean an Emmy nomination, so..." she trailed off and sipped her coffee.

Joey nodded in agreement.

Aggie stretched. "Oh my my my I don't know why I can't wake up today, I slept for nine hours!" She put her sunglasses on the table and reached in her purse for lip-gloss. "What did you do last night?"

"Not much." Joey lifted his mug of coffee up to his mouth and put it down without drinking it.

"You go out?" In the three months since Henry died, Aggie seemed to ask this every time she and Joey talked or got together. Joey reddened and shook his head no.

"Anyway," Aggie continued, "the only person I know who is crazy is my brother-in-law's mother."

"Who, Peter?" He wasn't sure why Aggie was now talking about people he'd met more than a few times as if he'd never heard of them before. Perhaps she thought his brain wasn't capable of keeping up.

"Right. Peter." Aggie applied gloss to her lips between each word.

"Diane's husband: Peter."

"Right. Peter."

"Peter and Diane, whose house I've been to several times."

"Right. PETER. What's your point?"

"Just that, you know. I do know who Diane and Peter are." Joey even knew that, while they still pretended to, Aggie and her sister Diane hadn't gotten along for years. He knew that Diane thought this was because Aggie was jealous of her having a husband, which was true, and Aggie thought Diane was jealous of her job as a television actress, which was also true.

"I didn't say you didn't."

"Okay, well then just say Peter's mother."

"Fine, sorry. Peter's mother."

"And diners don't have specials."

Aggie squinted at him. "Yes, they do."

"Not at brunch."

Aggie looked at the exit, then at her watch, then took a sip of her coffee before looking back at Joey.

"What about her?"

"Her who?"

"Peter's mother."

"I'm spending Wednesday afternoon with her. With Peter's mother."

"Oh?" His flares of unjustified rage were one of the reasons Joey didn't trust himself in social situations.

"I volunteered, as an anniversary present to them, to Peter. And Diane."

"That's nice of you." Joey was embarrassed by his outburst.

23

"Well. Ever since she moved in with them, Diane's been complaining that she and Peter never get to do anything alone together anymore. So I thought, if they could go to a matinee and dinner while I hang out with Alice, that's her name, Alice…" she trailed off again, probably waiting to see if Joey was going to get upset again. He did not. "Anyway, I'm not filming that day so it's no big deal. That kind of thing can put a lot of strain on a marriage." Aggie had never been married.

"You're a good sister." Joey had a passing instinct to reach across the small table to take her hand, but his stayed instead on his mug.

Aggie lit up at the compliment with an expression she'd perfected by the age of eight when she'd won a child-modeling contest. Her family had gotten to go on a cruise. "Anyway," she continued, "I'm almost positive that Brian is gay." Aggie's expression changed to non-judgmental suspicion.

"Oh really?" This time, Joey didn't know who Brian was. He played along, hoping that he'd catch up soon.

"Yes. In fact I'm sure of it. You'd be sure too. Trust me. Oh, can we have some more coffee, hon?"

"This here's decaf." The waitress held up a pot with an orange handle that matched her hair as she passed.

"Sure. I'm sure I would. Wow." Joey flipped through a mental Rolodex of people he'd heard Aggie talk about but had never met. Most were from her show. He came up blank. "That's pretty…" He left it unsaid, what Brian being gay might mean to him.

"Yeah. It means he will *love* me!" Aggie looked devilish but pristine. Joey could imagine a casting director lobbing directions at her like Precocious but Not Bratty or Slutty but Monogamous and Aggie handling each one with ease. Had she been in his position last night, she could have handled Confused and Innocent with both hands tied behind her back.

"You have plans this weekend?"

"I'm not sure," Joey lied. "I might. What's going on?"

24

"Well, nothing yet. But I was thinking we should get a group together."

"A group?"

"Yeah. You know. Carey and Josh and Elise. Maybe Pam and Roger?" Aggie pursed her lips to the side like a pre-teen sleuth while she thought. "Eric and Downey. Brian D, if he's not on the Island. It's been light years since we've all gotten together. We can do it at my place. Or, like, cheap Chinese. Who gives a fuck, right? The important thing is that we'd all be together again. Doesn't that sound fun?"

"Sure." Joey raised his eyebrows in what he hoped looked like enthusiasm. What it sounded like was actually pretty abstract, a group of people he hadn't talked to in ages acting like they all belonged together still.

"I think it would be a blast."

Joey knew what Aggie was doing by trying to get him out of the house. She thought it was time for him to move on from Henry's death. Joey had the capacity to make good money, when he actually worked. In the last year, he'd taken more time off than he'd worked. The suggestion of cheap Chinese was aimed directly at him; Aggie had money to burn.

The waitress sloshed coffee into each of their mugs and slapped their check face down on their table without missing a limp.

"Turn and burn," Aggie commented as she reached for the tab. "No parking on the dance floor." She leaned in closer to Joey, "At least not for hams."

It seemed like a lifetime ago even though it wasn't even a decade, when Joey had spent every weekend with Aggie. Dancing and drinking and talking about everyone and everything they came across until they fell asleep in the same bed. Aggie spent her days selling leotards and making up excuses to run out to auditions. Joey would style her hair in his kitchen to specifically match whatever outfit she had put together for their night on the town.

Aggie pulled a five-dollar bill out of her wallet and put it on top of the check. "This place bums me out," she said.

Joey nodded in agreement.

Things were different now; now they got together every three or four weeks to talk about anything except how much everything had changed. It wasn't really their fault; they'd just grown apart. Once she had been able to afford him, Aggie had stopped asking Joey to cut her hair. He no longer even pretended to watch her show on television. She no longer confided in him how much she wished someone would marry her, and he didn't feel like he could tell her that he had gotten so drunk alone last night that he'd exposed himself in his bedroom window and now had a file somewhere in a police station.

"Aggie?"

"Hm?"

"Who's Brian?"

"My nephew. Diane and Peter's - "

"Oh, right. Brian," Joey remembered. "Isn't he, like, six?"

"He's fourteen. And a total homo. Poor Diane has no idea. She uses, like every euphemism in the book: sensitive, artistic... lithe."

Joey laughed.

"I'm not kidding. She called him lithe."

"Wow."

Aggie's eyes sparkled. Mischievous and protective. "Let's get the fuck out of here. You gonna take me up and show me the new apartment?"

Joey had a sudden psychic flash to the future: Aggie in a tasteful but alluring black dress, surrounded by and newly in charge of the unpacked clutter in his new apartment, devastated but businesslike.

"I don't know." He sighed and felt dizzy from even the slight motion this caused. He craved stillness. "I might have to move again."

Five

Joey awoke from his nap feeling tired. He'd come home alone after agreeing to consider Aggie's dinner party plan. He'd fallen immediately into a deep sleep, despite his breakfast of caffeine. He showered, brushed his teeth, put on some clean clothes, and walked into his living room to face the boxes. They were not going to go away on their own.

Two months ago, Joey's sort-of friend Milt, whose memorial service Joey had walked out of, had been released from the hospital. Milt had been upbeat, almost manic with enthusiasm about the business he was starting for himself as a Personal Organizer and De-clutterer. He'd handed Joey a stack of brightly colored flyers advertising his new venture to hand out in coffee shops and bookstores. Joey wondered, at the time, if Milt planned to charge by the hour or the bulk of the mess, but never asked for clarification, worried that it would be mistaken for an intention to hire him. Milt described his new venture as a real turning point while white foamy spit collected in the corners of his dry, cracked mouth. He was dead two weeks later.

Now, standing over his boxes, Joey imagined Milt there, encouraging him to pick up one item, just one, randomly out of any of the boxes left to unpack. It didn't matter what, since it all had to be dealt with. Joey took imaginary Milt's advice, opened a box at random and pulled out the first thing he touched: a sleek Braun coffee maker.

Excellent work, Milt said. *Now is that something that you want to keep or something that you want to give away?* He looked at Joey as if he knew what the right answer was but if asked would say that there was no right answer. Milt would have made his money by making his clients feel one step behind.

The coffee maker worked perfectly well. Joey didn't know exactly how much it cost because Henry had bought it, but it probably wasn't cheap. "Keep," he said out loud to no one but Milt. Definitely keep. Henry had brought it home and put Joey's Mr. Coffee out on the curb without asking.

All right then, Milt said without judgment, now you just have to find a space for it in the kitchen, preferably near an outlet. Joey's new apartment was a decent size, but the kitchen was small and had a serious shortage of electrical outlets, which had been a non-issue until now, since he never cooked. This reminded him of the bag of groceries in the fridge which made him think maybe he should be making dinner and dealing with the boxes later. Milt pointed out that Joey was getting distracted and Joey argued, *No, I am not getting distracted, the groceries in the fridge cost over thirty dollars and if they go bad then it's just like throwing money in the trash. Would you throw away thirty dollars, Milton? Would you?*

Imaginary Milt patiently asked Joey not to raise his inner voice. He pointed out that he was here to help and he'd only been doing the job that Joey had hired him to do. At that point, Joey put the coffee maker down where he stood, went into the kitchen and poured a slug of scotch. Resurrecting dead people for the sole purpose of bickering with them seemed like as good a reason as any to have a drink. He glanced out his kitchen window down at the windows of the apartment below the one directly across from him. They were dark. Just as well: Joey had a lot of work to do.

He'd keep the coffee maker. It made sense economically. *Of course it does*, dead Milt agreed entering from the other room. *You spend a lot of money on coffee and this would save you some of that.* As Joey turned back to the boxes, he saw a light go on in the apartment that he'd been eyeing and froze. Milt disappeared. Joey finished what was in his glass and reached for the bottle and his cigarettes. Planning for one's own probably imminent death, it turned out, was much less fun than it sounded.

———

The sun was setting. Joey was standing on the sidewalk, smoking a cigarette and watching the door of the building next to his;

their facades were identical. He ignored the people walking by him and they ignored him, which made him feel like a phantom, as if he and the world were practicing getting along without each other and discovering they were both very good at it.

To Joey, the word 'spying' implied hiding somewhere while watching someone who had every reason to assume his privacy. Since his neighbor had the option of closing his curtains or lowering his lights and had chosen not to, Joey felt that what he'd been doing for the past few hours wasn't spying so much as exercising his right to utilize his senses, like stopping to smell honeysuckle or humming along to background music in an elevator. It was simply a matter of being consciously aware of his surroundings. Joey had gotten adept at following the other man's movements as well as imagining his activities when he stepped out of Joey's view. About a half hour ago, the man had stripped down in the bedroom before going into the bathroom and then the shower. He had stayed in the shower for a long time during which Joey had stood in his kitchen watching the steam escape through his neighbor's window into the hot evening.

Finally he'd come back into the bedroom and dressed with what Joey thought looked like purpose. Realizing that he was running low on cigarettes, Joey decided it might be a good time to go out. He'd slipped on a pair of sneakers and snuck past the boxes, down the stairs to the street where he now waited. And just when he thought maybe he'd been mistaken, the man Joey now recognized as his neighbor emerged, his head bowed as he took the four steps down to the sidewalk two at a time. He turned left toward First Avenue at a pace closer to a jog than a walk, carrying a sweatshirt and a yellow plastic bag in the same hand. Joey flicked his cigarette into the curb and started to follow, trying to keep up without actually running, an awkward pace usually reserved for women in knee-length pencil skirts. Then, without warning, his neighbor turned around and doubled back toward Joey.

Joey froze, but as the familiar stranger strode toward him without any hint of consideration, Joey remembered that the familiarity only went one way, that tonight he was a ghost. He looked as the man passed him. He was shorter than Joey thought he would be, thinner too. His shoulders were broad but he was more defined and less bulky than he had appeared in the window. His dark hair, parted down the middle and still wet from the shower, hung in his face. He passed Joey, almost brushing shoulders, after having slowed to a pace closer to a walk than a jog. Joey turned and followed a few steps behind.

Joey trailed him to Second where he turned right and ducked into a cramped café, a few small tables with hard metal chairs. Joey followed him inside and got in line behind him, standing close enough that if he leaned only slightly forward he could have touched the tip of his nose to the vertebra that protruded like a knuckle at the top of his neighbor's back. Joey looked slightly above this spot where the man's coarse dark hair gradually changed texture, softening and lightening as it spilled over from his hairline onto his neck. He was reminded of the men's grooming portion of cosmetology school, straight razors and hot shaves on rough chins and soft lips. When his neighbor moved his arm to pull his wallet from his back pocket, Joey was able to glimpse the dark hair under his arm and a trickle of sweat sliding down his chest, disappearing beneath his white tank top toward his nipple. He stepped forward and mumbled something that sounded like "Gimme a medium coffee" before stepping to the left, leaving Joey face to face with an acne-ridden youth with a stud in his left ear asking what he could get for him.

The question caught Joey off guard and he pretended to study the menu behind the kid's head. The woman behind Joey exhaled audibly so Joey stepped aside to allow her to order, an offer she interpreted as rudeness rather than courtesy, yet accepted anyway. She paid and stepped away and another person stepped forward, while Joey continued to pretend to contemplate a menu of items he didn't want. A third person stepped ahead of him and he realized with relief that he was a ghost again; nobody was noticing his charade of participation. He turned and walked out of the café and looked north up the avenue for the object of his pursuit, trying to remember what he wanted from this stranger. Joey spotting him almost a block away, jeans and white tank top, carrying the sweatshirt and paper cup of coffee and making good time among the strolling couples.

As handsome as the man was, Joey suddenly had no more interest in following him. The stark realization of why hit him like a van-sized marshmallow, shocking for a moment, but then comforting. It was a realization that allowed everything recently nagging and unsaid to click instantaneously into place in the most freeing way. It was this: Joey no longer belonged in the world. There was a time when he did, when he'd mattered, and that time had simply passed. It wasn't that Joey was like a ghost; it was that he *was* a ghost. He and the world were not practicing getting by without each other, they had both actually already moved on. His exhaustion, he suddenly understood, was not from the thought of death but rather the waiting around for it to occur. Dying, purely based on how commonly it happened, couldn't possibly be a difficult task to accomplish in and of itself. It was all the trying to figure out what to do in the meantime that wore the body out. It was trying to avoid looking at death as it sat next to you and took your hand that dried the eyes. It was handing out business cards and talking too loudly about your renewed zest that tired the voice. And so, Joey made a decision.

The decision was not an I'll-show-you-world tantrum, nor was it detached indifference the way a toddler moves from one toy to another without indicating a preference. It was not a petulant, existentialist determination to prove there were no real connections, that life was merely a jumble of car crashes, coitus, and the food chain. Joey felt there actually were connections. On his first date with Henry, they'd gone to a movie then talked for a long time on the street afterwards. They'd kissed goodnight and Joey had gone home to bed, tossing and turning and grinning himself to sleep. Real connections existed, just no longer for Joey. It was why he could not sit through a memorial service or unpack a bag of groceries or picture a dinner party or focus on a conversation or open a book or sit through a play or put on a record or actually actually actually ever touch another living person ever again.

It was not a sad or an angry decision. It was just Joey and the world standing side by side on the street trying to decide if a hug or a handshake would be more awkward and settling for a light chuck under the chin. A lumbering city bus moved up the avenue, picking up speed to make it through the light.

We had some times, didn't we? Milt was beside him again.

As decisions went, Joey had faced harder. Like deciding to stay in New York instead of taking Henry to San Francisco where everyone said the hospitals were better.

We sure did. We had some very good times.

Deciding where to hold Henry's memorial service, who would say what and what to do with the ashes.

Milt took Joey's hand and together they eyed the approaching bus.

One step, urged Milt. *One little step to oblivion.* Milt let go of Joey's hand, turned his back to the street and took the Nestea plunge. The bus passed without slowing. There was no sound of impact. From the asphalt, Milt slowly opened his eyes to find Joey still very much alive as the bus ambled lazily away.

Joey registered Milt's disappointment. *Oh come on,* he said to Milt. *I'm not looking to get dragged and dismembered over a quarter mile of city street.*

Oh, said Milt. *I misunderstood.*

"Relax," Joey said aloud. "I'll make an elegant, painless exit very soon." He squinted into what might be one of his last sunsets if he got his shit together quick enough. "I just have some loose ends to tie up."

Six

"We don't want any porno."

The woman working in the Salvation Army had made a decision, or a string of decisions, about Joey.

"I know that," Joey answered even though he didn't. "It's just clothes. Not 'just clothes' as in old shit that nobody wants, there's a lot of pretty new stuff in here, good stuff." He looked around conspiratorially. "I won't tell anyone if you want to go through it yourself first, get first dibs."

She stared at him, uncharmed. "Put it on the scale." Joey hefted the large plastic bag at his feet. The needle sprung forward clockwise, then back, then forward again before timidly settling on fifty-seven pounds.

Joey had intended on doing a more thoughtful version of this chore before he'd moved, considering each article of clothing with care, inspecting them for stains or irregularities but had been unable to do this at the time. This morning he'd awoken with an energy he hadn't felt in a long time and attacked six of the boxes, dumping their contents without discrimination into one extra large, heavy-duty Glad trash bag. He'd pulled the bag to the elevator with the coffee maker under his other arm and put the three of them into a cab where he'd rolled down the window to feel the morning summer breeze. As they'd sailed downtown through surprisingly light Monday morning traffic Joey had thought about bridges and jumping off them before deciding that the idea of not having his body found for days or weeks or maybe ever was not preferable. Plus it would probably hurt. He'd crossed Bridges off his list of ways to die. He'd felt good; he'd felt fifty-seven pounds lighter.

The woman looked at the scale then back at him. "Fifty-five pounds."

Joey corrected her. "It's actually fifty-seven pounds."

She, in turn, corrected Joey. "Actually it's fifty-five pounds because we round to the nearest five pounds."

"Well, why don't you just call it fifty pounds then? Or four pounds?"

"Well, sir, if we rounded to the nearest ten pounds I would say that this is sixty pounds since fifty-seven is closer to sixty than it is to fifty. That's how math works. I didn't make it up."

Joey inwardly conceded her point, that she probably hadn't invented math. He knew he should let it go. "I'm just saying that we have numbers and words for a reason. What's the use of having them if we don't assign them to what they actually are? Why not call this 'Toughie's red thumbtacks' instead of 'fifty-seven pounds of used clothes' if none of it matters?"

"It's Monday morning, mister. I gotta do this shit all week long. Do you want a receipt?" She made a pad of receipts and a pen appear as heavy as dumbbells as she lifted them to demonstrate the amount of resentful effort this would take on her part.

Joey considered reminding her that ever since disco, black women and gay men were supposed to get along. They were supposed to cheer each other on and have playful dance-offs, not belittle each other's accomplishments. He smiled and said no, he did not need a receipt.

"If you don't want a receipt," she said, "then why do you care what stupid weight I call it?" She held out her hands for the coffee maker tucked under his arm. "Gimme that."

Joey had always cared what strangers thought of him, even ones who were indifferent or blatantly disliked him. While he had other plans for the coffee maker, he almost handed it over lest she think he was the type of person who'd stoop to using charity as a weapon before realizing he no longer cared what anyone else thought of him. He looked her squarely in the eyes and said, "I have a good idea, why don't you go fuck yourself?"

34

The woman's mouth split into a dazzling smile and she made a high noise that went Hoooooo and then broke into genuine laughter. "Well fuck you too!" She chuckled approvingly as Joey turned sharply on his heel and walked away.

Outside, Joey turned and headed up the avenue. He needed to be on foot for the next task on his agenda. He had a hunch that what he was looking for would be easier to find on the less-traveled side streets rather than the busier avenues, so he inched his way uptown, crisscrossing between First and Second Avenues every two or three blocks. He thought about ways to die. A bullet to the head seemed chancy, a good way to end up in a city hospital as aware as a radish. Something heroic, on the other hand - like jumping in front of a bullet headed for an orphan - sounded more appealing. But waiting for such an opportunity to naturally occur would most likely take longer than Joey wanted to wait, and orchestrating it would take more planning than he was willing to do.

He shifted the coffee maker to his other hip. He remembered when Henry had brought it home and how he had sipped from his mug and sighed, *Can't you taste the difference?* Joey had lied and said yes he could tell, this was so much better. He liked that Henry liked it, so maybe it was better. When they first moved in together, Joey had been fascinated by everything Henry owned. It all held an erotic charge and he was almost jealous of the time his things got to spend with him. Henry's socks caressed Henry's feet and his tee shirts rubbed his chest and stomach and armpits. His cologne lingered on his neck and his forks touched his tongue, and his couch felt his warmth, held his weight.

Several blocks from his house, he found what he'd been looking for. There had been other candidates along the way, but he'd been dissatisfied with each of them for one reason or another; either the size, color or overall shape had been not quite what he was picturing. He'd wanted the instant recognition a classic look provided, so he'd held out and it had been worth it. In the dirt surrounding a tree on East 49th Street, Joey found the most quintessential pile of dog shit

35

he had ever seen; the collective clump was a rich chocolate brown with strains of mahogany in the sunlight. If he could recreate this color in a dye bottle, Joey would have some very happy clients. The pile didn't appear to be so fresh as to have any warmth to it, but neither had it been allowed to sit long enough to dry out and lose any of its sheen. Joey covered his hand with the plastic bag he had swiped from the Salvation Army and scooped up the whole mess, careful not too get too much dirt along with it, then slipped the bag inside out and tied it loosely, a knot that could be quickly undone. He was close to accomplishing everything he had set out to do that day, and it was still only morning.

———

Because he had once entered the wrong one by accident, Joey knew that the key to the front door of his building also unlocked the door to the building next door with the identical facade. As a result, he knew that inside the two buildings were mirror images of each other. This first time had happened a couple of days after he'd moved. He hadn't realized his mistake until he'd come face to face with the mailboxes where the elevator was supposed to be. He'd spun around to see the elevator where the mailboxes had been that morning, as if the world had been flipped inside out. His knees had buckled while his brain took a couple of seconds to unravel what must have happened, at which point he'd gone outside and vomited in the street before continuing into his actual building. For someone expecting to probably lose his mind any day to lesions, it had been a monumental experience.

This time, he purposefully unlocked the wrong building and strode confidently down the hall, finding the elevator exactly where he expected it to be. He stepped in and pressed the button for the sixth floor. Based on what he was able to see from his apartment, it occurred to him that there were really only three apartments that could see clearly into his. The one directly across from his was curtains 24/7, which pretty much ruled it out. The one below the one directly across was the one he had been watching so intently the other night and he felt fairly certain he would have noticed if his neighbor had looked up at him. So that left only one other viable suspect.

In the elevator, Joey ruled out hanging and instead settled on pills chased by booze. He'd suspected all morning that this would be his method. His main concern, besides the fact that it sounded both grand and expected, was that it might be misinterpreted as an accident. He wasn't planning to leave a note.

The elevator opened on the sixth floor and, after taking a moment to orient himself, he figured out where to go. He stood silently next to the door to apartment 6A, the apartment with plants that hung from the ceiling in macramé plant holders. He stayed to the side, against the wall, figuring the residents of this apartment were probably the type who rushed to look out the peephole every time the elevator opened. He set the Braun coffee maker down quietly, undid the loose knot in the plastic bag and carefully deposited the contents onto the doormat. One of the turds rolled away from the others as it landed and Joey used the plastic bag to push it back into place. He crumpled the bag and shoved it in his pocket, picked up the coffee maker and headed for the stairs. He turned back one more time to admire his artful installation, confident that he had made his point. Someone in this apartment had kicked him when he was down. Someone in there had witnessed him in a moment of loneliness and longing and had called the police. It was a shitty thing to do and now they would know it.

He walked down the stairs to the fourth floor. If he took the pills on the couch, sitting up and fully dressed, it would probably read as an intentional suicide. Maybe he'd wear a tie. He found the door to #4A, the apartment below the one directly across from him and set the Braun coffee maker down at a pleasant angle for his sexy neighbor to find. Something looked off. Should he have bought some sort of ribbon, something that clearly stated Gift?

Showered, clean shaven, hair combed. Shirt and tie. Empty pill bottle with the lid screwed back on. A lone, empty glass rinsed in the sink. No note required, right?

He didn't need ribbon. As early as the Trojans, people understood that Item on Doorstep equaled Gift. But something was off. The doormat was wet. Very wet. Looking closer he noticed that water was seeping out through the tight crack at the bottom of the door. The apartment was flooding. He stood back up and knocked on the door. He tried to call out hello but the word caught on itself and he had to clear his throat and try again. He'd meant for it to sound authoritative but it sounded thin and scared. He knocked again, louder this time, but still heard nothing. He tried the door handle, which turned easily and opened.

Joey had seen parts of this apartment from his window, but only specific triangular chunks due to the angles from which he looked. Being inside, the space looked both familiar and foreign. He'd imagined furniture and an overall aesthetic for the areas he wasn't able to see, and the first thing he noticed was all the ways he had been wrong. It must be similar to how people felt after meeting Aggie after only ever seeing her on television, not disappointed necessarily, but certainly thrown off-kilter. Joey felt for a light switch on the wall behind him, then stopped. He was standing in a quarter inch of water and wasn't totally sure how electricity worked. He could hear a faucet running from the bathroom, so he called out hello again before heading down the dim hall.

His body reacted to seeing the young woman in the tub before his mind did. His knees buckled and he fell against the bathroom wall, smacking the back of his head. A low, guttural moan sounded like it came from someone else. He slid all the way down the wall, dipping the seat of his pants in the overflowing water, a perfect wet circle around his ass. He realized that while walking down this hall, he'd been fully expecting to find a dead body in bathtub. Immediately after came the thought that he hadn't predicted it at all, but had added the idea retroactively in an attempt to deal quickly with the shock of actually finding a dead body in the tub. He should be very specific, he decided, about who would find him after the pills. It should be someone equipped to handle this sort of thing; it could potentially change a person.

He stood, surprisingly calm and efficient, and shut off the faucet. He didn't have an instinct to revive her; she was way beyond that. She'd been beaten badly; her eyes swollen, her nose smashed. Her pale, bloated skin looked as if it had softened to the point where one could poke a hole in her with a chopstick, creating an escape route for whatever was causing her puffy disfigurement. Joey imagined the fetid air oozing out and away, restoring her disfigured appearance to something prettier, something closer to what it had been in life. It would be unpleasant, but a favor he would have been happy to perform as long as he could be assured that it would work.

Who should find his body? His super? A jogger? Maybe the mayor?

Joey knew he had to call the police and that once he did, this girl would quickly become just a body, evidence. While there would ultimately be kindness in their collective goal of justice, there would also surely be aggression and bureaucracy, metal tables, and a case number. Since he couldn't attend to her appearance it seemed only right that Joey take a moment to think a few compassionate thoughts. Not that she didn't deserve more than a few, but Joey had been to enough memorial services in the past couple of years to appreciate short and sweet.

When, exactly, did this grisly end become inevitable for her?
I hope it didn't hurt.
Was it when she walked into this apartment? Was it when she first trusted the person who did it to her?
If it did hurt, I hope it didn't last long.
Was it the day she moved to New York?
I hope someone loved you and you knew it.
Who should find me?
Joey closed the bathroom door to give the girl a few last moments of privacy. As someone who'd been spending a lot of time lately wondering if life had any meaning, Joey had also been thinking

about fate, a concept both comforting and restricting. He wondered if this girl had ever had a chance at something better or if her demise was decided the day she was born. Maybe even before that.

Seven

1958

Dorothy Schiff's dinner party had been a success and, as usual, her least favorite guest was the last to leave. Dorothy was beginning to think the blurry socialite might be planning to just stay there, reclined on her chaise, forever. The looseness of the woman's drunken posture was deceptive, the look in her eyes was entitled and proprietary and feline. A Dior pump dangled carelessly from the foot of her crossed leg.

"I've got something for you," the socialite said in a taunting singsong voice. "It's very rich. It's very, *very* rich." She punctuated each word with a flex of her toes; as if the Dior pump was something unpleasant she'd accidentally stepped into. "It's so rich," she sat up suddenly and reached for her martini glass, "that I'm not sure you can even print it. I mean, I'm not sure that even *you* can print it, as fearless as you are in that regard."

Dorothy sipped her tea. This was neither a dance, nor a woman, that she was overly fond of. The socialite had only ever demonstrated zero loyalty to the people she called friends, a kamikaze pilot among the jet set. Dorothy preferred substantiated facts to rumors and this had the familiar build-up of tasteless, common gossip.

"It has to do with someone *very* high up. Politically. In a... *compromising* situation." The socialite paused before and after her innuendos, drawing out her words unnecessarily as if Dorothy would otherwise not understand her.

"I'm not intimidated by powerful men." Dorothy set her teacup back into its saucer without a sound.

"Powerful men." The socialite closed her eyes then let out a throaty laugh. "*Powerful* men. Powerful *men*. Oh, you have no idea."

"Will I ever?" Dorothy asked politely. "Perhaps you're expecting me to write you a check." The socialite had more money than France.

"What do you know about the homosexuals in this town?"

Dorothy understood that this was aimed to throw her off balance, but she was genuinely unfazed. She thought for a moment for the right words. "Tragic. Terrified and tragic. Justifiably so, I suppose."

"Oh Dorothy." Another throaty laugh. "*Honey*. You haven't been going to the right parties. It's much, *much* worse than that."

And then the socialite began to talk.

————

Christopher sat alone at the end of the basement bar nursing his third drink and feeling very old. It was the fourteenth anniversary of his first visit to New York. In the summer of '44, he'd been one of countless boys on their way to fight a man's war. It was that New York, the one of exuberant young boys, which he'd foolishly tried to return to. In its place was a city of lonely men. There were occasional gropes in subway bathrooms and nights spent alone at the end of darkened bars, his head down, sipping and bobbing his head off-rhythm to the music. It was depressing, but so was home. His wife no longer waited up for him.

"Care to dance, Helen?"

Christopher didn't need to look up to know who was asking. Many of the queens in this particular establishment called each other Mary or Eleanor or something more obtuse like Sister de la Charcuterie. "Rose," as the other queens called him, was tall and thin with a big nose and stubble dark enough to make people think the workday was over at ten in the morning.

"I said," Rose dragged out the ess, "Would you care to Dance, Helen?"

Christopher risked a glance up. Rose was tossing a feathered boa around his shoulders like he didn't want it to get comfortable and fall asleep on him. A clutch of queens huddled in the near distance, watching in anticipation of his reaction to Rose's advances. Several of them were dancing in place effortlessly, as if to further the challenge.

Christopher opened his mouth to say something clever in return but his lips only moved like those of a snagged fish and no sound came out. He knew he couldn't hear the music like they could. His head bobbing was clumsy, forced and off-rhythm.

"You know, you won't explode if you discover friendliness, darling." Rose turned dramatically and sashayed back to the others where they collectively collapsed into a fit of loud guffaws. Christopher finished his drink, stood and walked to the bathroom at the back of the basement bar.

At the trough-style urinal he unzipped his pants. Christopher knew the queens in the bar weren't laughing at him. Not really. He knew they were gaining power, which would soon shift back to him in this bathroom if he chose to allow their hands or their mouths or their asses on him, wherever they wanted him most. The door to the bathroom opened and closed. Christopher kept his head down, his eyes on himself.

He recognized, peripherally, Rose's long frame beside him. He looked up at the taller man's unfortunate profile. The boa was gone and so was the bravado. Christopher looked back down and saw Rose shaking a large erection up and down and all around like it was doing the Hokey-Pokey. Rose lifted his hand and touched Christopher's face, caressing his jaw. Christopher felt a mixture of rage, desire and revulsion at this tender gesture. His mind flashed to an image of him fucking Rose from behind, thrusting with enough force to bloody the man's ugly face on the marble in front of them and he knew Rose was wrong; he would explode if he discovered friendliness. Christopher zipped up his pants and walked out of the bathroom, hearing Rose call him a sissy as he left.

———

Christopher had never been in a bar raid, but he understood what was happening as soon as the two uniforms turned on the lights

43

and plunged the room into silence. Though he was near the exit, the cops blocked the stairs up to the street. They each took one step toward Christopher.

"Identification?"

Christopher knew to hand over his entire wallet.

"Are you aware that this is a known meeting place for inverts and homophiles?" The cop pulled Christopher's identification out and studied it.

"No, sir." Christopher knew to keep his head down and his answers short, like he would have back in basic training.

"I'm sure you ain't. I'm sure you ain't. This your current address?"

"Yes, sir."

"Why ain't you home tonight, Chris?"

"My old lady was giving me a headache. Needed some air. Went for a walk." It was a feeble excuse but it showed compliance. Christopher wanted this to be over, quickly and painlessly as possible.

"Well," the cop reached into his wallet and pulled out the cash. "You'd better get back. You don't want your old lady getting worried and calling us on you." He handed the wallet back, significantly lighter.

"No, sir."

"Run on home then." As aggressors, the cops were half-assing it, almost polite, as if they were made from a recipe that called for equal parts malaise, menace and benevolence.

Christopher was two steps closer to freedom when he heard Rose's bluesy baritone behind him.

"Run Rabbit… Run Rabbit… Run, run, run…"

The song he hadn't heard since the war stopped Christopher in his tracks.

"Run Rabbit… Run… Rabbit…" Rose's version of the upbeat ditty was slurred and torchy.

Christopher looked over his shoulder as Rose danced his way toward the cops. The boa was back.

"Well well well. What do we have here?" The cop who talked asked the cop who didn't.

"Bang! Bang! Bang!" Rose punctuated each lyric with another step toward them, each step accompanied by a shimmy. "Goes the farmer's..." Directly in front of the cops, Rose's voice trailed off. Christopher knew that the next word in the song was Gun.

"Oh, sweetheart," the cops eyed Rose up and down. "I guess we don't need to ask whether or not you are aware this is a known meeting place for inverts and homophiles..."

"I'm more than happy to answer any and all of your questions, officers," Rose purred. "But let's turn these lights back down." Rose draped her long, hairy arms over the talking cop's shoulders. "I'm far prettier in the dark."

The way Rose fell reminded Christopher of the boys he'd watched die in the war: forced surrender on the heels of absolute confidence. The cop hit Rose a second time even though he'd clearly gone limp. He yanked Rose's arm and twisted it behind his back.

"Let her go." Christopher wasn't aware he'd forfeited his safe exit until he found himself directly behind the two cops. His demand was quiet but obliterated his prior defense of ignorance. Without thinking, Christopher had referred to Rose as Her, giving himself away as someone who belonged there, in a known meeting place for inverts and homophiles.

Eight

Christopher's stomach growled as he walked out the doors of the 17th Precinct. While he'd never spent the night in jail before, he'd been in scarier places during the war. Jail, it turned out, was nothing more than a safe haven for a few belligerent men to sleep off their drinks. He turned his back on the hopeful morning sun and headed west toward Times Square, like a blood cell drawn to a heart.

Christopher had imagined this day and always thought it would devastate him. Instead he felt oddly freed by his arrest. He hadn't felt so unburdened since his weeks of strictly regimented basic training. He had never felt so sure of who he was as when every effort was being made to strip away his individual identity. He had never felt so sure of what he possessed as when he wasn't allowed to own anything.

He'd met Daniel only days out of basic. They passed each other on a base in New Jersey where they'd both been shipped for a week before heading overseas. Daniel changed directions to follow him, smiling and chatting effortlessly, as if they had known each other all their lives. To this day, Christopher still didn't know how Daniel had recognized him.

That week was intended to be, and had successfully become, an extended send-off party for the young soldiers. The nights became a blur, Christopher flying blind as Daniel pulled him away from the other soldiers to bars and house parties from the West Village to Harlem, the likes of which Christopher had never imagined. There were other young men in uniform at these parties, more than Christopher would have thought. Daniel said that a war was the perfect excuse for a boy to run away from home.

Christopher remembered the nights of waiting, listening for their third bunkmate to start snoring as they crept across the Atlantic on a cramped former passenger liner. He remembered holding Daniel's body, warm and slick as they moved together, shuddering uncontrollably from the keeping quiet. When Daniel's waist was at its most contracted, Christopher was sure he could get his hands completely around it. He could feel his fingers barely meet around the slimmer boy's middle for less than an instant before his inhale would expand it again.

He remembered holding Daniel's bloody body on a field in Germany, after they'd marched for weeks through mud and rain and bombs and minefields. He remembered being able to actually see the bullets flying around him as if they were in slow motion, knowing with absolute certainty that one of them would find him. He'd pressed his mouth to Daniel's dead lips so that he'd be kissing that beautiful boy when he died. But then the bullets stopped. An eerie silence followed by shouting, a hand under his arm pulling him, dragging him from somewhere bad to somewhere that should have, by definition, been better but ended up a 14-year succession of nights spent alone, often at the end of a bar. He bought a pack of cigarettes at a newspaper stand while freshly scrubbed people bustled past, ready to meet another day.

Christopher had been happiest being told what to do, being on the same side, fighting a common enemy; that was the beauty of war. Now, without the Nazis, America was left to pick from a longer list of lesser evils: communists, Negroes and perverts. It was still Us against Them and, while both groups had become less defined, Christopher had officially joined Them. It felt almost good.

Let her go.

He didn't regret saying it. He didn't regret any of it, except getting married. He tried to picture his wife and, although he'd last seen her yesterday morning, he couldn't be sure the face he had in his mind was hers or a younger version of his own mother. Not that it mattered. Tomorrow morning his name would be in the paper along with his address, the name of his employer and his crime. Everything he was in the world would instantly be nullified by one word: Homosexual. They meant to imprison him, but Christopher had learned from Daniel how to break free.

Iris was luxuriating in the perfectly cool summer morning. A light breeze passed through her open window providing just enough chill to make her reach down and pull up the blanket she had kicked off in the night. She tucked it under her chin, reveling in the softness and weight of it. She bicycled her legs to find new coolness in the sheets, enjoying the extravagance of having the queen-sized bed to herself for the second night in a row. She was wide-awake, yet decided to keep her eyes closed for as long as possible.

She heard the front door of the apartment open. Her husband often worked late, past her bedtime, even on the weekends. He often fell asleep on the couch in his office. She heard him trying to walk quietly but not being familiar enough with the apartment to know where the floorboards creaked in the hallway. They had lived there almost two years and she knew every nuance of the charming two-bedroom. She knew that the walls were so thick she could host a jamboree in there and the neighbors that surrounded them on every side would be none the wiser. She heard him open the door to his study, which she was already calling The Nursery in her mind. Not that she particularly wanted children, but she was almost 28.

Iris heard her husband settle into his recliner. She thought she should call to him that she was awake, but then she thought maybe he wanted to get some sleep himself. She'd get up in a few minutes and peek in on him and if he was sleeping she'd put a blanket over him. If he was awake she'd make him some breakfast. She had her share of complaints about her husband - who didn't? Christopher was too quiet and would often act as if he was listening to her when it was obvious he wasn't, which she suspected had to do with the fact that he was eight years older than she was and she did have a tendency to ramble sometimes. Not that he ever deliberately tried to make her feel childish; he was far too polite for that. She could have done a lot worse. Christopher was responsible and reliable, kind and gentle. He'd fought in the war but didn't like to talk about it.

Just a few more minutes, Iris thought as she allowed herself to drift, I'll get up in just a few more minutes. She was almost completely under when she was startled awake by a loud bang. Though she had never heard one before, there was no mistaking it for anything other than the gunshot that it was.

Nine

1985

Joey had been trying to touch his eyeball to the two-way mirror when the two detectives entered the interrogation room. He'd waited alone patiently for forty minutes before getting antsy. He remembered hearing somewhere that the way to tell a two-way mirror from a regular mirror was to touch it. If a small gap existed between the tip of your finger and its reflection, then the mirror was just a mirror, but if your two fingers appeared to be touching, you were probably being watched. Joey had only tested this in hotel rooms and public bathrooms and only ever found regular mirrors. Finally faced with what was most certainly a real live two-way mirror for the first time in his life, he'd wanted to settle the matter once and for all. He'd touched it and, sure enough, his finger met itself. His next thoughts had come very fast, one on top of each other: Was there anyone watching him right now? Could he see them through the mirror if he got close enough? If he could make his eyeball touch itself, would he see into his own brain or perhaps the gateway into another world?

That was when they'd walked in.

The one with the blond mustache introduced himself as Detective Inspector Flowers, but just barely, mumbling and looking at the floor. As Joey sat down across from him, as instructed, he wondered how he would go about it if part of his job were to intimidate people. Flowers's technique, so far, relied mostly on a gruff, paternal persona. Joey wondered if this came naturally to him, or if it was born as a survival technique to a man with an overly cutesy surname in a testosterone driven profession. Either way, Joey doubted he could pull it off if he were in Flowers's position. He'd have to make do with uncomfortable silences and judgmental eye contact.

Flowers introduced the man leaning lazily against the beige wall behind him as Lieutenant Collier. One of Collier's arms was propping up the other at the elbow, allowing his chin to rest in the palm of his propped hand and the fingers of that hand to push his upper lip up under his nose like a birth defect. He struck Joey as the kind of man who had probably breezed though life, excelling at team sports and school dances. He was handsome in a non-threatening, all-American way even as he screwed up his face. Joey felt his presence unnerving. Joey wasn't sure if he was supposed to include Lieutenant Collier or pretend he wasn't there, a dilemma that was proving to be a moot point since neither one had looked at Joey since they'd entered.

As Joey watched Flowers pick repeatedly for an opening in the cellophane wrapping on a new blank cassette tape, he began to suspect that he might not like the man on a fundamental level. He seemed completely indifferent to the potential emotional or psychological repercussions Joey might have been experiencing after stumbling upon the body of a young woman who had most likely died violently. He seemed unimpressed by Joey's willingness to put his personal feelings on the back burner for the time being, in the interest of aiding the criminal investigation.

After calling the police, he'd waited downstairs to let them into the building and had shown them up to the apartment like a realtor would. He'd led them to the bathroom after reminding them to watch their step in the watery hall. He'd complied with not even an iota of offense taken when they'd asked him to step outside, then back down the stairs and outside into the backseat of a patrol car with no handles on the inside, no way to get out if the car had suddenly caught on fire, which did happen to cars, by the way, often without warning and for no good reason. As his bladder had gotten fuller and his stomach emptier, he'd sat patiently for two whole hours, reading a newspaper left on the seat beside him. Outside the obituaries, he'd been unable to find even a tiny update on the disease that had killed Henry. The newspaper, like the mayor and the entire city, had been pretty silent on the whole matter. There was, however, oodles of coverage on the FBI's process of cornering and arresting the most powerful members of the top-five mafia families on trafficking and racketeering charges. The newspaper rehashed months of secretly recorded meetings and phone conversations that had led to seized evidence, padlocked buildings and detained men. After decades of inaction or inability, the government had finally found a way to prosecute the Mafia. The government could do a lot when it chose to.

Flowers called the stubborn cassette tape a motherfucker before handing it over his shoulder to Collier who took it without a word, making Joey suspect that this had happened before. Collier made a quick slit down the length of the tape with a small pocketknife attached to a key ring. He pulled the cellophane off in one fluid motion and handed the tape back to Flowers with one hand while closing the pocketknife with the other. Flowers jammed the tape crookedly into a waiting portable recorder, then pulled it out and jammed it in again. He pressed play and record at the same time before aiming a small microphone somewhere between Joey's mouth and left shoulder.

"Monday, July 15th, 1985, approximately 4:15 PM in the afternoon. D.I. Flowers, NYPD 17th Precinct interviewing male witness to the suspected homicide of unknown female victim found inside residential location located at 343 East 54th Street, apartment 4A."

Joey kept his elbow on the table but raised his hand in a subtle attempt to interrupt that either went unseen or was ignored as Flowers continued, reading from a small notebook.

"Also present is Lieutenant Collier -"

Joey tried again to get attention, this time by clearing his throat. Since his throat was already clear, the noise that came out sounded just like Ahem, sassier than he'd intended. Flowers looked directly at him for the first time and raised his eyebrows without granting or denying Joey's request to speak.

"Hi." Joey smiled. A big part of his job as a stylist was making people feel comfortable, whether they were innately rude or saddled with a cartoon skunk's name. "I was just thinking that sounds misleading. Saying that I was a witness *to* the suspected homicide makes it sound like I, you know, watched... it happen. Which I didn't. I just

52

saw her after. After she was already, you know. Dead. And stuff." Joey wished he hadn't said *and stuff*. "I think it's probably more accurate to introduce me as a witness *in* the suspected homicide, blah blah blah."

Flowers squinted as if Joey were fluently speaking a foreign language that he'd only studied in a class. Then he chuckled and rubbed his eyes. "Introduce? What do you think this is, some kind of cabaret show?"

It did sound weird, Joey thought, when he said it like that. He smiled too, like they were on the same side. "That's funny, but really I think -"

Flowers startled him by slapping his hand down on the tape recorder like it was a rowdy puppy. The tape stopped recording and he leaned in. "No. You don't think. You don't ask questions. I think. He -" he gestured over his shoulder at Collier, still in his harelip pose, "thinks. You only provide answers. You got it? This isn't one of your little cocktail parties." Flowers glared at Joey, Joey looked at the table between them. After a moment Joey looked directly at Collier.

"I'm sorry to bother you, but was that a question I'm supposed to answer? It sounded rhetorical."

Collier shrugged his shoulders silently. He had long, dark eyelashes and a little dried crusty sleep in the corner of his left eye. Joey thought he was smiling beneath his hand.

"That was a question, yes." Flowers spoke slowly with practiced patience that Joey felt was completely unearned; he was only here to help. "Do you understand the way this works?"

"Yes, I do." Joey was beginning to understand completely.

"Excellent. Let's continue." He pressed the buttons on the tape recorder and it began to whir. "Detective Inspector Flowers resuming the questioning of male witness *in*," he looked pointedly at Joey, "the suspected homicide of female unsub, 343 East 54th." He flipped his notebook to a clean page. "Lieutenant Collier, can you confirm that this recording was only stopped to clarify the purpose of this meeting, and that no questions pertinent to the investigation were put to the witness during this time, and also that no information pertinent to said investigation was extracted from said witness during said time?"

"I can." Lieutenant Collier surprised Joey with a voice that was dangerously close to one that could be described as high-pitched.

"Would you like to have a lawyer present for this interview?" Flowers looked at Joey with a knowing gleam in his eye. Minutes before, this question would have caught Joey off guard. But he'd prepared himself.

"No. I'm fine." Joey only knew one lawyer; she dealt with tax law.

"Suit yourself." Flowers looked very pleased with Joey's bad decision. "State your full name and address for the record."

Joey leaned in and slightly to the left, speaking directly into the microphone. "My name is Joseph Stuart Broderer. My address is 345 East 54th Street, apartment 5F."

"How long have you lived there?"

"About a month."

"State your occupation and place of employment."

"I'm a stylist and I work at Slate on East 61st street."

"Which is what? What is *Slate*?" Flowers was acting confused, manufacturing frustration with an invented lack of cooperation on Joey's part, performing for the record.

"Slate is a high-end salon."

Flowers sneered. "So you, what, you cut hair?" He sounded as if he'd maneuvered though something very convoluted to uncover the truth.

"Among other things, yes, I do cut hair."

"So you're a hairdresser."

Joey was no stranger to this sort of condescension in regards to his profession. He had received it from people whose opinions meant much more to him than this jerk's. Even Henry had made jokes from time to time about the cliché of the gay hairdresser and, while jokes were just jokes, Joey knew that Henry was actually embarrassed by it, especially around his finance friends.

"No. I'm a stylist."

"That distinction is only in your head, buddy." Then, from underneath his notepad, Flowers pulled a thin manila folder and put it on the table between them. Joey hated being called Buddy by someone who clearly wasn't a friend almost as much as being called Big Guy by somebody bigger than he. Joey glanced at the folder and saw his own name neatly typed on the white-labeled tab. He knew that in it was one copy of the traffic-like ticket he'd gotten the night before last, a translucent slip of paper that proved he was capable of questionable, and possibly outright criminal, behavior. It occurred to Joey that he hadn't been arrested only because they didn't have any real evidence against him, but they were planning to find some soon.

He felt incredibly naïve for having misread the situation so badly; it wasn't that Flowers was rude or worried about appearing soft in front of his colleagues, it was that he saw Joey as a faggot who had killed a girl and therefore despised him.

"I guess you could think of it this way, if this puts it into perspective for you." Joey stayed deliberately calm and conversational. "Let's say being a Detective Inspector is equivalent to being a hairdresser."

Flowers looked up from his notebook.

"Being a stylist," Joey continued, "would be more like being a Lieutenant."

Collier laughed out loud, assuring Joey that on his second pass, he'd more successfully assessed the circumstances. He'd assumed, at first, that Flowers was the one in charge, mostly because he'd taken control. He'd assigned them the roles of coach and quarterback based on their appearances. But Flowers's cockiness combined with his overly formal verbiage now looked to Joey like someone who had something to prove, someone determined to win a bet. He'd noticed that Collier had been watching Flowers much more than he'd been watching Joey, so Joey decided that the Lieutenant outranked Flowers's fancier sounding title. If Collier's laughter wasn't enough, the way

Flowers hit the tape recorder twice to stop it from spinning told Joey he was right. The interview went downhill from there.

Ten

It seemed to Diane that she would never, ever, ever be done picking up after people. Raising two teenaged boys, three if you counted her husband Peter, it was just non-stop picking up the things they left trailing behind as they moved through the house. Peter's senile mother, Alice, didn't add to the mess, since she didn't really do anything, but she was certainly one more person to care for. Diane had chosen to be a stay-at-home mom; both she and Peter felt it was important to raise their boys that way. She'd agreed with Peter that his mother shouldn't be put in a home. She didn't regret it, but she did feel as if she'd been cleaning up everyone's messes for the last seventeen years.

That afternoon Kyle had invited friends from his soccer team over to play Atari. Five sweaty sixteen-year-old boys with muddy cleats had crowded the den; whooping and hollering like a pack of wild monkeys. It had taken them barely forty-five minutes to eat all the food in the house, dirty every single glass and clog up the downstairs toilet. She'd coughed up ten dollars for pizza, just to get them out of the house, for which she'd received a peck on the cheek and privilege of an afternoon spent washing dishes, washing scuff marks off the wall behind the couch and discovering the bit about the toilet and dealing with that. At least Kyle had friends. It was her fourteen-year-old, Brian, whom she worried about.

As Diane bent down to pick up the clothes that her husband had left in a crumpled heap next to the hamper, she heard his laugh from the kitchen. "Peter?" she called out. He didn't answer. She separated his underwear, socks, and shirt from his pants, which could be worn again tomorrow, and headed for the laundry. "Peter? Are you done?" Still no answer. She passed the upstairs bathroom, still hot and damp from Alice's bath. She noticed Alice's rings next to the sink and pocketed them before turning off the light. She used Peter's undershirt to dust the banister as she trudged down the stairs. She heard him laugh again. "Peter? You on the phone?"

"Well, be careful," Peter was saying. "Don't drop the phone into the tub." He turned to Diane and mouthed *It's your sister.* He was leaning against the counter, shirtless, absentmindedly pestering an ingrown hair next to his nipple. Diane put the hamper on the floor and held out her hand for the phone. "Anyway," he said, "Diane's here, so I'll hand you off and get back to my workout." He smiled, looking down at the floor. "I don't know. Honey," he looked at Diane. "Do I look more built to you?" He flexed his pecs and Diane rolled her eyes. His glasses were smudged and greasy so she pulled them off his face as she cradled the phone between her ear and shoulder.

"Hi, Aggie, hold on one sec."

"Bye, Peter!" Aggie yelled in her ear. Diane heard water splashing on her sister's side of the line.

"Bye, Aggie," Peter called out, then quieter, to Diane, "Is mom asleep?"

"She's in bed, I don't know if she's asleep." She pulled his hand away from his chest. "Stop picking at that."

"It hurts."

"You're making it worse."

"Okay." Peter left the kitchen for the garage to finish his workout.

Diane turned on the kitchen faucet and rubbed dishwashing liquid onto the lenses of her husband's glasses. "Hi, Aggie, what's up?"

"Ooh la la, lucky lady! I didn't know Peter was pumping iron!"

"It's not for me, he made a bet with someone at work." Diane sounded more impatient than she meant to. It wasn't Aggie's fault that she was completely ignorant of the realities of married life. "What's going on?"

"Nothing, just doing the dishes."

"Why did Peter say you were in the tub?" Diane rinsed his glasses under warm water.

"We were just joking around. Anyway, I was just calling to see if you were excited for Wednesday."

"Wednesday. Wednesday. Wednesday?" Diane dried the glasses with a dishtowel.

"Wednesday." Aggie sounded a little hurt. "You guys are coming into the city, remember? Your anniversary present?"

"Oh right, Wednesday." Why had they been joking about Aggie being in the tub? What was so funny about that? "I'm sorry, I'm doing a million things at once here."

"You're still coming right?"

"Yeah, yeah. I mean, I guess." Diane looked at the sixty-foot phone cord that Peter had bought just last month for convenience, already impossibly knotted, twisted and tangled around itself.

"You don't sound so sure."

"Well, uh, I'm not sure this is the best time for this -"

"Diane! You said you wanted to! I bought the tickets already! It's *CATS*!"

"I know I did but that was months ago when it was very... abstract." Diane picked a particularly gnarled part of the cord and went to work on it. "Peter's got a lot going on at work and Alice, well, I'm not sure Alice is up for it."

"She doesn't want to?"

"Um... It's not really a question of want... you know. Her mind is loopy. Sometimes she knows what's going on but usually she doesn't. She gets confused easily."

"Can she go to the bathroom by herself?"

"Of course she can." Aggie's mind went to the most extreme places. "I mean, I usually go in with her in case she falls or something."

"You go into the stall with her?"

"Well, no, there are no stalls in our bathrooms here at home. I just go in there and clean the mirror or something until she's done. I don't wipe her or anything."

59

"I'm sure I can handle it for a few hours. I made her an appointment to get her hair done at Joey's salon! So that will be fun, right?"

"Oh. Well. That would be..." Diane's efforts to untwist the cord, no matter which way she went, only seemed to make the problem worse. "How is Joey doing?"

"He's good," Aggie sighed. "You know, considering. He could use some cheering up. Come on, Diane, please let me do this for you! You never let anyone do anything nice for you. You never treat yourself."

Diane didn't feel like arguing. "That's really thoughtful, but I'm just worried about Alice." Diane heard the front door to the house open. "She could be a challenge even for a trained nurse, with really nurturing... instincts, you know?" She heard the door close quietly and knew it was Brian, her younger son, coming home. Kyle wouldn't have cared how much noise he made.

"You don't think I have nurturing instincts?"

"Hold on Aggie," Diane put the phone down by her hip. She managed to stretch the knotted phone cord out long enough to catch Brian headed up the stairs. "Hey."

Brian paused halfway up and looked over his shoulder. "Hi."

"Where have you been?" She tried her best to sound conversational and not accusatory. She could smell the cigarette smoke on him from where she was standing.

"Just out," Brian offered from under his long bangs as if that were an adequate explanation.

"Oh. Okay. Did you have dinner?"

Brian moved his head in a way that could have been both yes and no. "I'm not hungry."

"I'm almost done with the kitchen. Do you want to watch a movie?" Diane knew that fourteen-year-old boys didn't get excited about watching movies with their mothers, but she thought she'd try.

"I'm just going to listen to some music." He turned and ran the rest of the way up the stairs.

Diane put the phone back up to her ear and could practically hear her sister pouting. "Hi. Sorry."

"You know," Aggie said, "I do play a nurse on television..."

Diane laughed.

"So I'm not entirely ill equipped..."

"Can I call you tomorrow and tell you then?"

"Absolutely." Aggie and Diane both knew that Aggie had won. "You just need one day off, you'll see."

"Hm. Alright. I'll call you tomorrow."

As Diane ended the phone call, she felt herself getting annoyed. It felt ungrateful to be annoyed with someone who was giving you a gift but, honestly, Aggie was oversimplifying and misreading the situations at hand, wasn't she? She was being incredibly presumptuous and masking it as generosity. Had being on television really made her sister so out of touch with reality? It wasn't a treat for a woman to go out to dinner in the city when she hadn't bought a new dress since 1978, nor was it exciting for Peter to go to a Broadway matinee when he hated musicals. Alice didn't know her ass from a hole in the ground; the last thing she cared about was a new hairdo. And, honestly, Joey's partner had died of AIDS; Joey didn't need cheering up, he needed a medical miracle. She'd always known her little sister was self-centered, but this was something else. Diane shook her head, opened the fridge and began to make dinner for a son who wasn't hungry.

Eleven

The upside to not eating anything all day was that if Joey vomited, probably not much would come out. So little, in fact, that he'd surely be able to hide it quickly. He was perched on the lip of a dumpster behind the coffee shop around the corner from his apartment. The dumpster was full of white trash bags and the kid with the bad skin and the stud in his right ear told him he was pretty sure it got emptied on Tuesdays and Fridays. Joey hoped he was right or this would be a futile, as well as disgusting, exercise. The bags had been tossed into the dumpster haphazardly. It was reasonable to assume, if Zits was right, that some were from Friday, some were from Saturday, some from yesterday, and some from today. He wanted the one that held the trash from the end of the day yesterday; it seemed logical that this bag should be near the top of the pile.

Climbing into a dumpster was not at all how Joey had pictured ending his weekend, but then he also hadn't planned on becoming a suspect in a murder investigation. True, he hadn't been accused outright but even the insinuation was offensive. Flowers's opinion of him as a pervert was a loose label that encompassed many evil possibilities. His initial indignation hadn't worn off; for the rest of the interview he'd been a mildly hostile witness.

Joey gave up trying to assign order to the garbage bags and picked one up at random, untied it and peered inside to find what one would expect: empty cardboard cups, wadded-up napkins in various states of wetness, newspapers, paper plates and muffin crumbs. The only seemingly out-of-place object was a Matchbox toy car that looked practically brand new. Joey shook the bag and kicked the outside of it in an attempt to jostle the contents enough to see more of what was at the bottom.

He'd gone over and over the details of his morning while Flowers took notes and Collier smushed his lips into a variety of unattractive positions. He'd been as honest as the situation called for and in return was repeatedly badgered by a man who obviously didn't understand the difference between niggling details and ultimate truths, someone who couldn't recognize which questions didn't need to be answered and which answers didn't need to be analyzed.

Joey considered putting his arm into the bag but imagined there was probably snot on some of the wadded up napkins so he re-tied it and placed it as much to the side as he could before opening up another one.

Yes, it was technically a lie that he'd walked into the neighboring building by mistake this morning, but not a lie that he'd made that very mistake a couple of weeks before, so why was it so hard to believe? Honestly, what was the difference? Joey hadn't killed the girl in the bathtub. That was the truth. Sure, it was a truth that he'd framed with some lies about his actions and intent that morning, but that didn't matter.

He'd returned home after running errands: true. He'd found the Braun coffee maker on the street and was taking it home to see if it worked: false but not important; he'd just needed a simple explanation for why he'd been holding it when the police got there. He'd not been paying attention and gone into the wrong building by mistake: false today but true of another day, so mostly true. He'd taken the elevator to the fifth floor where he'd realized his mistake: sort-of true, sort-of false, but also not really relevant. He'd decided to take the stairs down: absolutely true. He'd noticed the water coming from under the door to apartment 4A: true, he'd knocked on the door several times before trying the handle: truest yet, followed the source of the water to the bathroom, found the body, called the police and waited: true, true, true and true.

He tilted his head back to take a breath of air that smelled like anything other than coffee grounds. Zits called out to him from the back door to the coffee shop where he stood. "You find it?"

63

"Not yet..." Stupid question. If he had would he still be in the dumpster?

"Maybe you should come back when my boss is here."

Joey pretended he didn't hear this. He couldn't imagine what misadventure this kid was worried he might be perpetrating, but he'd had enough inferred accusations for one day.

Do you know a Raymond Nunez?

No.

Do you know anyone named Raymond?

No.

No one at all named Raymond.

Not that I can recall.

Anyone named Ray?

Not, no. Not personally.

So you do.

No. Not in the way that you mean. Not personally.

Don't decide what I mean. Just answer the questions. Do you know in any way someone named Ray or Raymond?

Yes.

Now we're getting somewhere. Ray who?

Ray Bolger and Martha Raye.

Joey picked up a fourth bag and held it up without opening it. The plastic was white and thin; basic shapes and colors of the waste that filled it could be seen it in the fading summer sunlight.

Do you know any resident of apartment 4A at 343 East 54th Street?

No.

Have you ever had any contact with any resident of apartment 4A, 343 East 54th street?

No.

Have you ever seen any resident of -

Nope.

This was all absolutely true, from Joey's point of view. It was pretty easy to deduce from Flowers's pointed questions that the apartment was rented to someone named Raymond Nunez and Joey was ninety-nine point nine percent sure he didn't know anyone by that name. The point oh one percent was reserved for people he might recognize, like a mailman, but didn't know by name. He was equally certain that the man he'd seen through the windows, the man he'd followed on the street the night before was not Raymond Nunez, no way. The name didn't fit him at all, he didn't look like a Ray or a Raymond and he didn't look Latin or Hispanic.

Flowers's mistake, if he was unhappy with Joey's version of events, was allowing him to sit for two hours in a locked patrol car with the newspaper as his only company. He'd gone into the meeting with the detectives completely ready to participate yet had had plenty of time to decide what he was and wasn't comfortable sharing about watching and following a man who most likely did not live in apartment 4A, but had very probably drowned a girl in a bathtub. Truth was subjective and often created by simple repetition and volume. The FBI had successfully boiled down the myriad violent crimes of the top New York mafia families to Racketeering, and the newspaper willingly peddled this version of the truth. Inspired, Joey had decided to create his own truth. He'd been willing to tell the cops what he knew while leaving himself out if it. Not only had Flowers not appreciated Joey's ingenious retelling of the facts, he'd challenged Joey with a version of the truth he'd already decided on and slid Joey's own file towards him as proof of his criminal deviance. Like the government to the Mafia, Flowers had already determined Joey deserved whatever he had coming to him without a trial. That was when Joey decided that none of this was his problem.

Can you identify the woman whose body was found in the bathtub of apartment 4A, 343 East 54th Street?

No.

Do you know the woman whose body was found in the bathtub of apartment 4A, 343 East 54th Street?

Nope.

Do you recognize the woman whose body was found in the bathtub of apartment 4A, 343 East 54th Street?

No.

It hadn't been difficult to deduce that the police didn't know the first thing about the dead girl, which meant she must have been in the apartment without any identification.

Joey saw something bulky and yellow through the plastic of the sixth bag of garbage he picked up. He untied it and peered inside. Unlike the other bags, which were relatively neat as far as garbage went, this one had obviously been used to dump out the remains of something like soup at the end of the day. Having had a day in the hot sun, the mess had congealed into a rancid slime with an unavoidable stench, even if he'd been able to breathe through his eyeballs. Joey gagged silently and put his mouth over the fabric of the tee shirt on his shoulder.

Once Flowers accepted that Joey's story wasn't going to change no matter what imagined curve-balls were thrown at him in the form of re-worded questions, he made Joey list everything in the apartment he'd touched (front doorknob, bathtub faucet, bathroom doorknob, telephone) before sending him to get his fingerprints taken. They'd released him and warned him not to leave town, which felt very much like living in a movie.

"You find it?" Pizza Face called out as he took a step back, as if there were any room for the foul odor in his already clogged pores.

"I think so," Joey managed to squeak out.

"It's about fucking time," the kid muttered.

It had only been about six minutes, but Joey was too busy concentrating on the task at hand to climb out of the dumpster and slap him. He reached his hand, still blackened at the tips from the fingerprinting ink, through the slimy, hot purification up past his elbow until he touched what he hoped he was looking for.

Sitting in the car that afternoon, he'd replayed what he knew about the man who wasn't Raymond Nunez, deciding how to give the police his description. The more he'd thought about the fact that he'd developed a crush, however fleeting, on a probable murderer, the less it seemed like that big of a deal. Once Flowers had alienated him, Joey decided it was none of their business if he'd seen the guy and followed him. If Flowers had been even a little bit polite, Joey would have found a way to tell him that he'd followed the man who wasn't Ray into this coffee shop, that he'd been carrying a sweatshirt and a yellow plastic bag when he'd entered and only the sweatshirt and a cup of coffee when he'd exited. Joey would have made it sound like a coincidence that they'd been in the same shop and that the memory didn't strike him as odd until the body was found.

Joey untied the yellow plastic bag and looked inside. Satisfied, he climbed out of the dumpster, holding his own filthy arm as far away from himself as possible all while trying to smile at the kid waiting.

"Yep this is it. This is what I lost." Joey held the yellow bag through one of its handles by the crook of his finger. He had no intention of handing it over to the police now that he'd touched it and his fingerprints were on file, just what was inside. He would drop it off anonymously like a baby on a doorstep, and then just walk away and forget all about it. He'd forget about the dead girl and the murderer and the fat asshole cop and the cute quiet cop and the government that had a boner for the Mafia and the mayor who was choosing to do nothing to help dying citizens and the shitty newspaper that was obsessing over one and ignoring the other. Fuck them all.

The kid sidled up to Joey, his curiosity winning over his cool blasé. He peered inside the bag. "How did you throw away your purse?"

Fuck you, Joey thought. And fuck the mafia too. Even though they had nothing to do with anything at all.

Twelve

Fuck this.

Giancarlo finished his bourbon and signaled the shirtless kid with the muscles behind the bar for another. Because he had tipped well on his first one he was handed a second right away. He traded a five-dollar bill for the drink and told the kid to keep the change. The kid smiled and lowered his eyes seductively in a show of thanks. That's what a one dollar tip on a four dollar drink bought you, good service and two or three seconds of flirting from a kid young enough to be your grandson.

Carlo could remember a time when he was a young man, a long time ago, when bars like this were a gold mine for the men he worked for, or used to work for. Bars like this used to be, like any other illegal but necessary commodity, money factories for people who didn't mind getting their hands dirty and playing a little rough. As a young man Carlo had never minded either, in fact he'd often sought them out. The desire was still there, only faded like the color from a favorite pair of blue jeans. Carlo was 61 and long retired from the business of hurting people; tonight was just a favor for his old friend Del. The favor was turning out to be much more involved than Carlo was comfortable with, and his anger was making him consider getting back into the business of hurting people one more time.

Carlo looked at his watch again. The favor had sounded simple when his friend had asked: some ledgers needed to be recovered. Carlo hadn't asked what kind of ledgers, he wasn't the least bit curious. The ledgers could have been a stack of phonographs, a smoking gun or a starving newborn infant as far as he was concerned; Carlo required no measurement of urgency for his participation. The favor would be done on the principle of itself, unquestioned, because the old man named Del who was asking had once been a young man with Carlo and together they'd done some frightening things. Even so, his friend had felt the need to explain.

Some very sensitive bookkeeping records that may or may not be potentially incriminating should they fall into the wrong hands, Carlo's old friend had muttered from behind a newspaper that he pretended to read. Completely uncurious and disinterested in the particulars, Carlo had kept his eyes on the pigeons at his feet, snacking on the breadcrumbs he'd scattered for them from a plastic bag of stale Wonder. Carlo knew the place his friend described well, though he hadn't been there in years. It had once been a bar like the one Carlo was now waiting for Anthony in, and had later become a social club of sorts, owned by the men Carlo used to work for and, until very recently, used for meetings and events or just afternoon card games. His friend hadn't needed to say that the place was under surveillance. Since the indictments had been handed down by the feds in January, everyone Carlo used to work for was either in jail or being watched, which was the reason his old friend couldn't recover the sensitive ledgers himself.

Carlo doubted that he was of any interest to the feds; he'd been out of the life for a long time. While the excitement level of the collective branches of law enforcement was off the charts at the prospect of being able to nail all the major players in New York City's five major crime families, their resources were not without limit. He could probably have broken into the shuttered social club himself one night to retrieve the ledgers without incident. Probably. But Carlo hadn't lived through his dangerous youth to make it to 61 by betting on the odds of probably. Which is why he'd enlisted Anthony, a decision he'd made with more than a little hesitation. Carlo had known Anthony from the neighborhood, watched him grow up. The kid was cocky as hell, dumb as dirt and had no light in his eyes whatsoever, but had other qualities that eventually won out over his complete lack of moral character.

Carlo had picked this bar on purpose for the exchange; two men could meet here, have a drink and no one would think anything of it. But forty minutes past the agreed on time there was still no Anthony and no ledgers. For the first time, Carlo wondered what was actually in the ledgers. Was there something in there valuable enough to make Anthony cross him?

Carlo stood up. Getting back into the business of hurting people one more time to teach Anthony a lesson might feel good. He'd even do it for free. He looked around the dark bar with lights flashing in time to the disco music. A lot had changed about these bars since Carlo had been a young man. Carlo had never had any particular opinion about fags; he'd always been a live-and-let-live kind of guy. The men in the bars back when they were run by the men Carlo worked for always seemed so ashamed, like they'd been forced onto their barstools as a punishment for something beyond their control. The men in here seemed different somehow, evolved yet directly descended from the others, their desperation masked by a layer of confidence as transparent as a veil as they rubbed against each other on the dance floor, talking and laughing and kissing, forgetting themselves in drinks and promises of sex. If they had any common instinct that there was a killer in their midst, they sure weren't acting like it.

———

The light on Carlo's answering machine was blinking in sync with his heartbeat, two pulses then a pause. Carlo wondered if this were intentional, if the contraption had been designed to subliminally make you feel it was something human doing you a favor, instead of slowly squeezing you out of the world. He didn't like machines that did things people could do, but it was a gift from his nephew who was getting a master's degree in biology and not only thought he knew everything, but that he had invented knowing everything. Carlo's nephew had plugged the phone into the machine and the machine into the wall. Now it was like life support that the phone couldn't live without.

He pressed the button he was supposed to press when the light was blinking and heard a series of clicks and then the whir of something spinning and a pause, followed by his own voice emanating from the plastic box. *Hello. This is Giancarlo* - he pressed the button again and his voice, stilted and formal sounding, stopped speaking to him. What the fuck had he done wrong? The stupid buttons didn't even say what they were, just arrows pointing in different directions. One was a square.

He pressed the button that was an arrow that pointed to the left and heard more clicking, more whirring, a beep, another pause and then, finally, Anthony's voice. *Hey, it's me.* This much, Carlo already knew. *Sorry I didn't make it tonight, but some shit's going on, going down. Not with your ledgers. Your stuff, I mean. I got that.*

Dumbshit. There was noise in the background that sounded distorted but like music, Anthony's voice sounded thick.

I just need to lay low for a couple more days, it's a personal matter. I took the week off work, for a personal matter, so don't call me there.

Like he would in a fucking million years.

Give me a couple of days, thanks babe, and I'll get in touch with you then. Don't worry. I'll call you back.

The machine made more clicks then the heartbeat light stopped blinking. Carlo stayed impeccably calm as he lifted up the hard plastic cover that protected two miniature cassette tapes. One contained his own voice, the other contained Anthony's message. He didn't know which tape was guilty and which was innocent, so he took them both out of their protective slots and went to get his hammer.

Thirteen

1958

Iris stared at the bed. She had never been to Eddie's apartment before; it was different than what she'd pictured. But then, everything looked different to Iris, even the familiar things like sidewalks and ladies' hats, things that made perfect sense yesterday, suddenly looked bizarre and purposeless.

Was your husband a homosexual?

The police officer's question had confused her; so had the scene in the study after she'd heard the gunshot. She hadn't seen the gun at first and, for a split second, thought she'd been mistaken, that the smoke coming out of Christopher's mouth was from a cigarette. That there was a perfectly rational explanation for the blood splattered up the white wall behind him. A doctor had given her some blue pills to take. The pills didn't take away her thoughts, but allowed her to view them like a collection of statues that someone else had made, statues that she wasn't expected to have an opinion about.

"Clean sheets." Eddie stepped behind her in the doorway of his own bedroom, gesturing toward his own bed. Iris nodded as if this simple fact required agreement. The bed was covered by a quilt, the kind that gets handed down from one generation to the next, tucked in tightly, hospital corners they called it, mastered by nurses, women in crisp dresses and white hats. Was Eddie a nurse? No. He wasn't.

Iris squeezed her eyes shut and tried to focus on what she did know. Eddie was Christopher's friend from the army. He was a lawyer and a bachelor and he'd grown up in Newark. She and Christopher had had him over for dinner probably ten times in the last two years since they'd moved to New York; each time it had been Christopher's idea and each time Iris, as his wife, had been the one to extend the invitation. Eddie had never reciprocated their invitations; nor had he ever refused them. Iris had never thought twice about this. She knew

Eddie lived alone and worked long hours. Truth be told, she'd rarely thought about Eddie at all. Christopher would sometimes say *I wonder how that old boy Eddie is doing*, and Iris would straighten his tie or refill his coffee and suggest they have him over for dinner. When the policeman had asked her that morning if there was anyone she could call who could take care of her, she thought of Eddie. She didn't know if Eddie could help, but she did know his phone number.

"Are you hungry?"

Iris always thought Eddie spoke too loudly, and almost exclusively about his own political opinions and often while someone else was speaking. She'd been very happy, the times he'd been over, to have a reason to get up and down from the dinner table, serving and clearing while he and Christopher talked. Now, alone with him in his tiny one-bedroom, he seemed like a totally different person, unsure and nervous.

"I don't have much here. I could make you a peanut butter sandwich. Or toast. I could scramble some eggs..."

When he'd picked her up from the police station, Eddie had taken control of the situation. He'd begun barking orders as if everyone within earshot worked for him. He'd insisted they cease and desist all the questions, putting the documents they'd shown her in his jacket pocket. He'd called her His Client and demanded a doctor be brought in to prescribe something for her nerves. He threatened each of the policemen individually and as a group with lawsuits for not complying. Iris hadn't known why they'd taken her from her apartment to the police station; it hadn't occurred to her that it might not be completely routine until they'd started asking questions about Christopher that she didn't know how to answer.

Was your husband a homosexual?

The hand that held the gun had been in his lap, beneath his crumpled jacket. Christopher had covered his head with the jacket before sliding the gun into his mouth. He hadn't wanted her to see the mess. His plan hadn't worked. Iris had squinted at the arrest report

73

they'd shown her from the night before, completely unable to comprehend their questions, let alone answer them.

"I can go up to your... to get some things of yours," Eddie said from the doorway.

Iris looked down at the nightgown she'd been wearing all day. She didn't remember when she'd put on her slippers. She'd been barefoot when she'd jumped out of bed. Iris pulled her purse from the crook of her arm and realized that it wasn't her purse at all. It was a crumpled paper bag that held Christopher's personal effects, everything that had been on his person, the policeman had said when he'd handed it to her. Where was her purse?

Are you aware that your husband was arrested last night in a bar that's a known meeting place for homosexuals?

"I can't go back there." Her voice was even quieter than Eddie's, her speech thick from the blue pills.

"Of course not. You don't have to. I'll take care of everything." She saw that he was holding her purse.

Eddie's promise sounded familiar to Iris. It was the same thing Christopher had said to her when he'd accepted a job in New York.

Don't worry, he'd said. *We'll make friends. I'll take care of everything.*

He hadn't taken care of anything and they hadn't made any friends. Well, she hadn't. Christopher, it seems, had made some. After two years, Iris had only fashioned passing acquaintances with several neighbors and made dinners for Eddie. She'd read books and gone sightseeing, planned to turn a study into a nursery, and constructed an imagined familiarity with a husband she hadn't known at all.

"Iris. I'll take care of everything."

Iris sat down on the quilt-covered bed. The mismatched fabric remnants clashed close up, but from even a short distance made something cohesive, intentional and beautiful. It would be easy to let Eddie take care of her. Let Eddie feed her soup and scrambled eggs and blue pills and marry her. Let him tell her stories of Christopher in the war and how they had crossed the Atlantic in a huge ship together and how Christopher had been one of his best friends, how the war had turned them into men together.

Iris emptied the contents of the bag onto the quilt. A nearly full pack of cigarettes, a Zippo lighter, some coins, a set of keys, and a leather wallet. His watch and his wedding ring. She opened his wallet and began to place its contents in front of her like cards in a game of solitaire.

She and Eddie would be the only people who would remember these few days and they would do their best not to think of them. They would work to forget that the police said Christopher had been arrested in a bar the night before his death, a bar that was a known meeting place for inverts, meaning homosexuals, and had long been under investigation by the good men of the New York City Police Department. Not even Eddie would know about Christopher's business trips and late nights at the office. She alone would be left to remember the Christopher of their marriage and if only one person remembered something, then it very easily never happened. It would be so easy.

From the wallet she pulled a small sepia-toned photograph of a young man smiling and squinting into the sun. She felt Eddie take a step towards her.

"Danny," he said, as if that were explanation enough.

"You know him?"

"He died in Germany. He was a great kid."

"Do you have a picture of him in your wallet?"

Eddie didn't respond.

Iris nodded. "So he and Christopher were close?"

Eddie sat down on the edge of the bed and took the picture from her hands. "We all were."

"I think you know what I'm asking."

Eddie stayed focused on the picture. "It's hard to know for sure. There's something about a war, being together for weeks and months on end. We were all so scared and acting so brave. It was sometimes necessary to forge relationships that wouldn't make sense in the outside world. It wasn't talked about. It was just... needed."

"Did you?"

"Did I?"

"Did you have those kinds of relationships?"

"No."

"So not everyone did."

"No."

"Would you say that half of the soldiers did?"

"I don't know. That sounds like maybe a high estimate. But I know that it happened. The army knows that it happened. It doesn't make them..." Eddie didn't finish saying what it didn't make them. He handed Iris her purse like a barely competent babysitter offering a different-but-not-better toy to a distressed toddler. Once her hands were occupied, Eddie reached down for Christopher's belongings.

"No," Iris stopped him. "Don't." She opened her purse and dropped the watch, wallet, keys, and coins into it. She leaned back onto the pillow and curled onto her side, pulling the purse into her stomach like a football, all the while staring at the picture.

Eddie rose. "Iris? Do you want me to close the curtains? Iris?" Iris?

Fourteen

1985

Joey was awakened from something resembling sleep by a persistent banging on the door. He got up off the couch and made his way to the peephole; Lieutenant Collier waved to him from the other side. Joey took a deep breath, in and out. His lungs were heavy, like someone had put a dictionary on his chest. The cloud of elation and confidence he'd experienced after deciding to kill himself had left. In its place was the familiar voice of hypochondria. The nag perched somewhere at the top of his spine suggested that while the heaviness in his chest could be the direct result of having smoked nineteen cigarettes in a row the previous night, it could just as easily be the beginnings of pneumocystis pneumonia.

Realizing the window of opportunity to pretend to not be home had closed, Joey let his forehead hit his side of the door with a dull thud. Collier raised an eyebrow and smiled again as he lifted his hands to shoulder height and turned his palms to the ceiling, an unexpectedly theatrical way of saying, Well, whaddaya gonna do? Joey opened the door.

"Good morning." Collier was chipper and scary at the same time, like a head cheerleader who knows you lost your virginity the night before and plans to use it against you. Joey didn't think he could talk so he squinted and gave Collier a thumbs-up. Collier stepped inside without an invitation and headed directly for the kitchen. Joey waited in his own entryway, attempting to assess what, exactly, was happening. Collier walked out of the kitchen with a tall glass of tap water which he handed to Joey, then waited patiently while Joey drank it down and accepted the empty glass when Joey handed it back to him. "Feel better?"

Joey took a deep breath. His head was throbbing. "Yes," he cleared his throat. "All better."

77

"Good. So, where did you get the purse?"

Joey held his arms out from his body and looked around his hips where a purse would be if he were carrying one.

Collier pressed his lips together into a thin line then turned the corners up like a child's drawing of a smile. "Cute." He stepped into the living room and looked around at the boxes. He nodded his head in time for a bit as if he were hearing a song he liked or an opinion he very much agreed with and couldn't have said better himself.

Joey spoke to his back. "I don't know what you're talking about. What... purse... are you... I don't know what you mean." Confused and innocent, confused and innocent. Collier sat down on Joey's couch and leaned back like he was testing it out at a furniture store. Joey tried to pretend that they were just two friends having a visit. "Why didn't you bring Flowers?"

Collier put his feet up on a box and folded his hands in his lap. "If I'd brought you flowers would you level with me?"

"No, your friend. The mean one, Flowers."

Collier barked out a laugh, "Flaars. Not Flowers, Flaars. F L A A R S."

"Oh. Well I heard Flowers." Somewhere deep inside Joey's head there was a thin, distant, high-pitched whine like some high-pressure air was escaping. He wondered if it was the onset of progressive multifocal leukoencephalopathy, lesions eating away at his brain. Collier's laugh made him smile.

"That's funny. You're funny." Collier put his hands behind his head, deliberately casual. "You're a funny liar."

Joey tried to make himself as still as possible.

"I have a damn good bullshit detector and it's going off like crazy around you. But here's the thing: you could be lying because you killed her, or you could be lying because you're scared. If you are scared, I feel bad about that, but I'm not in a position to make that my priority. Does that make sense?"

Joey didn't know how to respond without somehow admitting Collier was on to something. Collier leaned forward. "So. I have couple of options here. I could arrest you." He looked at Joey for a reaction and Joey continued to try not to have one.

"For what?"

"For lying. Lying a bunch yesterday. It's uh... lying during a murder investigation is... well, it's frowned upon by judges."

"I didn't lie."

"Come on, man, this building and the one next door are completely flip-flopped, there's no way anyone wouldn't see that after walking two steps in, so give me a little bit of credit here."

"I get disoriented easily. That's not a crime."

"Technically, you're right. It's a fine line. Just like there's a fine line between walking naked from the shower past your window and standing in that window with an erection."

Joey felt his face get hot. "I can't control what you think. Or what anyone thinks, for that matter. But, if you are going to arrest me, this would be a convenient time to do it. I've already taken the day off work."

Collier put his hands up to his mouth and made the weird harelip face. "I haven't decided."

"Can I go back to bed until you make up your mind?"

"Nope, sorry. See, every hour that goes by right now takes us exponentially further and further from finding the person who killed this girl. I think, because you paid that indigent ten bucks to walk her purse into my precinct and ask for me by name, that you want to help." He sat back again and crossed one ankle over the other knee, deliberately casual. "Mindy Shorent was 24 years old. She was a dancer, five-foot-three, one hundred and two pounds. Little. The medical examiner said that the left side of her skull had been hit so hard with something that it had gone soft. Her right collarbone was shattered beyond repair and her nose was broken in more than one place. She died from drowning, which means all that happened while she was still alive."

Resisting the urge to reach up and touch his own head drew Joey's attention to the ache behind his eyes and blurred vision. It could be nothing; it could be his hangover. It could be cryptococcal meningitis.

"I need to know where you found Mindy Shorent's purse and how you knew to find it there. I need to know what you were doing in Raymond Nunez's apartment. The rest of it, whether or not you're a flasher or a coffee machine thief or why you're completely incapable of unpacking after almost a month of living in a new apartment, if it has nothing to do with Mindy Shorent, I'll agree to drop it."

Joey nodded, slowly. Guessing that Collier was watching him very closely, he figured he needed to tell the truth, at least about something. "The man I was living with died a few months ago. He'd been sick for about eight months, I mean longer than that, but really sick for about eight months. He didn't want to die in a hospital, so when it became clear that there was nothing more they could do for him there, I brought him home. The other residents in the building, not all of them, but some of them, enough of them, signed a petition to get us kicked out, to make us take him back to the hospital. It wasn't clear if they had any legal legs to stand on, or how they intended to enforce this, but it was soon a moot point because he died. And I thought that was the end of that until I heard that there was another petition being circulated to get me out of the building. Technically since my name wasn't on that lease, I was a squatter. That was their point of view anyway. Not as many people signed that petition, but still... Anyway, the stuff in these boxes, a lot of it, is his."

Collier stood up but looked down at his tie. He half extended his arm to Joey in a non-specific gesture. "I'm sorry for your loss. People are assholes."

Joey waved the sentiment away like an unappealing passed appetizer. "I'm sorry it's not the answer you're looking for, but I can't help you." Collier looked uncomfortable; Joey felt sure he'd successfully deterred further questioning. "I didn't pay a homeless guy to give you a purse and I don't know who murdered Mindy Shorent."

Collier pursed his lips. "Well, then. I guess we're done here."

He headed for the front door and Joey did too. Did the distant whine in Joey's brain get louder? Did brain lesions make noise? Joey opened the front door like a proper host.

"Just out of curiosity," Joey asked Collier's back, "how do you know she was a dancer?"

Collier turned in the doorway. "What's that?"

"I was just curious. I guess I assumed she was a hooker."

"What made you assume that?"

"I don't know. I just... made that assumption. It's probably not a fair assumption."

Collier shrugged. "It's as fair as any. We know she was a dancer because she had a bunch of old school IDs in her wallet, from high school and from NYU and some dance place. Some dance school. Oh, and she had a key chain with little pink ballet slippers on it."

"Which place?"

"What do you care?"

"I told you. I'm just curious. I have a friend who used to dance. Sort of."

"A friend, huh?" Collier reached into the inside pocket of his blazer, pulled out a little notebook and read from his notes. "Let's see... she had a class schedule in her purse for a place called Broadway Dance Center but it was from last winter, I don't know how often they change schedules but I have someone looking into it -"

"Flowers?"

"Yep. Flowers. And," he turned a page in the notebook, "let's see... one of her student IDs was from a place called A.B.I."

"A.B.T.?"

Collier squinted at his own writing. "Yeah. Maybe that. Why?"

Joey considered dropping it, but it was weird. And he did still feel bad for lying about what he knew, but at the time he really believed that the little he knew wouldn't really help. Now he wasn't so sure. "Do you think I can see the body again?"

"Absolutely not."

"Why not?"

81

"Because."

"Because why?"

"Because technically, you could be the killer."

"Give me a break."

"You give me a break. Also you reek of a hangover."

"Just give me two minutes." Joey ran down the hall and into his bedroom where he changed his smoky tee shirt for a clean one. He skirted into the bathroom, brushed his teeth, splashed cool water on his face and ran some through his hair before pulling on a baseball cap. He sprayed two sprays of Colors by Benneton in his own general direction and walked through the mist before running back to the door where Collier was, for some reason, still waiting. "Better?"

Collier inhaled deeply through his nose. "Mmmm. Booze and cologne. I never said the guy was homeless."

Joey swallowed. "What?" The handsome detective was really close to his face.

"The guy you paid to bring me the purse. I never said he was homeless."

"Yes you did." Joey's brain whined a tad louder.

"I did?"

"Yep. You did."

"Hm. You sure?"

Joey smiled, having suddenly figured something out. "Rewind the tape, Lieutenant." He patted Collier's side pocket where the small handheld device whirred away, hardly louder than a bumblebee, but completely distracting when you're hypersensitive to signs that your body is giving up on you. Collier took the recorder out of his pocket and pressed the stop button and the whirring in Joey's brain, as well as the threat of cryptococcal meningitis and progressive multifocal leukoencephalopathy, disappeared. At least for today.

Fifteen

Collier put his hand up, as if to stop Joey from charging forward. The Korean man in the morgue reached for the handle of the drawer containing what they were still referring to as Mindy Shorent. Collier tented his hand and put his fingertips to Joey's chest as if he were a volleyball. Joey looked at Collier's face.

"What?"

Collier kept his hand on Joey and put the other one on his hip, pulling open his blazer to reveal a glimpse of a gun in a shoulder holster and a badge attached to his belt. It was probably subliminal but he also probably wanted to remind Joey who was in charge here. He met Joey's gaze. "Have you ever seen a dead body before?"

"Yes." It was almost cold enough in the morgue for Joey to see his own breath, cold enough to wish he'd had the sense to bring a cardigan.

"Okay, well an embalmed body that's been prepared for viewing is different from one that... one in here."

"It's okay. I've seen dead bodies before. In fact I've seen this dead body before."

Collier nodded. "Right. Just, um, if you have to throw up or anything, it's not a big deal, just try to get some distance..."

"Also, no touching," the morgue employee said.

Collier nodded in agreement. "Also I'm going to stand behind you in case you faint."

Joey looked from Collier to the other guy, "I'll be fine. I appreciate your concern," this to Collier, then to the attendant, "but really. I'll be cool."

Collier nodded and the drawer was opened to reveal a lumpy mass covered by a white sheet. The morgue attendant pulled it down to just above the body's breasts. This part happened a little too quickly for

83

Joey and he realized he was counting on a tad more build-up, perhaps a short speech about mortality or a drum roll. He looked at her face, beyond slack, discolored and veiny, eyes only half closed. His mouth filled up with saliva that he swallowed only to have it fill back up immediately. He swallowed again.

"You okay?" Collier's voice sounded as if he were close enough to place his chin on Joey's shoulder with very little effort. Joey put his hands up to his shoulders and turned his palms up and waggled them back and forth as if he were trying to get the attention of someone on the ceiling.

"I'm fine, I'm fine." He clasped his hands together in front of his crotch mostly to stop himself from involuntarily making another little old lady move. He took in a deep, meditative breath and tried to think of dry toast as he exhaled slowly. Collier stepped beside him but kept one hand out, lightly on Joey's back. Whether it was there to catch him should he fall or gently urge him forward was unclear. Joey tried to fuzz her face out of focus and just concentrate on what he needed to see.

"What are you looking for?" Collier was beside him again.

"I was wondering who gave her her last haircut."

"Seriously?" By now Joey didn't have to look at Collier to know that he was lifting one eyebrow up and regarding him warily out of the corner of his eye. It was one of his looks.

"Seriously. Look at this." He reached out toward the bleached hair around her face.

"No touching," the attendant stepped forward.

Joey jerked his hands up to his chest and clasped them. "Sorry."

Collier spoke up with authority, "Get him some gloves."

"He's not allowed to touch her."

"I don't have time for this shit, Junior, just get him some gloves." Collier's voice went deeper and he spat out his words through gritted teeth. The young man shrugged and turned away to do as he'd been ordered. Collier widened his eyes at Joey and grinned. He put back on his serious face a moment later as Joey was handed a pair of latex gloves.

Gloved Joey took a step closer to Mindy's head. He tried to imagine that she was just another client, freshly shampooed and toweled off, relaxed and waiting to be beautified, but it was awkward. Because of the drawer he couldn't get entirely behind her so he had to attack half from above, half behind, reaching his left hand across her face to the hair on the right side of her head while his right hand took a lock on her left to test his theory. He pulled each lock of hair straight, just about even with her chin, although in life, with her head up and her mouth held shut, they probably looked a bit longer. He looked at Collier. "See?"

"No."

"Look." He did it again, pulling his fingers down the lengths of hair to their ends, trying not to focus on the squeaking feeling the latex made against the damp hair.

"What?" Collier stepped forward as well and tried to position himself so that he could look at her head on.

"The left side is shorter than the right. Like, shorter shorter."

Collier squinted. "Oh yeah. A bit."

"It's not a bit, it's, like, get your money back and never return to that salon shorter."

Collier put his hands up in mock defense, "Ooh, take it easy, tough guy."

Joey ignored him. "Also," he put his hands under her shoulders before realizing what he almost did without thinking. His knees buckled a little. He looked at the miffed, neutered employee. "Sorry. Can we, can you sit her up for a sec?"

The attendant stepped forward and took her right shoulder before facing off with Joey. "On two." Joey realized his hand was still touching her left shoulder. "One, two -" Together they lifted her to a sitting up position and the attendant stepped away immediately, leaving Joey to steady her alone as she slumped forward off balance. He steadied her with his left hand splayed out on her solar plexus and his right on her back like he was comforting a friend who'd had too much to drink. The sheet slipped down to her waist. Collier took over, holding her by the shoulders to keep her in place.

"What do you see, Joe?"

"Don't call me that." Joey ran his fingers through the back of her hair.

"Call you what?"

"Joe. Sounds like a truck driver."

"No, it's a good, strong name. No frills." Collier watched Joey studying Mindy's hair. "Joey's a little... young for you."

"Shut up."

"Start talking, Joe-ee."

"Okay, her hair is a wreck. It's a total hack job."

"Meaning what?"

"Meaning it's all hacked up. Really badly. And look at the color."

"Blond."

"Yeah, but look back here, underneath, the color variation. It's shades darker in the back. It's really, really sloppy. Plus it's like butter yellow. It needs a full second process plus a toner to be considered blond. This looks to me like she did this all herself. And in a hurry."

Collier shrugged. "So what? Maybe she's a punk. Maybe she wanted to be Cyndi Lauper."

"I don't think so."

"You don't? How come?"

"I think... I think if this girl was a ballerina, it's... that's a specific look. Classical. This looks to me like a girl who..." he trailed off, knowing that if he finished his thought it could possibly derail his entire day.

"Who what?"

Joey sighed. Fuck it, it's just a day. "It looks to me like she didn't want to be recognized. Like she was scared, on the run maybe."

"Her hair looks like she was scared, or did she tell you she was scared before she died?"

"Didn't we do this yesterday?"

"We tried."

"Look, all I'm saying is that my professional opinion is that it appears that she cut and dyed her hair herself within a week of the time of her death, probably less. Probably within days. Do what you want with it. Personally, I think it would make sense to at least pop by ABT and see if my theory makes sense to anyone who knew her."

"That makes sense to you, huh?"

"Yes, it does. Why, does it not make sense to you?"

"Are you a detective, Joe?"

"You asked for my opinion."

"Are you a dancer?"

"Me? No. But I'm flattered by your mistake."

"Flattered?"

"Have you seen a male dancer's body?"

"I don't recall. Why?"

"They're pretty spectacular, so I'm flattered that you would mistake me for one." Their chaperone made a sound somewhere between a cough and a laugh. Joey turned to him. "Can you get out of here?"

"I'm not allowed to leave you alone with the body."

Collier stayed on Joey. "You're skinny like a dancer."

"No, I'm skinny like a worrier who smokes."

"So you've never taken classes at AT..."

"ABT," Joey interrupted. "No."

"So you're not a dancer, but you happen to have this very specific knowledge..."

"I don't have any specific knowledge, I have some general knowledge that might get me through a polite conversation on the subject at one of my little cocktail parties."

"Aw, you still mad that Flaars said that?"

"I'm not mad. Not at all. It was an insulting and small-minded generalization, but you'd know if I was mad."

Collier smiled, skirting the edge of condescension. "So if we go to this ABT place, there won't be anyone there who recognizes you, is that what you're saying?"

"No, I'm not going. You should go but I have stuff to do." Joey took off the latex gloves.

"Like what?"

"Well, I have a pretty busy day planned, full of minding my own business. You?"

Collier surprised Joey and the attendant with a loud, full laugh. "Cute. That was cute. Come on, tough guy, it'll take a half hour." Collier put his hands on Joey's shoulders and turned him toward the door. They took a couple of steps like this, a two-man conga line, and then Joey felt Collier's hand pat him on the butt, one quick encouraging pat, like a teammate.

"I'll buy you a drink afterwards," Collier continued as he stepped up even to Joey. "It's almost noon, you must be dying for one."

Sixteen

The topless waitress smiled at Carlo, like she recognized him, which he knew she didn't; he would definitely remember a previous meeting. He smiled back, mostly because it was easier to get information from someone who didn't see you as a threat. Since he wasn't there for entertainment it was easy to observe the scene as a whole. He thought of the way his nephew talked about observing behavior in groups of insects or reptiles, which is what he spent his days doing. The girl on stage was knee-deep in her uninspired performance, listless to the point of belligerence, on her stomach facing away from the audience, windshield wipering her legs from side to side like she was watching television in the family den. These clubs made you forget what time of day it was. Outside, the sun was just beginning to think about setting for the evening; inside it was sometime between midnight and 5 am. Always.

Sometime that afternoon, Carlo started thinking. He wondered if he'd been a little rash in destroying the tapes, if he shouldn't have listened to Anthony's message one or two more times. As it was, he had to remember what he could. There had been noise in the background, maybe muffled music, or traffic, but most likely music. Anthony had said he was *laying low,* which to Carlo was something one stayed home to do; but Anthony was not home; Carlo had already checked. There was no hard and fast rule or distinction between the terms, but Carlo felt that he usually heard people say hiding out when they were talking about laying low somewhere other than home. Anthony saying that he was laying low but not being home meant that he was hiding out. The fact that he didn't tell Carlo where he was hiding out meant that Carlo was one of the people he was hiding from. It occurred to Carlo that the Feds might be paying good money for the kind of information Anthony had in his possession. If Anthony were trying to go behind his back for a payday, well, that would not be good at all.

Not seeing Anthony at any of the tables, Carlo passed the stage and made his way to a hallway that led to the restrooms. Along one wall was a bank of pay phones. Carlo picked one of the receivers up and held it up to his ear so he could keep his eyes on the bathroom door without looking like he was. He'd wait for a few minutes, and then hit the next place on the strip.

"Can I get you something to drink?"

Carlo turned to see the same waitress he'd passed on his way in. She looked older than he'd first thought, but her tits were still in great shape. Carlo started to say no but then thought of the way Anthony had said *thanks, babe* during his message. The way it had sounded more like an aside than an actual part of the message. He hung up the phone.

"Yeah. Actually, I'm looking for someone."

The waitress raised an eyebrow.

"I'm looking for a friend of mine that was in here yesterday."

Her expression didn't change but she shook her head from side to side ever so slightly.

"He's a good looking guy named Tony, comes in here pretty regularly. Maybe you seen him? It'd be worth your while if you had." Carlo took a hundred dollar bill out of his pocket.

"Mister, I don't sell information," she looked at the bill like it was beneath her but leaned into him a little. "I sell gin and tonics."

"Oh yeah? How much for a gin and tonic?"

"For you? A hundred bucks."

Carlo laughed and put the money on the tray. He liked this girl. If he were younger he might tell her.

"It's good you're here. He got fucking hammered last night. He gave me two bills to let him sleep it off in the back, but Brian found out and now he's pissed."

"Two bills?" Carlo whistled. "You're making out like a bandit in all this."

"Yeah," she turned and walked toward a closed door that he'd passed on his way to the phones. "Lucky me." She shifted the tray to her other hand to open the door. "Good luck waking him up."

Carlo knew that Anthony was brash. He knew that Anthony thought he was a lot smarter than he actually was. The ease with which Carlo had found him was troubling, it made Carlo wonder what other stupid mistakes Anthony would make, what stupid mistakes he'd already made. "Don't worry," he assured her. "I'll wake him up."

———

"What do you mean you don't know?"

Carlo was sitting in a folding chair that he'd pulled up alongside the small dirty looking couch that he'd found Anthony curled up on covered by a sweatshirt that looked more like it had been thrown at him than used to cover him, a magazine rolled up in his hand.

"I mean I don't fucking know, okay? I had them -" Anthony was sitting up, rubbing the side of his face and rocking back and forth, his right hand nervously fussing with the watch on his right wrist. "I think they got stolen."

"Hm." Carlo nodded. He'd noticed the watch when he'd walked in the bleak little office, pissed-off Brian's office, he assumed. It was a nice watch. A watch like that could cost five hundred dollars, he'd thought, before slapping Anthony's passed-out face about as hard as he'd ever hit anything with an open hand. "Where'd they get stolen from?"

"My apartment. They were hidden, I swear. Man, you didn't have to fucking hit me like that."

"Watch your language."

Anthony grimaced and started to say 'fuck' but stopped himself. It sounded like pffff, a petulant exhalation.

"Anything else stolen? Or just the hidden books."

"Just - look, I know it sounds like bullshit, but there was this girl that I was seeing. I think she took them."

There's always a girl. "She a Fed?"

91

"Gimme a break."

"Trust me, I am giving you a huge break."

"I know. Look, I don't fucking know why she took them, okay? She and her friend fucked me over."

"Okay." Carlo stood up and handed Anthony his sweatshirt that had fallen onto the floor after the wake-up slap. "Let's go ask her."

"She's dead."

"You kill her?"

"No."

"Where's the friend?"

"I don't know."

Carlo nodded, thinking about how he was going to explain this to Del.

"Look, it's fucked up," Anthony said to the floor. "I thought I could get it out of her, what she'd done with them, but she wouldn't tell me. I left her on the couch for a while and when I came back the place was crawling."

"Anyone see you?"

"I kept walking."

"Okay, let me get this straight. A girl you're dating, completely unrelated to the situation at hand, steals my ledgers and gives them to a friend of hers who disappears with them into thin air. Then the girl turns up dead."

"Yeah," Anthony nodded. "Yes, sir."

"There's something you're not telling me. Like the fact that you beat the shit out of her. Am I right?"

Anthony shook his head just slightly, like the topless waitress had.

"How can you be sure you didn't kill her?"

"I swear to you, when I left her she was on the couch. When they found her, she was in the bathtub."

Carlo stood up. "Okay, go home. Take a shower. Go to work in the morning and try to act normal. Anyone know about you and this girl?"

"No."

"Anyone at all? Besides her friend?"

"No."

"Good. Don't bring it up, even as a story you heard about. If someone else brings it up, you say yeah, you heard about that. Got it?"

"Yeah. Carlo, I swear there's nothing I ain't telling you."

"We'll see." Carlo stood up.

"Where are you going?"

"To find out what you're lying about. What, you think you're the only asshole I know?" Carlo picked up the magazine Anthony had been sleeping with. "When this is all over, you and I will have a little talk about hitting women."

———

Carlo dialed a number he knew by heart from a pay phone. He had contacts in the NYPD, guys who were eager to make a quick buck for a piece of information without asking questions. He flipped through the magazine he'd taken from Anthony, which turned out to be a catalogue for sailing boats.

"Mike Dawes," announced the voice on the other end, rushed and inconvenienced.

"Hello Mike Dawes, it's Mike Dawes here, too," Carlo replied. Each of his contacts knew him by their own name, which made it easier to remember.

"Mr. Dawes!" the real Mike Dawes relaxed. "It's been a while. What can I do for you?"

"Mike, I'm wondering what you can find out for me about a girl who went and got herself killed. Very sad. A girl by the name of Mindy Shorent."

"Sure thing, Mr. D. Give me just a sec."

Carlo heard himself get put on hold. The real Mike Dawes didn't need to know why Carlo was asking. He knew that in a couple of days he would get a card in the mail with anywhere from one to three hundred dollars in it depending on the extent of the favor. The fake

Mike Dawes knew that the money would be lost at the Off Track Betting office by eight o'clock in the evening the day the real Mike Dawes received it. Addicts made for discreet contacts.

Who gets a catalogue for boats?

"You there?" Mike Dawes's voice was quieter now.

"Yessir."

"Okay. Doesn't look like they have much of anything. They got an APB out on someone named Raymond Nunez and they have a person of interest, but not in custody."

"If he's a person of interest to them, Mike, he's a person of interest to me." Carlo's biology studying nephew told him recently that it was close to impossible to observe natural behavior in the field or the laboratory without interference, that the act of observation itself was enough to affect behaviors.

"You got a pen?"

"Yeah." Carlo didn't need to write anything down.

"Alright, guy's named Joseph Broderer. You want his address?"

"Sure." Carlo planned to do some observation himself. Level of interference to be determined.

Seventeen

"Joey? Joey Broderer!? My word, it's been ages!" Joey and Collier had barely set foot inside the lobby of the American Ballet Theater's studio space. "Hasn't it been ages? My goodness, how are you?" The balding, dapper gentleman with matronly hips held a thin stack of files in one hand as he opened his arms to Joey. Joey stepped forward like a child obligated to hug a distant uncle.

"Hi Barry, how are you?" The hug was brief and Barry kept his hand on Joey's elbow. "I didn't know you worked here." Joey said this more to Collier who was looking like he just won a bet.

"Oh yeah. Fundraising. Almost a year now. Well, thirteen months." Barry looked at Collier. "Hi, I'm Barry."

"I'm sorry," Joey remembered his manners. "Collier this is Barry Hoegle. Barry this is Collier.... Collier."

Collier stepped forward as he opened his jacket and put his hand on his hip next to his badge as he extended his other for a shake. "Lieutenant Collier, NYPD."

"Oh my." Barry actually blushed as he adjusted the arms of the periwinkle sweater draped over his shoulders in a loose half-knot. "Is everything okay?"

"That depends, Barry."

"No, it doesn't." Joey stayed between them like a couples counselor. "Everything's fine." He turned to Collier, "Would you put the badge away?" Then back to Barry, "He's just kidding."

"No, I'm not."

Joey hit Collier on the shoulder with the back of his hand. "Yes, you are kidding."

"You just hit a police officer," Collier widened his eyes at Joey, then looked at Barry. "Did you see that?"

Barry looked from Collier to Joey, not sure what was going on between them. "I did see that." He settled on Joey. "How's Henry?"

"He's fine, thanks." Joey deliberately changed the subject. "Barry, do you know a dancer named Mindy Shorent?"

"Mindy Shorent, Mindy Shorent..." Barry tucked the folders under one arm and tapped his pursed lips with his index finger while looking up and to the right. "Doesn't ring any immediate bells. She's definitely not in the company."

Collier interjected, "How do you two know each other?"

Barry looked surprised, as if Collier had just materialized out of thin air. "Gosh, we've known each other forever. How *do* we know each other?"

"Through Brian, I believe. Originally."

Barry touched his index finger to Joey's shoulder. "That's right. We met at Brian Duvret's share on the Island. My word, what year was that, '75? '76?"

"Something like that." It wasn't Brian Duvret who had introduced them, it was Brian Magnussen, but Joey didn't feel like correcting him. Brian Duvret was the one who had introduced Joey to Henry, several years later. Brian Magnussen was the type of person to start talking about his share on the Island as early as January and insist all winter and spring that *You absolutely must come out, I insist,* and then act mildly inconvenienced when the offer was accepted. Joey was, apparently, the type of person to hold a grudge, or at least remember it, even after the perpetrator was dead.

"Is this back when you were dancing?" Collier asked Joey.

Barry lit up. "Back when we were all dancing! I was thinner then," he stage-whispered to Collier.

"Do you know, Barry, who we might be able to talk to about Mindy Shorent? To ask some questions about her?"

"What kinds of questions? Is there some sort of trouble?"

"No, no trouble -"

"Yes," Collier cut Joey off. "She was murdered." Joey hit him on the arm. "You know it's a felony to hit me, right?"

Joey stayed focused on Barry. "But we are in a little bit of a hurry..."

"Oh. Well if she's a student here, I suppose you could ask Holly for starters." Barry pointed with his folder toward a young woman in an oversized sweatshirt behind a reception desk. "She might know her."

"Thanks, Barry. We will. It's nice to see you." Joey smiled warmly and found that he meant it.

"Great to see you, too." They hugged again and Barry patted him on the back with the folder. "Give Henry my best."

"Deal."

Barry turned to Collier. "Nice to meet you, Lieutenant." Collier saluted and Barry saluted back then giggled and walked away, shaking his head. Collier turned to Joey.

"Who's Henry?"

"Would you be willing to let me do the talking here?"

"Sure," Collier said. "If you'd be willing to let me give the haircuts."

"I'm serious. You have a very accusatory air about you. It's very off-putting. It makes people who haven't done anything wrong feel like they have."

"Everyone's done something wrong. Well, except maybe that guy." He gestured in the direction that Barry had penguined off in.

"Shows how much you know. He got mugged a few years ago by two fifteen-year-olds."

"That makes him guilty?"

"It happened at one A.M. in the Rambles when his pants were around his ankles."

"Aha. Well, still, he definitely didn't know or murder Mindy Shorent."

"You're that confident in your ability to read people?"

Collier nodded. "Yup."

"Okay, let's try this. Let me talk to Holly and you can gauge her reactions. Does that sound fair?"

Collier considered Joey's offer for only a second. "Okay, sure. After you." He held out his arm for Joey to go first, like they were entering a restaurant. Joey strode confidently ahead up to the desk. Holly looked to be about nineteen. Her long blond hair was pulled up into a combination of a bun and a ponytail atop of her wide, open, mid-western face and her legs were tucked up under her. Sensing Joey and Collier's presence, she put her magazine to the side.

"Can I help you?"

"Hi." Joey liked her. "I hope so. Did you go to Princeton?" Joey pointed to the block letters across the front of her sweatshirt.

"No. My boyfriend did." She smiled and her eyes crinkled.

Collier put his chin on Joey's shoulder. "Hi." Startled, Joey jerked his shoulder up, which made Collier's teeth clack together. "Ow! That's three -"

"That was a reaction, not a hit."

Collier winked at Holly, jerking his thumb in Joey's direction like a vaudeville comedian. "This guy's been beating the crap out of me. You recognize him?" She looked at Joey's face with concern.

"I don't think so. Do I?"

"No, you don't," Joey reassured her. He turned to Collier. "I thought we had a deal."   Collier brushed him away like a gnat, still charming Holly with his smile. "Do you mind if I parade him around and see if anyone here recognizes him?"

Holly looked at Joey again. "Do you have amnesia?"

"No, I don't have amnesia," Joey sighed. "But I'm hoping to get some later today." He leaned in toward Holly in an attempt to shut Collier out. "Holly, do you know a dancer named Mindy Shorent?"

Holly's eyes widened for a minute before she caught herself. "Oh. I'm not supposed to talk about her."

"You're not? How come?"

"I'm not sure. There was a man in here about an hour ago asking about her... a detective."

"We're not cops," Collier lied.

"We're just friends," Joey added. "Not of each other, friends of hers."

"I didn't know her. I heard that she died or something, is that true?"

"Yeah, she did. Do you know anyone who knows her?" Joey leaned in and got a little quieter. "Have you heard anyone talking about her, any rumors or anything?"

Holly thought. "Well, not really. She auditioned for the corps de ballet but didn't get in. She took classes a lot, but then stopped like six months ago."

"Why didn't she get in?" Joey was legitimately curious. He had been thinking of her as a skilled ballerina. The idea that she'd maybe only been mediocre challenged his theory about her hair, but also made her somehow more interesting or complex, more real to him.

"I'm not sure why. But I could go get Mistress Tatiana. I'm actually supposed to get her if anyone else comes by asking about this. I mean her. Mindy."

"Who's Mistress Tatiana?" Collier asked Joey, still trying to catch him in some elaborate lie.

"I don't know. Holly, who's Mistress Tatiana?"

"She's the Ballet Mistress. Let me go try to find her." Holly got up and propelled herself down the hall with a quick series of graceful, perfect, tiny jumps strung together to form a jog.

Joey turned to Collier. "A detective was in here about an hour ago?"

Collier shrugged innocently, "Perhaps."

"Flowers?"

Collier smiled. "You're not the only one with the good ideas."

"You could have just told me instead of wasting my morning."

Collier opened his mouth to respond but was cut off by a flurry of commotion coming toward them quickly from down the hall where Holly had pranced moments before, a raspy voice with a thick Russian accent. "... refuse to take any more time away from my dancers to deal with this bullshits. Perhaps I was not making myself completely clear earlier..." Collier and Joey turned to see a tiny woman of indeterminate age marching swiftly toward them in a black leotard. She carried what looked like a walking stick, but she clearly didn't need it for support. It was as if someone had thrown an ice pick in their direction.

"These guys aren't cops, they're just friends..." Holly trailed behind.

The sinewy woman silenced Holly with a sharp glance before coming to an abrupt stop in front of Collier and Joey. She smiled, revealing nicotine stained, sharp teeth. "Good morning gentlemens. I understand you have questions?"

Joey considered the duality of her face as he looked down at it, damaged by years of smoke and sun, yet very well-moisturized and almost dewy looking. "We do haves questions. Have. Questions." He had unintentionally mimicked her accent and didn't want her to think he was making fun of her. If she noticed, she didn't show any sign of it.

"I see. And you haves a warrant for these information?"

Joey tried not to blink as he smiled. "We're not police."

Tatiana offered a throaty chuckle, flirtatious and disturbing. "Is true in America, yes? That when you are police you must say you are police?"

Joey glanced at Collier who was smushing his lip up. He nodded once, barely enough to be noticed.

"Okay. He is police. He's a policeman, a detective actually. But I'm not."

Holly hung her head in shame. A whole year in New York and her street smarts hadn't begun to develop. Joey wanted to apologize.

Tatiana's stare turned from ice to steel. "The American Ballet Theater does not offer any informations about its students or its dancers. Good day, gentlemens. Please see yourselves out the way you came in." She turned on her heel without making a sound and started to glide away. Collier stepped forward, taking his notebook and pen out of his pocket in one fluid movement.

"Fine, we'll be back this afternoon with a warrant. What did you say your full name was?"

Tatiana turned back, suddenly mere inches from Collier's face. "My name is Tatiana Gofuckyourself -"

Collier overlapped, holding his hands up like he was being mugged. "Whoa, whoa, language!"

"You think I am scared of you? You are a just a little boy who wets the bed."

"Wets the bed?"

"You are in my house now," she spat out each word.

Joey got in between them like a referee. "Okay, everybody calm down." He turned to Collier. "You know what? This lady is absolutely right, you're out of line." He glanced over his shoulder to see the Ballet Mistress glaring defiantly at Collier, her thin muscled arms folded defiantly across her bony chest. He hoped that Tatiana's knowledge of police work was as effectively tainted by her experiences behind the Iron Curtain as it appeared to be. "My family is paying you a lot of money to find my... niece. And we've given you a lot of free rein. But I draw the line at you bullying my niece's friends. If you can't behave yourself, I'm more than happy to hire a different detective. Do you understand?" Joey hoped that what he was doing was clumsy enough to be felt by Collier but sly enough to be missed by Tatiana.

Collier looked down for a moment, then met Joey's eyes. "Well, you don't have to fire me, because I quit." He pushed his finger into Joey's chest. "You got it? Huh? You got it?"

"Yeah, I got it." Joey pulled the small cassette recorder from the pocket of Collier's blazer.

"Good. I quit. This is bullshit." Collier turned like a soldier and stormed out, kicking a metal wastebasket by the door over onto its side where it rolled back and forth, spilling out garbage in a neat arc.

Eighteen

1958

Backlit by the afternoon sun, Iris struggled to focus in the dim bar.

"We're closed." A bartender with a blond pompadour didn't lift his head as he spoke.

"I'm not thirsty." Iris's heels scuffed along the wood floor of the room where Christopher had spent the last night of his life. She approached the handsome, if slightly weathered bartender who still hadn't moved; a cigarette burned in an ashtray next to a newspaper spread out in front of him. Iris thought of the Tin Man and wondered how he could read anything in such dim light.

"Even if we were open," the bartender looked Iris up and down, "I don't think we're your kind of place, doll."

As he spoke, Iris realized the handsome man was a woman. A square jawed woman with a man's haircut and a man's short-sleeved shirt tucked into pleat-front slacks cinched by a worn leather belt. Iris realized she'd never seen a female bartender before so she wasn't sure what an appropriate title for the blond woman might be.

"I'm not a doll." Iris said this quietly, more to herself, and wondered if she'd said it or only thought it and then didn't care. The blue pills made the concept of consequence feel far away and abstract. "I'm not a customer, I'm looking for information." This, Iris made sure she said aloud. Nothing about the blond woman's expression changed. "About a man. He was arrested in here. Maybe you remember him? It was two nights ago."

The woman's steeled eyes jerked once towards the door then jumped back to Iris.

"That man was my husband." She took in a deep breath. "My name is Iris."

The blond woman shrugged. "Talk to your husband then. I don't get involved in domestic disputes." She looked back down to the newspaper and turned the page. Conversation over.

"He shot himself." The bartender remained frozen in place, lacking a heart or perhaps just oil. "Christopher lied to me every single day since I met him. Eddie thinks I should stay in bed like a Goddamn invalid. And you won't even look at me. I just want to know why." Iris opened the door, allowing the sunny day to spill in. "I guess everyone must think I'm pretty stupid."

"Wait."

Behind her, Iris heard the newspaper rustle.

"Sit down," the bartender said. "If you want to, I mean. Let me pour you a drink."

Exposed momentarily to the bright daylight, Iris saw only darkness when she turned to look back into the bar.

"My name is Libby. What happened to your husband, what he did to himself, it might be my fault."

———

Iris missed the keyhole altogether using the spare key Eddie had given her, then jabbed and missed again. She held the doorknob with her left hand and slowly guided the key toward it and was on the cusp of making a successful connection when the door pulled open from the other side, yanking her off balance.

Eddie stared at her. "Where have you been? I've been worried sick, I was just about to call the hospitals and the police..."

"Don't call the police, the police are not our friends." She let herself fall into the couch. The lamp on the end table was too bright so she reached up and turned it off.

"Whose friend? Are you drunk?"

"Our friends. Friends of Dorothy's friends." Iris was reveling in feeling wise, in the know. She liked being in on a secret. She wanted Eddie to be scared of her instead of scared for her and she enjoyed the look of concern on his face.

103

"I'm going to make some coffee." Eddie went into the kitchen. "Who's Dorothy?"

Iris had asked Libby the same question. *Who's Dorothy?*

I don't know, Libby had answered. *It's just something we say. It's code, for people in the know to talk to other people in the know without anyone else understanding.*

Is it Dorothy Dandridge?

I don't know if it's about a real person at all. It might be made up. Anyways, it's not part of the story. Do you want to hear this or not?

"Iris?" Eddie poked his head in from the kitchen. "Who's Dorothy?"

Iris sat up straighter on Eddie's couch and licked her lips. She was done with this loose feeling now. It had been fun but now she wanted her mind back, her ability to focus. "Nobody. It's not important." Iris willed herself to feel crisper, to clear the haze away. "Eddie? May I ask you a legal question?"

"Sure, Iris." She could hear him putting the kettle on.

"If you pay a person, or a group, to provide a service and they fail to provide it, you can sue them, right?"

"Theoretically, yes, of course. Do you have proof? Or a contract?"

"I don't think so. It's more like an oral agreement I'm talking about."

"Oral agreements can be tricky..." Eddie came back into the living room with milk and sugar, which he placed on the coffee table in front of Iris. "It can be difficult to prove and enforce an oral agreement."

Iris thought of her marriage vows.

"Can you tell me what you're talking about?" Eddie stood in front of her, rumpled slacks and bow tie, his sleeves rolled up and a dishtowel over his shoulder.

Iris thought of Libby's eyes, how she'd watched them remember, refocus and finally resolve to share her story with a practical stranger. She hoped her eyes held the same confidence as she turned to Eddie. "Here's how it works."

———

"Here's how it works." Libby refilled one of the two glasses with the amber liquor she'd poured and left the bottle open on the bar. "I have to make payments. To the police."

"For what?" Iris had taken only one sip from her glass and could still feel it burning on her lips.

"Hold on, sugar, let me get it out. Jeez, who are you, Brenda Starr?"

"Hardly," Iris smiled. "Although I did edit my high school newspaper during my senior year. The most exciting story we did was about a dog who dialed the operator on the telephone after his elderly owner fell down a flight of stairs."

"You don't say."

"I'm sorry. Please continue... you make payments to the police."

"Right. The price of doing business. See it's against the law for us to congregate here, or anywhere for that matter. Technically."

"For who to congregate?"

"Us: Pansies, dykes, sissies, queers. Sodomites."

"Friends of Dorothy."

"Exactly. It's against the law for us to get together in a bar like this or a clubroom or anything, so when we do, technically the police can come in and break up the party. If they feel like it, they can arrest everyone in the room, just for being here. Anytime they feel like it. But if you pay them off, they tend to not feel like it."

"How much do you pay them?"

"Five hundred."

"Five hundred dollars?" Iris almost fell off her barstool. "How often?"

"Mondays. They come after the weekend when they know the till is full."

"Every week some men come in here, take money from you in exchange for looking the other way so you can run your business?"

"Not every week. Not at first. At first it was every other week. The fine officers come in while I'm setting up. Plain clothes, but might as well be wearing a badge out in the open, the way they act like they run the place. I give 'em their drinks with their envelope and that's that."

Iris was unconsciously shaking her head. It wasn't that she had never considered corruption, but this sounded so juvenile, schoolyard bullies and lunch money.

"Then a few months ago, maybe eight months," Libby continued, "Frankie comes in."

"Who's Frankie? Sorry. Go ahead."

"Frankie works for my landlord. A few months back, Frankie comes in on a Monday and tells me he's there to collect. And I remember thinking to myself that it wasn't the week to collect, but I don't say anything, I just pour him a drink while I get the money together. Now, I never had no trouble with Frankie; he's not a bad guy, he's just short. Every once in a while he gets a little too confident and start saying things like, Hey Libby, why don't you go out with a real man, or something like that, but I know it's just jokes, so I just give it back to him. I tell him something like, you know, Frankie I ain't going with a man until I find one with a johnson bigger than mine. And then he laughs and that's that."

Libby downed her third glass in one gulp. Iris wondered if she really had a penis before deciding she was more comfortable without knowing all the answers.

"So that's how it goes. One week the brass comes, next week Frankie, so on and so forth. Then, a couple weeks back, another guy who works for my landlord comes by, just to see how I'm doing. So I pour him one, we talk a bit, and as he's leaving, I say Tell Frankie I'll see him Monday. This guy smiles like that's the funniest thing he's heard all day and he says Oh yeah? Frankie likes to spend time here? And he's laughing, see, cause he knows what kind of place this is. So then I say No not like that, he just comes by to collect for the cops. And then this guy says Oh right. I'll tell him. But he's not laughing anymore. And I think, by something about the way he looks, that this is new information to him."

Libby looked down at the bar and cleared her throat. She picked up the bottle and poured a bit more in the glass, which she held tightly in her other hand. She lifted the glass halfway then set it back down. "And I thought, fucking Frankie. He's not collecting for the cops at all; he's keeping it. And the more I thought about it, the more pissed off I got. I don't know why. It didn't bother me when I thought the money was going to the cops, but just to Frankie? That ain't right." Libby's body was rigid, like she was steadying herself to take a punch. The ice in Iris's glass released and shifted as it melted, almost in sympathy with Libby's inability to do so. She cleared her throat.

"So, Monday, Frankie comes and I pour him drink like usual but I tell him I don't have any money for him. He says why not and I tell him it was a slow weekend. I tell him he's shit outta luck. And at first he just nodded and then, before I know it, he's halfway up on the bar and he's got me around the neck -"

"He hit you?"

"Nah. I hit him. I got in three good shots. He stayed down for a good minute. I told him that he had that coming. He nodded again, like he agreed, stood up, finished his drink and walked out. And that night, the cops showed up and the rest is history."

They both stared at the bar, maybe even at the same swirled knot of wood.

Iris took a sip of her drink; what had burned now just warmed. "I don't see how any of that could be considered your fault."

Libby smiled. "That's the right thing to say, but I happen to disagree. I have a responsibility to make sure my people are safe in here. I let everyone down. And now your husband is dead."

"Libby -"

"I should have just paid him."

Iris shook her head vehemently back and forth. "No, that is not the solution."

"I should have at least let him win the fight. It wouldn't have been that bad. If I'd have just let him feel like a man, maybe none of this would have happened."

"Libby, these men are extorting you, you have to tell someone."

"Tell someone? Who am I supposed to tell?"

"The... tell the newspaper! Call the newspaper. I'll call the newspaper." Iris reached for the folded pages that Libby had left on the bar between them.

"The newspaper? You think the newspaper cares?"

"They should care. It's an injustice."

"You know what the newspapers do every time the cops feel like busting in and arresting us for having a drink with some friends? The newspapers print the names of everyone the cops arrest. They print their names, their addresses and where they work. They ruin lives, dolly. They ruin lives. That's why your husband killed himself."

———

Eddie sat slack-jawed, listening to her story.

"You're talking about organized crime, Iris." Whether intentionally or not, Eddie had lowered his voice.

"I'm glad you agree." Iris picked up her coffee and took a sip. It seemed to clear her head the very instant she swallowed.

"No, I don't mean... that wasn't my complimentary opinion of their methods. I mean you're talking about... something way over your head. This is... you need to just forget about all of this."

Iris had left out Libby's outburst about the newspapers. She left out that the tirade had left the handsome woman shaking. She left out that she'd wrapped her hand around Libby's clenched fist and squeezed it.

Eddie shook his head. "I think I should draw you a bath. You can have a good soak while I turn down your bed. This is bad news,

Iris, all of it, just put all of it behind you." He looked down at her black coffee. "You need some cream and sugar."

Iris had left out that Libby had put her other hand on top of Iris's and the two women had stayed like that in silence. She knew, suddenly, that along with the anxiety Christopher must have felt about keeping so many secrets, along with the panic and terror, certainly there must also have been exhilaration.

Nineteen

1985

There is a tendency here in America, Mr. Shorent, to romanticize the dead. Then came a pause where Mistress Tatiana inhaled and exhaled smoke from what Joey knew was a brown, European cigarette, as long and thin as a conductor's baton. *I'm not sure why this is. Qualities and abilities you would never attribute to a living person are suddenly, in death, theirs for the taking.* Collier looked up at Joey, his head bent to bring his ear closer to the speaker of the small tape recorder that Joey had lifted out of his jacket during their fake fight. *Is not true so much in Russia. Here, is like everyone feels so entitled to life, so angry with death, so indignant that they not only do everything they can to outrun it, but continue to fight against it, even after death has so very clearly won. Is as if you think you can somehow lessen the power of death by celebrating the dead after they are gone. I don't know, is very strange to me.*

"Damn." Collier's eyes widened as he took a small sip from a cold pint of beer, leaving a circular ring of condensation on the wooden bar.

"It gets better." Joey was glowing, still high on adrenaline after getting Mistress Tatiana to talk on tape. He swallowed the last of the scotch in his glass, surprised that he had finished it so quickly. He jiggled the ice in the glass and the bartender picked up on his signal.

This niece of yours, this Mindy... I am sorry for your loss. Is perhaps sadder when a younger person dies than an older person, however should you choose to somehow elevate her position in life now that she is gone, I regret to inform you that I cannot offer the assistance of the American Ballet Theater in this matter.

"What does that mean?" Collier smiled in disbelief. Joey grabbed his wrist, knowing what was coming next.

"Just wait, this is my favorite part." They listened to Tatiana's long exhalation of smoke. When she began speaking again, Joey mouthed her first few words along with her, remembering them perfectly. *She was not a good dancer. Here, we like girls who dance like women, not woman who dance like little girls. Was of no use to me here, but perhaps was very successful down on 42nd Street.*

42nd Street? Joey heard his own voice through the tiny speaker and wondered if that's what he really sounded like.

This is just what I hear, you understand. Is not American Ballet Theater that tells you this.

You mean she was dancing... you mean stripping?

Like I said, is just rumor.

Do you know where?

I do not concern myself with such places. Mistress Tatiana had dismissed the entire distasteful notion as if she hadn't been the one who'd brought it up. *I only say this so you will understand my position that I do not wish to have the American Ballet Theater mentioned in any public way. She was a student here some time ago, is true. We cannot always control who chooses to be student here. Taking some classes is hardly an achievement alone, so is not worth mentioning.*

Joey stopped the tape. "So. She's a tough cookie, but did you hear what she said?"

Collier nodded his head but it somehow looked more like no than yes. "Yeah. I heard her."

"So that's good, right? I mean not good, but it gives you somewhere to look next, right?"

Collier looked at Joey with a mixture of pity and sweetness, the way one might regard a person naive enough to include Santa Claus in their life-sized lawn Nativity scene. "You really think any answers can be found in those places down on 42nd Street?"

Joey felt himself starting to blush. He took a sip of his fresh drink. "Sure. Maybe."

"Girls down there don't use their real names. There're no employment records and no one sees or hears anything. We'd have better luck interviewing fire hydrants in the area. If that is, in fact, where Mindy ended up, it's a complete dead end."

Joey nodded. He took another sip and realized that he had finished his second drink in two gulps. He looked at Collier's beer, still almost full. "So now what?"

Collier stretched his back as he put the tape recorder back in his pocket. "Now? Now I go back to the station where I find anywhere from one to four new homicides on my desk."

"So that's it?"

"No. That's not it, but it's it for now. I mean, what do we have: A dead stripper and a missing Raymond Nunez. Until he turns up..." Collier seemed to realize that he was sounding overly callous. "I mean, listen, we'll do what we can, it's an open case, but the fact is there are only so many of us and only so many hours in the day and given what we have to go on so far, there isn't really a way that I can justify to my bosses putting a substantial amount of muscle behind this."

Joey stared at Collier's barely touched beer, a prop to establish a false sense of camaraderie between them. When Collier said *we*, he meant the NYPD, not him and Joey.

"Look." Collier pulled a paper napkin from a stack on the bar and a pen from the inside pocket of his jacket. "Here's my direct number. If you think of anything, anything at all, feel free to call me." He put the napkin in front of Joey.

Joey nodded, keeping his eye on the beer, worried that if he looked up Collier would see the disappointment in his eyes.

"My friend -" Collier raised his hand to the bartender. "One more for my buddy here." He stood and put some bills on the bar and turned to leave. "See ya, Joe."

"Collier."

Collier turned back. "Yeah?"

"Can I borrow your pen?"

Collier looked at the pen still in his hand, then held it out for Joey. "Sure. Keep it."

Joey took a sip from his fresh Scotch and began to draw on the napkin that Collier had left. He drew a box around Collier's phone number. It was a nice pen, probably expensive; the ink flowed out in a steady, thick line, bleeding through the thin layers of paper. Joey noticed that Collier had actually grabbed two napkins. He put the phone number aside and began to draw on the clean, white one. He drew one arc, then another and a small dash and a dot. With only a few strokes he had what looked like a three-quarter profile of a woman's face.

Even a mediocre ballerina should have made for an above average stripper, a limber one with some actual skill. Surely her coworkers would remember her.

Another small squiggle suggested an ear that Joey decorated with a geometric earring.

Was Collier right? Would they really hit a dead end if they went to the strip clubs to ask about a dancer who was murdered? Sure, maybe the men who ran the clubs wouldn't want to get involved, but the other girls? Wouldn't they want to help one of their own? Or were they all like Collier, no sense of "us", all untouched beers and pens given, not lent? Even so, wouldn't they be scared enough of the same thing happening to them and want to help?

It'd had been a while since Joey had drawn anything and he paused to remember how to move his arm to translate the image in his mind. He drew swirls of hair around the minimal suggestion of a face that now had a pert nose and pouting lips. The swirls had movement to them, like she was posing into a fan or caught mid-run. He began to write across the top of the sketch, angular lettering that might be found on the cover of a New Wave album by a young band from England.

Maybe Collier was right, maybe even the other women who'd danced with Mindy would be too uninterested or too scared or too self-centered to want to help. But Joey was willing to bet that he could find a few of them who'd at least be willing to gossip.

The bartender cleared his third empty glass. "You want another one, man?"

Joey stayed focused on his drawing and the offer printed above it: Hair Models Wanted.

"No, thanks. I'm good."

Twenty

1958

Dorothy Schiff took a private elevator to her penthouse office in the New York Post building in lower Manhattan, passing the lower floors where the paper was laid out and printed, then the middle floors where reporters worked in cramped quarters, competing for typewriter ribbons and desk space. Dorothy toured these floors regularly. She knew that the elevator operator's name was Darcy and that he had two grandchildren. Darcy knew that, beyond a pleasant salutation, Mrs. Schiff preferred not to converse on the ride up. As she stepped off the elevator, Darcy took no offense at his employer's attempt at eye contact that only made it as high as his shoulder. He knew that this was no reflection on his station in life or the color of his skin. Everyone who read the newspaper that put food on his table, as Darcy himself did everyday, was well aware of the liberal politics of its publicly outspoken, but privately shy publisher.

Behind the large desk where she wrote her weekly column, Dorothy reached instinctively to the upper right-hand corner for the neat stack of phone messages before realizing there were none. She'd never once, that she could remember, had no messages. Just as Dorothy was about to buzz her secretary, she saw the messages right under her nose, square in the center of her desk, the one on top from a Mr. Clyde Tolson along with the number for the New Yorker Hotel, both in Kathleen's clear-as-day handwriting. As well as not being able to recall a time when she'd had no messages, Dorothy couldn't recall a time that Kathleen had ever put the messages anywhere other than the upper right-hand corner of the desk. She picked up the message.

Dorothy already knew where Mr. Tolson and his boss J. Edgar Hoover were staying; her reporters had been keeping close tabs on the two men's vacation together. They'd printed inconsequential details of it in the society pages the past two days. They'd been doing this before the distasteful socialite had told Dorothy her wild story about the two men. The story the socialite had told was garish and crass, ludicrous even. There was no way to print it, even as a blind item in the gossip pages. Even if there had been a way, people would think that Dorothy had lost her mind.

But the story had kept her up.

The socialite had also been right; the story was very rich, not in a juicy way, but in a troubling way. Very troubling. It left Dorothy feeling frightened, and very little in life came close to even intimidating her. She'd written countless editorials and held influence over both local and national politics. She was on her third marriage and had taken lovers on the side. She was 55-years-old, not a child. She'd dined with presidents. And yet, the socialite's gossip troubled her. So she'd called Mr. Tolson at the New Yorker Hotel that morning. She'd not expected to have her call returned. Come to think of it, she didn't know what to expect. She dialed again, and her call was put through.

"Miss Schiff, how do you do?" Clyde Tolson answered the phone himself. Dorothy had been expecting an assistant, before remembering that technically, Tolson was the assistant.

"Very well, Mr. Tolson, and you?"

"I'm well as well. Before we go further," Tolson continued, "I do hope you might clear up my confusion. Is it Miss Schiff or *Mrs.* Schiff?"

Dorothy had never spoken to this man before. She'd been in his company on two different occasions, but both had been large functions and they had never been formally introduced. She found his voice, while more than slightly condescending, warm and rich. "Why don't you call me Dorothy, and we'll take it from there."

"But you are married..."

"Yes. I am."

"I see... and yet Schiff is your maiden name, is it not?"

Dorothy could hear papers shuffling on the other end and wondered if it was one of the FBI files that Tolson's boss was infamous for compiling. "It is my maiden name, Mr. Tolson. It's very astute of you to notice that." Dorothy hadn't considered that there might be one of these files with her name on it. She'd never thought of herself as a security threat, but perhaps her politics and platform were enough to qualify. She felt oddly flattered. "Should you ever tire of secretarial work at the Bureau, I do hope you'd consider a career as an investigative reporter. Observational skills such as yours should not be put to waste."

"Thank you, Dorothy, for the invitation," he chuckled. "And while my confusion surrounding your marital status has not been entirely cleared up, your mention of reporting provides a convenient segue to the matter at hand."

"The matter at hand?" She hadn't said, in her message, why she was calling.

"Looking for more fodder for that cage-liner you call a newspaper?" His calm, pleasant tone did not waver.

"I don't think we need to insult one another."

"Is this really what you do? *Mr. Hoover dined on lamb chops at the 21 Club Sunday night with traveling companion and long-time assistant Clyde Tolson...* is this really the kind of exciting gossip your readers crave?"

"What I do, Mr. Tolson, is chronicle the events in what is arguably the greatest city on earth." Perhaps it was her newspaper, not her FBI file that she'd heard rustling.

"What you do, Dorothy, is irresponsible. J. Edgar Hoover is not a stage and screen star, he is a man of great power. Printing the details of his daily minutiae is a direct threat to our national security."

"Forgive me if this sounds challenging, but I really don't see how they could be both."

"Both?"

"The details of your boss's life are either mundane or incendiary. Only one poses potential threats."

"My time is valuable, Miss Schiff, so I will make myself clear. You are to cease and desist at once any and all inquiries into the personal and professional life of the director of the Federal -"

"You know you have no authority to make such an outrageous demand," Dorothy cut him off. "Even the FBI can't overturn at will the Constitution."

"You're so very naïve."

"Clyde!" Dorothy barked loudly, silencing her accuser. "I'm calling as a friend."

Though he didn't say anything in response, Dolly could swear she heard what sounded like whispering beyond a hand-covered receiver on his end. She waited a moment before continuing. "My time is valuable as well, so I'll get to the point. There's a woman, a well-connected woman, here in town. She's neither respected nor is she even well liked. But she is connected. And rich. And, well, unfortunately she is talkative."

Silence.

"She's claiming, Clyde, that she was at a party Sunday night. She's claiming that there were sexual activities, group sexual activities. Naturally, she claims she didn't participate in these, just observed. She claims that you were there, Clyde. That you were both there. She claims that your boss was dressed in women's underwear and a wig, as were several others. At first she thought there were both men and women involved, but she claims that everyone involved in the sexual activity was, in fact, a man."

Silence.

"I don't believe her story, nor do I plan to print it. She's not a reliable source. But, like I said. She is talkative. I do not know to whom she has also spoken about this. But I can imagine. I thought you both should know."

More silence.

"Are you a communist, Dolly? That is what your friends call you, isn't it?"

"It is. Yes. And you know that I am not. My politics are not a secret."

"Your politics, Dolly, are suspect. As are your motivations here. Open, as they say, to interpretation. And now, as a potential enemy of the state, officially under review."

She'd hoped he would laugh. Or be stunned. She'd hoped that the socialite was a liar, or simply a bored, misinformed drunk. She'd hoped that he would not be so prepared. "I'll admit, your response to this matter, Mr. Tolson, has me concerned."

"You should be concerned. You should be frightened. We can destroy you."

"You misunderstand. I am not afraid of you. I'm afraid for you."

Silence.

"There's a lot at stake here, Clyde."

Silence.

"Consider yourself warned, Miss Schiff."

The line went dead. Dorothy hung up and gazed down at her desk at nowhere in particular. The phone messages had always waited for her on the upper right-hand corner of her desk. She wondered if that alone shouldn't have told her that something bigger had shifted.

Twenty-one

1985

"I'm sorry, Lieutenant Collier is unavailable at the moment. Would you like to leave a message?"

Joey was between appointments, using the phone behind the reception desk at Slate. "No. Thank you." He'd already left a message yesterday to tell Collier his idea after leaving the bar with the cocktail napkin he'd drawn on. His next appointment, he knew, was Aggie. Or, more accurately, Aggie's sister's mother-in-law, Alice. They were twenty minutes late.

Hair Models Needed No Experience Necessary. Must Be Sexy and Now, was what he had written above the face he'd drawn on the napkin at the bar. He'd taken the napkin to a do-it-yourself copy shop and xeroxed it onto a piece of paper while thinking of Milt and his aborted career as a personal organizer, enlarging the image to fit the page. He'd made a hundred copies on hot pink and neon green paper, copies that were now hidden at his styling station, in a drawer under a hairdryer.

He hung up and dialed his own number, then hung up after it rang twice; his answering machine was designed to pick up after one ring if he had any messages; it did not. That morning he'd changed his greeting to reflect the cool, European feel he'd aimed for on the flyer: *You've reached JB, if you're calling about modeling and you have what it takes, leave your name and number. Ciao.* He'd done everything but distribute the flyers along 42nd Street. It was an idea that sounded fine in theory, but a task that was easy to procrastinate. And he wanted to tell Collier but Collier wasn't calling him back.

"Surprise, surprise!" Joey heard Aggie's voice while he was still looking down at the phone.

"Dear God, this is completely unexpected!" Joey looked up and pretended to stagger in shock.

"Did I get you?" Aggie beamed. "Did I really?"

"Not a bit."

"I didn't?"

"You made the appointment under a fake name but used your own phone number."

Aggie plopped her purse onto the counter. "I used my dressing room phone number."

"I know. I know that one, too."

"Oh. I didn't think you did." She looked a little disappointed, but then rallied. "Well, Diane and Peter are at their matinee, and these two foxy ladies are out on the town!" Aggie stepped aside to reveal a shrunken wisp of a woman in a plaid blouse and beige, elastic-waist clam diggers. "Joey, this is Alice." Aggie spoke loudly and clearly. "Alice, this is my good, good friend Joey."

Joey stepped out from behind the counter. "Hi, Alice. How are you today?"

"She doesn't talk," Aggie warned.

"Hello, sailor!" Alice greeted Joey in a warm voice.

"She's..." Aggie whistled like a cuckoo clock before registering that Alice had, in fact, spoken.

Joey offered Alice a small salute and Alice grabbed his forearm. "You're looking terrific today." She patted Joey's cheek with her other hand as she reassured him. "Very strong. Are you sleeping well?"

"So that's what she sounds like," Aggie muttered.

"I am, thank you. I'm looking forward to doing your hair today."

Alice looked at her shoes. Aggie raised her eyebrows at Joey, "And... she's gone again. That's honestly the only thing she's said in the last hour."

Joey led Alice by the elbow. "Maybe I remind her of someone." He glanced at the back of the elderly woman's thinning hair, a circular white patch of scalp exposed by wiry strands like a child's pencil drawing of a sun. "C'mon Alice. Let's get you washed and then we'll..."

"Give you a giant afro," Aggie finished as she breezed past them. She dropped herself into a vacant shampoo chair and picked up a glossy magazine as she waited for Joey and Alice to catch up. "Do you think I'm a nurturing person?" Aggie asked, a little too loudly.

"Who said you weren't?" Joey settled Alice next to her.

"My sister." Aggie flipped through the pages quickly. "She says these things to me, these incredibly hurtful things, so casually. She just tosses them off as if they're, you know, accepted facts, like owning a car or something. Like, 'You know Aggie, how you never cry at movies like a normal person'."

"You don't cry at movies."

"I know, but not because I'm some heartless not-normal person. It's because I watch them from a technical point of view. I can't help it. You should have seen how nervous she looked about leaving Alice with me. Like I'd let her wander off or something. I'm not a moron. I think I have at least basic nurturing instincts." She tossed the magazine aside and looked up at Joey. "How are you? Doing."

"Okay."

"What. Are you sick? I mean, like, a cold or something? A summer cold?"

"No. It's just been a weird couple of days."

"When. Since Sunday?" Aggie said this like she was surprised to learn that Joey didn't freeze in suspended animation between their visits.

"Yeah."

"Why. What happened." Aggie narrowed her eyes. "Are you okay?"

"Yeah, I'm fine." This was true if you didn't take into consideration that only two days ago he'd been planning his suicide. "It's not really got anything to do with me. Not directly. Or, I guess it does now. In some ways. Not really, though." He figured from Aggie's concerned expression that she was probably thinking his babbling was the onset of some AIDS-related dementia. There was no reason to think she too wouldn't be steeling herself for that inevitable day.

121

"Sorry." He collected his rolling thoughts. "I'm fine really, I swear. I just found a dead body is all."

"Oh, thank God." Aggie exhaled in relief. "You were starting to freak me out."

———

Aggie reached for the cigarette Joey had just lit. She took a puff of smoke and let it spill out of her mouth. "Holy shit, Joey. That's intense." She handed it back with stiff fingers splayed out like they too found the toxic fumes unappealing.

Joey shrugged. "I guess." He glanced through the window of the salon to make sure Alice was still under the dryer.

"That's an incredibly passionate way to murder someone."

"It is?" Joey hadn't thought of it quite like that.

"Absolutely. It's a lover's crime. Just the nearness of it, holding someone at arms' length until they -" Aggie handed the cigarette back. "She must have really gotten under someone's skin. Who do you think did it?"

"No idea."

"No idea?!" Aggie's eyes sparkled with something that was most likely not stemming from a nurturing instinct, but Joey didn't call her on it. "You can't have *no* idea."

"I don't. I mean, I do. I do have no idea."

"Joey!" she grabbed his arm. "You could catch a murderer!"

"I can't catch anyone - I don't know anything."

"Bullshit you don't. You were in the apartment, you know a lot more then you think you do, you're just not allowing yourself to access the information."

"Uh-oh," Joey knew what was coming. Aggie had once taken a series of self-help seminars that pedaled the notion that everyone on the planet was capable of attaining greatness through the release of false, self-imposed restrictions.

"Close your eyes."

"No way. You're not going to brainwash me."

122

"It's not... Just do it."

"Nope."

"Come on! Nobody's even paying attention to us."

"And it's killing you, isn't it."

"Haha. Come on, do it. I never get to help!"

Joey stepped on the cigarette butt and took one more glance through the window at Alice dozing, under the lowest possible setting. "Okay fine." He folded his arms and closed his eyes.

"Yay! Okay." Aggie's voice got warm and comforting. "Okay. In front of you is a short flight of stairs leading down to a door. Do you see it?"

"Sure."

"Joey, really see it."

"I do. I really see it."

"Promise?"

"Promise." He could see it. It was a dark stairway with moss-covered, stone walls lit by a single, dirty light bulb on a rusty chain.

"Good. Behind that door is the day you found her; whatever that means to you is right. I'm going to count backwards from five and when I reach one you will be in front of the door. Okay?"

Joey made an okay sign with his thumb and forefinger.

"Okay. Five, four -"

In his mind Joey put a Norman Rockwell-esque print of a newsboy and a puppy on the stone wall. The moss immediately ate it up.

"One. Are you there?"

"Yep." The door was made of rotting wood and big corroded hinges.

"Okay. I'm going to take you inside. Once you're in, you can go anywhere, through walls or doors. I'm going to ask you to tell me what you see and when I say 'Describe' I want you to say the first three words that come to your mind, even if they don't make sense to you. Got it?"

"Sure."

123

"Okay. Open the door and tell me what you see."

In his mind the door more dissolved than opened. He saw Raymond's apartment as he'd seen it the other day. "I see the hallway. The hall."

"Describe."

"Blond, brick, shunt." The first three words that popped into his head.

"What else."

"Um... there's a window. Over there... it's dark."

"Remember you control everything here. Turn up the lights." She paused to give Joey a moment to do it. "See an object in the room, any object."

"Wall picture. I mean a picture on the wall. It's a calendar."

"Describe."

"Flower, off, nail." Joey's palms were starting to sweat. Was this actually working? "There's a door at the end of the hall that leads to the bedroom. It's closed. There's a bookcase in the hall -"

"What's on the bookcase?"

"Books."

"I know. But what books?"

"Paperback ones. Books. They're just books."

"Describe."

"I don't... I'm -"

"Three words, don't think. Go!"

"Flap, Jack, Flapjack. This is... this feels dumb."

"Okay fine, but hold on. Don't open your eyes yet."

"I'm done."

"Fine but just – don't open them. Just... one more thing while you're still under."

"You do know I'm not actually hypnotized."

"Be quiet, you are under my power," Aggie giggled and then Joey giggled, too. "You know I didn't mean that earlier." Her voice sounded less confident now. "That being sick thing. I didn't mean that."

"It's okay."

"No, it's not. It's really important that you hear this. And that you tell yourself that you're healthy."

"Okay." Joey knew not to argue that cells don't have ears. "Thank you." It wasn't that Joey actually found the visualization exercise dumb; he found it surprisingly effective.

"Mean it."

"I do mean it." Before coming to the bookcase in his mental version of the apartment where he'd found Mindy, Joey had glanced out the kitchen window, out and up.

"Say 'I'm not sick'."

"I'm not sick."

Through that window he'd seen himself looking down from his own window. The version of himself in the dark, imagined apartment knew nothing; the one above knew everything. Joey felt Aggie's hand touch his cheek. When he opened his eyes she'd gone back into the salon.

Twenty-two

1958

Libby had been stuffing envelopes when the young woman named Iris came back into her bar at about the same time in the afternoon as she had the day before. She wasn't open for business, but neither had she been yesterday, so she poured Iris a white wine and 7-up after she'd asked for something sweet. The young woman didn't seem to want conversation, so Libby went back to work. Fold, stuff, lick, stamp.

"What's this place called?"

Libby shrugged. "Everyone just calls it Libby's. It's my place."

This wasn't entirely accurate. Libby referred to a man she'd never met as her landlord, but he was technically her boss. She'd met a handful of men who worked for the same boss. Libby was not naïve; she knew these men were criminals. She'd gotten into business with them because it was necessary. Yes, she might technically work *for* criminals, she'd rationalized, but she didn't work *with* them. There was no sign outside of the door to the bar that Libby's boss owned, but everyone who came there knew they were safe to be themselves and everyone who came in there called it Libby's.

"What are you doing?" Iris asked after a few minutes.

"Stuffing envelopes."

Fold, stuff, lick, stamp.

"May I see one?"

Libby winked, "You sure? It's criminal material; once you read it, there's no turning back."

Iris grinned slightly and held out her hand. Libby handed her one of the mimeographed sheets of paper with the minutes of last week's meeting typed onto it.

"Where do you stand on the butch/femme spectrum?" Iris read aloud. "This is illegal?"

"Revolutionary, even. I already told you it's illegal for us -"

"Friends of Dorothy?"

" - to congregate. Right. Even when it's just seven friends eating pecan pie and drinking coffee while discussing the butch/femme spectrum."

"What's the butch/femme spectrum?"

"Well, that's something else that's illegal. See it's also against city law for a woman to be dressed entirely in men's clothing, or a man to be dressed in women's clothing."

"Do people do that?"

"Sure. Look at me."

Iris did. "I think you look good."

"Thank you." Fold, stuff, lick, stamp. "But here's the worst part. It's against federallaw to distribute homosexual material through the mail. So this," Libby held up a sealed envelope, "is revolutionary."

"I don't see why anyone would care."

"Because they, meaning The Powers That Be, do not want us to organize and become a political force with a common vote. But they're on the losing side. Our women's organization has chapters in San Francisco, Los Angeles, Washington DC, and here in New York. Plus the mailing list." Libby held up a stack of sealed envelopes. "Lesbians all across the country are getting ready to stand up and be counted. The world is about to change. So get scared."

Iris burst out crying.

"Hey, whoa there," Libby dropped the envelopes. "Not you... I didn't mean *you* get scared. I meant them -"

"I know. It's not that. I'm supposed to be shopping for a dress for Christopher's funeral."

"Oh. Well, shit." Libby hated to see young girls cry and not know how to comfort them. But then she got an idea. "You want to see something nifty? Come on. It's downstairs."

———

"Take a look at that." Libby had rolled back the area rug in the basement of her bar.

"What am I looking at?" Iris stood at the bottom of the stairs. Libby had fixed the basement up to be a bar of its own when it became clear that past a certain hour her male patrons preferred to self-segregate from the women. It was the room where Iris's husband had spent his last free night on earth, which Libby hadn't considered before bringing Iris down here. She'd only been thinking of giving Iris something else to think about.

"Look again. What do you see?"

"A floor. A hardwood... floor."

"Exactly. You ever seen a basement with a hardwood floor?"

The way Iris cocked her head to the side made Libby think of a bird. "I'm not sure if I have. Is that unusual?"

"Damn right it's unusual. Basements have concrete floors. I keep waiting for someone else to notice and say something, but no one has."

Shortly after Libby's opened its doors for business about a year and a half before, some men who worked for her boss had pounded on the door while she was setting up. Two bigger guys carried in a third guy who'd been shot in the shoulder and took him downstairs. A few minutes later, Libby let in a nervous looking doctor. Neither she nor the doctor had looked at each other as she directed him to the stairs. Libby had waited and smoked until the doctor came back up and let himself out. Shortly after, the two bigger guys came up and told her their associate needed to rest and she would have to open late that evening. They'd tossed twenty bucks onto the bar as they left, not waiting to see if she'd take it. They didn't need to; they knew that they all worked for the same man.

"What does it mean?" Iris toed the floor without putting any weight on it, as if she'd just been told the surface was made of water.

"It means that this," Libby knelt down and rapped her knuckles on the boards, "is not the real floor."

"It's not?"

"Nope. Lookie here." Libby knelt down and began running her hand along the boards, stopping at the spot she knew well. Her fingernails dug in and with only a bit of effort she pulled up about a two by two foot section of flooring to reveal a hole underneath.

"What's it for?" Iris asked.

"Beats me." Libby lowered herself into the hole until just her head and shoulders were sticking out. "I think it's from prohibition. It's not a lot of space, but you could hide stuff down here. You want to get in it?"

Iris took a tentative step forward, keeping her weight back like she was afraid she might accidentally fall in. "I don't know. I don't think so."

"I'll get out if you want to." Libby stepped on something that raised her up a good foot. "I put a crate down here so I could get back out easier."

"No that's okay you can stay in. I just want to look." Iris took another step, then another, then lowered herself down until she sat on the floor, her feet and shins dangling into the dark.

"It's a dirt floor down here, but not muddy or anything."

"Libby?"

"Yeah?" Libby standing on the crate was about the same height as Iris sitting on the floor.

"What is it, exactly, that two men do together. For sex. Sexually." Iris's hands were folded in her lap. "What do two women do together?"

Libby thought for a long moment then took Iris's hands in hers. "Maybe you should go home, Sugar."

"I can't. There's still blood on the wall."

"I mean home home. To your family."

"My parents are both gone."

"Oh. I'm sorry to hear that."

"My father died when I was twelve. His heart stopped while he was driving home from work. The doctor said that it was probably a defect he had since birth."

"I'm sorry."

"He dropped dead at the steering wheel and then his car drove into the front of a house a few blocks away from where we lived. They ended up having to rebuild most of that house."

"That's… gee whiz. That's pretty…" Libby scrambled to think of something to say that didn't make her sound somewhat impressed.

"No one was hurt. Unless you count my father, which I don't since the doctor said he didn't feel any pain."

Libby nodded, unsure how to contribute to the conversation at this point.

"Now I don't have anyone. I have Eddie."

Libby wondered what had happened to Iris's mother. She wondered who Eddie was.

Iris was staring off into space. "He probably wants to marry me, but only because it would be easy since I don't have anyone else. He knows it's too soon to ask." Iris glanced down at her hand in Libby's. "I wish I was strong like you. I wish I was a lesbian."

Libby looked in the younger woman's eyes; there were questions in them, confusion and also a yearning. "You're as strong as anyone I know," Libby said.

"No." Iris shook her head. "You all have each other, and I have no one."

Libby hadn't meant for this to happen. She'd been trying to make herself feel better about everything, not make Iris feel bad.

"You have a whole mailing list," Iris sniffed.

"That mailing list has forty-six names on it."

"That's a lot."

"It's a nationwide mailing list. With forty-six names on it. We're a long ways away from scaring anybody. We're all too goddamned scared ourselves."

"Is that why you let them steal from you?"

Libby thought about it. Because they both worked for the same man, Libby hadn't questioned Frankie when he'd first come in to collect on behalf of the police. Even when she'd started to suspect he was taking the money for himself, there was part of her that was ready to chalk it up to an additional price of doing business. But instead she'd confronted him and as a result the police had come and now Libby was twice as scared as she'd been before. "Yes," Libby said. "That's why I let them steal from me."

"I'm tired of being scared," Iris said. Libby nodded in agreement. The two women talked for a little while longer. Libby explained to Iris how, because they both worked for the same man, Libby hadn't questioned Frankie when he first came to collect. She hadn't resisted him at all. But she had followed him. In fact, Libby explained, following Frankie had become something of a hobby of hers, and now she knew where the man liked to spend his time. But she could only get so close, could only follow him so far. When Iris left Libby's bar a little later, she had the illegal envelopes addressed to Libby's mailing list in her hand. She headed to the post office, via the dress shop.

Twenty-three
-
1985

"I'm actually more of a Warhol girl. But, like, the real Warhol. Factory Warhol. Even Warhol isn't Warhol anymore."

By the time Joey got home from work he'd had eleven messages on his answering machine. He listened to each one, young women offering descriptions of themselves and leaving their names and phone numbers. He wondered, as he copied these down, if the names they left were real; if they felt any apprehension about leaving their numbers on a stranger's machine. He'd sat for a bit with a drink in his hand, looking at the list of eleven names, realizing where this plan of his fell short. If he called one back, how would he broach the subject of Mindy's murder? As he dialed the first number on the list, he realized he hadn't thought this through and hung up before the call was answered.

"New York is over, officially over. Done. It's not like the sixties anymore, or even the seventies when people actually did something."

After three more calls, two of which resulted in brief conversations and promised follow-up calls, Joey realized what he needed was a talker. He found her fourth on his list. The number Heather left was for her answering service. Joey left a message and she called him back ten minutes later, asking him to call her back, claiming she was on a payphone and was low on change.

After quick hellos, Heather had begun to talk about Art, a rant that required no fuel from Joey's end at all.

"You know what I mean? It's like, New York used to be about something. Even if that something was undefined in the present, it was, like, a fucking citywide collaboration in the moment. It was a fucking controlled chaos, it was like a mosaic that could only be viewed, *should* only be viewed from a distance created by time. Or space, I guess. But mostly time."

132

Joey knew from experience when he was talking to someone on cocaine.

"It's really sad," Heather continued. "It's really fucking sad. When the future looks back on us, on this moment now, there won't be a recognizable picture for them to hold. There's no Factory, there's no 54, there's not even... fucking Harlem. Jazz, right? You know what there is? Empty Greyhound busses, bands with no fucking talent, smack, and people sitting alone in their apartments afraid to go outside."

Joey took a sip of his scotch and nodded in silent agreement. People on cocaine could be very persuasive.

"And people wonder why everyone's sitting in a park with a needle in their arm or getting stabbed up in a bathtub or moving to L.A. It's because we just can't dance to one more fucking Madonna song and pretend like that's enough."

Joey had just begun to wonder if Heather was becoming unraveled to the point of nonsensical when she dropped this into her tirade.

"What did you just say?" he asked her.

"What did I say when?" Heather's voice was practically vibrating from the speed coursing through her system.

"Something about stabbed in a bathtub?" It seemed too close to be purely coincidental.

"Oh yeah, that. Fucked up, right? Girl I know got stabbed in a bathtub."

Joey made quick calculation: drowning plus gossip equals stabbed. In two days it could be skinned alive. "That is, yeah. Fucked up. When did that happen?"

"The other day. Which is my exit cue, right? So I'm going to L.A. I have experience."

"Experience?"

"Modeling. Isn't that what we're talking about?"

"Right." Joey lit a cigarette.

"This pays, right?"

"Yeah," Joey tried to think how to back up the conversation. "It pays. Who - do you know who killed her?"

"Who killed who." Heather's stimulated attention span had ceased to function completely.

"The friend of yours. In the bathtub."

"I don't know man, maybe she pissed off the wrong chorus boy. We just worked together, it's not like we were friends. What the fuck do you care?"

"What color was - " Joey was wondering if his theory about Mindy's hair was correct, but he realized that it was an odd question; people on cocaine could get pretty paranoid. "What color is your hair?"

"My hair is blond right now, but you can dye it whatever. I really don't care.

"Where - um. Where did you say you worked?" He could hear Heather breathing. Fuck. He'd gone too far.

"Tony?" Heather sounded pissed. Whoever Tony was, she didn't want to hear from him.

"I'm not Tony." Joey tried to sound the opposite of creepy and totally failed. "I promise."

"Fuck you, man." Heather hung up.

Joey sat with the phone to his ear, listening to the dial tone. It had to be Mindy she was talking about. But had she even said anything besides the wrong method of death?

...*Stabbed or something in the bathtub.*

The pleasant hum of the dial tone changed suddenly to a louder, more abrasive noise that let Joey know that he'd had it off the hook too long, at least in the phone's opinion.

Maybe she pissed off the wrong chorus boy.

Everyone had an opinion.

———

Joey paused outside the door to Raymond Nunez's apartment and considered the big yellow X made of caution tape that blocked the doorway. He wondered if he was about to break a law. He'd already reached through the wide gaps in the tape and discovered the door was unlocked, reducing the potential crime of Breaking and Entering to simply Entering, which didn't seem menacing enough to be a crime by itself. And he wasn't planning to take anything; he just wanted to look around. The X wasn't the same as a sign specifically saying Stay Out of Here Joey; in fact as moats went, this one was fairly half-hearted and probably an afterthought, much like the way Collier and the rest of the police were treating this whole thing. If they were serious about it, they could have posted a guard or some attack dogs. Or at least locked the fucking door.

The first thing Joey noticed, as the door clicked shut behind him, was that the floors were still wet. Not wanting to turn on a light, he waited for his eyes to adjust to the dark. Once they did, he closed them again and compared the version of the apartment he'd envisioned earlier with Aggie. His memory hadn't been that far off; he'd only made it slightly larger and colder. In reality it felt tight and airless, in need of an open window to exhale, refresh and start to dry out. He looked at the wall where he'd pictured a calendar hanging to find nothing displayed there. He thought of the words he'd used to describe it: nail, off and flower.

He walked down the hallway slowly, so as not to splash the water, his hand against the exposed brick wall. The door to the bathroom, which was open the last time he'd been in here, was now closed. The door to the bedroom at the end of the hall, which was closed last time, now stood wide open in invitation. It was almost as if the apartment itself knew where Joey was headed. From the bedroom's doorway, still hesitant to turn on a light, Joey identified the few blocky shapes barely illuminated by streetlights below: a bed, a dresser, a nightstand. Something in the corner that might be a guitar. He walked to the top of the bed and touched the bedspread where it had been pulled tight and smooth over two pillow-sized lumps with expert hospital crispness. Gently, so as not to mess it up, Joey sat down and slipped out of his shoes, pulled his feet up and lowered his head onto the covered pillow.

135

He heard Heather. *Maybe she pissed off the wrong chorus boy.*

The taut bedspread disguised a well-used and dented mattress. Joey could feel his body being pulled into the negative space created by another person's favorite position. He relaxed into it and turned slowly onto his side without being aware he was intentionally moving as his knees curled up like a fetus's. It wasn't that the mattress was uncomfortable, but rather that after years of use it was only comfortable in one specific way. Whoever had slept here, Joey imagined, had done so facing out, turned away as if wanting to be held, closer to the edge of the bed than the middle. There was only one nightstand and it was on this side of the bed.

He heard Aggie. *It's a lover's crime.*

Just pick up one thing and start there. Milt's voice startled Joey, but only slightly, coming from somewhere in his own head, but also distinctly from the corner of the room. Joey glanced in that direction and the unidentified Rorschach shape he'd thought might be a guitar case was now clearly Milt the organizer, sitting against the wall with his elbows on his knees. *Pick one thing.*

"One thing?" Joey whispered.

One fact, then.

Joey didn't know if anything that he knew about Mindy qualified as a fact so he grabbed onto an assumption.

"She cut her hair herself right before she was murdered."

Why?

"She was on the run."

From who?

"The man who killed her. The one who threw her purse away."

Raymond Nunez?

"No." Joey knew this was another assumption on his part. "Not Raymond Nunez."

So Mindy gets murdered by mystery man in an apartment that belongs to neither of them. Is Raymond her lover? Is it jealousy?

"I don't think so." Joey's whispers were gaining confidence if not volume.

The other way around? Mystery man is the lover? Raymond is the boyfriend?

Joey sat up. He fumbled around the lamp on the nightstand until he found the switch and blinked while his eyes adjusted to the sudden brightness. He stood on top of his shoes without putting them fully on and pulled back the bedspread to reveal just a mattress, no sheets, like the bed had been made up in a model home to show potential buyers. The mattress itself confirmed what Joey had imagined from lying on it: well worn and stained from at least several good years of sweat and body oils. The other side was much cleaner, almost pristine by comparison. He opened the one drawer on the nondescript nightstand and found a watch, a couple of pens, and a saucer with some coins in it. No crumpled receipts or books of matches. No books. He knelt down by the bed and pushed his hand between the mattress and the box spring as far as he could, up to the shoulder, then slid his arm down the length of the bed, dipping his knee onto the wet floor as he did. Nothing.

Joey's head was buzzing with thoughts that swarmed like bees, moving too fast to focus on individually. He didn't hear the front door to Raymond's apartment open and close or the footsteps coming toward him down the hall. As a result he was startled by the man's voice from the doorway saying "Well, well…" and fell back onto his butt while a grunt convulsed from his belly. Having no way to explain himself, Joey simply stood and slipped on his shoes before allowing Detective Inspector Flaars to lead him to the front door.

And there, just before exiting the apartment, Joey saw the flower calendar hanging on a nail by the door, directly opposite from where he'd pictured it, open to the month of June, off by one month. Had nobody been in here since June?

137

"Good evening gentlemen." Collier's tone was friendly and upbeat. He left the door open as he walked into his office where Joey had been waiting with Flaars sitting guard. Collier was casually dressed in jeans and faded tee shirt, evidence that he'd once participated in some softball league.

"Sorry," Joey said as Collier moved behind his desk and started shuffling through paperwork. He took the contents of Mindy's file out of their folder and placed them on the edge of his desk in front of Joey, a photograph of her dead body on top.

"Sorry? What are you sorry for, Joe?"

"It's your night off, yeah?" Joey saw the neon green of one of his flyers beneath the picture. "No suit."

"I don't get nights off. Not your fault." Collier folded his hands on his desk like a kind guidance counselor. "Are you sorry that you broke into a restricted crime scene area? Or are you sorry that you printed up these flyers -" Collier pulled the green sheet out.

"Why should I be sorry for that? It's part of my job to recruit new clients." At no point had it occurred to Joey that he might be being followed. He wondered if he'd done anything that looked suspicious. Besides distributing the flyers, which surely looked at least a little weird.

Collier didn't say anything, which was much more intimidating than if he had. Joey instantly missed the casual banter and the illusion it provided.

"I guess I owe you an explanation," Joey said. Collier stayed silent so Joey continued. "Okay, well, I was thinking today, while I was at work that the apartment, that Raymond's apartment, looked... clean." He wondered if Collier or Flaars or someone else had witnessed him outside of Slate, eyes closed through Aggie's guided meditation, even weirder than the flyer distribution.

Collier leaned forward. "Clean?"

"Yeah. Clean."

"What does it look like normally?"

"I don't know"

"I'm confused," Collier furrowed his brow in mock confusion. "How could it look particularly clean to you if you don't know what it looks like normally?"

"I didn't say it looked cleaner than usual, I just said it looked unusually tidy for an apartment with a dead body in it. Did you guys... did you guys search it? Did you guys, like, confiscate anything? Any... evidence?"

"That's classified. You have about ten seconds to explain what you were doing in there."

"Okay, fine. Have it your way. We're all guys here, right?" Joey heard Flaars snort from his broken chair behind him. "Fine. Two guys and a Saint Bernard."

Collier smiled. "Five seconds."

Joey got to the point. "Where do you keep your porn?"

"My porn?" Collier's eyes opened wider for a second.

"Yeah. I'm sure you have at least a couple worn out issues of Penthouse Letters tucked away somewhere. Where do you keep them? Close to your bed, right? Like in a nightstand or under your mattress."

Collier narrowed his eyes and put his hand to his mouth to make a harelip. "Go on."

"Well, I looked in Raymond's bedroom and there's nothing there. So I was wondering if you guys confiscated any and, if you did, what kind of porn it was."

"What kind of porn?" Flaars asked from over Joey's shoulder.

"Yeah. What kind."

"Maybe he didn't own any," Collier said. "Maybe he had a girlfriend named Mindy Shorent -"

"I don't think so. I mean, it's a possibility but I doubt it. I actually think Raymond Nunez was single and probably gay."

"Was?"

"Is. Is."

"Why do you think this?"

Joey thought of the calendar and the mattress, Heather's particular wording. All tenuously strung together. "Just a hunch. Don't you get hunches?"

"I prefer evidence." Collier leaned back and stretched his leg out. "Okay, say you're right and someone cleaned the whack-off mags out of Ray's bedroom. Why?"

"I don't know yet."

"Okay. How about when?"

Joey thought. "Before Sunday night, I guess?"

"Where were you Sunday night?"

"I was home alone like I told you before. Can we get past this? You don't really think I killed her or you'd have arrested me by now."

"I don't have anything concrete to arrest you for, really." Collier leaned forward again. "Nothing that would keep you off the streets for more than a day or two and frankly, so far, it's been far more interesting to see what you get up to on your own."

"I'm just trying to help," Joey said.

"Why now? People die everyday in this city in horrible, violent ways." Collier picked up a stack of case files and dropped them onto the center of his desk. "Until now, to my knowledge, you've yet to offer to help apprehend their killers, so why now?"

"Are you serious?"

"Dead serious. See, Joe, sometimes a certain kind of criminal sociopath will want to get caught. Either they feel excited or they want the credit for the crime. Sometimes, if they feel the police are getting off track, they'll find a way to help them out."

"Oh, come on," Joey threw his hands up. "You really think I'm a sociopath?"

"I didn't say that. Flowers," Collier winked at Joey. "Did I say that?"

"What did you call me?" Flaars asked.

"I said *a certain kind of criminal.* You made the leap from that to you."

"Stop that. That's condescending," Joey said.

"Or incriminating."

"No it's condescending. Implying something and then making it my idea when I pick up on the implication is insulting. I'm not a fucking sociopath."

"Who's Henry?"

"Henry?" This time it was Joey's eyes that opened in surprise.

"Is Henry dead like you told me or is Henry 'fine' like you told your bald friend at the dance school."

"Oh, that," Joey shook his head like he'd been slapped. "No, that's just something I say. Sometimes. It's something I have said to people, acquaintances, who don't know yet. Sometimes I'm not in the mood."

"Not in the mood for truth?"

"Not in the mood for sympathy." Joey matched Collier's cool stare. "Besides, that particular bald friend happens to be a churchgoer, so technically, to him, Henry is fine: up in the sky playing with his childhood dog in a field of daisies."

"Fine. What else do you 'just say,' meaning 'lie about'?"

"Nothing."

"Flowers," Collier looked past Joey. "When I say 'indigent,' what do you think I mean?"

"You mean, like offended?" Flaars answered.

"Close enough." He looked back at Joey. "I listened to the tape again. I said 'indigent,' you knew I meant 'homeless'."

"Isn't that the definition? Doesn't that mean 'impoverished'?"

"It technically just means 'deficient'."

"Do I have to be here for this?" Joey turned to Flaars. "You're the by-the-book one here, right? Have I been arrested or anything or can I just leave -"

"You can't leave," Collier answered.

Joey ignored Collier. "Can I walk around maybe? Maybe see your office?"

"Flowers doesn't have an office," Collier said to Joey's back. "Not anymore. Maybe one day. Were you sleeping with Raymond Nunez?"

"What?" Joey spun back around to see that Collier had stood up and was leaning forward towards him, hands on his desk.

"Were you sleeping with Raymond Nunez? It's a yes or no question."

"No."

"Did you get jealous of his relationship with Mindy Shorent?"

"Nope."

"Did you get jealous of their relationship and kill her?"

"I'm leaving." Joey stood and turned toward the door but Flaars stepped into his path. When he turned back, Collier had come out from behind his desk.

"Were there pictures of you and Raymond together that maybe he used to keep in his nightstand or under his mattress and now they're not there? Come on, we're all guys here." Collier put his hands on Joey's shoulders. "You can tell us, we all get jealous. Maybe you and Ray were having a good time, doing whatever you guys do. It's going great, maybe you even move into the building next door to be closer. Maybe he starts messing around on the side, which is a hurtful thing to do; I know I wouldn't like it. Maybe you didn't mean to hurt her, maybe you just meant to scare her." Collier moved his hands closer to Joey's neck, like a coach encouraging a waning boxer. He used his thumbs to gently tilt Joey's chin up so he could look him in the eye. "Who knows?" he shrugged lightly. "Maybe you killed Ray, too, and we just haven't found him. Maybe you even killed Henry."

Joey didn't know how to punch well, but he was fast. He got two solid hits against the side of Collier's face with a closed fist before Collier got his hands up to block the third. He felt Flaars grab him from behind and pull him back. One of Collier's hands pressed against Joey's jaw, forcing his head to the side while his other tried to undo Joey's gnarled grip on his shirt. Flaars lifted Joey off the ground completely, giving Joey the opportunity to lift his leg up like a Rockette and bring the heel of his shoe down onto the side of Collier's head. Collier got his arm in the way just before Joey's foot connected, but the kick still dropped him to his knees. Then Flaars pulled Joey's arm behind his back and applied learned pressure that shot pain from his shoulder through his entire body and made him go limp.

Twenty-five

1958

The gin martini had been Libby's suggestion. She'd pointed out, and Iris had agreed, that a woman with enough confidence and devil-may-care attitude to sit alone at a bar in the Village would order something a tad more sophisticated than white wine mixed with 7-up. Libby had followed Frankie to this particular jazz club in the Village more than a few times, but had never followed him inside. Iris had followed Libby's script to the letter without knowing what, exactly, she was saying and ordered a dry gin martini straight up with two olives. Thankfully, the string of words had meant something to the man behind the bar. The first sip had startled her.

"A conundrum? What the hell is that?" A man that fit Libby's description of Frankie sat one stool away from Iris, hunched over his drink like a hyena who'd found a dead rodent too small to share.

"A conundrum. It's a pickle. Or a jam. It's a puzzle." Iris had not been sure, after sitting down at the bar, how she would strike up a conversation with him. Hopeful that the opportunity would present itself, she'd ordered her drink and concentrated on looking mysterious while a trio of men on a small, raised platform played music that had no definite beginning, middle or end. The melody flowed and intertwined and doubled back on itself or jumped ahead to an unexpected new place as if to suggest that time, in here, was either less relevant or more complicated than in the rest of the world. *Conundrum,* they'd said, was the name of their band.

"Like a riddle or something?" He was looking at Iris almost sideways, his head slightly cocked like he didn't quite trust her. He was grinning though. Libby had described him as short and fat. Iris didn't think he was all that short and would have probably replaced 'fat' with stocky or solid. She considered that he might not be Frankie at all.

"Sort of like a riddle. It could be a hypothetical situation."

144

After her martini, Iris had gone to the ladies' room. When she'd returned, her seat had fortuitously been taken, allowing her to take the stool right next to him and order another.

"I don't know what that means. You a teacher or something?"

"Hardly," Iris rolled her eyes. "I didn't even go to college." She didn't want him to think she was snooty, so she recalibrated her vocabulary. "It's like a situation that you imagine yourself in, a complicated situation where every possible avenue has an up and a down side."

"Yeah, okay," he was following her now. "I think I know what you mean."

Iris took a sip from her second martini. "I'll think of an example." She smoothed the skirt of the new black cocktail dress she'd purchased that afternoon with Eddie's money after leaving Libby's. She'd told Eddie she needed something for Christopher's funeral and he'd been happy to open his wallet. Iris had plenty of money of her own in the bank, but she'd accepted Eddie's. She'd found a dress that looked equally appropriate for both a jazz club and a wake. "Okay. I've got one. It's a bit morbid, I'm afraid."

"I think I can handle it," He turned to fully face her. Libby had not said that he was handsome. Maybe this was not the sort of thing that Libby noticed about men.

"Okay. There's a button you can press. Once you press it, you receive a large amount of money. However," Iris paused for suspense, "as a result, someone, somewhere dies. Do you press it?"

Before she finished the sentence, he pressed his finger four times into a swirl in the wood of the bar that resembled a button. Iris surprised both of them when a whoop of laughter jumped out of her throat, a juvenile sound for the femme fatale she was playing. She clapped both hands over her mouth. "Well," she recovered, "apparently it's not such a conundrum for everyone."

He smiled, "Nah, I was making a joke. Sort of. Sort of a joke. He swallowed the last of his melting ice, signaled to the bartender and pointed to both his and Iris's glass. "Alright, so how do they die?"

"You can't be sure. It may be quick and painless in their sleep or it might involve agony."

"Can I pick the person?"

"Absolutely not, otherwise you'd pick someone very old or very sick which would absolve you of all but a sliver of guilt."

He raised his eyebrows. "That's not necessarily who I'd pick."

"Oh, really?" Iris tried to mimic his expression as the skin on her arms turned to gooseflesh. Libby had not said that his eyes seemed able to not only see what was in front of him, but also, vividly still, something that had disappointed him long ago. Maybe she'd not looked closely. Maybe he'd never looked at Libby like this.

"Okay, so you're saying I press this magic button and I get some cash, but an otherwise healthy person, who I don't know, meets his maker."

"I didn't say it would be someone you don't know. It could be your brother or your childhood piano teacher or a mountain man in Tibet. That's what makes it a conundrum."

"How much money we talking?"

"Enough to live on for the rest of your life. You'd never have to work again if you spent it modestly." Iris was practical, even in her fantasies.

"Yeah," he nodded. "I think I could press it."

"You do?"

"Sure, why not? There's a lotta people in the world and most of them are dirt, so why not?"

The bartender placed fresh drinks in front of them. "I know what you mean," Iris said as she lifted her glass to meet his. "I believe I'd press it too."

"What's your name?"

"Iris," she replied before she could think to lie.

"Iris," he repeated. "That's a pretty name."

Iris tried to picture this man grabbing Libby but couldn't quite see it.

"And yours?" She couldn't decide which she wanted more, for it to be him or for him to be someone different. She realized she was holding her breath.

"My name?" he was looking at her sideways again. "You ready for this?"

Iris nodded.

"Galterio."

"Galterio?"

"Yeah. It's a family name. There's been a few of us."

Iris couldn't tell how she felt; She'd wanted him to be Frankie and then at some point she'd wanted him to not be. She was both disappointed and relieved but couldn't tell which one she felt more.

"Galterio Dante Franzese the fourth," he said. "But everybody calls me Frankie."

He looked directly into Iris's eyes; she couldn't look away. "Hello Frankie."

"Hello, Iris." He lifted his drink, touched the rim of it to Iris's then took a sip. "I was just fooling around before."

"Before?"

"Yeah. About the button. The conundrum."

"So, you wouldn't push it?"

"Wouldn't need to," he turned on his stool so that his legs were on either side of Iris's. "I got a bag full of money."

———

Iris woke up in a strange bed, too disoriented to feel any sense of alarm. She'd been dreaming of a cold bottle of Coca-Cola, slippery with condensation. In the dream she'd been drinking, head tipped back like she was on a billboard, swallowing gulp after gulp of the sweet liquid from a bottle that seemed to have no end. Was she at Eddie's? She didn't think so. She was so thirsty, thirstier than she could remember ever being. Had she not been in a dark room, in a strange bed, she'd have gone to get some water, but as it was she didn't know which direction she'd need to go to find some. She began a silent,

147

motionless diagnostic assessment of her situation starting from the feet up. Shoes off, stockings on, dress on but twisted uncomfortably, arm asleep.

Whoever's responsible for you being alone at a bar, she remembered him saying, *well, I don't know whether to teach him a lesson or thank him.* She remembered that him saying that had made her think of Christopher who was past the point of learning lessons. It had also made her feel good, which had made her feel guilty.

The pillow was too soft and did not smell like the one on Eddie's bed. The shadows were different as well. A siren cried in the distance.

One, two, three, he'd said as they each held a shot glass full of a liquor she didn't recognize. She remembered holding it in her mouth, afraid to swallow it while her eyes burned. She remembered grabbing his arm and being surprised by how strong it felt.

"You awake?" The voice came from next to her, rough and phlegmy, barely above a whisper.

Iris remained motionless. Oh no. Oh no no no. Had she wound up in Frankie's bed?

"Me too," he said.

Had she moved? How did he know?

"Damn, you're a bad influence on me Iris Milligan."

He used her maiden name. She didn't remember telling him that. She didn't remember leaving the jazz club.

"In case you were wondering," he cleared his throat, "I was a perfect gentleman." She felt Frankie's finger touch lightly to her shoulder and gently trace a line down her upper arm. "I was a perfect gentleman," he repeated. She could tell by the way he was forming his words that he was smiling. "No matter how much you tried to get me to go to bed with you, and you did try, I was a grown-up."

What had she done?

"But not because I didn't want to." His finger traced the stitching on the side of her dress where a seam bisected her ribs, down to her hip, then slowly all the way up to her armpit. "I just thought you might regret it in the morning."

She felt a flush of relief hearing this. If she'd ended up in a criminal's bed, and she had, she was really one terrible spy. That she'd not had sexual relations with a total stranger hopefully meant she was still a decent person. But this relief lasted only as long as a blink and was replaced by the realization that she'd only felt it because she thought she should. It was a remnant of the person who recently believed that decency was what civilized people strove for. That it was, in fact, required in order to walk down the street with your head held high. But this clearly wasn't true for everybody; was it even true for anybody? Frankie, she knew, was not a person concerned with decency. So why had he suddenly developed a conscience where she was concerned?

She thought of Libby, waist-deep in the hole in the floor of the basement. How Libby had glanced at Iris's mouth, just for a second, less even. She realized that what startled her was not the idea that Libby might kiss her, but rather her own acceptance of it. She'd actually wanted Libby to kiss her, but Libby hadn't. And now Frankie. Iris suspected that Frankie's decency was a lie. She suspected that the truth was that there was something off about her, something ugly. Maybe it was something recent, left smudged on her soul by Christopher's death. Maybe it had always been there.

"I gotta use the can." She felt him roll over, the weight of his bed shift as he got off of it. How would she get home? Where was she even? Where exactly is Brooklyn? She wasn't totally sure, beyond a general 'over that way' notion, across a river.

Untouchable in Brooklyn, it couldn't get any worse. Iris wanted to cry.

"You have any aspirin in this joint?"

It took some seconds for Frankie's question to sink in.

"What?" She asked.

"I said you got any aspirin in here?"

Iris's spiraling thoughts snapped back like a Slinky as she realized what she'd done; she'd brought him home. She'd brought him to her apartment and begged him to sleep with her in her dead husband's bed. She'd begged the man who'd attacked Libby to take off the dress that she'd bought with Eddie's money for Christopher's funeral. And now he knew where she lived.

Oh, how she suddenly wished for Brooklyn.

Twenty-six

1985

After a night in a holding cell, Joey had been told he'd be free to go as long as he could make bail. He couldn't, but he knew someone who could.

"Cash or check?" a tiny policewoman with thick glasses asked him in a pinched voice after typing his answers to her questions onto a form in triplicate. After a life completely undocumented by the law, Joey realized he now had a rap sheet.

Aggie was standing next to him, tapping her foot, running her fingers through her ponytail and exhaling audibly. "Cash or check?" Joey repeated the question to Aggie who glared at him like he was a moron.

"Cash. Do you really think I want a paper trail tying me to this?"

Joey wasn't interested in making his night in jail all about her, so he took the mature route and mimicked the face she was making back to her, intentionally exaggerating it to make it ugly, like a witch.

"Don't." Aggie squared her shoulders to face him. "Don't even try to make me the bad guy here."

"Fine," Joey backed off. "Just..." he waved his hand over her purse like it was a pot of soup he wanted to smell.

"Fine." Aggie pulled out her wallet and slammed it onto the counter. "How much?"

"Two hundred dollars." The tiny officer looked from Joey to Aggie like she was watching a Ping-Pong match.

"Wow!" Aggie smiled brightly at Joey while she removed the cash. "What an expensive temper you have!"

Joey whipped around and strode through the precinct's entryway, pushed through the double doors and took the steps to the sidewalk two at a time without waiting to see if Aggie was behind him. After a moment he heard her high-heeled sandals slapping on the steps.

"Joey. Joey! Hey!" She grabbed his arm. "What the fuck is your problem?"

"What's my problem?" He stopped and faced her. "I just spent the night in jail is my problem. I'm fine, by the way. Thank you for your concern."

"I can see that you're fine, okay? I can see that you're not physically injured. Don't act like I'm insensitive. I'm not the one who punched a cop." Joey started to walk again, but at a pace Aggie could easily keep up with. "I mean, did you stop to think what would happen if Page Six got a hold of this? I have a fan base, Joey. I know it's not a big deal to you. I know that you think it's all... my job and my fans... that it's all some sort of big, funny joke -"

"I don't think it's a joke."

"Of course you do. You think everything is a joke. You roll your eyes more than Stevie Wonder."

"Now that is a funny joke."

"But, you know, it's not a joke. It's a job. Are you going to make my co-op payments if this little stunt of yours makes me late and I get fired?"

"I'll pay you back." Joey turned the corner of his block. Aggie followed. Unspoken between them was the fact that Aggie had also given him the money to move: first and last months' rent plus a little extra to help the transition. While Joey had been working more in the past month, more was still a relative term. Most of his regulars had moved on after his year of spotty availability.

"It's not... it's not the two hundred bucks. I don't give a shit about that. It's about growing up, Joey. I know it's hard, I know you're grieving. I know. But you're making me worry about you all the time. Do you know that my heart I think literally stopped when I got that phone call this morning? You can't make me worry like that. You have to start taking some care of yourself. Do you want to tell me what's going on?"

"Shit." Joey stopped in his tracks.

"What?"

Joey pointed to his stoop, forgetting that Aggie, who had yet to see his new apartment, would recognize neither it nor Collier sitting on his steps, holding a bunch of flowers. "That's the cop I punched."

"He's cute."

"Yup." They started walking again.

"Why is he holding flowers?"

"Because he knows he's cute."

Collier stood as they approached. He let the bouquet of cheap daisies drop to his side and smiled at his shoes then looked back up at Joey. "Truce?"

Joey bit the side of his cheek. "Sure. Truce." He was uncomfortable with all aspects of conflict, including resolution.

"Can we talk?" Collier gestured to the front door of Joey's building with the flowers.

"Sure." Joey turned to Aggie. "I'm sorry I worried you. I'll call you after I've gotten some sleep, okay?"

"No. Absolutely not. I'm coming up." Aggie turned to Collier and stuck out her hand. "Hi. I'm Aggie."

Collier took her hand in his. "Hi. Lieutenant Collier."

"Didn't you say you were late for work?" Joey asked Aggie.

Aggie pushed her sunglasses up on top of her head; her light brown eyes sparkled in the morning sun. "Late? No, I meant that as a metaphor. Or a hypothetical... what do you call it?"

"A guilt trip." Joey crossed his arms.

"You look familiar." Collier didn't seem to hear any of Joey and Aggie's debate.

"I was just thinking the same thing!" Aggie said as if that were the most insane coincidence on the planet. "That's so funny! Have we met somewhere before?" Joey knew Aggie's checklist: eyes, wedding ring, teeth, physique, hair, grooming, and manners. Collier was passing with flying colors.

"Maybe I can help sort this out," Joey interjected. "Collier, Aggie is a very successful actress with an extremely influential fan base. You've probably seen her on television. She doesn't recognize you from anywhere. She's just flirting."

Collier looked back at Aggie. "Sounds like somebody is grumpy."

"He's such a pill," Aggie agreed.

Great, Joey thought. Now their opinion of him was something else they had in common. He turned and let himself into his building as they followed.

"So you're a detective? That must be exciting."

"It has its moments. It's a lot of paperwork, actually. You're an actress?"

"Guilty. A card-carrying member of the second oldest profession. Do you have a gun?"

"Fully loaded at all times."

Aggie laughed suggestively at his innuendo as she stepped into the elevator. Collier looked at Joey as he followed and mouthed the words 'She's gorgeous'. Joey gave him the finger.

Joey could hear them behind him as he faced the elevator doors.

Collier: "One for you."

The paper around the cheap flowers rustled as he pulled one from the bunch.

Aggie: "My hero, I do declare!" in a bad southern accent.

Collier: "Oh my, had I known…"

A deep inhale.

Aggie: "Mmmm. I love flowers. Someday I want to have a big garden so I can just lie there surrounded by beautiful flowers."

"If that's all you want," Joey said as the elevator stopped on his floor, "you could just have a funeral." He stepped off without looking back.

"Ha ha, very funny. But not me, I'm going to be cremated."

"Oh yeah?" Collier seemed to find even this morbid detail about her interesting.

"Definitely," Aggie said. "Ashes to ashes, baby. Besides, it's really bad for the earth, all that embalming fluid..."

"Huh." Collier sounded impressed. "I guess I never thought of that."

"It's true," Aggie stepped into Joey's apartment. "Formaldehyde is incredibly toxic - Oh Joey I love it! You have a sunken living room!!"

Collier and Joey both looked down at the one step that led to the box-filled area to which Aggie was referring.

"You can give me the tour later," she continued. "You boys need to talk. Go, sit. I'll make some coffee."

"I don't have any coffee." Joey thought of the bag of groceries. "I have some tea. In the refrigerator."

"Perfect!" Aggie was pulling out all the stops now, the perfect housewife: efficient but playful. "Tea for three!" She walked into the kitchen leaving Collier and Joey alone. Joey took the chair by the window and Collier sat on the couch. They sat in silence for a couple of minutes.

"So," Collier said. "You punch harder than I would have thought."

"You were being an asshole."

"I was doing my job."

"I didn't kill her."

Collier lifted an eyebrow and tilted his head from side to side.

"If I'm still a suspect, why did you let me go?"

Collier sighed and stood. "Well, that's a tough one, Joe. I'm still not sure, I guess. My problem with you is that you either know a lot more than you're admitting, or you're figuring shit out in real time by conducting your own little side investigation, which I can't really allow." Collier had crossed the room and now stood behind Joey's chair, looking out the window at the apartment where Mindy had been found. "Either way, you clearly have some knowledge of the players in

155

this and you seem hell bent on feeding me that information in dribs and drabs and the whole time I keep wondering why you are not simply cooperating with me."

"I am. I tried to. I did call you, you know." Joey tried not to sound too defensive. "You're the one who's doing stuff behind my back, keeping me out of the loop."

"I'm not keeping you out of the loop," Collier laughed. "You are out of the loop. You're a civilian."

"You said you were giving up on it. That there weren't enough resources to follow up on what we -"

"Yeah. I partly said that to see what you would do."

"Okay, fine." Joey stood up and looked around the room for his cigarettes. "Do whatever you need to do. I'll stay out of it. Done." He spotted a half-empty pack on a box near the couch and went for it.

"It's too late now. You can't stay out of it. Now, you're in it."

Joey lit a cigarette. He felt Collier walk up behind him but didn't turn around.

"Why did you say the apartment was clean?"

"Because it looked clean. I told you that already."

"In Mindy's purse, the one that some Samaritan paid a homeless man ten bucks to bring directly to me, was a bag containing what appears to be the contents of a vacuum cleaner. The apartment had been cleaned."

Joey had not looked inside the purse before handing it off to the homeless man with explicit instructions.

"Can you – can you guys… get evidence from that?"

"We can. But it takes time. Or you could talk to me. What is it, Joe? Just tell me. I promise I will do everything I can to ensure that you are treated fairly."

Joey took another deep drag. He closed his eyes and pictured the man in the window who wouldn't look at him. He saw Henry's face in his final moments; the frightened expression as he realized death was pulling him under, panicked gasps from lungs that no longer functioned.

"Talk to me, Joe."

Joey opened his mouth. Just tell him, he thought. He'll think you're pathetic, but he won't think you're a killer. "I -"

"Joey?" Aggie called from the kitchen. "Where do you keep all your vases?" She pronounced it vah-zes.

"I don't have any." Raising his voice made him realize how quietly he and Collier had been talking.

"You don't have any?"

"They all broke in the move."

"Oh. Okay." Aggie accepted this easily while not being able to comprehend a person not owning vah-zes. "I'll find something."

Aggie's interruption provided the moment that Joey needed to snap to his senses. Collier couldn't promise fairness; no one could. Henry had been an avid runner his entire adult life and had drowned at the age of forty-four in fluid produced by his own lungs. Collier wouldn't accept Joey's drunken sexual desperation as an alibi, he'd see it as deviant and suspect. Joey pictured the rest of his life in jail, waiting to be executed for a crime he didn't commit even though the trail of circumstantial evidence led directly to him. While it was not so different from the way he was living now, and maybe even less challenging in some respects, he still wanted to avoid it. He took another drag from his cigarette and turned to Collier.

"I'll tell you what I know. It's just – it's nothing useful; I feel pretty stupid about it, actually. I'm... embarrassed that I wasted your time even."

"Try me."

"I talked to some girl that I think worked with Mindy and she made a vague reference to Mindy hanging out with gay guys, that's all. It's... see? It's nothing."

"She said that? She said 'gay guys'?"

"She said 'chorus boys'."

"And from that you extrapolated -"

"Yes."

157

Collier studied Joey's stoic expression. "Are you trying to get arrested?"

"Aggie," Joey called out.

"Yeah?" She sounded very busy, cupboards opening and closing.

"What's the difference between a male dancer and a chorus boy?"

"Um, amount of gayness?" Aggie called back.

"How so?"

"Well, I think a male dancer could be gay or not, whereas all chorus boys are gay."

"Okay, thanks." He held Collier's now amused gaze. "Also, when I say 'indigent,' what do you think of?"

Aggie entered from the kitchen carrying a metal baking sheet with three steaming mugs of tea and a plate with a sliced orange and some vanilla cookies from the groceries in the fridge. "You mean, like, a hobo?"

"Close enough, thanks. One more." Joey watched Collier sneak a look at Aggie's cleavage as she bent to put the tray on one of the still-packed boxes.

"Sure." She handed both of them a mug. In the kitchen she'd found a minute to brush her hair and put on a little makeup.

"What do guys keep under their mattresses?"

"Oh that's easy. Beat-off magazines. Right?"

Collier laughed into his tea. "No! Not all guys -" He wiped his mouth with his hand.

Aggie laughed, too. "Whatever you say, officer, but it's not a crime. Not in my book, anyway." Aggie perched on the ottoman that went with the chair by the window. Collier sat on the couch, shaking his head.

"Beat-off magazines... sheesh. Where did you come from?"

Aggie laughed again, bailing Joey out for the second time in less than an hour. Joey knew she'd find a way to keep the conversation about herself and Collier wouldn't challenge her because he wanted to get in her pants. Basically, Joey was off the hook, at least for the moment.

"So." Aggie nibbled the corner of one of the cookies. "Are you guys talking about that dead body Joey found?"

Twenty-seven

It had been a long time since Diane had had wine with dinner. It had been even longer since she'd had a cocktail before dinner; last night, courtesy of her television star sister, she'd had both. She'd gone to bed feeling giddy and then slept through her alarm, not waking up until 7:45. She'd leapt out of bed like a firefighter on call, certain that everything had fallen apart, to find that Peter had already left for work and Kyle and Brian were both up, showered, and eating breakfast. Alice sat on the couch in her nightgown staring at a morning news show with no volume on.

"Did your father take something for lunch?" Diane asked her older son. Both he and Brian were in the middle of a summer session, extra classes that were supposed to beef up their college applications.

"Mom, relax." Kyle answered as he handed her a cup of coffee, "I'm sure he'll figure it out."

"Don't be surprised when he calls here at noon asking where his lunch is."

"How would I be surprised when I won't even be here?" Kyle teased good-naturedly.

"Ha ha, very funny. What about you? Should I make you a sandwich?"

"I'm gonna buy."

"Oh." Diane wet the dishrag and wiped up around the coffee maker. "Do you need money?"

"Mom, chill out." He kissed her quickly on the cheek. "I have money."

Oh. Well. Excuse me. She looked at Brian who was buckling black suede ankle-high boots that she'd never seen before. "What are - what about you?" He was wearing blue and red plaid pants and a tee

160

shirt that went past his knees. "Do you want me to make you something?"

"I'm gonna buy, too."

"When did everyone suddenly become so self-sufficient?"

"Brian!" Kyle called from the front door. "Let's roll!"

"Go. I don't want you guys to be late," Diane said to Brian.

"Come on, Byron!" Kyle called again.

"Hey, be nice!" Diane called back.

"I am being nice! He knows I'm joking."

Diane looked at her younger son. "Should he become a comedian?"

"Probably not."

"Bye-bye By-ron!" Kyle let the door close as he jogged to the driveway.

"Okay, go," Diane said. She didn't get the joke so she didn't really know whether she should laugh too. "Kiss your mother."

Brian rolled his eyes as he did. She was pretty sure it was in reaction to his older brother rather than her. "Bye, mom."

———

Diane was tidy and particular and, yes - maybe slightly neurotic, as her family often teased her. The teasing didn't bother her much. She knew that without her the house would look like the town dump, which would probably be fine with Peter and the boys as long as there was pizza, Atari, and a stereo. Boys will be boys. Diane's daily chores were self-imposed, rigorous, and non-negotiable, even if she might have a little bit of a hangover. She tried to remind herself that it had, after all, been an enjoyable night as the noise of the vacuum cleaner set her teeth on edge.

The audience at *CATS* had been mostly tourists, many of whom didn't speak English. It wasn't until they'd gotten to the Italian restaurant where Aggie had made reservations that Diane had begun feeling like she and Peter stood out, and not in a good way. Everyone in the place had looked so cosmopolitan, so chic. Even the waiter

161

looked like he'd stepped out of Benson and Hedges billboard. When he first came to the table, Diane had automatically ordered a Sprite. Peter, who had dozed through most of the musical, ordered a coffee. The waiter reminded them, with a wink, that they'd not be receiving a check and that their host had specifically asked that they be encouraged to go 'all out'. Diane had probably sounded more defensive than she'd meant to when she'd explained that not everyone could go all out on a Wednesday night - that some people had jobs and children and had to drive home.

Very well, the waiter said with a slight nod and another wink, leaving Diane to wonder if he had some sort of a tic and if 'chic' was even a word that anyone was using anymore. When he'd returned with the drinks they'd ordered, he also set down two tall flutes filled with something bubbling but purple, like no champagne she'd ever seen before. *Kir Royales,* he'd called them.

Diane finished the carpet in Kyle's bedroom and parked the vacuum in front of Brian's. She made his bed and pulled the clothes out of his hamper to add to the small pile of Kyle's in the hallway. There were a slew of cassette tapes out of their cases on his nightstand, bands imported from Europe with spiky hair and dark smudged make-up. It was easy to see where Brian was getting his fashion tips. She matched one tape with its cover and smiled; if they were The Cure, she shuddered to think what the disease was. Some of the cases felt gunky so she decided to get some Windex from the kitchen and wipe them all down.

She wasn't really worried about Brian; at least she didn't think she was. He was doing well in school and had some friends who were actually sweet and polite despite their collective intention to look criminally insane. She guessed that this was just some teenage phase, some attempt to let the world know that you invented feeling different. It might just be a reaction to having an older brother who excelled at everything. It was actually Kyle's total acceptance of Brian's kookiness that gave Diane some relief, some hope that it was less of a big deal to other teenagers than it was to adults. Kyle, who was popular, was quick

162

to put a protective arm around his weird younger brother unabashedly, in public. This phase of Brian's would surely pass. She just hoped that it passed before the world agreed with him that he was different.

Once the tapes were all wiped down Diane realized that there were too many to fit in the top drawer of the nightstand. She opened the bottom drawer to see if there was room in there and well, well, what do you know, that drawer was a mess, too. Diane sighed and got to work. Loose change, a variety of eyeliners, which didn't make her happy but she didn't know what to do about it. Peter said they should draw the line at makeup and Diane said *Fine, tell him. I'm tired of always being the bad guy.* A cigarette lighter, perfect. She'd take that, thank you very much and put it right in the trash. Some things she didn't mind being the bad guy about. And now look at this: bits of what appeared to be... oh great. Tobacco. Loose bits of tobacco all over the bottom of the drawer, which means everything gets taken out and the drawer gets taken outside and Oh My God what is that.

"Miss?"

Diane started at Alice's voice and dropped the magazine back into the drawer like it was a curling iron she'd grabbed at the wrong end. She slammed the drawer before Alice could see it and think it was hers.

"Yes, Alice?"

"I didn't eat any breakfast." Alice's new thing was forgetting that she'd eaten. Alice's doctor said that it was okay to be firm with her; that in fact it was better not to capitulate.

"Well," Diane stood and wiped her clean hands on her jeans. "Let's get you some."

———

After the dishes were washed, Diane stood outside Brian's room, biting the fleshy part of her thumb like she'd done since she was a teenager while taking tests or reading something hard to follow, knowing that going back in there would mean crossing a line. It was't the line of privacy she was worried about crossing; Brian was only fourteen years old. It was something else she couldn't name. She knew they were growing up, making breakfast and driving to school and paying for their own lunches and looking at colleges and planning to move away. She and Peter would grow into comfortable, aging, out of shape suburbanites who got too loud in Manhattan restaurants once a year. Growing up was all part of the plan, a necessary step before getting married and making grandkids and Thanksgivings and Christmases and summers by a lake. It was not the growing-up line she was afraid of crossing.

She opened the drawer and pulled out the magazine with the blond boy on the cover; he couldn't be much older than Kyle. The magazine fell open naturally in her hand to its center where the same boy grinned over his shoulder against a blue background. He was reaching back to expose a pink anus, so bright that Diane briefly wondered if there was makeup on it. His expression was innocent and eager, as if he were offering something useful and unattached to a neighbor, something to be borrowed and later returned.

Diane's memory replayed a scene - a holiday party at Aggie's apartment in the city last December, seeing Aggie's friend Joey and meeting his friend Henry. Aggie had told her in advance that Henry was sick, but had not warned her about his alarming appearance. No one spoke about it, everyone so clever and above it, as if it were all so normal. Diane had felt tricked, furious and tricked and trapped by politeness. She'd pretended to mingle but stayed focused on the two of them across the smoky room: Joey on the arm of a chair, holding a plastic cup of white wine that couldn't have weighed more than a hummingbird so that Henry could sip from it. She'd made an excuse to follow Joey into the kitchen to make sure he threw the cup away, to see if he'd carelessly set it down where someone else might accidentally pick it up. It was not prejudice or small-minded suburban thinking; it was preservation. It was making sure that she or Peter didn't inadvertently bring something dangerous home to their children.

Diane dropped the magazine and closed her eyes. Behind her lids the boy from the magazine took his hand from his behind to wave to her. Then the boy turned into Brian and Brian turned into Henry and Diane began to shake.

Twenty-eight

Aggie had many talents; among them was the ability to speak with absolute confidence and authority in situations where she had none. Once, years ago, when she and Joey had been eating dinner together, Joey had burned his mouth on his first bite. *Be careful,* Aggie had said as if she were a scientist or a chef, *broccoli really retains heat.* It wasn't until much later that Joey had stopped to question whether her statement was based on anything factual, if broccoli actually did stay hot longer than the other vegetables from the same pan.

"He didn't do it." Aggie stated, strident but not emasculating, like a tough district attorney who'd learned to juggle a demanding career and a less successful husband. She was looking at a Xerox of Raymond Nunez's employment record that Collier had gotten from Actors' Equity. Collier was accepting Aggie's expertise unchallenged while Joey smoked and sipped lukewarm tea.

Collier had gone to the stage actors' union for background information on Mindy, but they'd had nothing on file under her name, which Aggie found 'not surprising'. Almost as an afterthought, Collier said, he'd asked about Raymond and had been given the printout.

"Why not. Why didn't he do it?" Collier was leaning forward, practically taking notes.

"Dancers don't kill people." Her eyes scanned the page. "Broadway, Broadway, national tour, regional, national tour. Summer Stock. He works a lot."

"His last job ended six months ago," Collier pointed out. Aggie's eyes shot back to the top of the page.

"Swing in *CATS*," she read aloud.

"What's that. Like swing dancing? World War II stuff?"

"No it means he covered more than one role. Most likely filling in when someone's injured or on vacation."

166

Joey silently made note that this was the third time this week that this particular show had been brought to his attention.

"So where is he now?" Collier asked Aggie the expert. "He's steadily employed for years then drops off. Where does he go?"

"On tour?"

"Wouldn't it be listed here if he was?"

"He could be scabbing. He could be on a non-union tour." Aggie said this as if it was an unpleasant but manageable truth that they had to consider, like diabetes. "It would be less money, but if it's the right role..."

"I don't know. It doesn't sit right with me. I mean the guy was in a Broadway show. Isn't that what you guys all aspire to?" Collier looked to both of them for confirmation, either ignoring Joey's repeated insistences that he was not a dancer, or lumping them together: dancers, actresses and gay people.

"Yeah, but a Broadway show with no guaranteed stage time? Sometimes it's worth it to take a bigger role in a smaller production if it means building a solid resume and eventually getting out of the chorus." Aggie's current job required her to regularly utter ludicrous sentences with a completely straight face, but Joey could not suppress the laugh that jumped out of him, a quick hiss of admonishment. "What?" Aggie defended. "It's true." No one said anything for a moment. The silence made Joey look up to see that Collier was looking at him instead of Aggie.

"What. Why are you looking at me?" The scrutiny was becoming tedious.

Collier shrugged lightly. "No reason. I was just wondering what you thought."

"What I thought?"

"What you think. What do you think?"

Joey was beginning to see that Collier was always a couple of steps ahead of where he pretended to be.

"I think you went to the Winter Garden."

167

"I did." Collier pointed at Joey like he was calling on him at a press conference.

"And?"

Collier took a small notebook from the inside pocket of his blazer. "Did you know that show is really just about cats?"

"Yes," Joey and Aggie said in unison.

"I guess I hadn't really thought about it. I mean, I've seen ads for it and everything, but I guess I thought it was a metaphor or something." He flipped through the notebook.

"They're cats with people problems," Joey explained. "There's no reason for them to be cats other than if they weren't, the show would have to be called *PEOPLE* and everyone would see that it's mind-bogglingly inane."

"Well. There is a really big tire on stage. I thought that was pretty neat."

"You would."

"Yes," Collier found the right page in his notebook. "I did. Okay. I also talked to a few people. I got the impression they knew where he was but didn't want to tell me."

"I'm telling you he's scabbing! They're covering for him." Aggie's DA had a stubborn streak.

"Then, as I was leaving, a girl stopped me... a young woman by the name of -" he squinted at his own writing. "Marlene. Marlene asked me if I'd been sent there by his dad."

"His dad?" Aggie picked up a cookie, broke it in half and put both pieces back down on the plate.

"Yep. Said his dad was there a few weeks back, from Maryland, looking for him too. His family hasn't heard from him either. He left a phone number in case anyone had any information on his son."

"She give you that phone number?" Joey crushed out his cigarette.

"Yep. Said she didn't want to get involved, that it was Ray's business, but she thought his dad should know."

"Know what?" Aggie was rapt, her mug suspended halfway between her lap and her mouth.

"That about six months ago Ray had to leave the show due to an infection in his foot that required hospitalization."

"She say which hospital?"

"St. Vincent's."

"So you called them..." Joey thought back through the morning, being released from jail with a slap on the wrist after being openly accused of murder.

"They said he's not there."

"Which, of course you know, does not mean he's not there."

Collier's apology, the cheap flowers, his sudden willingness to share information.

"I know."

Joey added up the other suggested implications: The calendar that hadn't been turned in a month, an infection that required hospitalization. *The wrong chorus boy.* He looked directly at Collier. "You can't get into the hospital, can you."

"Not in an official capacity."

"They want a court order?"

"Yup. It'll take a week, if I'm lucky."

"You're trying to make me think this is my idea, right?"

"It could be both of ours, Joe. Our idea. You know people there, right?"

Joey tried to remember if he'd told Collier that Henry had been at St. Vincent's before asking to be taken home to die. He didn't think he'd mentioned that specific, which meant he was really being investigated. He stared coldly at Collier.

"Flowers found your... partner's -"

"Henry."

"Henry. Found Henry's obituary." Collier's voice had gotten quiet with respect.

"Flowers hates me."

"It's not hate. He's just doing a job."

169

"Who's Flowers? What does Henry have to do with this?" Aggie was left confused by the swift turn the conversation had taken.

"I would have given you his obituary. You should have asked. You should start trusting me."

"You should start giving me a reason to trust you."

"You should stop fucking with me. You want me to help you or not?"

"It'd save a lot of time."

"Yes or no."

"Yes. I'd like you to help me."

"Admit that Flowers hates me."

"Yeah. He hates you."

"Fine. I'll call work and tell them I won't be in today."

"Is that going to cause a problem for you?"

"No, it won't," Joey stood. "They happen to like me."

Twenty-nine
-
1958

Libby had left the front door propped open when she'd stopped sweeping to let Iris in for the third day in a row. Jack had invited himself in right after Iris had finished telling her about her conversation with Frankie in the jazz club. Libby had told Jack that she wasn't open and Jack had claimed that if Libby was open enough to serve some chickadee at the bar, then she was open enough to serve him a martini, extra cold, hold the attitude.

"You're lucky to have any business at all, Miss Libby, after letting those coppers in here the other night. Don't worry, I'm not going to interrupt your little ssseduction sssscene," Jack purposefully lisped as he waggled his fingers in Iris's direction as he passed. "I'll just sit quietly down here and mind my business." He dragged Libby's newspaper down the length of the bar as he walked, perched himself on the barstool at the far end, crossed his legs and began to read. Libby made him his drink and then got back to Iris.

"Sorry 'bout him."

"Who is that?" Iris whispered, looking over Libby's shoulder.

"Jack's a regular. The other queens call him Rose. He's a pain in the ass."

"Why do they call him Rose?"

"Beats the hell out of me. They should call him Nose if you ask me."

"Libby!" Iris caught her laugh before it jumped all the way out. "That's terrible!"

"So's that honker." The two women giggled as quietly as they could; they were both excited by Iris's story of the night before. "Sorry," Libby continued, "where were we?"

"Where?" Iris seemed confused, still smiling at the joke at Jack's expense.

171

"What happened after that?"

"Oh." Iris took a sip of her white wine and 7-up. "Um... we finished our drinks and then I left."

"Oh." Libby tried not to sound disappointed by the abrupt ending to the story. "You went home then?" She toyed absentmindedly with the baseball bat she kept behind the counter in case she ever needed it. She'd never needed it.

"Yes. Well, to Eddie's. I went back to Eddie's. I would have called you, but he would have overheard -"

"Sure, sure."

"I sssTILL," Jack said loudly from the other end of the bar, "can not get over it! I know it's been two months, but *The Music Man* over *West Side Story* for best musical?"

"Hey Jack - " Libby shouted over her shoulder.

"I know, I know. It just needed to be said." He mimed zipping his lips shut and throwing a key over his shoulder.

"But Libby," Iris leaned in, "he told me he had a bag of money. That can't be a coincidence, can it?"

"Isn't that a thing people say? Bags of money? Moneybags?"

"But he didn't. That's why it stuck out to me. He said it as if he had one specific bag. That's odd, right?"

"Maybe. Maybe not. I just don't know what to do about it."

"We... we tell someone."

"We?" Libby looked down at the bat. It was a long time since she'd felt like part of a team.

"Yeah. We."

In 1943, when Libby was twenty-nine, a man had come up to her after a neighborhood baseball game in which she'd hit two home runs. He'd asked her if she wanted to try out for an all girls' professional league. She'd been living outside Chicago at the time. Libby took the train to the tryouts on her own dime. Libby had never played softball, only baseball. Her father had taught her how to hit and throw and they'd listened to the games on the radio together, cheering when their favorite teams won. She hadn't expected the field to be so distorted, shrunken. The distance between the bases had been shortened, as had the distance between the pitcher's mound and home plate. The ball was big, like a grapefruit. It seemed insultingly easy to smack it with the wide, lightweight bat, sending it sailing over the heads of the other women trying out for the league. After the drills, the man told her he'd pay her sixty-five dollars a week with a bonus every time she knocked one out of the park. With the sun in her eyes and the smoke from the man's cigar in her nose, Libby had quickly done the math. He'd offered her more than three thousand dollars a year. Her father, when he'd died a decade earlier, had been making under one thousand dollars a year.

"Who should we tell?" Libby lowered her voice more even though Jack was too far away to hear the details of their conversation.

"Well, if he's taking money that's supposed to be going to the police, maybe we should tell them."

"I don't think they'll care. Besides, we don't know which ones of 'em are in on it and which one's aren't. If there even are any that aren't. I don't think they're gonna care that some lezzie's getting the shake down."

The man had told Libby she was expected to go to a training camp first; that all the gals had to. He said there'd be a ticket waiting for her at the train station the following Friday, all paid for.

Oh, the man had said. *You have dresses, right?*

Libby did not. She spent her days working in a factory, her evenings playing ball with men who were too old to go fight, and her nights with a married woman whose husband was not.

Get some dresses, he'd said. *All my girls gotta look pretty. You can do the bulldagger thing on your own time, capeesh?* Libby had not recognized his last word and she'd stared at his mouth as if she'd been confused by the entirety of the rules he'd laid down. That night she'd gotten drunk with the guys and told them about the bullshit game they wanted her to play, how the bases were all crammed together and the ball that was the size of a grapefruit which made them laugh.

173

No, bigger than that! It was the size of a goddamn cantaloupe! which made them guffaw.

It was the size of a fucking cow's head! She'd mimed hitting something that big which made them howl. She knew even then that Tom and Jim and Big Jim and Dale and Jimmy weren't only laughing because she was being funny. They laughed because no one had ever offered them sixty-five dollars a week to do anything; they were happy to hear it was a shit deal.

"What about your landlord? Frankie's boss?" Iris asked.

"What about him?"

"If Frankie is taking money that's supposed to go to him, maybe he'd like to know that."

"Who's Na-*sah*?" Jack interrupted from across the room. "Maybe I'm mispronouncing it. Maybe it's Naysay. NaySAY. Well," he flipped the page. "Whoever they are, they plan to put a man into outer space in two years. I wonder if perhaps they'll let me select the man."

"I don't know," Libby shook her head and ignored Jack. "I thought that was the case, but I don't know if it is anymore." She thought of the man who worked with Frankie for her landlord, the one she'd tried to rat Frankie out to. He'd seemed at first to find it odd, the idea of Frankie collecting from her, but then seemed to not find it odd. And Frankie had still shown up to collect. "If the money's not going to the cops, then how come they showed up when I didn't pay it, huh?"

"I don't know," Iris said.

"So I guess that's it." Libby reached for the bottle to refill her glass. "Can't tell the papers, can't tell the cops, can't tell the mafia."

The Friday after the man offered Libby sixty-five dollars a week, the paid-for train left without her. Libby spent the rest of the war as she had been, her days, evenings, and nights with no regrets. When the day came when the entire country celebrated victory together in the streets, Libby stayed home and drank alone. For her, the end of the war meant that baseball would once again be played by men, and her lonely, married lady wouldn't be so lonely any more.

"He did tell me he had a bag of money. I know he said that."

174

"No one to tell." Libby downed the pour in one gulp and leaned the bat back in its resting place before picking up the broom again.

"J. Edgar Hoover and his companion, Clyde Tolson take in a show at Radio City Music Hall," Jack said from his end of the bar. "Now there's some ex-sssitingnews for the serious reader."

Libby and Iris exchanged a look. "What did you say, Jack?"

"It's right here on Page Six: 'The director of the FBI and his assistant continue their tour of the finest New York City has to offer on the fifth day of their vacation...' and so on and so forth, where they ate dinner, what they ate for dinner. Oh Mary, this isssss riveting news."

"They're in town right now?" Libby took two steps in Jack's direction then looked back at Iris.

"That's what it says! Do you even read this rag? Or just carry it around as to appear literate." He continued reading, "'The two finally retired to their suite at the New Yorker Hotel well after midnight...' Well." Jack closed the paper and finished his drink. "I bet they're just now waking up."

Thirty

1985

Collier double-parked on Seventh Avenue and put a placard on the dashboard that told other cops and the rest of the world that he was allowed to break whatever rules he wanted even when there were actual parking spaces within walking distance.

"Hold on."

Collier had been about to open his door. "Why?"

"Because I have an idea." During the drive downtown Joey had gotten Collier to agree to downgrade his status from Suspect to Person of Interest. He still wasn't completely happy with the term, but compromise was rarely fully satisfactory for either party. "You should take off your shirt."

"Take off my shirt?"

"Aren't we trying to pretend you're not a cop with an attitude problem?"

Collier looked down at his outfit. "Don't you think shirtless is a little aggressive?"

"I mean I think we should trade shirts. I get that you have to wear your nerdy blazer to conceal your gun, but if you wear it with my tee shirt, it will look more casual. I'll wear your button-down, but leave it untucked. I also think you should take off your socks and roll up your cuffs a couple of times. It's not a look I'd normally encourage, but in this case I'll make an exception."

Collier shrugged. "Okay. Sure."

"Really?" Joey had expected more resistance.

"Why not?" Collier took off his blazer and went to work on his holster, leather straps that went over both shoulders, allowing the compact gun to fit snugly under his left armpit. "You think I have an attitude problem?"

The holster's straps made Joey think of fetishes that involved harnesses and motorcycle boots.

"You guys all have attitude problems."

"Us guys?" Collier unbuttoned his shirt. He wasn't wearing an undershirt; Joey deliberately looked out the window, not wanting to give Collier the satisfaction of being admired. "That's a generalization and it's insulting and small-minded. Shame on you."

"Very funny."

"Ha ha. Here." Collier held out his shirt for Joey with the ease of someone who'd only ever been shirtless around other men in non-sexual situations. Joey allowed himself only a glimpse of Collier's bare torso; not overly built, but natural muscles shaped by a youth filled with sports, a patch of effortless, untrimmed dark hair in the center of his breastbone. Joey kept his arms as close to his body as he could while he slipped his faded, salmon colored tee-shirt over his head, his back rounded in a tortoise-like apologetic curve. "Fabric softener and cigarette smoke," Collier commented as they both redressed. Joey could feel cold wet spots under his arms where Collier's sweat had cooled. "Now what?" Collier asked as he buckled his holster back into place.

"Socks and cuffs."

"Right." Collier slipped off his dress shoes and pulled off his socks. "This feels dopey."

"That's the point."

They each climbed out of their prospective doors. Collier glanced at Joey as they met up and started walking together. "Okay. We good?"

"Almost. Do this." Joey wiped the inside corner of his own eye to make Collier do the same.

"Do I have scudge in my eye?"

"Pretty much all the time."

———

Joey ignored the fact that his heart rate jumped up a couple of notches as he and Collier walked through the automatic doors that he hadn't been through since the day they'd wheeled Henry out into a private ambulance, Joey's hand on his bony shoulder to keep him from trying to sit up, Henry's eyes wild with panic. They stepped into the elevator, where he'd once vomited after leaving Henry's room while a nurse changed shit-covered sheets; Joey realized he was holding his breath. He made himself inhale, then exhale. He heard Collier ask him if he was okay and he nodded in reply. Joey's vision tilted sharply to the right as they stepped off the elevator onto the sixth floor. A young, muscular black man nearly collided with them as he ran down the hall toward some commotion, a woman's voice calling out that it was happening again, somebody hurry, it's happening again.

Joey focused on putting one foot in front of the other as if on a tightrope to get to the same reception desk where he'd been told that Henry's kidneys had shut down, that it was only a matter of days now. The desk seemed to stay the same distance from him even as he walked closer. His teeth started chattering from the cold, he wondered how they'd made it so cold here in July. He heard Collier ask him again if he was okay, but this time his voice came from somewhere else, from down the hall. A middle aged woman in blue scrubs stood in alarm as Joey finally made it to the desk and he wondered what terrible thing was behind him to make her look that way. He saw the ceiling, square tiles made of some material that could be easily crumbled by hand, a sprinkler that could burst to life and cover them all.

Then he saw only white.

———

Joey heard voices before he opened his eyes. He didn't know where he was or what he was lying on, but it felt lumpy and awkward. He was shivering, the muscles in his body tense and cramping, and he tried to focus on relaxing them. His hands had seized into gnarled talons; he flexed his fingers and then slowly made fists, then flexed them again.

178

He distinguished Collier's voice. "He's awake." He realized he was lying half on the floor and half in Collier's lap. He struggled to sit up and felt Collier's arms tighten around him, one hand across his chest and the other pressing a cool, damp cloth to his forehead.

"Stay put, Joey," another voice said, a cool, raspy alto that he recognized, a slight southern twang that got stronger after several shots of tequila. He peeled his eyes open and looked into the stern but caring face of Dr. Carolyn Mortensky. "What are you doing here, Joey? Didn't I warn you that I'd beat the living shit out of you if I ever saw you again?"

"Did I faint?"

"You did." Dr. Carolyn, as she encouraged her patients to call her, was shining a penlight into Joey's face. "Lucky for you Mr. Blue Eyes caught you before you hit the floor." Joey squinted and looked up at Collier who nodded back down to him.

"Can I sit up?" Joey asked and then did so. He felt embarrassed. He thought of the time, several years before, when he'd passed by a phone booth and had heard a woman saying *Just be grateful you didn't wet your pants*. "How long was I out for?" He saw that the cloth Collier had been holding to his forehead was really just a wet paper towel.

"Not long." Dr. Carolyn studied him with clinical concern. "Come here." She reached up and pressed hard with her fingers behind and then up under his jaw for swelling. "Your glands feel okay. How are your lungs?" She put the earplug ends of the stethoscope around her neck into her ears.

"They hate cigarettes but I love them, so we argue sometimes," Joey said. She slid her hand up under Collier's button down shirt covering Joey's chest.

Carolyn Mortensky had once been a pulmonologist who dealt mostly with the elderly. When young, gay men started suddenly developing pneumonia in droves, she quickly became one of the city's leading AIDS doctors.

"Breathe in," she instructed as she moved the cold disc around his chest. "Well. Your lungs are right about the smoking. But they're clear." She put the back of her hand to his cheek, probably just to feel his temperature, but it felt maternal and welcome. "You're too thin. You need to eat."

"I'm not hungry."

"Eat anyway."

"I'm sorry I fainted. I'm fine, I'm... we're here looking for someone."

Dr. Carolyn cocked her head and looked at Joey's mouth like she was reading the words coming out of it. "Looking for someone?"

"A friend who's a patient here. Ray Nunez? He's a patient here, right?"

Carolyn's lips flattened out briefly before pursing in admonishment. "Joey. You know as well as anyone that I can't just give that information out." Her patient protection eclipsed her patient compassion.

"Why not?" Collier asked.

"Because many of my patients, if not all of them, are dealing with incredibly complicated situations. Not only in terms of their health, but also their privacy, their employers, their families and their insurance." Her speech sounded like she'd given it often. "It's not my place to discuss their situations with anyone except them and people they personally introduce me to." She stood up. "Sorry Joey."

"Carolyn." Joey and Collier both got to their feet. "Come on. It's me you're talking to."

"If he's a friend," her eyes darted from Joey to Collier and then back, "find out from another friend where he is. Go home, I can't help you."

"He's not really a friend," Joey said to Dr. Carolyn's back. "I don't actually know him at all. But Henry did. I was going through some of Henry's things and I found this phonebook that I'd never seen before. Names of people, men, I'd never even heard of. I've called some of them."

Carolyn turned back around. "Why? What on earth for?"

"I'm not sure. Maybe for closure or... to see if they're okay."

Collier wrapped his arm around Joey from behind and placed his hand on Joey's chest like he was pledging allegiance to the flag.

"They're not. Okay?" Carolyn stepped forward. "They're not okay." She looked at Joey with a kaleidoscope of emotions: rage, pity, anger, disgust and wonder. "None of you are okay." She shook her head.

"If he's here, he's on this floor, right?" Joey asked.

Carolyn squinted at him. "You haven't been here since -"

"February."

" - since we ran out of beds," she finished. "He's on the fourth floor. Come on."

Dr. Carolyn led them to the stairs, to the fourth floor and into what appeared to be a supply closet that had been partially emptied to make room for two cots, one of which was ominously empty. She gestured to the body on the other cot. "Private room, as of this morning. Lucky guy."

Collier and Carolyn stood in the doorway while Joey approached unconscious Ray. The information that Collier had gotten from Actors' Equity said that he had been born in 1958, which made him 27. The person in the bed more resembled a mummy than a living person, yellowed skin with deep purple lesions stretched over thin bones. The little bit of living that Ray was doing at the moment was courtesy of a variety of machines he was hooked up to. A collection of pill bottles stood vigil on a cleared supply shelf. Joey had been right, the man he'd seen in the window had not been Raymond Nunez.

"The hospital isn't accepting any more AIDS patients. There's no room. If they're smart, and your friend here was smart, they come in through the emergency room and we can't legally turn them away. Gotta put 'em somewhere."

"How long has he been here?" Collier asked from the doorway.

"This time? A week, maybe. Something like that. Said he woke up and couldn't see, called a cab instead of an ambulance, otherwise he'd have ended up at Bellevue."

"Is that bad?" Collier wasn't familiar with the nuances of AIDS care at the city's various hospitals.

"No. But we're better," Carolyn said. "He's in a medically induced coma. He was having seizures, too. Bad ones. Untreated Psitticosis. The only way to stop them is to keep him under."

"Is that contagious?" Collier took a small step backwards.

"Not really. It's an infection parrots usually get." A beeper went off from somewhere on Carolyn's person. "Shit," she said. "You boys are gonna have to show yourselves out."

"Sure." Joey turned and waved. "And thanks. For this."

"Sure." Carolyn nodded. "Eat something."

"Well," Collier stepped up behind Joey after the doctor walked down the hall. "Looks like we're back to square one."

Joey looked at the bottles of pills labeled with long but familiar names. One was for nausea, another an anti-fungal that was hard on the liver.

"Come on," Collier said as he turned to leave. "Let's get out of here."

One was for pain, a strong narcotic that was only to be used sparingly. Joey put them in his pocket.

Thirty-one

1958

Frankie sat alone in the back of the diner and ordered a chicken salad sandwich, choosing his seat so he could see the front door, out of habit. He had just been thinking that if he played it cool, this whole thing would blow over, when the door opened and Carlo and Del walked in casually, like they weren't looking for anyone in particular. Frankie saw them see him, lifted his chin in salutation and took a sip of his coffee. Carlo and Del were attached at the hip; Frankie had worked together with them for years, but never one without the other. Frankie hadn't seen them since Sunday, when Carlo had mentioned offhandedly that the man they all worked for thought someone inside was stealing. Frankie had gotten angry after Carlo had said this, irrationally furious even, but he'd since calmed down. He knew he had to stay focused and act normal if he was going to live through this. Carlo and Del sat down, one on each side of him.

"Hiya, Frankie," Carlo said smiling.

"Hey, Carlo," Frankie nodded. "Del." He'd never heard Del utter more than a few mumbled words at a time.

"Your mom told us you'd gone out for lunch." Carlo's tone was friendly but formal, like he was pretending not to know Frankie beyond a passing acquaintance. Like he was establishing a distance between them.

Frankie kept his hands in plain sight, loosely wrapped around his coffee cup like a man with nothing to hide. "Yeah. Well. Here I am."

"Here you are," Carlo repeated.

"I just ordered, you guys hungry?"

"Nah. We only have a few minutes," Carlo spoke for both himself and Del. Del was big and always acted as if he wasn't paying attention. He looked like a grownup sitting at the kids' table.

"There something I can do for you guys?"

"I hope so, Frankie. You think anymore about what we talked about on Sunday?"

Frankie took a sip of his coffee. "Sunday? What did we talk about on Sunday?"

"About Mr. C figuring out that someone's been taking money from him."

"What's there to think about? I ain't the one doing it. How would I even do something like that?"

"Well, apparently what you would do, or what someone would do, if they were so inclined, is go to one of the establishments Mr. C provides protection for and collect money on his behalf -"

"That's what we all do."

"Right. That is what we do. But someone has apparently been collecting... extra."

"Extra?"

"Yeah. Extra."

"Well, it's not me," Frankie widened his eyes like he couldn't even fathom such a concept.

"It's not you?"

"You know I ain't smart enough to come up with something like that."

The gray-haired waiter came by and put Frankie's sandwich in front of him. Carlo waited until the man walked out of earshot before continuing.

"So you're saying you neverdone anything like that?"

"Never."

The first time Frankie had stolen money from Mr. C was probably five years ago. At the time he didn't think of it as stealing since he'd done it with every intention of paying all two hundred and forty dollars back.

"That's good to hear, Frankie. That's really good to hear. I like you."

"I like you too, Carlo." Frankie tried not to audibly exhale with relief.

"Now all we have to do is convince Mr. C, who seems to think his source doesn't have any reason to make this up."

Del reached out his big hand and took half of Frankie's sandwich.

"Who. Who's saying that. You gonna tell me who's out there saying these things about me?"

Carlo didn't.

"I mean, these are some serious accusations, I should be able to know who's talking about me."

Carlo shrugged as if it didn't matter to him either way. "This case isn't exactly going to be argued in front of a judge, Frankie."

"So what, I'm guilty now? Just like that?" Frankie snapped his fingers. "What are we talking about, a twenty or a fifty here or there? Sure, yeah. I done that. We all done that." They'd done a lot more than that, the three of them, and they'd done it all easily without hesitation or question at the request of their boss, often while cracking jokes or discussing where to get a burger after they were done. "All three of us have done a lot worse than pocket a coupla bills here and there, so don't act like you're better than me."

Carlo considered this then looked at silent Del. "I don't think I know what he's talking about. Del, you know what Frankie here is talking about?"

Del shook his head no.

"I've never taken any money. Have you ever taken any money Del?"

Del shook his head no.

"Have you ever seen me take any money?" Carlo looked back at Frankie and waited for an answer they both knew wasn't needed.

Frankie had taken the two hundred and forty dollars because Deandra had said she needed it and Deandra was the most beautiful woman he'd ever been with. She was beautiful enough to be only moderately talented and still get gigs in clubs that took pride in booking

185

talent over beauty. He couldn't remember now what her first reason had been; it may have been something to do with her rent or her mother. There were so many reasons that came later, once Deandra had pegged Frankie as a bottomless well of cash. At first, Frankie had been foolish enough to believe that her trusting him with her intimate problems meant that she loved him. Later, he'd been foolish enough to believe that if he could get her away from the needle, and keep her away from the needle, he could use the money he'd started tucking away to build a new life for the two of them, somewhere far away. He'd given Deandra the choice and she'd chosen the needle.

"Alright, listen," Frankie leaned forward. "You known me since before we could stand up to piss. Whatever this is, whoever is saying this about me, you owe me a few days to figure out why they got it out for me. How much money are we talking about here?"

"A lot. In the tens of thousands."

Frankie whistled. "Come on, Carlo. You think I'm the kind of guy who could peel away ten thousand dollars?"

Deandra had gotten her heroin from a cat who called himself The Doctor, a skinny little fuck who made a show out of it, calling the junkies his 'patients' and making himself available for house calls for an extra fee. After Deandra OD'd, Frankie caught up with The Doctor and put two bullets in the back of his head.

"I didn't say ten thousand. I said tens of thousands. We don't know exactly how much."

Del swallowed and reached for the second half of Frankie's sandwich.

"Alright give me a couple of days," Frankie leaned back. "I'll see what I can find out."

It was exactly fifty-seven thousand, nine hundred and fifty dollars. It was neatly stacked in The Doctor's black bag in the back of a closet in his mother's upstairs sewing room. Frankie had actually been surprised at how easy it had all been. He figured that the people he collected from were cowed enough to not challenge his demands and he'd been right. Perhaps he'd underestimated one of them.

"I can give you a couple of days, Frankie, but you have to come back with something good. If I put my neck on the line and you don't deliver, it might look like I have an interest in helping you stall here."

"I understand, I understand," Frankie said. He understood that even if he gave all of the money back with a hundred percent interest it would only mean the difference between a fast death and a slow one. "I'll get to the bottom of this and then we can all laugh about it after I find the person who's saying this about me."

Carlo nodded and stood up. Del stood up at the same time and the two of them walked out of the diner. Frankie looked at the crumbs on his empty plate. He was actually fine with being done with it all; he had enough to start over somewhere. He just needed to get the money and get out of town, all while being watched, a target as good as painted on his forehead.

Frankie knew that the hit out on him, when it came, would not be personal. It would be good business. Were Frankie in his employer's position, he would order the same action, even on a brother. He would mourn the departed and curse his mistakes, but he would do it. Once word got out that Frankie had stolen, his body would have to turn up pretty quickly. Mr. C made a business of people owing him money and paying large amounts of interest. Any hint of forgiveness or give where money was concerned would collapse the whole structure.

Frankie had seen other men in similar predicaments make poor choices that had ended up getting them killed. The poorest of these was usually the one to run. People who ran made mistakes and left trails; people who walked had a better chance. In many ways Frankie had it easy. He had practically nothing that he'd mind leaving behind. He didn't even need a change of clothes. He just needed the bag from the closet in his mother's sewing room. The problem was, if Frankie was seen walking out of his mother's house carrying anything that looked remotely like it could possibly contain cash, he'd be stopped by Carlo or Del, or someone even less sympathetic. He needed a conspirator, and he needed one fast.

But they knew everyone that he knew.

Except for one person. He barely knew her himself. She was pretty enough, in a naive way. Not so pretty that he'd have a difficult time getting rid of her when the time came. He'd get her some flowers. Girls liked flowers.

Thirty-two

-

1985

Joey followed Collier out of Ray's room, to the elevator and out onto the street. His light-headedness was gone; in its place was an overall lightness. Collier was walking towards his car, moving faster than Joey. Joey called out to him.

"Hey."

Collier motioned for Joey to catch up. Joey smiled and stayed his course and used his hands to make a megaphone. "I was right, you can say it. You owe me a drink," he said to Collier's back. Joey squinted his eyes into the bright sun beating down; there was a breeze keeping it from becoming oppressive. It was one of the maybe six days a year where the weather in New York reminds you that yes, it can actually be perfect when it wants to be. In spite of fainting, it was sort of a perfect day, the kind where everything good and bad in your life all seems to make sense. He looked back to see Collier back in the sedan, talking on the radio. Joey took his time, allowing Collier to finish up what he was doing before making it to the driver's side window.

"What were you yelling at me about?" Collier asked.

"I was just saying we should go have a drink."

Joey reached into his pocket for his cigarettes. An indecipherable voice muttered again in a flat tone through the radio in Collier's car. Collier spoke low and rapidly into the CB before turning back to Joey.

"Sorry. What'd you say?"

"Drinks. Us. To celebrate."

"Celebrate?" Now Collier was squinting into the sun as he looked up at Joey.

"We did it. We found Ray."

"We did do that. Yeah. But we haven't found the person that killed Mindy."

189

"But we did good. We should celebrate."

"I can't. I'm working." Collier started his car.

"Okay. But admit that we did good."

"We did okay," Collier said. "What's wrong with you? You're smiling really… oddly."

"I'm fine," Joey said. He lit a cigarette.

"You're not going to pass out again?"

"I'm not. I feel good, I swear. You need your shirt back?"

"Later." The police radio in Collier's car garbled something else unintelligible. "I gotta run."

"Okay. Later." Joey took a step back as Collier shifted the sedan into drive. "Hey."

"Hey," Collier put his foot back on the brake.

"Thanks. It's been a while since I felt good."

"Wait till we catch the bastard," Collier smiled. "You'll feel even better."

As Collier pulled into traffic, Joey realized that he suddenly had a free day; he couldn't remember the last time he'd had one of those. Free days were different than days off. Days off were, at best, spent relaxing or doing chores. At worst, they were spent caring for a dying person, cleaning out a dead friend's apartment, or lying in bed in shock. Free days, on the other hand, were days that had been earmarked for some purpose, which was then unexpectedly wiped away. They were days when you realize you are not needed or expected anywhere by anyone including yourself. Totally free. They were days in the middle of the work week where you could wander your way from the West Village up to Central Park and sit in the grass of Sheep's Meadow and take in all the young men who, for whatever reason, had nowhere else to be but under the sun, shirtless and beautiful. You could walk barefoot to the edge of the park and then venture back out onto the pavement and find the restaurant where six years ago you went on a first date with a man named Henry and eventually fell in love.

We did okay.

It had been a long time since Joey had felt like part of a We.

They were days when you could sit at the bar and drink a Scotch or four and feel no self-pity, no sadness, only gratitude. That there was beauty. That you knew him. That you loved him. That you tried.

We did good.

———

Although he was a little drunk, Joey knew immediately upon walking back into his apartment that something was wrong. The cheap white roll-up blind on his living room window that came with the apartment had been pulled down, and he never pulled it down because it was ugly. The light in the hall that he left on all the time had been turned off. Joey knew that the light wasted energy but he had a strong aversion to coming home to or falling asleep in a completely dark apartment based on a long menu of fears that included this particular situation: someone was in the apartment with him. He stood frozen for just a moment too long, his arms limp and useless by his sides, before turning to try for a quick escape through the door swinging shut behind him. An open hand jumped out of the shadows and slammed him in the chest, pushing him up against the wall as the door closed with a dull click.

Joey's feet stumbled over a pair of shoes he'd left there. His ankles wobbled and his knees buckled, causing the hand to press into his chest harder to keep him from sliding down the wall. He dropped his house keys and felt them hit his foot and slide to the floor as his attacker's other hand reached out and closed tightly around his neck.

"Where is it?" The intruder's voice was low and gruff and came from an arm's length away in the darkness. Joey didn't know what *it* was, much less its whereabouts, so he didn't say anything. The hands pulled him an inch away from the wall just for a breath before slamming him back against it with more force than before. "Where is it?"

"I don't know what you're talk -" Joey managed to choke out before he was spun around and pushed again. He turned his face to the

191

side just in time to make his cheek hit the wall first instead of his nose. His legs hadn't caught up with his torso and twisted beneath him offering even less support than before. His arm was yanked and wrenched up his back behind him just as Flaars had done the night before. Joey gritted his teeth to keep from crying out as he slammed the heel of his free hand into the wall to steady himself. How, he wondered, did everyone except him seem to know how to inflict this incapacitating hold?

"Do not fuck with me, man." Joey's attacker's voice stayed low and whispered, as if intentionally disguised.

"I don't know what you're talking about I really really don't know. I don't. I don't know." Joey waited, pressed against the wall, for the man holding him there to decide what to do next. He'd probably pictured a more straightforward transaction: he'd rough Joey up a little and Joey would hand over whatever it was he was asking for, knowing that whatever it was wasn't worth more than his life. Maybe he was only now considering the possibility that Joey really might not know. It was hard to breathe.

"The money. My money. Where is it?"

Still unsure of how to answer the whispered demands, Joey stayed quiet, trying to match his breath with the rhythm of his assailant's while he waited for the man holding him to decide what to do.

"Where's the fucking money?"

Joey wondered whether his attacker was intellectually limber enough to consider another angle of interrogation.

"It's a lot of money and it's mine. She fucking stole it and I don't know what or where and I don't give a fuck. I want it back. So find it."

Only one of Joey's feet was flat on the floor. The other had landed in a sickled bevel in the melee. He wanted to pick it up and right it, but he was nervous any movement would be mistaken for an escape attempt. Not that he didn't want to escape, he just didn't believe that he'd be able to.

"Find it," the man repeated his simple demand. "Do you understand me?"

Joey nodded and grunted out something that sounded vaguely affirmative. He actually did sort of understand. He had a good nose for health and beauty products and recognized the same deodorant that the man who'd thrown Mindy's purse away at the coffee shop had been wearing. They were also the same height and, Joey was fairly certain, probably the same person. He understood that the man who'd killed Mindy Shorent was now in his apartment demanding stolen money under the assumption that Joey would know what he was talking about. Piecing it together, Joey understood that this guy had once had some money and believed that Mindy stole it. The fact that he'd killed her in Ray's apartment probably means that they'd gone there because this man believed Ray would know where the money was.

"If you go to the police, I will find out and you'll regret it."

What the man didn't know, that Joey did know, was that Ray was not involved in stealing any money because he was too busy dying. How did he and Mindy get into Ray's apartment? Mindy must have had a key, which would be on that key ring with the ballet slippers on it. He wondered if Collier or Flaars had thought to test Mindy's keys in Ray's locks. If Mindy were a good enough friend to have a key to Ray's apartment, she would have known that Ray was in the hospital. If she brought this man who killed her to Ray's apartment, did that mean that she believed the money was there? While this man was beating her up and drowning her in the bathtub, wouldn't she have told him where the money was if she knew? If the money really wasn't there, did that mean Ray did something with it?

The man who killed Mindy pushed Joey against the wall again, for emphasis. Joey did not know how this man came to believe that he would know anything about Ray or Mindy or the money.

"I don't know where you faggots have my money, but I'll fucking kill you if you don't have it back the next time I come here, you understand?"

193

Joey grunted. He both understood and believed that this man would fucking kill him. Joey had watched this man through the window for two consecutive nights the previous weekend. What he didn't know then was that Mindy was also in the apartment, most likely in some state of distress, beaten, restrained. Joey knew now that while this man waited for Ray to show up, he spent his time alternately beating Mindy and beating off. This made him, in Joey's opinion, a certain kind of messed up. Either the violence turned him on or he was able to completely detach from it. Either scenario made him dangerous.

"I'll kill you."

The man did not know how closely Joey had come to killing himself. He did not know that Joey had just had four scotches and had ten powerful pain pills in his pocket. Would this man really know if Joey went to the police? It sounded like something anyone in this guy's desperate position would say. How would he know if Joey told Collier about all of this?

"I'll kill you as easily as you killed her. I'm going to hit you now."

Joey didn't really hear the second part. Or at least he didn't process it. He was too busy registering the fact that even Mindy's murderer seemed to think that Joey killed her.Before he could think a subsequent thought, a closed fist hit the back of his head, bouncing his forehead off the wall just a few inches away. Joey lost consciousness for the second time that day, but unlike the whiteness of fainting, this time everything went black.

Thirty-three

The gin martinis had been Aggie's suggestion, as had the place. On the 35th floor of a hotel in midtown overlooking everything, businessmen and their wives sipped cocktails alongside tourists while a pianist played Cole Porter in the background. Many of them were in tuxedos and gowns, coming from something important like a fundraiser. This venue was not that event; it was the after-event. Dim chandeliers and flickering candles flattered everyone. Aggie had arrived fifteen minutes late to see that Collier was waiting at the bar, leaning noncommittally on a barstool with a beer in front of him. When Aggie suggested martinis, Collier pushed the beer aside.

"So," Collier said after they'd taken their first sips. "When did you do it?"

"You mean my phone number?" Aggie watched him study her face, one eye than the other, then her nose, her chin and back to her eyes.

"Mm hmm." He looked bemused as he slowly and absentmindedly traced the knuckle of his index finger back and forth across his own lips.

"Well. I wrote it down while I was making tea in the kitchen, but I didn't slip it into your pocket until we were leaving the apartment."

"That's very…"

"Forward?" Aggie raised her eyebrow.

"Modern. I was going to say modern."

They sipped their drinks.

"Well. I'm a strike-while-the-iron-is-hot kind of gal. I don't mind making the first move."

"I imagine you must have to; men must be pretty intimidated to ask you out."

"It's less complicated than that. I have an unlisted phone number."

"You think that would stop me?" Collier's laugh caught Aggie off guard. "It's my job to find people."

"What do you do when you find them?" God he's handsome, she thought.

"Expose them."

It wasn't an answer that Aggie expected, especially as it was delivered with no hint of innuendo in it. "Expose them," she repeated. He was handsome, but it wasn't just that. He was confident. He was solid.

"Yep. Find 'em, catch 'em, expose 'em."

"How do you do all that?" Aggie took a sip of her drink then dabbed a drop of gin off the rim with the tip of her tongue.

"Lots of different ways," Collier shrugged. His eyes dipped almost imperceptibly to her mouth.

"What's the best way?"

Collier's expression changed. He still looked impressed by her, but also a little surprised. "No one's asked me that before."

"It's the actress in me. I've been trained to investigate motivation."

"Hm," Collier nodded as he sipped his drink. "You and me both. I guess the best way is to get people to talk to you. You figure in every situation, someone somewhere knows what happened. The trick is finding the right person to talk to and getting on their good side."

"How do you go about that? Getting on their good side, I mean." Their initial flirtation had shifted seamlessly into a more relaxed conversation. Aggie found herself actually interested in the question and Collier seemed to be carefully assembling a thoughtful answer in his head.

"Give people what they want."

"Hm," Aggie nodded as she tucked her hair behind her ear and pulled it around to fall over her shoulder.

"Everybody wants something. Even if they don't know it. If you can figure out what it is, what they are missing, and offer it to them? Well, then you're on their side."

"You sound like you're good at your job. And also like you'd be a natural in my business."

"Well thank you kindly," Collier smiled. One of his front teeth was slightly and perfectly crooked. "I guess I shouldn't make it sound so much like conscious manipulation. It's more like just paying attention. Most people just want to be heard without being judged."

"But you do, don't you? You do judge them."

"I don't. There's a whole legal thing in place for that."

"Right."

"I just try to figure out what happened. Then, you know, the lawyers get involved and it all goes to hell anyway, but at least I feel like I tried to make the world a little bit better."

Aggie nodded like this was something she too was actively trying to do on a daily basis.

"Of course, you have to also talk to a bunch of insane people and people who are perfectly nice but don't know anything."

"You just perfectly described the writers on my show."

Collier laughed. "Well it isa soap opera, isn't it?" Aggie had told him that on the phone earlier when he'd called and they'd made these plans.

"It is that, yes. Don't get me wrong," Aggie looked up as if addressing God or the universe. "I'm lucky to have my job and I love it very much. I love it, I do. But sometimes…"

"Tell me about it."

"No," Aggie lifted her glass and took the tiniest sip ever taken in the history of drinking. "I'll spiral out. Suffice it to say, writers are the worst. I'm enjoying hearing about your work. Really. Tell me about your insane people."

"Ha ha. Okay, well…" Collier put his hand on his hip, exposing the badge attached to his belt loop by his hip as he thought.

"Okay. Here's one for you. Today I get a call from a guy who claims to know something about one of the cases I'm working on."

"The one that Joey -"

"Yeah. That one." Collier lifted his glass and tilted it in Aggie's direction. "This guy tells me he has a name for me to look into, Anthony Somethingorother. So I write it down and ask him how I might find this guy, and he says 'Look around'." Collier widened his eyes and pretended to look around. "So I thanked him and asked what his name was so I could contact him in case there's reward money, and he tells me his name is Lieutenant Collier."

"Isn't that your name?"

"It is. It is my name."

"What did you say?"

"Nothing. I just hung up on him."

"That's it?" Aggie laughed. "That's the end of the story?"

"Yeah. I guess it wasn't that great of a story."

"I liked it."

Collier took a little bow. "I probably shouldn't try to write for your show."

"No, probably not." They were both smiling and looking into each other's eyes. Collier looked like he was about to try to kiss her; Aggie tilted her chin slightly and looked at his mouth.

"Can I ask you a question now?" Collier said.

"Yes."

"It's about your friend. Joe."

"Joey?" Aggie was suddenly reminded that she'd only met this man about twelve hours before. It seemed like they'd known each other much longer.

"Yeah. Joe. Is he... uh...do you trust him?"

"Do I trust him?"

"Yeah. I mean. Is he trustworthy. I'm saying this wrong. I feel like he knows something - something more than he thinks he does."

"I told him the same thing!" Aggie touched her finger to Collier's chest right between his collarbones. "I did. I said Joey you were in there. You know more than you think you do. It's like repressed. Maybe. Like you know, your mind can only experience so much tragedy at one time."

"Right." Collier ran his hand through his hair. "Did you know his -"

"Henry? Yeah. Oh, yes, incredibly well. I knew them both. I knew... I thought they were an unlikely match at first. Henry was so buttoned up, I guess. And Joey was so -"

"Wait, Henry was the buttoned up one?"

"Yeah. Totally." Her finger was still touching him, right above where his shirt was buttoned.

"And Joey was the not buttoned up one? I can't picture that."

"You think Joey is buttoned up?"

"Tight. Tightly buttoned. Up. He used to be fun?" Collier winked.

"No. Well, maybe I guess if you're just meeting him now - after." Aggie didn't see Collier's wink; she was focused on the bar. "Joey was not just fun." She lifted her glass but did not drink. "Joey was the most fun."

"Oh shit," Collier put his hand under Aggie's chin and tilted her face up. "I'm a jerk." He handed her a cocktail napkin. "I'm sorry. I didn't mean to upset you."

"No, you didn't," Aggie dabbed the napkin at her eyes. "It's not your fault."

"I really feel for the guy. I - this probably sounds crazy to say about a guy who punched and kicked me in the head - but I like him. I feel like he needs a friend. Another friend. It's a weird position to be in, kind of catching me off-guard. I don't know how to say to a basically - to someone who is basically a stranger - you know, 'you can talk to me if you need to'."

"Why don't you just tell him?" Aggie looked at the napkin and felt confident she had not totally ruined her eyeliner. "I think he'd like that."

"I don't know. It feels a little presumptuous on my part. I barely know the guy."

"Do you want me to tell him?"

"No, that's nice of you to offer -"

"I don't have to make it sound like you askedme to talk to him. I think you're right. I think that's exactly what he needs. Sometimes I think - you know when you know someone so well I don't know if I'm able to… I don't know if I'm the right person for him to talk to."

Aggie felt like the conversation had taken a morbid turn. He'd been about to kiss her, she was sure of it, then they'd started talking about this. She put her hand on his. "You're a sweet man."

And then he did kiss her.

"So what about you?" Aggie said after their lips had barely separated.

"What about me?"

"You can tell what everyone else needs, what do you need?" She put her finger on his belt buckle.

"To catch the bad guys."

"You do judge them! I knew it."

"Okay… to catch the -" Collier drew a blank line in the air with his finger " - guys. To catch 'em."

"Mmm." Aggie smiled and tilted her head back again.

"And what about me? What do I need?"

Collier looked at each of her eyes again, and then her mouth. "That's a good question. I'm actually stumped."

"Really? You mean you can tell what everyone needs except forme? That's not fair."

"You look like the type of woman who can get anything she wants."

"Looks can be deceiving. And they fade."

"Not yet they haven't." He leaned in and kissed her again.

"But they will."

"That might be a good thing, you know." Aggie felt his lips break into a smile. "Honestly. Because right now, it's a little intense."

Aggie bit his bottom lip gently and felt his belt buckle press against her finger.

"Okay," Collier took her hand in his and cleared his throat as he looked around. "That almost got… wow. Should we get one more?" He raised his hand to get the bartender's attention.

"I think we should." Aggie reached up and took a hold of his index finger with her own. "Maybe back at my place?"

"Yeah?"

"Unless that makes me come across as too… modern."

"You should know," Collier pulled a twenty-dollar bill from his wallet and put it on the bar, "that I'm a little old-fashioned."

"Oh yeah?"

"Yep. If I come over, I might not ever leave."

Thirty-four

Joey was pulled into consciousness by the discomfort of something digging into his hip. He realized that his head was throbbing and his arm was numb, pinned beneath his fallen body. A wave of nausea rolled through him and he took a deep, jagged breath and whimpered aloud. Joey had never been a crier, but there were circumstances that called for whimpering. He managed to peel his eyes open one at a time. The room was still dark but he could somehow tell it was morning. Maybe it was the birds chirping outside, sounding exactly the way they did in a cartoon when someone fell in love or got knocked out. His eyes weren't focusing properly, but that sometimes didn't happen for a little while on a good morning, nothing to get alarmed about in and of itself. He squeezed them shut and then open again. One of the shadows around the small step that led down to his living room looked a little like a rounded shoulder of a person sitting there calmly, facing away from him. As Joey watched it, the shadow seemed to gently pulse as if taking in and exhaling air. The longer he watched, the more Joey became convinced that it was alive.

Do you remember that day that one summer...

Milt.

... That we roller-skated all around Central Park, and then aaaaall the way downtown to that Eye-talian place that had tables outside with umbrellas like we was in the French Riviera.

Milt was putting on some kind of vocal affectation that Joey had never known him to do in life. It wasn't appealing.

What was that lil ole place called? I cain't recall.

Neither could Joey. It was somewhere on Bleecker. Or Carmine. The umbrellas had been blue and white.

Do you remember those three jaded muscle queens at the table next to us? With their tennis visors, fanning themselves with those Chi-nesey fans? I swear we must have had thirteen gin and tonics apiece that afternoon. Remember those queens? Remember how bitter they were?

Joey did remember them, but slightly differently than Milt's recollection. Joey remembered that two of them had looked like a couple and the other one looked like a friend of theirs. Only one of them had had a fan. They'd been having a very loud conversation while developing a shared thesis that by the age of forty, a person has met everyone of significance in their life. Sure, other people would be met, but none would play a substantial role. To thirty-one year old Joey at the time, that idea had seemed absurd. He and Milt had had a good laugh at their sad point of view, promising themselves and each other that they would never stop Living with a capital L. He didn't know why Milt was bringing it up now.

If your head hurts, Milt said, still facing away from Joey, *you could take one of those pills in your pocket.*

Joey realized the hard plastic container he'd taken from Ray's hospital room was what was jamming into his hip, the pea to his princess. He could take all of them. That was the plan, after all. Not necessarily the plan for today, but the plan.

You should call the police, man. Or at least, call the policeman.

"Hm?" Joey managed to croak out just the one questioning syllable.

You got attacked. You should call him. Call him and he'll come rescue you. Don't you want to be rescued?

Joey didn't answer. He was thinking about the thesis and realizing that it had been a long time since he'd met anyone of any real significance. Unless he counted Mindy.

Mindy. Milt agreed from the shadows. A rush of sleepiness suddenly pulled at Joey like a riptide. He saw the flight of stairs leading down to Ray's apartment, the stairs Aggie had led him to through guided imagery. He opened the door; this time it led directly to Ray's bedroom, as it was when Flaars had led him out of it the other night.

203

Pick up one thing, Milt said sharply. Joey's eyes opened. He couldn't tell if he'd lost consciousness again. *One thing, and decide where to put it.*

Joey rolled onto his back and dug into his pocket for the pills and held the bottle tightly in his fist. He suddenly felt like he couldn't get any air into his lungs no matter how much he inhaled. He wondered if this was what emphysema felt like. He wondered if this was actually emphysema.

Good. Now decide where to put it.

Joey set the bottle down on the floor next to his head and stared at it.

My, my, my. I wish I had a mind for dates. I cannot, for the life of me remember when that was that we roller-skated all day long.

1978.

I can't hear you when you talk in your head. I need you to talk out loud.

"'78," Joey muttered.

Louder please! Milt reprimanded from his perch on the step. *I can't hear you…*

"Nineteen hundred, seventy and eight years," Joey said as loud as he could.

Yes! 1978. How do you remember that?

Joey shrugged as best he could while lying on his shoulder. It was the summer he made a white afro out of white gardenias pinned to Aggie's head. She'd looked so stunning that they got pulled from the line at 54 and danced until dawn with celebrities. "I just do." It was the summer he was first introduced to a handsome banker named Henry at Brian Duvret's share on Fire Island.

That was a spectacular day. If I could go back and relive any one day of my life it might be that day. It was a day I felt like I would never get old.

"You never did get old," Joey reminded him.

True. God had other plans for me.

Milt was quoting the armless man on the subway platform. Joey had never heard Milt mention God when he was alive. He'd never heard Milt talk with a fake southern accent and he'd never seen Milt roller-skate. He and Milt had never spent the afternoon together drinking in the West Village.

The image of Ray's room was vivid in Joey's mind. The shape in the corner that he'd first thought might be a guitar case, the shape that had become Milt, he now clearly saw was one of those carpeted cat trees.

It wasn't you, he thought at Milt's back.

Whaahht?

It wasn't you that I roller-skated with that day. It was Davey Matthers. I hadn't met you yet. I didn't meet you until probably a year after that.

Who's Davey Matthers? And stop talking to me in your head. I can't hear you.

Joey hadn't thought about his friend Davey in a long time. "You don't know him. He moved to Arizona." Joey didn't believe in God; he didn't believe that God had a plan for him unless that plan was to get the shit beat out of him on a regular basis and possibly have to sit through *CATS* again.

Are you sure it wasn't me?

"I'm positive."

It wasn't?

"It wasn't."

Oh. Well then, how do I remember it?

"I don't know. Maybe I told you about it."

Milt was quiet as he thought about this possibility.

Protesting to the contrary aside, Joey could understand why Collier might find his character suspect. He had, after all, in the time that Collier had known him, gotten a ticket for indecent exposure, found a dead body, broken back into the crime scene, assaulted an officer of the law and fainted in a hospital. But, if he could somehow, on his own, figure out who had the money that the man who had attacked him wanted, Joey was pretty sure he'd find Mindy's killer. And then he could give him like a present to Collier and Collier would have

205

no choice but to change his opinions of Joey. That sounded, to Joey, like as good a plan as any.

Joey opened the pills he'd swiped from Ray's nightstand, fished one out with his finger, and dry-swallowed it. "Does that sound like a good plan?" Joey asked Milt out loud, so he could hear him.

No, Milt said from his shadow by the step, *I'm sure you're wrong. It was me.*

Thirty-five

1958

Clyde Tolson felt nothing but contempt for New York City. He buttoned his shirt in one bedroom of the two-bedroom suite in the New Yorker Hotel. It was a beautiful, sunny-but-cool, July morning, as if even the weather were putting its best foot forward, but Clyde was not fooled. A gentle breeze did little to make up for the city's pushiness and demands. He would have preferred a vacation in Miami, or better yet, simply staying in DC where no one cared to know you, only your politics. But Clyde never had his way, not in these matters.

Clyde stepped out of his bedroom at the exact same time that his boss, J. Edgar Hoover, stepped out of his. This was not uncanny or a coincidence, it was a direct result of the amount of attention that Clyde paid, the amount of attention that his job demanded he pay. Jay handed Clyde a pair of cufflinks, preferring tasks to salutations. Clyde knew that his boss saw little need for polite, empty words. He abhorred small talk and was enraged by minutiae. Hearing two people wishing each other good morning, discussing whether they slept well or, God forbid, of what they dreamt, would push his boss right over the edge.

Clyde had slept poorly. He'd tossed and turned after their late dinner, wondering what, if anything, should be done about Dorothy Schiff and her rumor. It had been two days since they'd spoken on the phone and he hadn't heard anything at all. Something told him that it wasn't over though. He knew Dorothy Schiff was a shrewd journalist. He suspected that Jay hadn't slept well either; it wasn't until well after two a.m. that Clyde had heard the rhythmic bass of his snores through the thin walls of the suite. He'd matched his breathing to force a sleep-like pace of his own until he'd slipped under. He'd dreamt of a gunfight he'd once been in in New York in his early days in the FBI, before he'd taken a more administrative role.

Even though they hadn't exchanged any words, Clyde could sense that his boss was grouchy. He knew that Dorothy Schiff's phone call was the source of it. More than small talk and pleasant, empty words, Jay hated feeling exposed. He was a man who loved information and secrets about others and the power that could be flexed with such knowledge. His job was fairly high profile and he was often photographed in public and written about. Anytime the subject of these articles strayed beyond reports of his job as the head of the FBI, Jay would be angry for days. Cuffs properly linked, Jay took a seat at the small dining table. A split second after his butt hit the chair, there was a sharp rap on the door to the suite, signaling that the room service Clyde had ordered for them had arrived right on time. As much as Jay hated being known, it did have some advantages.

———

One of the biggest headaches associated with being a public figure was actually going out in public. Everywhere Jay and Clyde went had to be thought through, choreographed and orchestrated. At home in Washington, there was a routine to it. Every morning their driver picked Clyde up first, then Jay. Every morning, unless the weather wouldn't allow for it, the driver dropped the pair of them off a short distance from the office so they could walk the last few blocks together. These brief and routine public walks served a couple of purposes. First, it allowed them to discuss the day ahead away from prying ears. Second, it gave them the appearance of normalcy, of everyman-ness. During those few blocks, it was as if they were just two regular guys stretching their legs, taking in the morning air, as if anyone could approach them. This was, of course, only an appearance.

While their security detail on vacation in New York was rigorously planned, there was something about the city itself that added elements of both stubbornness and surprise. Many people here had grown up inventing themselves, making their own rules as they went, collectively less convinced of and impressed by the power of the government in general. Cabs invaded motorcades, pedestrians ignored black sedans with blaring horns, maître d's acted aloof and ignorant, yet tripped over themselves to fawn over some minor stage performer or dancer having a post-show supper. The ass-backwards social ladder added to the overall chaos of the city. Clyde opened the door of their suite for his boss. He could tell that Jay was in no mood for the day ahead.

Jay ignored the "Good morning, sir," from the handsome young agent standing guard outside their room. He ignored the identically dressed agent who held the elevator door open as well as the two others who rode the lift down to the ground floor with them. Once the doors opened into the lobby, Jay pushed past the two escorts and marched quickly ahead, faster than normal, forcing Clyde as well as the six agents who now flanked them, to scramble to catch up. Jay pushed through the front doors out to the street without waiting for the doorman's assistance and bee-lined for the car door being held open by their driver.

"Mr. Hoover!" The female voice stopped Jay abruptly in his tracks causing a near pile-up behind him. One of the suits threw himself sideways, hands first onto the pavement to avoid running into the agent in front of him, bouncing back up off of the sidewalk as quickly as he'd gone down. The young woman stepped forward, causing the agent who'd fallen to step between her and his boss.

"Miss, stop where you are." He put his hand up like a stop sign a few inches from her shoulder. This was all probably unnecessary since she'd stopped on her own accord after the one step, but the agent was overcompensating for falling.

Jay glanced in her direction once, then dismissed her and continued into the car.

"Sir, if I might have a moment of your time -" she spoke over the agent's shoulder. "It's a matter of national security. Please."

Jay froze for a moment, then looked to Clyde, who'd caught up to everyone by then, as if to say 'Handle this'. Clyde stepped up and touched the agent lightly on the shoulder to get him to stand down. He looked the young woman up and down as it dawned on him who she must be. As strategic moves went, this one did have some ironic humor about it.

"I'm just asking for a few minutes," she shifted her request to Clyde, understanding that he was the man who could help her. She looked incredibly green, fresh out of journalism school. Clyde had been on the lookout for reporters since his talk with Dorothy Schiff. Her decision to send this pretty young woman did have the element of surprise; he'd give her that.

"Well, well, well. What do we have here? A friend of Dorothy's I presume?"

The young reporter squinted at him, obviously thrown off by being seen through so quickly. "I'm, uh… a friend of a friend, I guess you could say."

"I'm afraid Mr. Hoover is on a very tight schedule today."

"I understand. I think, though, that he will want to hear what I have to say. It's a matter of -"

"National security," Clyde interrupted. "I heard you the first time."

"That might have been an exaggeration. But it does concern a certain party, and certain criminal activities."

Clyde exchanged a quick look with his boss whose eyes were darting between the reporter and the agents overhearing this whole thing. Jay gave him a slight nod.

"I see. Well perhaps we have a few minutes to offer, Miss…"

"Milligan."

"Milligan." He smiled coldly at her. "I hope you don't mind chatting while we drive."

"I don't. Not at all."

After Jay ducked into the backseat, Clyde held his arm out to gesture for her to follow. As he got into the car after her, Clyde sensed an opportunity here. He didn't know exactly how, but he felt he could turn this young woman's gall to their advantage.

———

As Iris caught her reflection in the rearview mirror from the back seat of the black sedan, she thought that her mother would be proud of her. Her mother had always told her she could accomplish whatever she set her mind to and here she was, sitting in a car between two of the most powerful men in the country.

"Let's circle the block, if you don't mind." The man who Iris guessed must be Hoover's second in command and traveling companion spoke to the driver without raising his voice beyond a conversational tone, giving no indication that he was speaking to anyone other than the person closest to him, which was Iris. "Now then, Miss Milligan. How long have you worked for the New York Post?" She could see his reflection in the mirror as well as her own.

"The New York Post?" Iris was confused. "I don't work for the New York Post."

"Let's not split hairs, dear. Whether you are officially under Dorothy Schiff's employ or working freelance is of little concern to me." His dismissive words sounded gentle. He continued looking out the window. "Nor is the distinction one I find particularly interesting."

Iris's mistake dawned on her. Had her worldview really become so skewed over the last few days? Had she really thought that the heads of the Federal Bureau of Investigation would freely banter code used by homosexuals with her out on the open street? Maybe Eddie was right; maybe she should be in bed. "I'm... I'm sorry. I think there's been a misunderstanding."

"It's not me to whom you owe an apology; it's your boss. Perhaps your journalism professors. Someone who believed in you."

Iris's thoughts came like bullets from a machine gun. She felt silly, like a child. Sitting between these two grown men reminded her of all the nights she'd spent on the couch between her parents, reading. Like these two men, Iris's parents always angled their bodies slightly away from each other, a couple which always seemed slightly angry. Iris had been taught not to fidget and she obeyed easily, not wanting to add to the tension in the room. When Iris's father drove his car into the house down the street, her mother's only comforting words had been *Everything happens for a reason,* the agnostic's reliance on a higher plan. She repeated those words in her head. Iris's subsequent thought was that her mother had not taught her to apply such a perfect face of make-up only to see it crack.

"What I meant, sir, is that I have proof of crimes being committed against the citizens of New York by city employees. If that doesn't interest you, then I apologize for wasting not only your time, but mine as well. Feel free to drop me on the next corner."

"Call the police, Miss Milligan," he said in his now infuriatingly even tone.

"With all due respect, Mr. - "

"Tolson." His eyes met hers briefly in the mirror.

"Tolson, I'm afraid you don't know the extent of it. Neither do I, really. I know that members of the police department are committing these crimes. I don't know who or how many. Which is why I came to you." She said this last part to her right, but Mr. Hoover only continued looking out the window. Iris had no way of knowing if he'd even been paying attention.

"You have two minutes, Miss Milligan, to lay out your evidence."

Iris glanced at her own reflection again. She thought of her mother explaining her bone structure to her as they sat together at her vanity table. *You're like me, dear. Close-set eyes and a nose just a tad too wide. Nothing debilitating, just something to be dealt with.*

"I have a friend, a business owner and tax-payer, who runs a small neighborhood bar. The police constantly threaten to close her down unless she makes regular and substantial cash payments to them. We're talking thousands of dollars."

One afternoon, while Iris was in her senior year of high school, her mother discovered a pea-sized lump near her armpit. The lump was quickly removed with a sharp, clean knife, but then it came back, with something to prove.

"Liquor is a shady business." Tolson exhaled through his nose. "Whatever arrangements your friend might have with local law enforcement are not only insignificant in the big picture of National Security, but also impossible to prove."

In the years following high school, while her friends went off to college or married, Iris cared for her mother. She wondered what the pea-sized lump could possibly be made of that was crafty enough to consume a strong adult woman from the inside out. It started with her breasts and then, finding them too small to be completely satisfying, moved on to bigger things like lungs and stomach.

"It's not just the police who are involved. There are other men, criminals." Iris thought of Frankie's grin while the jazz band had played behind them. "I'm talking about the mafia."

Still hungry, the pea-sized lump moved on to Iris's mother's lymph nodes. Iris hadn't known, still didn't know, what lymph nodes looked like, but she imagined they couldn't be very big.

"Ah the elusive mafia," Tolson sounded amused. "An underground group of gangsters in hats perpetrating most if not all of the world's evils. And yet, no one has been able to prove that even one of them, let alone a whole network, actually exists. I suppose you think you can change all that?"

In the end, the lump revealed itself to be driven by spite more than hunger or need, a thief who takes something of much sentimental, but no financial, value.

Hearing it like that, Iris realized that her request did sound preposterous. Why would these powerful men help her? Why would they believe her? What she was telling them sounded far-fetched, as far-fetched as sitting in a car with the heads of the FBI, circling a midtown block, but it was happening. And what Frankie was doing to Libby was happening. And what Christopher had done had happened. It was all real.

"I can get proof. If I get proof, will you believe me then? Will you listen to me then?"

"I'm listening to you now, and frankly I don't know what to believe. You claim to be an innocent bystander in all this, a concerned citizen. For all I know, you could be a member of a rival group of gangsters, looking to squash the competition."

Iris's eyes flicked once more to her own reflection. "You think I look like a criminal?"

"I couldn't say. After all my years in law enforcement, I still have no concrete idea as to what, exactly, a criminal looks like."

Iris couldn't put her finger on it, but he seemed to be mocking her somehow. She leaned forward. "Could you pull over please?" The driver did not.

"There's no need for theatrics, Miss Milligan. The insinuation that your character is up for debate was intended as a compliment. And please keep in mind that I have not yet said that we cannot help each other."

Iris sat back and listened.

"You claim to have an innate sense of justice. Whether I believe that, or share it, is of no real consequence. As it turns out, there's a favor I need done as well. We just might be able to help each other."

For a moment the only sounds in the sealed car came from the outside traffic, horns blasting in combat and alarm.

"Do you really not work for Dorothy Schiff?" Tolson's eyes found Iris's in their mutual reflection.

"I really don't."

And then he smiled.

Thirty-six

1985

-

The pill Joey had stolen from Ray had dulled the pain in his head, but his body felt tight, sore all over. He got into the shower and let the hot water beat against the back of his neck while he thought through the facts as he understood them. After twenty minutes he started feeling possibly better enough to turn on a light and saw, in the steamy mirror, that he'd been given a proper black eye. It made him look tough and mysterious and he instantly liked it.

He threw on some clothes and went down to the lobby of his building. The entrance of the building had a foyer bookended by two doors. The door that led to the street was always unlocked and often propped open like it was now. The second door, just beyond a panel of buzzers, was locked but could be released for visitors from inside each apartment when buzzed. Joey held this door open with his foot while he studied the list of names next to the buzzers and wondered how up-to-date they were. The label next to 5F, his apartment, still read 'Bih'.

While Joey was in the shower, he'd thought of the man's body in the window of Ray's apartment. He'd thought of how he'd been hoping the man would look up to see him, but was thankful now that he hadn't. The man's head seemed to have been angled down. At the time, the man had looked to Joey like he was using the drapes to hide behind while spying on someone in an apartment below his, using them to cover himself if he thought he was at risk of being seen. Thinking back on it, and adding in what he now knew about the man who had broken into his apartment and knocked him out, the man's lack of respect for laws, Joey wondered if maybe the man didn't care if he was seen. Maybe the covering of the drapes was more of a performance than a shield. He wondered, as he'd stepped out of the shower, if the man maybe had known he had an audience after all. Since Joey had moved in, he'd had less than no interest in meeting his neighbors. Maybe, against his better instincts, it was time to get cordial.

215

"Hold the door!"

Joey groaned as he watched the old man huff up the stoop behind him in the reflection of the held door's glass without turning around.

"Thank you, son! You new in the building?"

Joey should have been more specific about which neighbors he wanted to meet. He decided to try out his new black eye, to see if it actually did make him look dangerous, turning so the chatty man could see it. "Yeah. I'm new." Badass.

"Haha! Nice shiner! Wow. Somebody got you but good." Joey's new friend kept pace with him through the lobby. "You should see the other guy, right? Hey, I'm Mack. Been here thirty years, I know everyone. You in 5F?"

"Yeah. 5F."

"Hey I'm right above you. I hope I don't wake you up during the night -"

"You don't." Joey stopped in front of the elevator.

"I gotta get up every hour to piss."

"It happens." The elevator arrived in the lobby and Joey held the door open for Mack.

"Thanks but no thanks. I take the stairs. Good for the ticker. Take my word for it, you take the stairs every day, you'll live to be a hundred. See you around!"

"See you around, Mack." Joey said as the door slid shut.

"You can count on it!"

Excellent. Can't wait. Joey had done a great job of avoiding his neighbors since he'd moved. At this new rate, by the end of the day, he might be organizing a block party or a concerned citizens meeting. Barf. The name J. Bernskin from the panel of buzzers was all Joey had to go on as he knocked on the door to apartment 3F, two floors below his.

———

"Put your face where I can see it," said the female voice from the other side of apartment 3F. Joey complied, knowing that the distortion of the lens would make his skinny neck and head look like a turtle without its shell. He smiled to convey friendliness. The door opened to reveal a young woman in her early twenties clutching a thin, pink terrycloth robe around herself. Her hair was messy from bed.

"Yes?" Her sleep-wrinkled face peered out beneath the chain latch, which she'd kept fastened.

"Hi. I'm Joey. I'm kind of new." Joey had already said he was her neighbor when he'd knocked on her door.

"Okay." The young women squinted. She was either suspicious or trying to wake up.

"Is your phone out? My phone is out and I'm not sure if it's just my apartment or the building."

"I think mine's working." Her eyes glanced back into her apartment. "It was last night."

"Mine was too!" Joey said this like it was proof that the two of them had some kind of crazy connection. "And then this morning, nothing. No dial tone or anything."

The young woman was not impressed. She held up a finger while stifling a yawn and let the door close between them. Joey waited about fifteen seconds before the door opened again. "Mine works."

"Shit."

"Yep. Sorry, man." The door closed again.

Joey knocked again. Shave and a haircut.

"Come on, dude." She said from the other side.

Two bits.

The chained door opened again.

"Hi. It's me."

"I know."

"May I use your telephone to make an important call?"

"I didn't get to sleep until six."

Joey raised his eyebrows. "Lucky lady."

"I was at work."

217

"Please?" Joey clasped his hands in front of his chest. "It's local, I promise, and then I'll be out of your hair, I swear."

"Are you a Jehovah's Witness?"

"Scouts' honor."

"Are you a Hare Krishna?"

"Honey. Please."

"Are you a homicidal maniac?"

"Close. Homosexual man-ee-ac."

The young woman puffed out a short laugh that sounded like *pfft*. "What's a maneeac?"

"I don't know. I was trying to be cute."

The door closed and the chain came off. It opened again. "Nice try." She gestured to her living room. "Come in."

"Where do you work?" Joey stepped into the apartment. It was identical to his in layout but much more lived in. The furniture was mismatched; a combination of found and handed down, typical of a first apartment. The couch had a bed pillow on one end and a blanket on the other. An empty Chinese food carton was on the floor beside it. Joey corrected his initial impression of her: her hair was messy from couch, not bed.

"I work in a bar." She stepped into her living room and picked up the phone from the coffee table by the couchbed.

"That sounds fun."

"Does it? Well, I guess if getting hit on while pouring shots for yuppie assholes until they're too drunk to get it up is your idea of fun, then yeah, it's a total fucking blast." She handed him the phone. It was connected to a long cord that trailed down the hall into the bedroom. "Knock yourself out. I have to pee. Don't steal anything."

Joey dialed the number he'd memorized from Collier's notebook and waited while it rang. The realization that Flaars had followed him made him wonder if his phone had been tapped. He wasn't sure what that entailed, in reality. Movies made it seem like someone had to break in and put something spidery in the actual phone but it made sense that it might be something that could be accomplished through the phone company. Better safe than sorry, Joey figured. He'd sworn up and down that he didn't know Ray Nunez and calling the boy's parents probably wouldn't look right. A machine picked up. There was no outgoing message, just a sudden, long beep. It was jarring. "Uh. Hi. Hello. I'm not sure if this is the right number. I'm trying to leave a message for Mr. or Mrs. Nunez. If you're trying to find your son, you should call Dr. Carolyn Mortensky here in New York."

Doctor Carolyn had given Joey her home number at some point during Henry's final weeks, in case Henry took a sudden turn for the worse during one of the five-hour periods she allowed herself to be away from the hospital. He sensed that she didn't intend for him to give it to others, but these were extenuating circumstances. Henry's parents didn't come to his funeral. Joey's parents sent a card that his mother signed for both of them. Ray was dying. Fast. Joey was tired of secrets.

"Her number is two one two, six seven six," Joey heard the toilet flush as he finished reciting. "Thanks," he said, knowing that it wasn't quite the best fitting pleasantry, and hung up.

"You done?" Joey's neighbor asked through a yawn.

"Yeah, thanks." Now that he was here, he was not sure how to bring up the subject of Mindy's murder. "You headed back to bed?"

"Yup." She glanced toward her sleeping spot.

"Or couch, I guess I should say. You're headed back to couch."

"Yeah. Might watch some TV."

"Cool. I'm Joey by the way."

"Julie."

"Hi."

Joey took a couple of steps to her living room window and looked up at what he now knew was Ray's apartment. "You hear about that girl that got killed up there?"

"Yeah. Bad news."

"For sure," Joey nodded. "The police totally questioned me; my window looks right down into the apartment."

219

"Yeah. They stopped by here too. My friend thinks it was the Nightstalker."

Joey laughed. "I doubt it. That guy's got a pretty good thing going in California. At least, from a psycho's point of view."

"Yeah, I guess." Julie pulled her robe a bit tighter, but didn't appear to be intimidated by the discussion.

"What did you say?"

"I just said, yeah, I guess he does have a good thing going out there," Julie repeated.

"No, I mean, what did you say to the police?"

She shrugged. "Oh. Nothing to say. I didn't know the girl. I don't really hang out with anyone in the building, let alone next door."

Joey nodded.

"I was at work the night they say it happened. So I didn't have anything to tell them."

"Yeah, same here."

"You were at work too?"

"No. I mean, I lied to the police also."

Julie's neck flushed with mottled redness that quickly climbed her neck.

"For probably a lot of the same reasons as you did. We both saw him, what he was doing. In the window."

She snorted through her nose. "I don't know what you're talking about, man. But I'd like you to leave now."

"Okay, I will." Joey didn't want to be creepy. He walked to the front door and opened it to convey non-creepiness. "Can I just tell you what I think happened?"

"No."

"I think," Joey ignored her, "that you saw him. And that he was watching you."

"I was at work."

"I don't think so. A girl got murdered next door just a few days ago and you weren't nervous at all to let me into your apartment."

"I wasn't nervous because I'm one hundred percent certain I could break you in half."

"You probably could. But you know that you don't need to. You know I'm not the guy you saw up there."

Julie stopped arguing, but didn't acknowledge he was on to anything.

"You know that he's not still up there, but it freaks you out to be in your bedroom since the night he watched you." Joey jutted his chin in the general direction of the couch. "You feel like you did something wrong so you don't want to tell the police what you saw. You don't have to."

"I didn't -" Julie started to argue, then changed her mind and instead arched her eyebrow at Joey while she gritted her teeth.

"You could tell me what you saw, and I could tell the police. Not just that night, but anything else that might help. I know the detective working on it. I could find a way to tell him whatever you know and make it look like I found it out some other way."

Julie shook her head.

"You didn't do anything wrong. You didn't do anything to be ashamed of. The only person who did anything wrong was the person who killed that girl."

"No, man." She stopped shaking her head. "You got it wrong."

"Okay. How so?"

"I didn't not talk to the police because I was ashamed. I didn't talk to them because the guy I saw was one of them."

"One of… a cop?"

"He showed me a badge. From the window. He held it up."

"When? Like to scare you?"

"Maybe. I don't know. It was more like he thought I'd think it was sexy."

Joey considered this new information. If the guy he'd seen in Ray Nunez's apartment who was not Ray Nunez but who was after money that Mindy stole from him was a cop, then, well. Then he didn't

221

know what that meant except that it explained why he and Flaars used the same arm-twisting techniques. He had to find a way to tell Collier.

"Anyway," Julie opened the front door for Joey to leave. "That's why I'm not talking to any cops. You shouldn't either."

"Did you…" Joey wanted to ask her more questions but he couldn't think of what else to ask. "Did you see anything else?"

"Anything *else?* I told you, man. I was at work. I didn't see anything."

Thirty-seven

Collier's phone was ringing. He had gotten to work later than usual, wearing the same clothes he'd worn the day before. He folded the newspaper he was reading and picked up the handset.

"Collier." He sipped his coffee.

"Hi. It's me."

"Joe?"

"If you insist."

Collier laughed. He didn't know why he found calling Joey 'Joe' so amusing, but he did.

"I'm busy. Can I call you back?" He wasn't really busy, but he suspected that his primary suspect would be chattier if he thought so.

"Yeah. Well wait. I just have something quick."

"Okay. Quick like a rabbit then." He pulled Mindy's folder from under another on his desk and opened it.

"It's two things, actually. One: did Ray have cats?"

"I don't know, did he?" As murder suspects went, Joseph Broderer was far more entertaining than most. And he did introduce Collier to Aggie, who was one of the most beautiful women Collier had ever slept with.

"I don't know. I think he did."

"And this matters because…" He jotted the word 'cats' on the inside of the beige file folder then added a question mark.

"I don't know."

Collier and Aggie had started on her white leather couch before moving to her large white bedroom. She'd woken him up that morning by climbing on top of him and then gotten in the shower with him afterwards.

"Great. What's the second thing?" Collier drew a box around the word 'cats'.

"Um. The bag of dust. In the purse. I was just wondering, you know, who would know to do that?"

"Vacuum?" Collier drew a bigger box around the first box then began filing in the space between the two with ink, tiny pen strokes back and forth.

"Yeah. You know at a crime scene. Is that something that's done often?"

"You sound like you do when you're pretending not to know more than you do."

"I don't."

"I'm hanging up or arresting you."

"Okay, here's my thought. It sounds like something a cop would do."

Collier's pen stopped. He thought of the phone call he'd gotten the previous afternoon, the one he'd told Aggie about. *Look around you* the crackpot had said after giving him a name to write down. Where had he written it down?

"Did you hang up on me?" Joey asked through the phone.

"I'll call you tonight," Collier hung up on him by pressing and then releasing the switch hook. The dial tone buzzed patiently while he leafed quickly though the pages in Mindy's file, trying to remember where he'd jotted down the name given to him by the man who claimed to also be called Collier. He had written it down, he remembered that for sure. It was Anthony Somethingorother, he remembered that much. He'd written it down but then thrown it away. He dialed the extension for the precinct's front desk as he pulled the wastebasket from beneath his own, grateful for the lax janitorial staff and wondering if he had hung up on the crackpot too quickly.

———

"Need some help with that?"

Anthony was in the break room at the precinct, taking out his frustration on a vending machine that had taken his fifty cents but had not given him his soda, wishing the machine was a human. He knew

224

how to hit a human. He turned to see a detective whom he recognized but had never talked to before.

"Sure." Anthony stepped aside. He knew the detective finding him here wasn't a coincidence, but he didn't know what the detective knew, or how much.

"I have a key." The detective winked as he closed the distance between them, holding up the proof, as if having a key to something made you hot shit.

"I'm not supposed to use it unless the janitor is off duty, but why call them when we can do it ourselves, right? Those guys have enough to do as it is." He unlocked the machine and opened it like a refrigerator. They'd never spoken before, and now the detective was acting like he respected everybody, even the janitors. "Go ahead," the detective offered. Anthony reached in and dislodged the stuck can.

"Thanks, boss."

"Take two," the detective winked again. "In fact, grab me a couple. We work hard right? The department can afford to buy us a couple of cans of pop, right?" Anthony didn't like people who winked. He reached in and tossed two cans to his superior, one at a time, before taking a second for himself. He could hit the detective in the forehead and bounce the back of his head off the hard plastic and metal of the vending machine.

"Thanks detective, I owe you one."

"It's lieutenant, actually. Lieutenant Collier." He held out his hand.

He could slam the butt end of the full can in his hand into the lieutenant's temple. Instead, Anthony shook his outstretched hand. "My mistake, now I owe you two."

"So," Collier opened one of his sodas, "my guess is you're a good enough cop to know I'm not here to talk about soda."

"What's on your mind, sir?" It would be suicide to try to fight the lieutenant in the police station, especially when he hadn't done anything to run from. But it made Anthony feel more confident to consider his options.

"Mindy Shorent."

"What about her?"

"You know her?"

Anthony took off his hat and put it on one of the break room tables. "Did."

The Lieutenant laughed, which surprised Anthony. "I don't suppose you know who killed her."

"Nah. I just fucked her a few times."

"She any good?" the lieutenant took a drink of his soda.

"Had better. Had worse."

"I saw her pictures; looked pretty good to me. How'd it end?"

"She fucked me."

Lieutenant Collier laughed again, but not like he was laughing at Anthony. More like he thought Anthony was funny.

Collier shook his head. "Fucking whores, man."

"Do I need to call someone?"

"What, like a lawyer?"

"Yeah."

"Last I heard it wasn't a crime to fuck someone," Collier said. Both men nodded as they each finished off their first cans. "You were smart to keep quiet about this. Really smart. I wouldn't have said anything either."

———

Collier felt confident that he'd gotten Officer Anthony Tandino comfortable enough to speak openly about his relationship with Mindy. He'd suggested that they take the conversation into his office, *In case this relationship between you and her comes out later, I can say you came clean to me about it and were never under any suspicion.* He was surprised to find that the suggestion had been interpreted as an invitation to conspire.

"Between you and me," Tandino said, "I'm not at all surprised that this happened." He was leaning back in the chair on the other side of Collier's desk, not a care in the world. "She treated other people the way she treated me? I'm not fucking surprised at all."

226

"What, she fucked around?" Collier often found himself falling into the rhythms of those he was questioning, mimicking their inflections and body language.

"How the fuck does a whore fuck around?"

They both laughed.

"You got me there."

"Nah man. What this chick did was worse. She stole from me."

"Money?"

"Yeah, money. Of course money."

"Ha ha, how much?"

"You sitting down?"

"Should I sit down?" Collier leaned forward; he was already sitting down.

"You should definitely sit down." Tandino was clearly enjoying this.

"Okay, hit me."

"Fifty."

"Fifty!" Collier shouted, then lowered his voice to a stage whisper even though the door to his office was closed. "Fifty grand?"

"I'm not shitting you, man. On my mother's life. That bitch stole fifty gees in cash and then went and got killed before I could find out what she did with it."

Collier thought about Joe saying she looked like she was on the run. "Fuck. Fifty gees. What I could do with that kind of money."

"You kidding me? The kind of money you make?"

"Trust me, don't let the private office fool you. I don't get paid near what I'm worth."

"I hear you, man. I hear you."

"How can I get fifty gees in cash?"

"You can't." Tandino was really smiling now. "I can, but I don't know if you can." Psychiatric buzzwords swirled around Collier's brain: narcissistic, sociopathic, delusional. "We're off the record, right?"

227

"We are way off the record," Collier laughed. He had pressed the record button on his mini-cassette recorder before entering the break room.

"I did a guy a favor. Guy from the neighborhood. I wouldn't normally get involved -"

"Sure, sure."

"But this guy's like an uncle to me. He spoke at my mother's funeral."

Collier thought of him swearing on his mother's life only moments before and added pathological liar to the list.

"So he tells me about these ledgers he needs, but the place they're in is possibly being watched, so on and so forth..." Tandino glossed over this as if they were niggling details, spices in a sauce no one wanted to taste again.

"The feds sure have their dicks hard for your uncle and his friends."

"That's for damn sure. So I go into this particular location, locate the ledgers, as asked, and while I'm in there I find this bag, full of cash to the tune of fifty grand."

Collier whistled in appreciation.

"Now the way I know the money's in the free and clear is this: you ask a guy like me to use his position to do you a one time favor like this, and you know there's fifty grand in there, you'd ask me to get that too, right? And trust me, this was hidden real good, and for a long time. I only found it cause I know how these people think. See?"

"I do. I see." What Collier could see was this guy beating the life out of Mindy Shorent over messing with his windfall. "So how does the stripper find out about it?"

Tandino shrugged and smiled. "I showed it to her."

"You showed it to her?"

"What can I say, man, I like pussy."

Collier laughed, caught off-guard by this base but honest confession.

228

"I thought she'd be impressed. I didn't think she'd fucking take it."

"You sure she did?"

"Absolutely. Two hundred percent sure. She admitted it. Didn't think I knew where she lived. Scared shitless when I catch up with her, saying she's sorry and she's gonna pay me back but that she needs it. Like I'm just supposed to be okay with that. So I tell her, Damn right you're gonna pay it back, but right now. That's when she tells me she doesn't have it. So I tell her she has two days to get it back."

"Or what?"

"I didn't think that far ahead. Didn't think I'd need to."

"Right."

"Next thing I know, she's getting ready to go on the fucking run. Bleached her hair out like I wouldn't recognize her. Like I was too big a dumbshit to catch up with her. That's when she tells me that she doesn't know where the money is, that she left it with her faggot friend and doesn't know what he did with it or where he went."

"She said that? She said 'My faggot friend'?"

"She didn't have to. She takes me to his place, but he's not there. So I say, Okay, let's wait for him to get back. But the guy never shows, and I become convinced that she really didn't know where he was."

Collier could picture Tandino knocking Mindy around to pass the time, fueled by equal parts anger and boredom.

"I needed to go out for a bit and by the time I get back, she's dead and the money's still gone."

Collier laced his fingers behind his head and looked up at the ceiling. "How do you know he's gay?"

"She told me. Plus the dude has a shitload of gay porn. Whole fucking box of videotapes. I put one in and saw some shit I don't ever need to see again."

Thirty-eight

1958

"That," Libby grabbed Iris's arm in the doorway to her bar and pulled her inside, "was insane." She'd been smoking and pacing since she'd watched Iris climb into the sedan alongside J. Edgar Hoover. She'd tried to follow the car on foot for a bit but soon gave up and came back to her bar where the two women had agreed to meet should they get separated.

"What happened? Did they believe you?"

"I'm not sure," Iris planted herself on what was now her usual spot at the bar while Libby got behind it. "I think so, but I'm still not sure."

"Tell me everything." Libby put a bottle of Coca Cola in front of Iris and listened while Iris explained what had transpired in the car. The story, as Iris told it, was neither entirely promising nor discouraging.

"So," Libby attempted to summarize once Iris had finished, "he didn't say he would help us, but he didn't say he wouldn't."

"No, he said he might, but not necessarily because he believed me." Iris appeared to be looking back over the conversation again for clarity. "He said he would help us if I helped him first."

"Do you believe him?"

"I don't know," Iris said. "I don't have any reason not to believe him."

"What's his name again?"

"Tolson. Clyde Tolson."

Libby poured herself a bourbon. Just a sip. "You know," she said after she'd swallowed it. "You don't have to do this."

"I know that. I want to do it. I want to help you."

"Why?"

"Because it's the right thing to do. Christopher was my husband. I loved him."

230

"Did you?"

"Of course I did. I wouldn't have married him if I didn't love him."

"Sure. I'm sure you did. But now?" Libby poured another sip. "Your husband was nothing but dishonest with you. I should think you'd be angry."

"Was he? He only vowed to love and protect me. And I believe he did both of those, to the best of his ability at least."

Libby shrugged. "I suppose it's how you choose to measure honesty. Is it by the number of lies told? Or is it the number of promises kept."

"Maybe," Iris said, "it's some sort of equation that involves both. Like the number of lies told subtracted from the number of promises kept."

"Well," Libby winked, "in that case, I'm a seven."

Iris smiled, "Lucky number seven!"

"How about you?" Libby said. "What's your honesty number?"

"I think I'm a thirteen."

"Unlucky thirteen," Libby clinked her empty glass against Iris's bottle of cola.

"What do you have to do?" Libby asked.

"Do?"

"What's the favor?"

"Oh, that. It's nothing really."

"Nothing?"

"It's… I have to meet with someone. Later. Maybe today, maybe tomorrow or the next day."

"What, you can't tell me?"

"I can, I suppose. But I said I wouldn't."

"You told him you wouldn't tell me?"

"Not you specifically. I just said that I wouldn't tell anyone."

"Oh."

"Trust me," Iris put her hand on Libby's. "This will all work out."

231

"I trust you, kid." Libby wasn't as convinced it would all work out. Still, she put her other hand on top of Iris's. "I have to. You're my ace in the hole."

"Just wait for me to get in touch with you; I'm not sure when the favor will happen."

"I suppose I have to," Libby said. "I wouldn't know how to find you if I tried. I don't even know your last name."

"You won't have to. I give you my word."

"Okay, good. Because I thought about how we could prove what Frankie's doing." As Libby outlined the simple plan she'd come up with while waiting for Iris to return that involved marking bills for Frankie to collect and then catching him with them, another part of her brain was picturing the equation for honesty as if written out on a blackboard. She wondered if the real equation weren't something much more complicated involving many more factors. Secrets weren't inherently bad; everybody had them, especially women. Especially married women. If you asked why too many times, sometimes you heard what you wanted to hear. Other times you heard words like lonely or lost. Broken. So Libby stopped asking.

It wasn't, in and of itself, suspicious that Iris wouldn't share with her what Clyde Tolson wanted her to do. But it was something around them now in a peripheral way, like a puddle. To be crossed soon; maybe harmless, maybe deep.

Thirty-nine

1985

"Wow!" Aggie kept her eyes bright and her smile broad, gripping the script in her lap, bending the sides of it in towards each other.

"You like?" Desmond, the head writer, stood in the doorway to her dressing room, a cup of coffee in his hand. His glasses balanced on his forehead, halfway between the bridge of his nose and the top of his head.

"I do. It's really…" Aggie looked at the ceiling for the rest of her sentence, rustling the tissue paper tucked into her blouse around her neck to protect the outfit from the television make-up applied a half-hour before by a woman named Doris.

"Thanks." Desmond plucked a compliment out of nowhere. "I told you it would be something awesome." He switched his mug to his other hand and hitched his thumb in the belt of his slacks.

"You did tell me that, yes. I was prepped for awesome." Aggie nodded emphatically twice before remembering the rollers in her hair. She stopped nodding, not wanting to shake them loose. Unwilling to make eye contact with Desmond, she focused on the small potbelly on his otherwise skinny frame. She reached up and felt the rollers one at a time, gently patting each one to make sure they were still secured. "You did warn me."

"Yeah, I thought this would be up your alley. Serial killers are very hot right now, but no one's doing a female one. That's the twist, see?"

"No, yeah. I totally get it. It's very… ballsy." She wished Beth, the hair girl, would come back to take the rollers out now that her make-up was done. It would rescue her from this conversation and she needed some time to process what this new storyline might mean for her career. She'd been told there was going to be a murder, a crime of passion. This was something else altogether.

233

"And especially one that specifically targets married men, other women's husbands. Newlyweds."

"Oh! I hadn't picked that particular detail up from the script." Serial killers weren't forgiven for their digressions and gently integrated back into polite society. Even in the fictional town of Ravenswood Heights where, admittedly, a lot of batshit crazy stuff occurred on a regular basis.

"No, I know, no one would. It's not in there yet. It will be revealed. Over time." His attempt to look suggestive as he said 'revealed' fell flat. "Over the next few weeks."

Next few weeks. A few weeks. Jesus, an eternity. Unless her character ended up dead at the end of those few weeks. Then it was no time at all.

"I think we're going to call you The Wedding Crasher."

Aggie's dressing room phone rang.

"That's catchy, right? The Wedding Crasher?"

Aggie held up her finger. "Yeah, that's... hold on one sec." She picked up the receiver. "Hello?"

"Aggie?" It was Diane. Thank God.

"Hi Di, hold on." She turned to Desmond. "I have to take this, it's a director. Of another project." She didn't want him to think she didn't have other irons in the fire. "A movie I'm doing."

"Oh. Sure." Desmond cocked his head slightly, probably wondering if this constituted show-biz infidelity on her part.

"But great work though," Aggie lifted the script up. "Really, really powerful stuff."

"Nothing but the best for you." Desmond glanced at her tits, then her crotch, then her tits again before turning and walking down the hall, whistling as he went. Aggie reached over and pushed the door shut behind him.

"I'm so happy you called," Aggie said into the phone. "You totally rescued me."

"I rescued you?"

"Oh my God. Diane. I'm freaking out. I think I might be getting written off the show."

"Really?" Diane sounded meek and Aggie made a mental note to ask why.

"I don't know. I don't know what this means."

"What... what did they - what happened? Did they tell you something bad?"

"I don't know. I'm not sure. Fucking writers, man. I bet this wouldn't be happening if I'd fucked him."

"Aggie, I don't think that's a good -"

"Don't worry, I'm not about to."

"Who... who are we talking about?"

"Desmond Levesque. He's the head writer."

"Did he make a pass at you?"

"Not in the way you're picturing. It's like a constant thing, it's like an open-ended pass. He's a total pervert. He's probably a child molester. Or a dog molester, I don't know. I'm sure he molests something, he has to, nobody would willingly fuck this guy. He probably molests inanimate objects, like shopping carts or... doorknobs. He has kids, but that doesn't prove anything, right?"

Diane didn't respond.

"It probably just means that his kids are fucking perverts too. Pervy parents make pervy kids, right? The Levesque family is probably a bunch of doorknob-fucking perverts -"

"Aggie!" Diane snapped.

"What?" Aggie snapped back.

"I'm sorry. I didn't mean to... um. Maybe this is a bad time. You sound like you have a lot on your plate."

Aggie realized that Diane was crying and then remembered that her sister had sounded meek and she was supposed to remember to ask why. "No. I mean, I do, but what - what's... is everything okay? Are you okay?"

"I guess. I mean, no one's died or anything."

"Well, that's good." Aggie waited for Diane to respond. She didn't. "Diane?" There was another long silence followed by a ragged breath from her sister's end.

"Yeah. I am. I'm sorry, I shouldn't have called you at work -"

"What's the matter?"

"We can talk later." Diane sounded completely defeated.

"No! We can talk now. Tell me what happened."

"Um. Well. Peter and Brian got in an argument. It was a pretty big argument and and I don't think he meant to, but Peter pushed Brian and Brian fell and then Kyle stepped up to defend his brother and I'm not sure what exactly happened next but Kyle ended up with a broken nose."

"Oh my God, Diane. What were they fighting about?"

"I'd rather not say, for now." Unlike Aggie's reputation as a man-stealing murderess, Diane's reputation as a terrible storyteller was neither exaggerated or unearned. But this wasn't the time to point this out to her.

"Okay. Wow. Is this… Is this sort of thing normal for Peter? His temper?"

"No, it's not normal. He's beside himself with guilt. He feels like a horrible father."

"He's not a horrible father. People fight. Do you want me to talk to him?"

"NO," Diane said a little too quickly. "Thank you, I mean. That's okay."

"Sweetie, I'm going to have to go in a minute, but I can call you later…"

"Okay. Sure. You don't need to if you're busy."

"No, I'll call after I get done shooting. And if there's anything at all I can do -"

"Actually there is."

A sharp, two-knuckled rap sounded on her door before a young, relatively new PA whose name Aggie had trouble remembering stuck his head in. "We need you."

236

"Hold on one sec, Di." Aggie looked at the PA and pointed to the rollers in her hair. "I need Beth."

"Right." He picked what looked like a CB off his utility belt and spoke into it. "Paging Beth to Ms. Appleton's suite. She's high and tight and needed on set." He winked at Aggie as his voice amplified throughout the halls of the studio.

Aggie put the phone back up to her ear. "Hi. Sorry. What were we talking about?"

"I was… uh. I was going to ask a favor. Of you. But, it's okay. It sounds like there's a lot going on there."

"Well, there is, but I can call you later." Beth stepped past the PA and began removing the rollers from Aggie's head with expert speed. "I don't really have a lot going on this weekend. I was putting together a dinner party with some friends but I don't think it's going to pull together so I'm free to talk whenever -"

"Can you take Alice?"

"*Take* Alice?" Aggie's head jerked back in a way that Beth, who was about to start brushing her out, had no way of anticipating. An onlooker might have thought that Beth bonked Aggie's head with the heavy brush on purpose.

"For the weekend. Just the weekend."

"Um…" Aggie's mind raced for an excuse but couldn't come up with one. Beth grimaced and mouthed 'sorry' to Aggie's reflection in the mirror.

"Please?"

"Sure. I'm… sure that's fine."

"Thank you." Diane exhaled in relief. "I'm calling a car service. What time are you done there?"

"Uh, six?" Aggie lied. She was done at two today, but wanted Alice to get there as close to bedtime as possible. "Better say eight, to be safe. In case we run late."

"Thank you. So much. I'll call you."

"Sure." Aggie hung up the phone with out saying goodbye. The Wedding Crasher: what a crock of shit. A man-stealing nymphomaniac, how original. Aggie chewed her lip while Beth brushed. She hadn't called Joey to tell him that she'd slept with the cop, even though there was no betrayal involved there. First of all, Collier was straight, obviously. She wasn't *not* calling Joey, she just hadn't called him.

She spotted Desmond walking by her dressing room. "Desmond!"

He poked his head in.

"Hi. I meant to ask you before…"

"Shoot." He made a gun with his thumb and forefinger and pointed it at her.

"Will there be a trial? Or jail time?" Aggie bit the inside of her cheek. My God, was she being fired?

"Trial. Don't worry; you get off. I just haven't figured out how yet."

She'd call Joey after this scene. Better yet, she'd go see him.

"Nice," the young PA nodded approvingly. Aggie and Desmond both looked at him. "I don't know what you guys are talking about," he winked at Aggie, "but I'd like to watch you get off."

There was the briefest of pauses as everyone in the room weighed the appropriateness of the blatant innuendo. But then Desmond, who was in charge, laughed because he was emotionally stunted. The PA laughed as Desmond patted him on the back because he'd just learned something about power and being on the right side of it and both felt strong. Beth laughed because she hadn't been paying attention but didn't want to be left out of a good joke, and Aggie laughed because that's what good actresses do.

Forty

1958

Iris had been a good student. While she had not gone to college, she'd always imagined she would have excelled in higher learning. She had always been quick to understand the questions being asked of her, the assignment, which in itself was most of understanding how to answer. That, coupled with innate desires to do a good job and please others would have lent well to an academic life, had she gone that route. Or so she imagined.

Iris had sent away for a brochure to Ohio State University at the appropriate time in her life. When her mother's illness had sidelined those plans, Iris took a part time job doing secretarial work at a local radio station in Cleveland and put the brochure in her desk drawer. Christopher had worked at the same station in sales, a job that required him to travel. When he was in town and their paths would cross, he and Iris would chat pleasantly. She'd been touched when he'd postponed a business trip to attend her mother's funeral, especially since he'd never met her mother. With her mother gone, Iris was left with a sizable inheritance, a large gloomy house, and a nagging feeling she'd missed the boat. One day, on a break from filing invoices at the radio station, Iris had thrown away the brochure. College suddenly seemed like nothing more than a prolonged invitation to not get married or have babies until she was thirty. She'd been so sure of her decision that she'd asked Christopher if he'd like to take her out to dinner. They were married a little more than a year later.

The instructions that Mr. Tolson had given her had been straightforward and easy enough. The part of the assignment that Iris understood without having to be told was all that was left unsaid. There was something at play that was over her head and she understood that part of the assignment was to not ask what she did not need to know. The only caution she'd felt as she phoned the offices of *The Post* came in the form of whether she would be so confident without the aid of the blue pills. But then that thought floated away because the blue pills were very good at what they did. As promised, Tolson's driver had dropped her off in front of the hotel where they'd gotten in, but a world away from where they'd started. Now, only a few hours later, Iris was in the penthouse office of the publisher of one of the most influential newspapers in the city, if not the country. If not the world.

"Thank you for agreeing to see me." Iris kept her hands in her lap and crossed her feet at the ankles.

"What can I do for you Miss Milligan?" The older woman was both stern and kind, and Iris was instantly reminded of her mother. The resemblance was not physical, yet it was undeniable.

"Please, call me Iris. Miss Milligan sounds so formal."

Dorothy Schiff said nothing.

Iris cleared her throat and focused on the assignment. "My uncle asked that I speak with you to clear up a misunderstanding regarding his schedule this past week. I hope I can be helpful."

Dorothy Schiff said nothing.

"Of course, as I'm sure you know, he's not really my uncle. More of a family friend. Mr. Hoover, *Uncle* Hoover became something of a father figure to me after my own father passed away when I was a teenager." These details hadn't been included in the original assignment, but Iris felt they added credibility. "Since I moved here with my husband a couple of years ago, we try to see each other whenever he's in town. Uncle Hoover, that is. Not my husband." Iris took a sip of the water that the secretary had given her.

Dorothy Schiff said nothing.

"Of course, his schedule is packed with professional obligations and often the window of opportunity that we have for visiting comes at an odd hour. Last Sunday, my husband was still away on business. Uncle Hoover, Jay, telephoned that he had some time to stop by and he did."

Dorothy Schiff said nothing.

"I understand that there is a rumor as to Uncle Jay's whereabouts that evening. He wouldn't tell me what those rumors were, exactly, only that they were scandalous and absurd and untrue. I'm sure it's something of a let down, since scandals sell newspapers, but the truth is fairly bland, I'm afraid. J. Edgar Hoover was with me Sunday night."

Dorothy Schiff spoke.

"Are you a prostitute Iris?"

"What?" Iris felt her chest get hot.

"Are you an actress?"

"Hardly -"

"Do you work for the FBI?" Dorothy Schiff suggested each of these without judgment, as if they were all viable means of earning a living. "You don't really need to answer. I'll find out on my own. Are they paying you?"

"No." Iris hadn't really considered the possibility that her story wouldn't be believed. "Like I said before, I understand that it's your job to find a story in this, but I'm afraid that the truth is fairly bland -"

"Yes. So you said. All right. What time did he arrive?"

"Sometime after nine. Nine-thirty perhaps?"

"What did you eat?"

"Nothing fancy, leftovers. Some cold ham and potato salad. Neither one of us was very hungry."

"How much are they paying you?"

"I'm -"

"Fine. What did you talk about?"

Like the previous two, Iris had anticipated this question and prepared a response. "I've been having some personal problems. In my marriage. My husband has been staying late at the office more often than not. He goes out of town. When he *is* home, he's quiet. Distant. I think he's having an affair. I don't know anyone here. I don't have any friends. I hadn't planned on confessing all this to a man who has known me since I was a child, but once I started talking, I couldn't stop." Iris wiped her eyes with the back of her hand. "That's mostly what we talked about. That and, of course, all the top secret government files he shared with me." Iris hadn't planned to make light of the situation, but Dorothy Schiff seemed to appreciate the joke and smiled.

"Alright," the older woman handed Iris a tissue. "First things first. In response to the state of your marriage, if I'm to take it at face value, which I'm not sure that I do, you do not need to be a victim in this situation. I've been married three times, and none of them have been what you'd call *traditional* by any stretch, at least in terms of fidelity. I've found that you can have companionship and great romance at the same time if you can do away with the fairytale notion that it will consistently be the same person giving you both. My advice, while you didn't ask for it, would be to get out and meet people. You're an attractive young woman."

"Thank you."

"You're welcome. There's no reason why you can't be experiencing all that life has to offer."

It wasn't the advice that Iris thought her mother would have offered but it still made Iris miss her.

"Now. As to the other issue at hand, the purpose of this meeting… You're in trouble, my dear. You're lying."

This time, Iris did not protest.

"The portrait you paint of Mr. Hoover as a sympathetic Santa Claus is laughable. I don't know what you stand to gain from this, or lose, but I can tell you that however he appears to you, whether as a friend, punisher, or savior, it is nothing more than a means to an end. Do you know what transvestitism is?"

Iris said nothing.

"It's when a man puts on women's clothing for sexual arousal. In this case, lingerie."

Iris said nothing.

"My source places your Uncle Hoover, as well as his assistant, at a private party Sunday night that devolved into a sexual orgy. You must understand, Iris, these kinds of tawdry rumors are not what I

242

choose to spend my time on. Normally. But this situation is not normal. Contrary to my own opinions, homosexuals are some of the most feared and hated members of our society. Your *uncle* is a very powerful man. Should there be any truth to this rumor, any truth at all, your uncle could be easily owned. Easily, by anyone who had proof."

Iris said nothing.

"Think about it, Iris. You can call me any time. I can give you my word; while I don't know exactly what you are dealing with, I can offer you protection. Mr. Hoover is a powerful man, yes, but there are others and I know most of them."

Iris was tempted to tell this woman everything, but something stopped her. She thought of Libby's newspaper, the one from which they'd gotten this whole idea in the first place. She thought of Libby describing how men's names and addresses and employers were printed after being arrested for being in her bar. Dorothy Schiff ran that newspaper. Her words were generous; her actions were different.

"Why are you doing this, Iris?"

Iris spoke.

"I have my reasons."

Forty-one

1985

I'll call you back.

That was how Collier had left it almost six hours ago. Since then Joey had felt closely tethered to his phone, not wanting to miss the call when it came. A couple of hours ago he'd gone looking for the bag of groceries in the fridge to find that Aggie had unpacked it while he and Collier had been talking in the living room the previous morning. The chicken legs seemed too labor intensive; he boiled a cup of rice and topped it with some of the Italian meat sauce. He washed the dishes and then smoked another cigarette while thinking about the bottle of scotch as he filled a glass with water from the tap. He wanted to have his wits about him if Collier called. When he called. He'd call.

———

Joey wasn't aware that he'd nodded off on the couch until he was awoken by a sudden and rude buzzing sound, like a loud angry bee being stepped on. The buzzing stopped for a moment and then started again. Joey followed the sound to the intercom mounted on the wall next to the front door. The device had three buttons; Joey pushed the one labeled Talk.

"Hello?" he said into the circular pattern of dots. He pressed the Listen button and heard nothing. Talkbutton. "Hello?"

Listenbutton. " - Oey?" Aggie sounded tinny and far away, miniature.

Talk. "Yes?"

Listen.

" ... Me! Just a little something. Can I come up?" Aggie seemed to be barreling through a conversation. Maybe she only had a Talkbutton on her side.

Talk. "Sure, come up." Door button. Talk. "Are you in?" Listen. "Ime. Is it?"

Talk. "It's not a bad time. Just stop talking for a second so I can buzz you in!"

Listen. Silence.

Door.Joey held it while he counted to five Mississippi in his head. Listen.

"Uzzer work?"

"I'll come down."

Joey left his front door ajar and, realizing he hadn't pressed the Talkbutton for his last message, took the stairs two at a time, gripping the banister and holding tight to the inside on the corners. On the second floor, focused on his feet, he almost ran directly into the same old man he'd seen that morning. Mack.

"Oops. Sorry," Joey said as he jumped to avoid a collision.

"Take the stairs! You'll live to be a hundred."

If only it were that simple. As he passed the elevator in the lobby, Joey could see Aggie looking into the building, shielding her eyes with a salute. He waved as he jogged toward her.

"Hi!" Aggie held a vase in her hands with a ribbon around it.

"What's this?"

"Just a little housewarming prezzie." The vase was matte silver with accents of black and white and grey that looked like drips of wet paint trickling down the sides, elegant and masculine at the same time.

"Wow. It looks really... beautiful." Joey led the door as Aggie passed. He'd almost said expensive but didn't want to be tacky.

"It's practical. Since all your other ones broke." Aggie could be a little self-involved, that was true. But she could also bail you out of jail and show up the next day with an expensive gift as an excuse to make sure you were doing okay. "You have plans tonight?"

"Yeah. Sort of. I mean yes." They stepped into the elevator.

"Oh my God, what happened to your face?"

Joey had forgotten about his black eye and consequently had forgotten to make up a lie about it. "I... fell. I tripped. Fell." He was not a great liar when put on the spot; given some time to concoct a good story, he was capable enough, but caught off guard he was less than impressive.

"On what?" Aggie took his chin in her hand and tilted his face to get a better look.

"On a… car."

"You tripped on a car?"

Saying that he had plans when he did not was a knee-jerk lie that he'd trained into himself over the last few months when the other stylists would invite him out for drinks after work. He'd perfected saying it with a look of slight regret, as if the plans he had didn't promise as much fun as those being offered, but came with a considerable amount of obligation. He'd said *Yeah* this way when Aggie asked if he had plans before remembering that he actually did. Sort of. Maybe. If Collier called him back. WhenCollier called him back. He'd call.

"Onto a car. I hit -" Joey pushed his ajar front door open and let Aggie pass through, hoping her flighty attention span would get distracted if he stalled long enough.

"Well that sucks." Aggie removed the ribbon from around the vase as she walked to the kitchen; already more at home in Joey's apartment than he was. Joey followed and watched from the doorway as she filled the vase with water. "Diane has to bring Alice over. Again."

"How come?"

"I don't know. A fight. Some… family fight." She transferred Collier's flowers into the vase from the pint glass she'd put them in yesterday and started absentmindedly arranging them. "Peter pushed Brian, Kyle tried to stand up for his brother and ended up with a broken nose. That's all I could get out of her. I guess she needs to get Alice out of there."

"For how long?"

"She didn't say. You have plans tomorrow?"

"I might. I'm not sure." This was Joey's knee-jerk lie for any invitation one or more days in the future. He'd perfected saying this as

246

if he'd only then remembered that he'd made some tentative plans and the present question served as a welcome reminder to follow up on them.

"Crap." Aggie filled two glasses with water and handed one to Joey. She carried hers and the vase into the living room. "What do you think, windowsill?" She centered the flowers, turning the vase to find the most attractive angle.

"Sure."

"What are you doing tonight?"

"What?" Joey's coworkers never asked for details.

"What are your plans? Hot date?"

Joey hesitated for just a hair. "No."

"No?" Aggie said with a taunting grin. "Are you sure about that?"

"I'm sure. Totally sure." Joey tried to sound as emphatic as possible while not sounding like he was lying. New love was one of Aggie's favorite topics; she could easily become relentless in her probing.

"Then why won't you tell me what you're doing?" Her eyebrow shot up.

"I'm just seeing a friend for dinner."

"New friend?"

"Yeah," Joey lied. "From a… support group." Joey began to regret that he hadn't just told her the truth from the get go: that he was waiting for Collier to call him back and that they maybe might get together for a drink. It was way too late to backtrack now; it would look really weird. Joey wasn't lying because he didn't want Aggie to know the truth; he was lying because he was aware that the truth sounded flimsy. He didn't want to look like he was sitting at home all day waiting for Collier to call him, even thought that technically was what he'd been doing. But he wasn't doing it because he thought it would be a datedate; Joey wasn't an idiot. He was doing it because they needed to talk about the case. There was a difference. In one version Joey was pathetic and in the other he had an impeccable work ethic.

247

"Oh!" Aggie had talked in the past about various support groups for men in Joey's situation, dealing with loss, that had sprung up all over town, just to make sure Joey knew there were resources out there. "Terrific!"

Joey had never taken the bait when she brought them up; a support group was the last thing he wanted to sit through.

"That is terrific!!" Aggie looked at Joey with pride.

Joey looked for his cigarettes.

"Speaking of new friends, Lieutenant Collier seems like a really good guy."

"You think?" Joey said this like he had no opinion of his own on the subject.

"I do." Aggie took her glass to the kitchen for a refill, talking as she did. "You two seem to get along really well. It's nice to see. I bet he's someone who would be good for you to hang around with, you know. Talk to. Or just hang out with."

"Yeah?" Joey glanced at the phone. "Sure. Maybe…"

"You know, as a friend."

"Cool." Joey smoked. He felt his face flush and his ears get hot.

"Oh," Aggie called out. "I put out some calls for dinner this weekend."

"Why did you add that last part?" Joey didn't care about the dinner.

"What do you mean?" Aggie came back from the kitchen.

"That 'as a friend' part. Do you think I think it could be something besides that?"

"No…" She looked as though she wasn't sure if she should take another step.

"Maybe you think I'm some sort of confused person who would think something else?"

"I don't know what you're talking about. I said I thought he'd be a good friend for you. That's all, end of story."

"Yeah, but like this emphasis on the word 'friend.'Like you didn't want me to think you meant boyfriend. You know, like I better not get my hopes up of maybe having sex with someone."

"Whoa, whoa. What is happening here? Have you lost your mind? Where did thatcome from? You're the one who made some weird martyrdom vow to not sleep with anyone until someone figures out all this AIDS bullshit."

"Maybe I changed my mind," Joey said.

"Good! I think you should change your mind!" Aggie flattened the palm of her hand into her chest. "I think you absolutely should, as long as you're being safe and responsible -"

"Why? What's the big deal? Didn't you just tell me the other day at work that I was healthy?"

"Yes. I did! And I really, truly believe I'm right. But the truth is, we don't know."

"We don't know if you're healthy either."

Aggie's chin jerked back into her neck. "You're right. We don't."

"I mean, based on sheer numbers, your chances are just as high of having been infected as mine are. Maybe even higher. You do tend to get around."

Aggie put her glass down on the floor. "Okay. I think I should leave." She went to the front door and picked her purse off of the floor while Joey continued.

"But you're right. You're probably fine and I'm probably toxic."

Aggie banged her fist on the front door and spun to face Joey, still seated innocently on the couch. "Do not put those words in my mouth. Do you hear me? Do not ever." She tried to open the door but it was locked. She twisted the deadbolt and yanked on the knob but it still wouldn't open. Joey calmly and silently watched her struggle. She flipped the bottom lock and tried again but it still wouldn't budge so she kicked the door three times, turned both locks and tried again to no avail. She put her forehead on the door. "I want you to be happy,

Joey, I really do. I want you to fall in love again and have lots of sex and get married and live to be a hundred and twenty years old and die peacefully in your sleep surrounded by family and friends. But I'm not calling the shots here. None of us are."

The word 'us' struck Joey oddly.

"I know you're angry. And I even understand why some of that anger would be directed at me. But you are not allowed to say whatever the fuck you want to me just because you're grieving. I am a person. With feelings. It is not okay with me." She turned the deadbolt once more and the door, as if it could sense she'd said what needed to be said, opened.

As Aggie left, Joey felt his rage evaporate as easily as it had engulfed him moments before. He almost couldn't remember what it had even felt like. He almost couldn't remember what they were fighting about. He almost didn't care. He looked back at the phone.

Forty-two

1958

The gin martinis had been Iris's idea; Frankie said he didn't normally drink gin, but sure, why the hell not? He was behaving like such a gentleman. He'd stood up when she walked in, held her chair out for her as he signaled for the bartender's attention. He'd kissed her hand and told her she looked beautiful.

After her meeting with Dorothy Schiff, Iris had gone to her and Christopher's apartment building. She knew she couldn't go inside there alone, she didn't even know why she'd ended up there until she discovered that Frankie had left a bouquet of flowers with her doorman. Her doorman, knowing that Christopher had killed himself in their apartment, had handed the flowers to her reverently along with a note from Frankie, asking her to meet him at the same jazz club. Iris felt then, and still felt here in that club, that she was on some journey not of her own making. It was as if she'd boarded a train with an inevitable destination not of her choosing and each odd encounter, Libby, Frankie, Clyde Tolson, Dorothy Schiff, were preordained stops along the way. She felt both necessary and not in control. She wondered if this is how people of religious faith felt.

On the small stage where *Conundrum* had played the other night was a black man at a piano playing either from memory or making the tune up as he went. A cigarette burned in an ashtray in front of him where sheet music would normally be. Maybe the piano player was the train's conductor. Maybe he was God.

"I'm happy you came to meet me." Frankie took her hand and held it. "I was worried I might not ever see you again." He kissed her hand again, Iris felt the sharp stubble around his soft lips. "I was worried I might not ever get to take you out to dinner. Or the movies."

"I would let you take me to dinner," Iris smiled. "And to the movies."

251

"Yeah?" Frankie leaned back a little. "You'd go out on a date with a guy like me?"

"I would, sure. Why not?"

He put his hand over his heart. "I feel like the luckiest guy in the world." He signaled the bartender to make them two more drinks.

Iris watched the piano player's long, dark fingers as they jumped around the keys. She felt certain that he was making it up as he went along. She wondered how far ahead of his fingers his mind was. Had he planned out the next hour of music ahead of time? The next ten minutes? Even if his mind was only two notes ahead of his hands, there was still intent there. There was still creation.

"Hey Iris," Frankie slid a fresh drink toward her. "I was wondering if you might be willing to do me a favor."

———

Because Iris knew what she knew about Frankie, she felt like she was able to detect the holes in his story. He told her that he had some money in the house that he shared with his mother, money that he hadn't wanted to put in the bank. Some men, he'd said, suspected that the money was there and Frankie worried that they were planning to rob him. He needed to get the money out without being noticed, and was hoping Iris might be able to help him.

"Your version of this sounds like it's open to some interpretation. I'll help you if you answer two questions. Honestly."

"Alright."

"Are you a criminal?"

Frankie looked taken aback by this question. "Yes, I am."

Iris was equally taken aback by his stark honesty, the contrast of it when she thought of Christopher.

"Do you have a gun?"

"Yes."

This was the answer Iris was expecting to hear. Christopher had also owned a gun. *For protection,* he'd said once when Iris asked what was in the locked box in the closet of his office. The idea of a gun in the house had bothered her and Christopher had read it on her face. *Don't worry,* he'd said, *it's not loaded and it's locked up tight, high on a shelf.*

"Do you have it with you?"

"That's three questions," Frankie said. "I get to ask you one now."

"Alright."

"I've made some mistakes in my life. I'll be the first to admit it."

"People can change," Iris said.

"No, they can't. Not really. But that's okay; I'm not a bad guy. I've done wrong, but I knew it was wrong when I did it. I know how that sounds, but believe me, there are people who don't know the difference. I'm a criminal, but I'm also honest."

"I don't know how to respond to that." Iris pictured the equation for honesty that she and Libby imagined. She wondered if their initial stab at it had been too simple. Maybe it should also factor in the number of lies one was told. Better yet, the number of lies believed divided by the number of lies caught.

"Fair enough. If the answer turns out to be no, if you can't help me, I'll understand. But I am honest. What I said before, about wanting to take you out on a date, that was all true. I want to treat you to nice things, Iris. I really do."

He could have, Iris realized, in his telling her about the money, tried to make himself sound more innocent. He could have involved his mother in the story, or said that the money was given to him by a dead relative, something to make himself sound better, somehow, than he actually was. He hadn't. It made Iris trust him. It made her trust that he'd also fallen for her.

"So do you?"

"I do."

"I meant do you have a gun with you."

"Yes."

"Yes."

This was the answer Iris hoped to hear. She was less intimidated than she would have thought by the dangerous possibilities that the nearness of such a dangerous object provided. She'd discovered the hard way that the safety of distance and obstacles between a man and his gun were mere illusions.

"Will you show me how to use it?"

"Yes," Frankie squinted at her. "If that's what you want."

The piano player began to sing along with his unmapped tune. There were no words to the man's song, just syllables: Doot doot dwaddle-endee. Shiba senda nevah nevah nevah know. Iris felt like his nonsensical intonation was directed at her and, in it, she heard a definite message.

"It is. I want to know how to use it."

"Yeah. I'll show you."

"Then I'll help you."

The conductor had let her know she was on the right track; the train was starting to move fast.

Forty-three

1985

-

Joey's need to pee got him up off of the couch. He looked at the expensive vase that Aggie had given him holding Collier's cheap flowers. *Beware of strangers bearing gifts*, isn't that what the legend of the Trojan Horse had warned? That story had always baffled Joey. It seemed like the Greeks had taken a pretty big risk that the residents of Troy would see a gigantic wooden horse parked outside their gated community and collectively assume it was a present with no strings attached. Heading to the bathroom, Joey rounded the corner and saw his neighbor Mack standing at the end of the hall, framed by the doorway to Joey's bedroom. The old man who planned to live to be a hundred by taking the stairs had his hands up, palms facing Joey.

"Don't be scared," Mack said.

Joey wasn't scared; at least he wasn't until Mack told him not to be. He'd been startled, yes, but his first thought was that the old man must have gotten confused and wandered into the wrong apartment. Now he was a bit scared.

"I just want to talk."

Joey didn't say anything. He calculated the distance to the front door behind him and attempted to gauge how fast the man at the end of his hall might be. He didn't appear nearly as old as he did when Joey let him into the building earlier in the day.

"My apologies for letting myself in uninvited like this," the man took a tentative step in Joey's direction. "I was led to believe that you might have something of mine and I figured we should have a conversation. My name's not Mack. It's Carlo."

Joey didn't say anything.

"You're Joseph, right?"

Joey nodded once.

"You go by Joseph? Or Joe."

"Doesn't matter," Joey said. The man must have let himself in when Joey had run down to get Aggie. "I don't have the money."

"Money?" the man looked genuinely surprised.

"Are you going to hit me?"

"Hit you?" the man raised his palms a bit higher, then clasped them in front of his chest. "No. I'm not in the business of hurting people. Not for a long time now."

Joey nodded, and relaxed a bit. For some reason, he believed this man who had lied about being his neighbor.

"I'm looking for some ledgers, financial documents. What money are you talking about?"

"I'm not sure."

"Were you friends with this poor young woman Mindy? Or maybe this Ray person?"

Joey shook his head no. It occurred to him that this man had been privy to his fight with Aggie.

"Let's sit down, is that okay? We can have a civilized conversation about all this and see if we can help each other. Does that sound okay with you?"

"Depends," Joey wondered how much he'd heard. "Do you drink Scotch?"

———

Carlo listened while holding the glass of ice and Scotch he'd been offered. He wasn't sure what to make of Joseph Broderer's story. He wasn't sure what to make of Joseph Broderer. His body language, Carlo thought, was defensive, or maybe he was just being protective. He seemed to be manufacturing a determined casualness that looked put on. His arms were crossed over his thin chest and his body was angled slightly away from Carlo. Carlo thought about the gay men in the bar where he'd waited for Anthony the other night, the way they danced. Carlo could count on his fingers the number of times he'd himself danced. Each time had been at a well-lit event, a wedding for instance, and each time he'd danced with a female partner. Carlo had

256

never stood in a darkened crowd and gyrated with his eyes closed and his arms raised over his head like the men in that bar. Those men danced with what looked like a determination to disappear.

As Joseph talked, Carlo raised the glass to his lips, but didn't actually sip. Carlo liked his mind clear but he also understood the implied bond of trust that accompanied a shared drink, the power of the ritual. Once Joseph finished telling him about how a man that could only be Anthony had broken into his apartment to demand the return of some unknown amount of stolen money, Carlo knew the glaringly missing piece of the story that Anthony had fed him. His girlfriend Mindy hadn't stolen Carlo's ledgers; she'd stolen money.

"I'll be damned," Carlo said.

"Yeah, you probably will be if you keep breaking into people's homes."

Carlo laughed. "Young man, breaking and entering is the least of my sins."

Joey smiled and lifted his glass toward Carlo before taking a sip of it. Carlo touched his own glass to his lips again in a show of camaraderie.

"I think I might have an idea what money that asshole is talking about," Carlo said.

"Finally, somebody does."

Carlo looked over Joseph's head at the blank, beige wall. In his life, Carlo had seen plenty of blood. There was something about that one night, though, that changed him. The change was not immediate, nor was it complete, but it was specific and definitive. It wasn't just the blood, though there had been a lot of it that night.

"Are you going to tell me about it?"

Joseph's voice snapped Carlo back to the present. "Yeah, sure. If you have time for a story, I'll tell you about it."

"I have time."

Carlo lifted his glass and took an actual sip. Then he took another. "Before I tell you this, it's important to me that you know I don't have any problems with you guys."

"Us guys?"

"Yeah. Homosexuals. I didn't have a problem with you guys back then either." Carlo took a third sip. "It was just a way to make money."

———

Carlo told his story of illegal bars, police kickbacks for protection, and his colleague who had taken it upon himself to take a substantial amount of money for his personal use under false pretenses. The story he told didn't have an ending per se, but there came a point where Carlo was clearly finished telling it.

"So, if no one ever found the money," Joey asked, "how do you know this Frankie guy actually took it?"

"I know he did. You can take my word for it."

"You said when you caught up with him he'd been beaten half to death, but not by you. Is he still alive?"

Carlo nodded and looked over Joey's head again. "He is."

"Wasn't it your job to find the money and kill him?"

"It was."

"You don't sound like you were very good at your job. At the business of - what did you call it?"

Carlo broke out into a wide grin. "That's funny. You're funny. I like you."

"Oh boy," Joey rolled his eyes. "Keep it in your pants, captain."

That made Carlo chuckle. "Funny guy," he repeated.

"Seriously, what did you call it?"

Carlo finished the liquid in his glass. "The business of hurting people."

Joey thought he saw a flash of this man's reconciliation with his history in his eyes as he said these words. There was both regret and a detached lack of judgment attached to the description of his former career. The description itself sounded like exactly what it was but also somehow made it clear that the hurting was never personal. "Okay. So just to recap, back in 1952 -"

"Eight."

"Sorry. Back in 1958, this guy steals some money from your boss at the time, it disappears, Anthony Whatever-his-name-is somehow finds it a hundred years later, someone steals it from him and a girl gets killed over it all."

"Sounds about right. And I'd think twice about trying to find it, if that's what you're thinking about. Tony Tandino is mean. Mean and dumb. He killed that girl over this money and he'll kill you too."

"He didn't kill her. He thinks I killed her. Also, he said he'd kill me if I didn't find it."

"I could help you."

"A gigantic wooden horse, how thoughtful."

"What's that?" Carlo asked.

"Just my way of saying what's in it for you?"

"We find the money, we find my ledgers."

"I'll have to think about it. I don't really know if I trust you."

"I don't blame you." Carlo gave the ice in his otherwise empty glass a little shake. "I suppose I did break into your apartment."

"Yep."

"Well. I'll give you my number in case you change your mind. I'd prefer not to write it down, how's your memory?"

"Alive and kicking, unfortunately."

Carlo recited seven digits and Joey repeated them back to him three times in a row. Carlo nodded, stood, and walked to Joey's front door.

"So," Joey followed him like a proper host, "if you're not in the business of hurting people anymore, what business are you in now?"

"The business of helping people."

"I bet that doesn't pay as well."

Carlo laughed. "No sir, it does not." He turned back to Joey. "Be careful. You should probably assume you're being followed."

Joey nodded. "That woman you talked about, the one who was with Frankie when you found him. Is she still alive?"

259

"That I don't know." Carlo easily opened the door that Aggie had struggled with. "I never saw her again."

Forty-four

Joey sat still, waiting, in a small, dark room downstairs in the Saint Marks Baths. The small cot was covered in a material that could easily be wiped down between uses. He wondered how many lives had ended here, how many men had entered these rooms healthy and left sick. Sick, but feeling fine. Feeling terrific. Feeling wanted. Joey knew, before the man named Carlo had told him, that the mafia had once run the gay bars in New York, but it was before Joey's time. It was less than twenty years since the law prohibiting homosexuals to congregate in public had been overturned after a weekend-long riot downtown. Left to do as they pleased, the homosexuals had built places like this and, before too long, the grim reality of the past faded to make way for the more gruesome one in front of them now.

For a Friday night, the place was nowhere nearly as crowded as it had once been, but there were still a significant number of men who either felt invincible or suicidal enough to show up like nothing had changed. There were also those who believed, in spite of the mounting evidence, that efforts to slow the transmission of the disease were right-wing, homophobic attacks. The men in that camp were defiant and outraged. On the other side, those who championed hand jobs and dry kissing were equally defiant and outraged. Joey's personal choice of abstinence was based more on terror than politics and, so far, had not been challenged by any real temptation. He'd read in *The Village Voice* that the city would be closing all the bathhouses in the fall.

The ex-mafia man, Carlo, had convinced Joey that he shouldn't underestimate Anthony's potential for violence or mistake him for a dumbass. Joey had climbed down his fire escape dressed in black jeans and a dark blue hooded sweatshirt, like he was in an environmental theater production of *West Side Story*. He'd called Collier from the pay phone in the changing room after renting one of the small private rooms.

Where? Collier had asked. *Why there?*

I'm being followed. Maybe. It was the only place I could think of...

Okay. Okay. Collier jotted down the address and room number. *Sit tight, I'll be there soon.*

That had been twenty minutes ago. Joey tried not to fidget on the small bed. He wished there was some clutter to tidy, a stack of mail to sort.

It could be really hot, Henry had said, sometime in 1980, after bringing up the possibility of a three-way. The two of them were eating in an Italian restaurant. *Hot for both of us.* Henry had tucked a cloth napkin into his collar to protect his designer shirt and tie. *Keep us both out of trouble,* he'd winked.

They'd been together for a couple of years at that point, and had settled into a comfortable monogamy without vows. Joey hadn't felt the need to reevaluate the situation. Most couples they knew had arrangements of some sort, but still the suggestion had caught Joey off guard. The next day Joey told Aggie, and she'd said that Joey should be flattered that Henry wanted to include him in his affairs, that this was a good thing. Henry suggested that they go out to pick someone up together. Getting ready, Henry had changed clothes three times. A few drinks later, Joey had watched from a corner of a crowded, smoky bar as Henry talked to a handsome Latin man in a tight tee shirt. He pointed toward Joey and the Latin man squinted in the same direction. A few minutes later, Henry rejoined Joey in the corner carrying fresh drinks for both of them, claiming that the man in the tee shirt was an asshole.

"Joey! Are you in there?" Collier knocked on the other side of the flimsy door Joey had locked from the inside.

Joey got up and opened the door to see Collier standing in the dim light wearing nothing but a towel around his waist, his hands on his hips. "Why are you naked?"

"Because they made me." Collier's voice was raised, either out of anger or just to be heard over the loud disco beat.

"They made you?"

"Yes. They made me. I went to pay the big guy for the the the the ticket, or whatever, and he said it was full. I told him I was meeting someone and he asked me if I worked for the health department."

Joey had never heard Collier stutter. "Did you wear your blazer?"

"It's a sports coat, it's very casual."

"Gun and badge?"

"They're in the car. I'm not an idiot. That guy had me escorted to the locker room by an even bigger guy who stood there holding this towel until I got undressed." Collier jutted his chin forward and crossed his arms over his chest. "Can I come in? I'm feeling a little... exposed."

"Yeah, come in." Joey stepped aside. "Do you want my sweatshirt?"

"Thanks."

Joey unzipped and handed it to Collier who put it on while Joey deliberately looked away.

"Who's following you?" Collier sat on the small bed.

Joey took a breath and sat next to him. "Okay, well. Somebody broke into my apartment."

"When?" Collier moved his ear closer to Joey to hear him better over the music.

"Twice actually. Two different people." Collier was close enough for Joey to smell his shampoo. It was a familiar smell, very distinct, but he couldn't place it. "The first was yesterday after I got back from the hospital with you. There was a guy in my apartment who kind of roughed me up, asked me all kinds of questions about Mindy."

"He roughed you up? Why am I just hearing about this now?"

"It's okay, I'm fine."

"No, you're not. You're withholding information about a homicide, that's not fine."

"No, I'm not." Joey had misread his concern. "I'm telling you about it right now."

"Fine. Keep talking." Collier shook his head in disbelief.

"And for the record, I have been trying to get in touch with you all afternoon." Joey couldn't remember ever smelling any hair product on Collier.

"I said fine. Okay?" Collier looked angrier than Joey had ever seen him. "Just keep - what was he asking you about?"

"Apparently Mindy stole some money from him. I don't know how much. He seemed to think that I would know where to find it."

"Do you?"

"Stop."

"Fine. What happened then?"

"He knocked me out and left."

"He knocked you out? You mean he assaulted you?"

"Yeah. I guess. He banged my head into the wall and I didn't wake up until this morning." Even being on the receiving end of it, Joey hadn't thought of it as assault as much as a solid getaway plan.

"This morning?" Collier looked directly into Joey's eyes.

"Yeah."

"We talked this morning."

Shit. "Did we?" Joey had somehow forgotten this detail.

"Yup. We sure as shit did. When you called to tell me that you figured out, completely on your own, that it might occur to a law enforcement member to vacuum the crime scene." Collier rubbed his temples. "And during that call you neglected to mention any of this."

"In all fairness, you practically hung up on me."

"How did you know he was a cop?"

"Was I right?" Confused and innocent, confused and innocent.

"How did you know? And don't even think about lying."

"Okay. After I woke up, I went downstairs to get some air and I ran into a neighbor." This was barely even mildly a lie. "We were talking about how creepy it was to have a murder so close and she told me that her window is across from Ray's and just one floor down. She says she saw a guy -"

"What's her name?"

"I gave her my word."

264

"What is her name."

"Why does it matter?"

"It matters because we interviewed everyone in that building and didn't learn jack shit. So if she lied, she's in trouble."

"Calm down." Joey was pretty sure that Collier had gotten loud enough to be heard over the music if anyone was listening. "Just take the information and stop trying to blame everyone all the time."

"Blameevery- are you insane? It's my job to blame. Someone did this, okay? Someone killed Mindy Shorent."

"Stop yelling."

Collier cooled it. "Someone killed her," he said more quietly.

"I'm telling you everything I know." Closer to a lie, but well intentioned. "This neighbor seemed to think the guy she saw was a cop. So you can see why she might be nervous to talk to the police."

Collier nodded as he leaned forward to prop his chin in his hands, elbows on knees. He smushed his top lip into his nose, which meant, Joey knew, that he was doing his heaviest thinking.

"I can ask her if she'd feel comfortable talking to you."

"These aren't rules that you or I can bend because we feel sorry for someone. There is a procedure that I have to follow here. It's cut-and-dried. If this woman can identify someone who was in Ray's apartment when Mindy was being beaten and drowned, I need to know who she is. That's all. If you don't tell me, I will have to arrest you right now."

"You're in a towel."

The look that Collier gave Joey allowed no wiggle room for charm.

"If you're going to hit me, keep in mind that I might have a concussion." No wiggle room at all. "You don't have to talk to her or arrest me, because I know his name."

Collier stood up, his muscle memory for interrogation overriding the awkwardness of his outfit. "If I don't know everything in the next thirty seconds I'm going to drag you out of here by force and embarrass you in front of all your friends."

"These aren't my friends."

"Twenty-six seconds."

"Fine. The secondperson who broke into my apartment today was a like a mafia guy."

"A mafia guy."

"Ex. Ex mafia guy. But a sort-of nice one. Not a mean one."

"Fifteen seconds."

"Jesus Christ, okay." Joey stood up to face Collier. "The cop is named Anthony Tandino. He sometimes does favors for the mafia guy so it's in the mafia guy's best interest that Anthony doesn't get arrested. Mafia guy knows Anthony, the cop, broke into my apartment and wanted to know what I know because the mafia guy, like everyone else in the world, thinks that I know much more than I do. He did not know that Mindy had stolen money from Anthony so I told him that part and then he left. The end."

"What's mafia guy's name?"

"Carlo."

"That's it?"

"Yeah. Oh." Joey remembered something else. "Anthony, the cop, said he didn't kill Mindy."

"He said that?"

"Yeah. He thinks I did."

Collier nodded. "Okay. We're leaving." He opened the door and stuck his head out while keeping his hand on Joey's shoulder as if to prevent him from running into sniper range.

"They're not…" Joey rolled his eyes. "They're not in here."

Collier walked ahead toward the locker room, keeping one hand on Joey's elbow.

"Where are we going?"

"I'm thinking." Collier planted Joey outside the locker room. "Wait here. I'll be right out." He left Joey standing in a spot that felt very familiar.

After another hour at the bar, that night back in 1980, Henry and Joey decided to go to the baths. *Less seduction, more action*, they'd

266

joked on the way. They'd both gotten a little drunk by then. Once in towels, they decided to split up with the agreement to find the other if they got a good candidate. The memory was boozy, compounded by an inescapable amyl nitrate contact-high and endless faceless naked bodies lit by shadowy red light. After some time, Joey found Henry with a hairy chested man who was the physical opposite of Joey in every way, opposite and superior. Henry motioned for Joey to join them. The hairy chested man grabbed Joey's crotch in lieu of a handshake. Joey didn't remember how he and Henry and the hairy-chested man had gotten home to their apartment or into the bedroom, but they had.

——

Diane stood outside her younger son's bedroom wondering if she should knock again. After the hospital, all three of the men in her life had sequestered themselves into their respective rooms. The confrontation between Peter and Brian after she'd shown the magazine to her husband had been brief but loud. She knew Peter would never intentionally hit one of their boys; he'd only pushed Brian against the wall because he'd been angry. And scared. When Kyle jumped in to protect his brother, Peter's elbow connected with their older son's nose and suddenly there was blood everywhere. Now no one was speaking, no one had eaten dinner; the house was practically vibrating with tension. Diane listened at her younger son's door for signs of something, anything. If only I could just keep him in there, she thought. If I could just keep him locked in his bedroom, I know he'd be safe.

——

Collier came out of the locker room dressed and handed Joey back his sweatshirt. "Okay. I have it figured out." He led Joey up the stairs to the street level.

"Good night, gentlemen," the big man behind the counter who had intimidated Collier cooed and batted his eyelashes like an approving yenta as Joey handed him the key to the private room.

Joey looked at Collier while the big man watched. "My place? Or yours."

"My place." Collier winked, looking more relaxed now that he was dressed.

Joey followed him out onto the street. "For real your place?"

"I thought of that. But it's not really safe." Collier's car was parked in front of a fire hydrant with the placard on the dashboard that told other cops it was fine for him to do this. "I'm going to lock you up."

"Isn't that a little dramatic?" Joey stopped short of the car.

"I don't think so, Joe. This is bad news."

"So I keep hearing."

"Joe," Collier put his hand on Joey's shoulder. "These are criminals who do not care about you. They will not think you are cute or funny, they will just get what they need from you and when they are done, they will kill you. Do you understand?"

"So you're going to lock me up."

"Think of it as protective custody. The problem is I'd need authorization for that officially, so we are going to pretend that I arrested you."

"Do I have a choice?"

"Yes. I can actually arrest you."

Joey looked at the late-night foot traffic on the busy street, drunk kids and punks in the prime of their lives.

"I'll make it really loud and embarrassing."

"Fine." Joey sighed as he walked to the passenger side. Collier was going to protect him. He bit the inside of his lip to keep from smiling.

They drove north in silence. He thought of Henry in the Italian restaurant, the gleam in his eyes as he said the idea of a three-way would be fun, keep them both out of trouble. 'Out of trouble' seemed to be the number one destination for Joey when leaving the St. Marks baths, even if it was consistently at someone else's insistence.

Forty-five

1958

-

Iris had never known, but was figuring out that there was a pocket of time in the early morning, well after midnight, where anything was possible, and none of it held any consequence. Christopher had never shared it with her. Her parents had never told her about it, maybe they'd never witnessed it themselves. She didn't know exactly how long it would last, since it was only her second experience in it. The feelings and exchanges in here were both tremendous and no good at all, absolute and yet too fragile to survive in the light. She knew it would be over before the sun rose.

Frankie was kissing her shoulder and her back, and now her neck. She didn't know if she was asleep or awake. She rolled over onto her back and felt his lips move to her throat and chin, his thumb tracking the line of her jaw. If she was awake, it was as close to sleeping as she could get. He kissed her side, where her zipper had been the last time they'd slept in her marriage bed together, and then her hip. It wasn't until she felt his rough stubble on her stomach that she fully comprehended that she was naked. She felt his hand between her legs and squeezed her thighs together.

Iris's experience with sex was limited. While her mother was dying in a hospital, Iris accepted a dinner invitation from a tall, redheaded resident. He'd taken her to a steakhouse in downtown Cleveland and told her that the sky was the limit. After dinner, on the couch where Iris had spent so many evenings reading with her parents in silence and stillness, the young doctor had buried his freckled face in her neck and grunted while gripping her breast like a proud shortstop.

That wasn't your first time, was it? he'd asked while buckling his pants. Iris had lied and told him it was not.

Frankie bit her hipbone when it arched up, then pushed her back down with his forearm.

She pictured Christopher, swaying on the edge of the bed on their wedding night, obliterated from champagne. *I'm sorry,* he'd said as he fell back. Iris thought he was apologizing for getting so drunk.

Frankie put his hand under the small of her back and lifted her pelvis up. It caught her by surprise and she gasped in a gulp of air as the muscles holding her knees together gave out.

Iris thought of the hole in the floor of Libby's basement.

Her thighs wrapped around Frankie's head. She didn't know what to do with her hands; one grabbed his ear. The gun sliding between Christopher's lips. Did he open his mouth wide like he was at the dentist? Or did he wrap his lips around it? Was his mouth wet? Iris closed her eyes even though the room was dark. The experiences here, in this pocket of time, were irrevocable but easily forgiven.

The blood on the wall behind Christopher as the smoke trailed out of his mouth.

———

Considering the long menu of potential hiccups, the favor Iris was doing for Frankie was going surprisingly smoothly. She'd almost laughed when he'd asked if she would do it, as if she had any say in the matter. She'd thought of the train they were on together, the inevitability of what was unfolding, and had almost told him about it. About how she'd already started doing him the favor, about how his asking her was just one of the stops. But instead she'd just said *Yes, I will help you.*

The subway ride had been easy, a little longer than she would have liked - only because it had given her time to imagine and play out a variety of potential outcomes for this errand, even though she knew there was only one. She found Brooklyn to be charming; seeing it for herself, she couldn't quite remember how she'd pictured it. She'd been a bit nervous about getting lost, but the directions Frankie had made her memorize were detailed and accurate. He didn't want her having to consult a piece of paper in her hand in a neighborhood where everybody knew everybody else. She hadn't realized there were parts of

New York full of modest, one-family homes like the rest of the country. She found Frankie's house easily and walked past it on the other side of the street, just as he'd told her to.

You live with your mother? She'd asked this more for clarification than anything else, not considering it might be a sensitive issue for a man in his early forties.

It's not like that, he'd snapped, then immediately softened. *I live in an apartment upstairs and she lives downstairs. It's like two different places. My ma's getting old. She needs a lot of help these days.*

Iris crossed the street at the corner then ducked into the small alley that ran behind the row of houses that Frankie and his mother's was a part of. She gripped her vanity case tightly. If anyone stopped her, she and Frankie had decided she should say she was selling cosmetics and giving complementary makeup lessons. She knew her makeup kit wouldn't pass inspection by a real professional, but Frankie assured her that his mother's nosy neighbors would be sufficiently impressed by the idea of free anything.

She took Frankie's key out of her purse as she took the last few steps towards his back door. The key slid easily into the lock, the handle turned and within seconds she was inside the unfamiliar house with the door shut behind her. Although she'd still not broken any laws, she felt she'd crossed some invisible line into criminal territory. And the world kept spinning. She listened for movement but heard none.

As Frankie had said, Iris found herself in the laundry room. The stairs in front of her led to Frankie's half of the house, his apartment; the doorway to her left led to his mother's. She tiptoed up, careful not to make any noise even though Frankie's mother, he'd assured her, was deaf. The second level was dark, considering that it was not yet noon. She paused in the doorway to a room that must have been his bedroom. The bed was not neatly made, but at least a nod toward order had been undertaken. She had a desire to go through his drawers before reminding herself that she knew all she needed to know about him for the task at hand.

The sewing room, as Frankie had referred to it, had clearly not been used in some time. A Singer sewing machine sat quiet and covered, thick with dust, fabric scraps in a basket on the floor, larger pieces folded carelessly, projects abandoned before begun. The closet was filled with boxes: family photographs, Christmas ornaments. In a back corner, behind a small rocking horse, was a black doctor's bag, as promised. She lifted it out and placed it on a rocking chair draped with a homemade afghan.

Frankie had described his crime as stealing from his boss, a crime lord millionaire, which had given the act an almost noble, Robin Hood kind of feel. In his mind, the money belonged to whomever he worked for, whatever they called themselves. Seeing the stacks of bills in the bag, grouped together and bound by rubber bands, Iris couldn't help but consider the thousands of hands, maybe more, that these bills had passed through. How many of them had been pulled from Libby's till, put there via hands sweaty with fear, perhaps trembling, eager to hide in a pocket. How many of these bills had passed through hands that wore wedding bands like costumes. How many of them had passed through Iris's own hands? How many had she accepted from the bank teller after depositing Christopher's paycheck and withdrawing his cash for the week, his allowance, they'd joked. When it came to the ownership of this money, any money actually, the concept was hazy, transient at best. It didn't surprise her that Frankie had a skewed, black-and-white view of what belonged to whom. He'd had no problem claiming he lived in an apartment above his mother's when it was clear they shared a house. Being able to close your bedroom door didn't mean you lived alone. She zipped up the bag.

Hung on the wall next to the door was a framed picture Iris hadn't seen on her way in, of a handsome man resembling Frankie, probably his father. He looked to be about Frankie's age in the picture, leaning against a wall with a sign behind him that she couldn't read, some kind of store, maybe. She wondered if this man shared Frankie's loose morals, if he'd handed them down through his blood or his teachings. Or maybe he'd fought against them, heartbroken to watch his boy fall in with a sketchy crowd, praying for a better life for his only son.

Now listen, Frankie had said. *My ma broke her hip, so she can't get up the stairs. She can't even really get around the kitchen, so don't worry about her seeing you or nothin'.*

Does she depend on you? Iris had asked. *If you go running off, will she be alright?*

He'd looked at her with a sort of amusement or condescension. *Who said I was running off?*

Back in the laundry room, Iris peeked into the kitchen; it smelled of tomato and oregano, of recent cooking. She heard low music from a radio coming from another room closer to the front door. Frankie hadn't answered her question; he'd implied that she was wrong, but she knew he was lying. Maybe it was none of her business. Maybe his doing so would be what his mother was hoping for. Maybe his leaving his feeble mother brought up resentment in Iris over her inability to leave her own while she was dying. Maybe his mother was a difficult person to be around and deserved to be abandoned. Maybe she had a million dollars in the bank. Maybe whatever obligation he might have toward her had been paid over a hundred times by now. Maybe it was time for them to part. Maybe.

Iris reached into the bag. She didn't know how much each bundle held, they were all different sizes. She pulled two of them out and placed them on the kitchen table. It was the right thing to do. Her son was planning on skipping town with money stolen from innocent men. Iris was planning on turning him in to the head of the FBI. Either way, he wasn't coming back. The train was going, on to its next inevitable stop, and Iris was merely a porter whose job it was to carry a bag.

Forty-six

1985

-

While letting him out of his cell in the morning, Collier suggested that Joey go to work and stay out of his apartment for the time being. Joey asked him how he was supposed to get dressed for work if he couldn't go home and Collier had made him promise promise promise not to go back there.

"It's for your own safety," Collier said, holding Joey's wallet and keys just out of reach.

"I know."

"I'm on the fence about even letting you out, you know."

"You can't be on the fence about it, this is still America, not Russia. We were just pretending I was arrested. Remember?"

"I do." Collier handed him his stuff.

"Besides," Joey said putting his wallet back in his pocket, "if those guys are trying to find me, couldn't they just as easily find me at work as at home?"

"That's a good point. Maybe you should go to the movies. Do you have any money?" Before Joey could answer, Collier pulled out his own wallet and handed Joey a twenty. "Here. Take this. Stay out of trouble."

"Thanks."

"Oh, and here." Collier sifted through his pocket change and handed Joey five dimes. "Check in with me every couple of hours, okay?"

"Sure."

"Promise?" Collier put his hand on Joey's shoulder and made a goofy-stern face.

"I promise! Sheesh!" Joey rolled his eyes and slumped his shoulders as he walked away.

Eating bacon and eggs at a nearby diner, Joey considered his promise. He really wanted to shower and change clothes. He'd promised Collier that he wouldn't go back home to his apartment; that was true. He couldn't remember if it was he or Collier who had used the term 'home,' but it had been used.

You know, said Milt from the other side of the booth, *they say you never can go home again.*

"I was thinking the same thing," Joey said out loud through a mouthful of food.

So that promise you made is null and void. You can't promise not to do something if it's impossible to do. There's no point!

"Right."

A woman in the next booth looked at Joey, maybe wondering if he was trying to get her attention.

And as for the term 'your apartment,' Milt looked longingly at Joey's bacon, *well, with everyone who's been breaking in and out of there these days, who's to say whose apartment it* actually *is?*

"Touché. And this from someone who's gotten quite comfortable there himself."

The woman in the next booth took a sip of her coffee and pointedly looked past Joey.

Moi? Mais je suis un tres bon ami for sure!

Joey couldn't remember if the affected French thing was something Milt had actually done in life. Either way, it was annoying.

"Quiet, Antoinette. We're being watched."

————

And perhaps they were.

The mess inside Joey's apartment was not unlike the mess in his head. It was there and it was real and it was almost insurmountable, but not quite. He thought of the stripper's coked-up rant, how she'd described New York City. 'Controlled chaos' was what she'd said. That described the mess in Joey's head and apartment, too. It was a mistake on someone's part to think that Joey wouldn't notice that things had

275

been moved. They were basically the same, but he was pretty sure the boxes in his living room had been unpacked and then repacked. Whoever had done it had either underestimated Joey's mind, or overestimated his mess.

He noticed the light on his answering machine blinking: Blink. Blink. One message. When he had two messages it went Blink Blink. Blink Blink. The only time he'd had more than two messages was the night he'd flyered the strip clubs on 42nd Street. He pressed the playback button.

"Joey, you little fucking asshole, I knew I shouldn't have trusted you." Dr. Carolyn's voice hissed at him through the tinny speaker. "Call me, you little shit, as soon as you get this. I'm at the hospital."

———

"Why the fuck did you give Raymond's father my phone number?" Dr. Carolyn walked up behind Joey, startling him. He'd agreed to meet her across the street from the hospital. He'd gotten bored watching the entrance for her exit.

"Because I think he has a right to know what's going on with his son, that's why." It's not exactly like he was hiding the fact that he'd done it; he'd given Ray's dad his own name as well as Carolyn's.

"Did you know there's a history of abuse there?"

"No."

"Did you know that even now, dying from the worst disease known to mankind, that kid is still terrified that his dad is going to find him?"

"No." Joey stayed defiant but was pretty sure he could feel himself shrinking.

"Did you know that he was so worried that his dad would find out he's gay that he made his friends clean everything out of his apartment that would remotely hint at that fact?"

Bingo. That's why the apartment looked so clean, why Joey wasn't able to get a sense of who Ray was, even while lying in his bed.

"Joey, the kid is dying. He's dying and he's scared that his own father is going to hurt him. Does that give you any sense of what we're dealing with here?"

"It seemed like a good idea at the time. I thought -"

"No, you didn't. You didn't think at all."

"I did give him your home number instead of the hospital's."

"Yeah, thanks for that. Now I'll have to change it." She turned and looked back at the hospital.

Joey pulled a cigarette from his back pocket and lit it. The wind shifted slightly just as Carolyn was turning back and the smoke blew right into her eyes.

"Goddammit." She waved her hand around her face.

"Sorry."

"The fuck you are." Carolyn snatched the cigarette from Joey's hand and threw it into the street before he could react. "Wake up, okay? Just wake up." She put her hands on his chest like she was going to push him, then took a step back. "I can't be the only sane person in this. I just can't. I won't... I refuse to care about you more than you care about yourself."

Joey didn't know what to say. His options all felt inadequate.

"I can not be the only one thinking straight. I refuse to be. You understand me?" She folded her arms across her chest. "You really don't know Raymond?"

"Really. A friend of mine said her friend Ray Nunez was in the hospital and his dad didn't know where he was. I remembered his name from Henry's address book and I guess I was curious. I don't know him at all. Calling his dad was just..."

"Fucking stupid."

"Right. It was fucking stupid."

"So I guess you don't want to hold on to some of his stuff." Carolyn said.

"Ray's stuff? Not really. What is it?"

"It's this..." Carolyn looked at her shoes and laughed. "It sounds, well, maybe it won't sound weird to you, I don't know. It's... I have a box of porn -" As she said the last word she started giggling, then stopped herself like it had happened in church. "Sorry. It's not funny. None of this is fun -" She broke again, another high-pitched girlish giggle that she managed to talk through. "I have a box of gay porn, a big box, in my apartment. Right now. As we speak."

Joey smiled, more at her reaction than her story. "Why do you have it?"

"I'm not sure," she wiped her eyes and got control of herself. "His girlfriend brought it to the hospital because Ray didn't want his dad to find it. I didn't think it should be at the hospital so I brought it home. And now it's there." Another giggle fit. "In my apartment."

"His girlfriend?" Joey tried to act nonchalant.

"Yeah." her laughter died down again.

"What was her name?"

"Her name?"

Joey thought quickly to backtrack the blend of lies and half-truths that had put him in this conversation. "Yeah. I wonder if it was the same friend as mine. The... mutual friend. Of ours. Mindy?" Joey went out on a limb. "Short girl. Long brown hair?"

"Maybe," Carolyn looked at the traffic, as if she'd lost interest in Joey's questions. "I don't remember. Maybe."

"Have you seen her lately?"

"Who."

"The girlfriend. Who brought the porn."

Carolyn looked slightly confused, like she'd only been paying half attention to him and now was lost. "No. I... she's a crazy person. I haven't seen her. For a while." She cleared her throat and wiped her face. "It's a fuck lot of porn. What is it with you guys, you know? How much is enough?" She chuckled, which sounded very different from her actual laugh.

"I don't know the answer to that." Joey took a cigarette from his pocket. "When Henry first got symptoms, there was a moment when I... he'd been going off so much on his own, sleeping with other guys, that there was a moment that I was almost grateful. It didn't last

278

very long, I mean I realized that whatever weird neediness I had was beside the point. But there was a short time there when he was still basically healthy, but also terrified. It made him faithful."

Carolyn nodded. Two soldiers who knew their side was losing but still wanted to be brave for each other.

"If I knew a way to go back and live in that snapshot with him, indefinitely..."

"We all make mistakes, Joey. But, it's just a disease. It's a smart, strong disease." She picked something off her sleeve, lint or a hair too small for Joey to see, and released it into the wind. "You didn't cause it."

"I know." They both stared up Seventh Avenue, like there was a parade coming their way.

"I tell ya," Carolyn shook her head, "if you believe in reincarnation and you want to have a long, healthy life next time around, hope that you come back as this virus. It's winning. It wants so badly to live."

"I don't."

"I can tell."

"I mean I don't believe in reincarnation."

"Suit yourself. From where I sit, you're moping around like you're a forgone dead man, yet you remain completely asymptomatic."

"So far," Joey interrupted.

"So far. Look, I'm not saying surviving is any easier than getting sick, okay? I'm just saying that right now you are healthy. Do what you want with it."

Joey lit his cigarette.

"Well, I guess that answers that." Carolyn took a step backwards, toward St. Vincent's, then turned away abruptly. "Don't give anyone else my number, understood?"

"Understood."

"Good. I don't want to see you again."

Forty-seven

1958

-

Clyde made young Iris Milligan wait in order to prove the point that he was still calling the shots here. Twenty minutes after the concierge had rung, Clyde folded his newspaper and sauntered to the door. He'd told the concierge: no calls and visitors for the morning. The pinched little man had been apologetic. He'd described the young woman as excitable and said she claimed to be a personal friend. Clyde had been angry at being interrupted having left such explicit instructions, but then saw the opportunity in the situation for restraint, for delayed gratification. Then it became an idea too good to pass up. He opened the door to the hall and saw her sitting on a bench with a worn, black doctor's bag in her lap, flanked by two agents in matching suits.

"Ms. Milligan. Please come in." He waited until she stood and walked to the door before stepping aside to give her room. He wanted to relish, even briefly, the moment she entered the suite.

"Is Mr. Hoover here?" she asked, looking around the opulent setting.

"Mr. Hoover is indisposed at the moment." Clyde resisted the urge to glance at the closed door that led to the bedroom, but intentionally spoke loudly enough to be heard on the other side.

"Did you hear from Mrs. Schiff? I did what you asked me to do." The bag in her hands looked heavy but she didn't set it down.

"I did not hear from her. Which is a good thing. I took her silence to mean that you had proven yourself a worthy ally."

Iris breathed a sigh of relief. "That's wonderful. I mean... it's – I'm – it's good that you trust me. I've brought proof of the extortion we spoke about before. The man responsible is at - I know where the man responsible is. But we should move quickly -"

280

"I'm sorry," Clyde moved behind a highly polished desk. "Did you say you wanted to see Mr. Hoover?"

"Yes. I would. Is that possible?"

"I couldn't quite hear you. You would like to see Mr. Hoover right now? Is that what you said?"

"Yes, I would like to see him," Iris said, louder and slightly more confused. "Is he available?"

"Not at the moment," Clyde sat down. "Perhaps soon." He put a leather briefcase atop the desk and pulled from it a typed document. "Perhaps soon, you will see him." He turned the document to face her.

"What's this?" Iris glanced down.

"It's called a non-disclosure agreement. It means confidentiality. In regards to our previous conversations, this conversation, any subsequent, third party conversations that might have been provoked like the one you had with Ms. Schiff..."

"I already gave you my word that I wouldn't talk about it, and I haven't."

"Yes, well, words can be retracted. It's ink, Miss Milligan," he winked at her, "that seals the deal. The document is necessary; it's our insurance. Once you've signed we can forget about it and discuss how to help you. But only once you sign it."

"Fine." She accepted the pen he was holding out and signed on the line where he'd placed his finger. "I don't know how much time we have. Frankie - Franklin, I mean – that's the name of the man who's guilty of this, although he has a more complicated name -"

Clyde stood from the desk and walked calmly to the sitting area and sat on the couch. He opened the single, thin drawer in the coffee table that matched the desk. The drawer contained several street maps of the city as well as advertisements for neighborhood restaurants and Broadway shows. Next to these was an envelope Clyde had planted after the concierge had rung.

"He's expecting me to return with this bag."

From the envelope, Clyde pulled five crisp one hundred dollar bills.

"This bag," she hugged it to her chest, "contains the proof. It's all the money he stole -"

Clyde stood and held the five bills out to her.

"What's that?"

"This, young lady, is five hundred dollars."

"For what?"

"Your services. It's for you." He shook it at her. "Go on. You can take it. I'll have a car drop you anywhere you need to go, within reason of course."

She squinted at him. "Go? Where am I supposed to go? Aren't you listening to me? I don't need five hundred dollars, I need protection."

"I can't go any higher than a thousand. And I believe that's being very, very generous."

"You just said you would help me."

"I did say that. Right after I said words can be retracted."

She took a breath and shook her head lightly. "I think, if you would just listen to the whole story, you might find that you have a personal interest in seeing this through."

"And why is that?"

"The establishments that he has targeted, they... cater to a particular clientele."

"And you think that would interest me because..."

"I'm not judging you, I don't care."

"What is it," he took a step toward her, "that you don't care for?" He should have guessed that Dorothy Schiff would have found a way to get her filthy gossip into this child's head.

"About. What I don't careabout. I don't care if it's true."

"If whatis true?"

"If you... or he... or you and he -"

"Say it, girlie," he whispered. "Let me hear you say it."

"If you or he is a homosex -"

Clyde slapped her hard across the mouth before she could finish the word. "You bite your tongue. I could have you killed for that." She didn't make a sound; the only indication that she'd been struck was her hand that jumped halfway to her face before she pulled it back down to her side.

"I only meant -" Her voice was small.

"I don't care what you meant. Words have meanings, young lady, specific meanings. Meanings you are, apparently, too stupid to comprehend. You'd be wise, Miss Milligan, to learn some definitions before you continue to speak in educated company."

There were, Clyde knew, dozens of categorized paraphilia and probably many others as well. He knew because he'd read the psychiatric journals to learn what exactly he and his boss were. What he found was so many variations labeled Perversion, that together those afflicted, he thought, must form a rather large group. It was easy to imagine that, together, the perverted must be in the majority.

"You'd also be wise," he continued, "not to listen to every rumor that comes your way. Or at least consider the source."

There were words for sexual attractions to mannequins, amputees, getting robbed, trees, insects, the elderly, raping and being raped as well as everything that could possibly come out of a human body including mucus, vomit, blood, and breast milk. Transvestism was arousal from wearing the clothes of the opposite sex. Transvestophilia was arousal from a transvestite sexual partner. Two very specific tastes, and yet ignorance caused most of the foolish world to lump these attractions in with homosexuality.

"Do you want the money or not?" He held the bills out to her again.

"I'm holding a bag of money."

"Yes. A bag of money you stole from a criminal. I wouldn't shout it too loudly if I were you."

Sadism was arousal from inflicting pain or humiliation on others. Masochism was the desire to be beaten or bound, humiliated. His sessions with Jay were not about affection or racing toward a climax. They were about control and discipline, testing limits and practicing restraint. They had no desire to fall asleep in each other's

283

arms like a couple of pansies. They were about power, the exchange of power, and homosexuals were some of the least powerful people on the planet. Clyde found the comparison insulting.

Iris looked past his shoulder. "You're done with me, is that it?"

She glanced at the closed bedroom door and he wondered for a second if she knew, but she couldn't. It was beyond her scope of knowledge, he could tell. She would have no mental map or language to imagine that right then, behind that door, one of the world's most powerful men was bound, face down to the bed with soft cord, wearing nothing but stockings, high heels, and a blindfold. Clyde could show her. He could show her Jay's erection straining against the tight nylon fabric. He could show her his ass, red from the paddle. He could let her watch.

"So what do I do now?" Iris asked.

Clyde smiled. "Life is short. In your case, maybe shorter than most, depending on how well you can hide. I suggest you try to have a little fun. Maybe fall in love. Pretty girl such as yourself shouldn't have any trouble at all in that department." He looked at his watch. "Now, if you will excuse me, I'm afraid the rest of my day is all tied up."

Forty-eight

1985

"Why do you hate me, Lieutenant?"

Collier had just explained to Lieutenant Lucy Jiminez in Internal Affairs everything he knew.

"Just following protocol, Lucille."

"Covering your ass is more like it."

"What do you care?" Collier leaned back and put his feet on her desk. "Aren't you out of here in a couple of weeks?"

Jiminez was eight months pregnant and made no attempt to dress it down with blousy maternity clothes. "You're a real piece of work, you know that? You've been in my office more in the last year -"

"It's an excuse to see you."

"Some of these guys have worked here for twenty-plus years, and I still haven't met them. But you? It's like every other week."

"I'm in love."

"I'm a house."

"You're glowing."

"Yeah right. So explain it to me again? You say the money is unrelated to the murder?"

"Well, it remains to be seen. The finding of the money is what I'm mostly talking about."

"And your question is, was Officer Tandino…"

"He was off duty when he first found it."

"Far off duty, sounds like."

Collier shrugged. "So call the feds. I'm homicide."

"Fine. Why didn't he turn it in?" Jiminez shifted in her seat in discomfort.

"Would you, Lucy?"

"Would I what, Lieutenant? Would I turn it in?"

"Yes. Would you turn in a bag of money with no obvious criminal ties to it."

She leaned her head over the back of her chair. "My fucking back hurts. How are there not obvious criminal ties here? You're making my entire back seize up."

"Who would you turn it in to?"

"Fine. Let's talk about the girl. He admitted to beating her."

"Roughing her up."

"Aren't we splitting hairs?"

"Again, I'm homicide, not domestic disputes."

"Sounds to me like at best he's an accessory to the murder." She unwrapped one of several pieces of hard candy scattered on her desk and popped it in her mouth.

"How so?"

"He beats her - sorry - roughsher up to the point where she can't defend herself -"

"That's a philosophical argument."

"How so?"

"I lend my car to someone who runs someone down. Am I an accessory?"

"You know there's a difference. Don't play stupid with me. I'm pregnant in July, I will shoot you in the dick."

"Okay, I smoke cigarettes for forty years around my wife and she dies of lung cancer. Did I murder her?"

"A lot of people would say that you did."

"We're talking about intent."

"You don't think Tandino intended for the girl to get killed."

"I don't. I don't think he's remorseful about it, but that's not a crime. When I look at it, unless the girl comes back from the dead and files a complaint against him for roughing her up, we don't have anything on him. I don't see a reason for him to lie about it."

"You don't?"

"I mean, not with everything he's already admitted to, no. I don't. I believe him." Collier felt it in his gut that Anthony Tandino was telling the truth.

"You have anyone for the homicide?"

"I think so. Maybe."

"That was unconvincing - if you're trying to make me feel good about this -"

"I do." As oddly charming as Collier found Joe Broderer, he knew that Joe was lying and, at this point, there was only one reason to lie.

"That was a terrible, terrible attempt."

"I do. Don't worry."

"Alright go wrap this up. Your ass is officially covered." Jiminez rolled herself to standing. "Get out of here. I have to go pee for like the fifteenth time today."

———

"Collier." Collier answered his phone like he was too busy to do so.

"Hi, it's me," Joey spoke into the pay phone receiver. He'd used one of Collier's dimes.

"Hey baby, you being good?" Collier's tone caught Joey off guard; it was chipper and winking.

"I am being good." After his confrontation with Doctor Carolyn, Joey had started wondering about who had been in his apartment the night before and Collier's motives for locking him up. It occurred to him that if Collier wanted to go through his apartment, putting him in a cell overnight would give him all the time he needed.

"Where are you?"

"Downtown," Joey said without explanation. "I'm going to a movie," he added. Before dialing, Joey had decided how he planned to handle this conversation. Part of him wanted to confront Collier face to face to ask him.

I would have let you in, Joey wanted to tell him. *If you had asked, I would have let you in.* But Collier's tone was throwing Joey off and he was suddenly relieved he'd decided on calling.

"That sounds fun! Get out of the heat for a little while..." He sounds like Henry, Joey realized. Not in a way that Joey would mistake one for the other, but he sounded like Henry.

"Yep. Double feature. What are you doing?"

"Saving the world. I should probably get back to it."

"Okay, I should go too. My movie's about to start." The tone that reminded Joey of Henry, Joey realized, was the one Henry would use when he was hoping Joey wouldn't ask him why he'd come home so late the night before, or where he'd gone on his lunch break. It was the tone that made Joey realize that no matter how dissatisfied you might have been before knowing the truth, *before* was way better than it was after you knew.

"Okay buddy, have fun. Call me after the movie."

"I will." Joey almost said: Wait. He wanted to tell Collier about his conversation with Doctor Carolyn. He wanted to sit next to him at the bar and watch his exposed forearm in his rolled up shirtsleeve lift a cold bottle of beer to his lips but not drink from it. He wanted to say something that would make Collier laugh so he could see his teeth. But he didn't. Instead he hung up the pay phone inside the 17th precinct, just down the hall from Collier's office. Between the phone and Collier's office was a row of five plastic chairs against a wall where three sketchy people were sitting, waiting. What they might be waiting for was unclear. They appeared to be junkies or homeless people, not really in trouble for anything specific as much as being the people that they were. Joey pulled his hood up over his head and joined the lost souls on the chairs, twitching and stinking. He twitched with them.

Before long, the door to Collier's office opened and the man he recognized from the window in Ray's apartment walked out. It was the same man who'd broken into Joey's apartment and knocked him out, the man that Carlo the mafia guy had said was named Anthony Tandino. He looked both ways down the hall and then walked right

288

past Joey. Joey considered that this might not be what it seemed. After all, he had told Collier Anthony Tandino's name; maybe Collier was investigating him. Maybe everything was still okay between them. But Joey knew that wasn't the case. If it were, Anthony Tandino would be in custody, not walking around freely. Joey suddenly recognized the shampoo he'd smelled on Collier when they'd been in the dark room at the baths. It was Aggie's shampoo. Collier's tone was the same that Henry would use when he'd just fucked someone else.

Forty-nine

1958

Iris left the New Yorker Hotel with no idea of what she should do next. She got into the car Tolson had readied for her because it was there. She gave the driver the address of Libby's bar because she'd made a promise. Christopher had promised he would take care of everything. So had Eddie. Clyde Tolson had said it, hadn't he? Some version of it, at least. Her parents had surely made some implied promise to take care of everything. Iris looked at the bag of money in her lap, collected from homosexuals and stolen from criminals before it could be given to the police in return for protecting the homosexuals. The police, she felt sure, had also promised to take care of everything.

The equation used to measure a person's honesty was determined by subtracting the sum of lies told and promises broken from the number of promises kept, multiplied by the sum of lies believed subtracted from lies caught. It now seemed to her that it would have to be expanded to account for lies told inadvertently, lies believed at the time. Like saying you loved your husband when all you really felt was a numb kind of safety - lies told to keep you afloat.

It occurred to Iris that when people said they would take care of everything, they really meant taking care of themselves. No one, Iris realized, was going to take care of everything, ever.

She'd made a promise to Libby, and had meant it at the time. It would be seen as a lie, but Iris no longer cared. The real equation for honesty, Iris imagined, covered an entire chalkboard and was only decipherable by the nation's top mathematicians, and Iris had not gone to college. When the sedan stopped at a traffic light, Iris stepped out on her own and walked away.

———

Iris hadn't realized how many of her clothes Eddie had brought from her apartment to his until she started trying to pack them. Two drawers of his bureau were filled with garments of hers; all her dresses hung in the closet next to his dress shirts. She'd thought that what she had there would fit in the doctor's bag on top of the money, but now the bag was full and there was still so much left, strewn around her as if the room had been ransacked by pirates and it was up to her to decide if they'd left behind anything of value.

"Iris!" Eddie's bark startled her from the doorway of his bedroom. Although the money was covered, she pulled the bag shut before turning around.

"What?"

"I've been standing here saying your name."

"You have?" She'd registered a noise in the background, come to think of it, but hadn't processed it as her own name. In hindsight, his claim sounded feasible.

"Yes. I have."

Iris looked at his rumpled slacks, his slippers, the newspaper folded under his arm. It seemed odd that someone so physically close could be having such a vastly different experience of this day, an unscathed house next door to one leveled by a tornado.

"What are you doing?"

"Packing." It seemed fairly obvious to her.

"Where are you going?" Eddie sounded less curious about her destination and more surprised that she would actually go at all.

"I don't know." Iris didn't know how to explain that her destination was beside the point.

"Then don't."

The plea in Eddie's voice made Iris freeze in place. She glanced first to her left and then to her right where she spied her own suitcase in the back of Eddie's closet, behind neat rows of shoes that belonged to both of them. He'd moved her in. She lurched forward and crawled to the suitcase, pulled it out and started filling it with her things.

"Iris, stop. This is a mistake. You're in no state of mind to be on your own."

Iris no longer cared what would get left behind. She closed the suitcase and pulled it and the doctor's bag toward the exit, grabbing the paper bag off the dresser that contained Christopher's belongings.

"Wait, Iris. Just hold on." Eddie walked ahead of her through the living room and into the kitchen while she bee-lined through the small apartment for the front door. She heard him open and then close a drawer then come up behind her as she reached for the knob.

"Iris, wait. Here."

She looked back to see that Eddie was holding a ring between his thumb and index finger like it was very hot or covered with ants, his digits meeting to form a tense circle.

"It was my – It's for you. It was my grandmother's."

Iris stared at the symbol of proposal.

"You don't have to wear it, of course. Not right away. You can keep it, put it somewhere safe, as a promise I will never back down on, no matter what. And you can stay here. I'll start looking for a bigger apartment, a two-bedroom, so you can have your own room for as long as you need it. You can take as long as you'd like, and I will take care of you."

"Eddie -"

"I'm a good man, Iris. With a good job and the potential to get an even better one. I can provide for you. And when you're ready you can wear the ring. I won't push you. You can let me know when you're ready."

Iris looked up at him like she was trying to read the bottom line of an eye chart at the optometrist's.

"We shouldn't be alone, Iris. Either one of us. People go a little crazy when they're alone."

When Eddie said this, Iris realized that she did, in fact, know where she was going. She also knew that she didn't plan on going alone. "Are you saying that you love me, Eddie?"

"Love you?"

"Yes. Is that what you're saying?"

"I can love you -"

Iris stood on her tiptoes and put her mouth on his, the soft inner part of her bottom lip scraping on his light, Saturday afternoon stubble. Eddie's mouth instantly tightened into something that could be called a pucker, but was really just a startled version of the shape it had formed to say the last word of his dubious promise. Iris lowered her heels to the floor.

"That was not the kiss of a man in love."

"We could grow to love each other," he said, his voice quieter. "Love takes time to grow."

Iris took Eddie's hand in hers and studied it. It was bigger than Frankie's, softer too. Cleaner. Well manicured. It was the hand of a gentleman, she thought. "I'm not sure if that's true." Her voice was barely audible. His was a hand of a man who would keep his promise. A man who would, barring any unforeseen tragedies, provide for her for the rest of her life, meeting all of her needs. She let their intertwined hands drop to waist level before, without warning him, pulling his hand and pressing it into her crotch.

Frankie's hand knew how to curve and form to both gently and firmly meet every soft edge of her. Eddie's hand recoiled in contrast, splaying out like he was going to trace it with a crayon and draw a Thanksgiving turkey. He pulled it away and took a step back. Iris heard the ring from his other hand hit the wooden floor with an insignificant plink. He looked shattered and Iris felt powerful. "I don't know who you love, Eddie, or who you wish for. But I don't think it's me." She pressed the paper bag containing all that was left of Christopher into his chest where he instinctively grabbed it. "Goodbye, Eddie."

"Shame on you, Iris."

Iris's confident, jutting chin cocked to the side as she heard his words behind her.

"That's not love, what you're thinking about, what you just did. You want to know about love? I can tell you a story about love."

Iris didn't turn around but she also did not leave.

"The day Danny died we were marching across Germany, through mud and rain, when we found ourselves trapped by snipers.

293

We couldn't move; behind us was all open and ahead was about two hundred yards of meadow before the next patch of cover. We waited until it got dark enough and then decided to make a run for it, one at a time. We only had a small window of time when it would be dark enough to make it hard for them to see us, but light enough to see where we were going. It was a real rabbit run; stay low and weave, they told us. It quickly became obvious that this was a faulty strategy. We lost a lot of good men that night."

Christopher had never talked about any part of the war.

"What got me to the other side," he continued, "was nothing I would call luck. Luck implies some sort of good fortune, some sort of blessing from somewhere, and to think that I was given that while better men than me were not - well. I think it was just math. Some of us had to make it and some of us had to die. Truth be told, I don't remember running. I just remember being on the other side, safe watching my friends, the only people I cared about in the whole world, scared shitless and running."

Iris heard his voice break before he cleared his throat to cover his suppressed emotions.

"Our orders were clear: one at a time at haphazard intervals. When Christopher started running, it didn't look good for him. He was tall, as you know. Not as tall as me, but broad. A bullet hit the mud a foot in front of him and stopped him in his tracks, just froze him in place while we all yelled at him to move. And then, out of nowhere, Danny hit that field like a flash of lightning. He got to Christopher and grabbed his arm and pulled him. They ran together. No one will ever know for sure what that kid was thinking, but from where I was it looked a hell of a lot like Danny was doing everything he could to keep himself between Christopher and the snipers. And Danny was good at everything he tried. Danny should never have died that day. If he'd just followed orders, if he'd have gone it alone, he'd be alive today. That's what love gets you, Iris."

Iris clutched the bag.

"That's a love story."

Fifty

There were others roaming the streets, some in groups, some cozy couples, arm in arm. Some, like Eddie, were going it alone. The western hemisphere was turning away from the Earth's closest star to face the darkness of space for the night. Eddie sat down on a bench in Washington Square Park facing west, with a view between the buildings of the pink and purple sky. Christopher's funeral was in the morning, and there was a very real possibility that Eddie would be the only one there. He'd phoned Iris several times after she'd left, but she either wasn't home or she wasn't answering.

"Excuse me," a woman's voice said, "have you got a light?"

Eddie turned to see an attractive, well-dressed woman holding a cigarette. He hadn't noticed when she'd sat down next to him.

"I don't smoke."

"I don't either." The woman looked at the cigarette in her hand. "Not really. But it does seem like the sophisticated thing to do." She opened the clasp on her purse and dropped the cigarette into it. "Just as well."

The woman looked to be in her late forties. Plain, but well dressed. Eddie went back to looking at the sky.

"It's a beautiful sunset," the woman said.

Eddie nodded in agreement, even though he did not. It was not the beauty of the spectacle that he took issue with; it was the woman's casual ignorance. But he wasn't in the mood to correct her.

"I'm just visiting for the day. Shopping." The woman had no bags. "New York City has the best of everything."

"The sun is not setting," Eddie had had enough romance for one day. "The sun is just sitting there, burning. We're the ones who are moving."

"Hm," the woman cocked her head. "I suppose you're right. I never thought of it like that."

Often, Eddie could feel people bristle when he started talking about what bothered him in the world. This woman didn't seem to mind.

"I mean, I knew that, that the Earth moves, not the sun. You have to admit that 'sunset' does have a catchy ring to it."

"Shops are closed."

"I'm sorry?" the woman scooted a bit closer.

"The shops are closed." Eddie pointed to a boutique behind them. The window was dark save for two dim spotlights illuminating well-dressed mannequins, a man and a woman. "You said you're shopping, but the shops are closed."

"You're very observant." Again, the woman did not appear ruffled by Eddie's directness. "The shopping is like the smoking. It's something I say I'm doing, I suppose to justify my being here. It's my son's birthday. I'm celebrating."

As an activity, this was even further from the woman's truth than shopping.

"By sitting on a bench?"

"Exactly. By sitting on a bench and watching the sunset. I don't know why I like to come into the city to do it. Maybe it's because no one knows me here."

"Where's your son?"

"Oh, he's dead." The woman said this as a matter of fact, without a trace of sadness.

"I'm sorry."

"Harold died in Korea, six years ago. It was his choice to go. His father brought him here into the city to enlist and bought him a beer afterwards."

"I'm sure he died a hero," Eddie said.

"I don't know about that," the woman squinted into the sun that only appeared to be setting. "He stepped on something, something explosive. He wasn't always the best at looking where he was going.

Once that happens, I think it's better to die than to live in pieces in some shattered body with stumps for limbs."

"I hope you'll forgive me for saying this, but you don't look very upset."

"Don't I?" The woman turned to face Eddie. "What is it," she smiled pleasantly, "that you think 'upset' looks like?"

The look on her face, while nowhere near upset, encompassed something much closer to rage.

"I guess I say that because I know what it's like to live like that. Not first hand, of course." The woman held up her hand and wiggled her fingers to demonstrate that they were hers and moved just fine when her brain commanded it. "I was a nurse at a VA hospital across the river, before I was married. This was moons ago. I was a very young woman." She sighed. "Then again for a couple of years during the second one. What I really wanted was to go overseas, but by then Harold was ten and I'd just had Peter. So it wasn't in the cards. But I wanted to."

"I was there," Eddie said.

"You made it out in one piece," the woman said, again without any sort of opinion on the fact. "I worked a lot with the boys that didn't." She seemed to let that stand alone as an explanation for her previous opinions of living wounded.

"Tomorrow morning is my buddy's funeral. We were over there together. He did not make it back in one piece." Eddie pointed to his heart and the woman nodded like she understood. "I think I'm going to be the only one there. It doesn't seem right, that a soul could slip out of the world with so little fanfare."

"I don't know about that," the woman said. "When you consider history, the sheer number of lives that have passed through it, it's very rare for anyone to be remembered for very long at all. Being remembered for any bit of time is actually quite a success."

"I would like to be remembered."

"Would you? I'll be forgotten like that," she laughed and snapped her fingers. "I plan to outlive my husband and I've only got one son left. I've not done anything in my life that will be talked about by strangers."

"I will."

"Well, good luck," she chuckled. "I'm not sure we're meant to be remembered."

"Then why are we?"

"I'm not sure that weare. Take Harold, for instance. Who will remember him? His father tries hard to forget, it's too painful for him. He'd love to rid himself of all of it. He's not been able to though, so he and I will both remember our son until we die or our minds turn to mush. His brother Peter will also, some. But who else? Classmates, the boys he fought with who did come back? They might, maybe. But their children won't. Even Peter's children, should he have them, won't. Their dead Uncle Harold will be just a framed picture on a wall of a handsome young man in a uniform. They won't know his favorite foods or the sound of his laugh or the smell of his hair. Nor should they. They shouldn't be expected to mourn someone so far removed from them. Nobody should. Think of how heavy we'd all be. Keeping Harold, what's left of him at least, belongs to his father and me. And when his father dies, I will be the only one, and then I will be the happiest woman on the planet. Just me and my memories, as long as they last."

As if on cue, the Earth rotated just enough more to block out their view of the sun.

"Anyway," the woman put her hand on Eddie's knee, "if you do want to be remembered, become a politician. You'll have a bridge named after you and everyone will say your name when they drive over it. They might not know what it was that you actually did, but they'll know your name. What is your name?"

"It's Eddie."

"Hello Eddie, it's a pleasure to meet you." The woman offered her hand to shake. "I'm Alice."

———

298

Once the woman named Alice left, Eddie stood and looked at the well-dressed mannequins in the shop window. At least he thought they were well-dressed. Eddie didn't know much about fashion, but he knew that this shop sold expensive, high quality merchandise. The mannequins had smooth, beige skin. Their features were petite and perfect, their expressions wide-eyed and unfocused.

When Eddie had told the woman, Alice, that Christopher's death didn't seem fair, he'd been thinking about Danny's. Since Christopher had killed himself and Iris had come to his apartment, Eddie had been thinking about his nights on the top bunk as they'd crossed the Atlantic, Christopher and Danny on the bunk below. He was thinking how loud keeping quiet actually was. He'd hoped that when all the dust settled, Iris might stay. Eddie's own keeping quiet would surely make some noise of its own one day.

A man stopped next to Eddie and looked in the same store window. Eddie knew that the men in this neighborhood did what he was doing when they wanted to initiate a sexual encounter with each other. Cruising, they called it. He'd heard that they would do some version of this, pretend to be looking in the same window and then tap a foot or strike up a conversation. Eddie had never participated. He'd genuinely only been looking in the store window. He'd also been thinking how the woman mannequin was nowhere near as pretty as Danny had been.

"Do you have a light?" Eddie was asked for the second time that evening. This time, he wasn't so sure of the answer.

Danny had never once looked at him, not really.

He thought of Alice who didn't believe being remembered was a possibility, the woman who believed it was better for her son to die than to live with compromise. Eddie, Ed, decided that he did not agree with her. He would live, albeit compromised, and he would be remembered.

He turned away from the man asking for more than a light and headed down the avenue alone.

Stay low and weave. One at a time, stay low and weave.

I'm Alice, saidthe woman who'd claimed that she'd do nothing with her life to be remembered for.

His own name, Eddie, sounded like a boy's name when he'd said it to her, so while they were shaking hands, he'd corrected himself.

It's actually Ed. Ed Koch. Nice to meet you too.

Fifty-one

1985

The first part of the plan was for Joey to get lost. He layered a pair of conservative canvas colored drawstring pants and a hooded sweatshirt over his first outfit, ignoring the dull ache lingering in his head, neck, and shoulders. He packed what he needed in a small duffel bag that he'd found in a yet-to-be-unpacked box inexplicably labeled Holidays. It was warm for the sweatshirt, but it was essential to the first part of the plan for Joey to look like someone who wanted to blend in. He stepped out of his building and stood at the top of the stairs in plain view, hoping that Carlo the mafia man was successful in his part of the plan, which was to make sure that Anthony the cop thought that Joey was on his way to get the money.

Joey and Carlo had come up with this plan after Joey had called the number Carlo had asked him to memorize the day before. Carlo had told him to use the number if he wanted to talk, and so Joey talked. He hadn't planned on telling Carlo everything he told him, but once he started it all just sort of tumbled out. Joey told him about Henry and Henry's cheating and Henry's dying and having to move and seeing the man in the window below the apartment across from him who he now knew was a cop named Anthony. He told him about his drunken desire, his vow of abstinence, the certainty of disease and the desire to beat that disease at its own game. He told him about Collier and Flaars and Aggie, he told him about Collier and Aggie, he told him about Collier and Anthony. He told him about Ray.

When Joey finished telling everything, Carlo the mafia man said, *Well. You should be pretty angry.*

Who should I be angry at?

Everybody, Carlo had said after thinking for a moment. *You should be angry at everybody.*

Joey finished counting to ten Mississippi before pulling up the hood and heading left toward the avenue, thinking about anger.

One day, when Henry was asleep in his hospital bed, Joey was visited by a well-intentioned volunteer counselor. He'd poked his head into Henry's room *just to chat,* but really to educate. He talked to Joey about the Five Stages of Grief and managed to emphasize twice that he wasn't getting paid to be there, as if it was important to point out that he, too, was experiencing loss. The volunteer presented his opinion as fact, that each of the five stages was unavoidable and, ultimately, necessary for catharsis. Joey had been more than a little put off by the idea that he was not only expected to steep in each of these unpleasant phases for unspecified amounts of time, but that he was also supposed to expend considerable energy thinking about each of them in advance. The volunteer described each of the phases slowly and in depth, pausing in case Joey needed to sob, and looking disappointed that this never happened. Once the volunteer left, leaving a number to call if Joey felt the need to talk, Joey decided he was completely capable of jumping ahead to Acceptance: voilà, graduation, the final stage.

Joey approached the entrance to the 59th Street subway. It was a hub where several different lines met, providing a maze of stairs and tunnels, entrances and exits, one of which led directly into Bloomingdale's. The first part of the plan, Joey's getting lost, also depended on the ability of New Yorkers to be surrounded by hordes of people while giving and receiving total privacy. Shielded by newspapers, books, Walkman headphones, and coffee cups, the commuters were collectively alone. Joey dropped a token into the turnstile and slid through into the crowd. Despite Carlo's suggestion, Joey didn't feel angry; he'd graduated to acceptance long ago. He accepted the situation as reality, as fact. He wasn't happy about it, but neither was he actively angry.

Joey found a particularly congested platform and merged in front of a lumbering man who was easily over four hundred pounds. Confident of his shield, Joey removed the sweatshirt with the ease of a fashion model to reveal the hot pink tank top underneath. He stuffed the sweatshirt into the bag, swapping it for the wig and baseball cap he'd packed earlier. The wig had been marketed as a Beatles Wig; Joey had worn it to a costume party years ago as Dorothy Hamill. He took a pair of sunglasses from his back pocket and put them on as he pulled over to stand against the wall. He scanned the people moving past him and spotted Anthony the cop searching for him in the same crowd. As Joey waited for Anthony to pass he continued scanning the oncoming faces.

After Carlo the Mafia man had prescribed anger, he'd started talking about his nephew, the biologist, again. *I called him after we talked yesterday, so I could ask again what it was that he said about bugs. He said the biggest mistakes made in biology are 'attempts to anthropomorphize the animal and insect kingdoms.' These are his words. He says this happens all the time when causality is assigned to observed behavior, like saying that a female insect behaves 'promiscuously' by having more than one partner, or that a virus is 'aggressive' when it's just doing what it does.*

Joey had nodded. It made sense even though he didn't know what it had to do with anything.

Promiscuous means slutty, in case you don't know.

Joey did know. He didn't bring up the coincidence that he'd just been saying basically the same thing about *CATS,* that cats with people problems was a ridiculous premise for an evening of theater.

You're probably wondering what this has to do with the price of rice in China. I'm not sure myself. I guess maybe I'm trying to say we know fuck-all about why things happen. We think we know what's going on, but we don't have any fucking clue. Even the scientists.

In the crowd of commuters, after Anthony the cop passed, Joey spotted the second familiar face he'd expected to find. He watched Flaars bump into and apologize brusquely to a diminutive Asian woman carrying a thermos. Flaars looked ahead, the same pissed off expression that Anthony had worn. When he passed by, Joey followed him. Once Flaars realized he'd lost sight of Joey, he climbed one of the many sets of stairs leading to the street. On the sidewalk, Joey stopped to pull a pair of rollerskates from the duffel. He quickly swapped his sneakers for the skates as he watched Flaars survey the masses in all directions to no avail. Joey put the wig and hat back into

303

the bag and skated slowly past Flaars. He stopped at the corner as if deciding which way to go, pretending not to see Flaars spot him. The second part of the plan was for Joey to be found. He headed west leisurely, making sure to keep a pace that Flaars could follow.

Joey had told Carlo the Mafia man about the three queens at the cafe on Bleecker Street all those years ago, their hypothesis that one has met everyone of import by the age of forty. Carlo had laughed and said that sounded like the theory of a young person. *Or a dumb person.* As he skated, Joey pulled his Walkman from his bag and slipped the headphones over his ears. He pressed play and heard the funk guitar's opening chords of his favorite Donna Summer song. The Walkman reminded him of Collier's recorder, of Collier's suspicions. Joey had told Carlo that Collier thought that he knew Mindy and Ray professionally, but that he, Joey, had never been a dancer. Which was both true and not true.

As a child, in his room, Joey would play records with the door closed and really go to town. His routines ran the gamut from classical ballet to frenzied rock and roll gyrations, performances abruptly interrupted by admonishments to stop jumping on the bed or else. When he was in high school the performances matured into thoughtful and expressive pieces, yet remained unseen by any other person. He knew he wasn't great, but suspected that he was good; the raw talent was there. After moving to New York, it took Joey two years to muster up the courage to go to his first real class. He pretended to let his new friend Aggie talk him into it and acted like he was being dragged. From the get go, it was clear that Joey was in over his head. He didn't know how to follow, what to do, so he'd made jokes, mimicked the teacher, and made fun of the other students after the seventy-five minutes were over. Everyone else was so accomplished and beautiful; Joey had waited too long, had been too scared. He was all of twenty-five years old.

For a time, bars and discos provided a suitable outlet for Joey to move, to lose himself in the music. But as he got older it seemed only natural to let others take the spotlight there. They were often younger, more beautiful. Sometimes they were just crazier, or on more drugs. For whatever reason, they were more deserving. Or needier. Joey was happy to let them have it, especially after he met Henry. The times they went out together, happy and stable, Joey was completely satisfied to sway to the music in place against the wall, no movement big enough to spill a drink.

Joey reached his destination with time to spare. He skated up to the box office window at the Winter Garden Theater and asked if there were any standing room tickets available for that evening's performance. There was one left. Joey bought it, confident that Flaars was watching from the sidewalk somewhere.

The overall goal that Joey and Carlo had come up with was for Joey to be able to get some information without being followed. He had to lose his tail without tipping anyone off that he knew he was being followed. The plan required that everyone think he was exactly where they thought he was. The first part was for Joey to get lost, the second part was for him to get found. The third was for him to get followed to something where he'd be necessarily occupied for a length of time. It didn't need to be a Broadway show, but Joey thought that made sense. It didn't need to be *CATS*, but Joey thought there should be some sort of poeticism if there could be. Joey fanned his face with the ticket he'd just bought, intentionally looking past Flaars who was doing a bang-up job of hiding behind a phone booth.

The overall plan also relied on Carlo's nephew's point that 'assumed causality' was the basis for many errors. Joey suspected that Flaars would see a fag in a pink tank top on rollerskates buying a ticket to a Broadway musical and jump to obvious conclusions. The fourth part of the plan was for Joey to slip out the stage door, run an errand, and be back in time to be followed to the precinct to be locked up in protective custody by Collier for the night.

Joey had about fifteen minutes before the show started. He skated in small circles, thinking about causality. He pressed the rewind button on his Walkman to go back to the beginning of his favorite song.

The volunteer thought that death caused five stages of grief.

Doctor Carolyn thought that Ray Nunez's seizures caused the need for a medically induced coma.

Collier thought that Joey knew Ray and Mindy and that his jealousy had caused her death.

Joey thought that something about him, some deficiency, had caused Henry to be unsatisfied and become promiscuous, *that means slutty in case you didn't know.*

Maybe they were all true; maybe they were just theories.

Joey pressed the play button and looked at the faces of the tourists all around the theater, people he'd never see again. Was there any harm in showing them what he was made of? True, he'd probably look insane, but so what? Among the faces, he spotted Milt, giving him a thumbs up. He waved as he turned the volume up in his headphones.

Joey had repeatedly told Collier that he was not a dancer. While this was true in a professional sense, it was also a lie. The truth was that Joey Broderer was not a dancer. And the truth was that Joey Broderer could dance.

Fifty-two

"That's *my* name, Louise. *I'm* Detective Inspector Flaars."

Flaars was collecting his messages from the woman who worked the front desk at the precinct. She was older than God's mother and just as useful and, for some reason, she had never retired. He pointed to the one message that had been in his in-box, a thin sheet of yellow paper with his own name next to a phone number. "It'd be helpful, next time you take a message, to get the name of the person who actually called. That might make my life a little bit easier."

"Kiss my ass, Lester."

"I didn't call myself, Louise." Flaars shoved the message into his pocket as he walked toward his office. He was relieved to find it empty. His office was a small room with four desks shared by six detectives who each referred to the space as 'my office'. Their shared use of the singular possessive did not stem from a sense of proud communal ownership, but rather a petty power struggle between six downtrodden lifers who each felt equally passed over by a system that not only refused to promote them, but had started to behave as if they didn't even deserve their current positions. When more than two of the six were in the office together, they achieved privacy by ignoring each other.

Flaars didn't mind working on a Saturday. What he minded was being told he was working on a Saturday with no notice and being treated as if his questions were evidence of a crap work ethic rather than clarification.

Tomorrow? He'd asked his boss when Collier told him late last night to be in by noon.

Yeah. Tomorrow. Unless you have somewhere else to be.

What Flaars minded was not being told why they were all supposed to genuflect every time their new boss walked into the room to treat them like rent-a-cops. Threats like *If you don't like it, there's the*

307

door might sound like hyperbole, but Flaars had seen two good cops forced into early retirement since Collier came on board last November. He took his one message out of his pocket and put it on his desk as he reached for the phone.

"Flowers." Collier's voice startled him from the doorway.

"Yeah?"

"What are you doing?"

"Nothing." Flaars said it more defensively than he'd meant to, but Collier's question had sounded accusatory.

"Great," Collier said cheerfully. "Maybe nothing*is* something you could do on your own time. Maybe I could convince you to do something while you're here."

"I don't mean nothing*,"* Flaars' stomach made a high-pitched whine, the sound a question mark might make. "I just got back -"

"I thought you were going to check in with me when you got back."

"I am, I literally just got back. Literally, like one minute ago."

"Relax man," Collier smiled. "I'm just playing with you."

"I know. I'm just... playing also."

Flaars was beginning to think that Collier had been playing with him all day, giving him small jobs without the benefit of knowing how they fit into the overall investigation. It was like being handed one piece of a jigsaw puzzle without being allowed to look at the picture on the box.

"How's our boy?"

'Our boy' had become Collier's nickname for Joseph Broderer. Flaars had spent the first part of the afternoon following one set of vague instructions only to be pulled off that job when Collier decided that 'our boy' needed surveillance.

"He's fine. He's at a show."

"A show?"

"Yeah. A show." Flaars was trying not to look exasperated, but after being marooned on a waste-of-time stakeout watching for a man named Carlo of whom he'd only been a vague description, followed by two hours of watching Broderer the fruitcake roller skate around the city, he had started to feel like he was not being utilized to his full potential. "He went to a musical. I asked at the box office and I know what time it gets out. I'll get back on him when he's out."

"Nah. Don't worry about it." Collier picked some papers up from one of the other desks and looked through them. "I'll catch up with him later. Any luck on that Carlo character?"

"Old tan man with gray hair? Yeah, I saw a few. None that were carrying a body or a smoking gun."

Collier laughed. "Fair enough." He looked at his watch. "Alright, why don't you go get some dinner. I need you back here at ten -"

"Tonight?" He thought of the videos he'd rented that were due back by midnight. Now there would be a late fee.

"Yeah, tonight." Collier tossed the papers back on the desk and looked at his watch again, forehead creased in thought as he pushed his lip up under his nose and nodded to himself.

Shit. Flaars cursed himself for walking right back into the same trap. He held his breath waiting for the reprimand. The joke about returning to a forty-hour workweek that would serve as yet another insinuation that he didn't have the dedication. But none came.

"Okay. See you in a bit." Collier rapped his knuckles twice on the doorjamb as he left the office.

Flaars looked at the message from himself and picked up the phone again.

"He really went to a show?" Collier's voice startled him again from the doorway.

"Yes. He went to a show. He stood in line and bought a ticket and went into the theater on rollerskates."

"He was on rollerskates?"

"Yeah. Fucking rollerskates. The asshole danced in front a crowd of tourists, all taking pictures and shit."

Collier broke out into a smile; he looked genuinely charmed at the thought of it, which was the exact opposite of how Flaars had felt watching the spectacle in real life.

"Was he good?"

"Good?"

"Yeah," Collier smushed his lip, "is he a good dancer?"

"I don't know how to answer that question."

"Fair enough. *CATS?*"

"What?"

"The show. He went to see *CATS*, right?"

"Oh. Yeah. *CATS*. Why?"

But instead of answering, Collier started laughing. He muttered "That little shit," under his breath as he looked at his watch and walked away, once again leaving Flaars in the dark as to what that meant at all.

Flaars shook his head as he picked up the phone for the third time. One day, he thought as he dialed, maybe one day I'll get some fucking answers.

After the second ring, the line on the other end picked up. "Hello?" The voice was male, gruff.

"Hello. This is Detective Inspector Flaars -"

"Yeah, yeah. Flowers. I've been expecting your call."

"It's Flaars." Flaars was really sick of this shit. "The name is Flaars."

"Relax," the man chuckled, "I'm just fucking with you."

"Who the hell is this?"

"Well Detective, that's the thing. My name is Flaars too."

———

Fuck you fuck you fuck this shit fuck you.

Anthony stabbed the knife again and again into the couch cushions, stuffing flying everywhere. He knew the couch couldn't feel it, but it made him feel better to destroy something. If the money was not in this apartment it meant he had to wait until tonight for Plan B. Anthony hadn't been told what Plan B entailed, but if it wasn't finding the money and beating the shit out of who ever had it, Anthony was going to start shooting people, whether they meant well or not.

Anthony could tell he'd impressed the lieutenant yesterday when he'd told him about the money. He knew that even assholes who tried to act like they were above it weren't above it all; when a free pile of money is up for grabs, it changes things. The lieutenant hadn't come right out and said he'd help, but Anthony could tell he'd been hooked by the suggestion of a payday by the way the lieutenant had nodded, telling him *Okay just act normal. Go home like you normally would, go out to the bar like you normally would. Don't spend more money than you normally would.* Anthony already knew that much. Yeah, he'd bought the watch, but that was it. After he'd gotten that out of his system he knew to lay low.

Sleep at home, the lieutenant had instructed, *like normal. Say hello to your neighbors so they see you. Show up to work tomorrow at your usual time.* Lieutenant Collier obviously liked to think he was always in charge. Anthony wouldn't have been surprised if Collier had started reminding him to eat, sleep, and wipe his ass. *Drop by my office in the morning,* the lieutenant had said casually, leaning back with his hands behind his head like he was sun tanning. *I'll see what I can find out between now and then,* he'd said, like they were old friends. Like they were equals. But Anthony could tell that he had the upper hand on the higher-ranking lieutenant. That was yesterday.

This morning was different.

Sit Down. Collier pointed to the same chair that Anthony had sat in yesterday as he closed the door to his office. *You know someone named Carlo?*

No, Anthony lied without thinking.

Well he knows you. And now he knows about the money.

Fucking Carlo. Anthony had been wondering when he was going to hear from the old man again.

So let me ask you again. Do you know someone named Carlo?

What the fuck does he have to do with you?

He has to do with me because you told me that no one but you and a dead girl knew about this money. And now this guy turns up, this Carlo.

Look, Anthony had said, *I know for a fact that Carlo doesn't know shit about the money.*

How?

Because Carlo is the type who'd be direct. He'd ask me about it himself, and he didn't. So it's not an issue. Anthony knew this was true or Carlo would have told him about the money when he told him about the ledgers.

The ledgers, Carlo had told Anthony, were in a lockbox that had been cemented to the underside of a pool table in the basement. The Feds had seized the keys to the lockbox as evidence, but evidence of what they'd yet to determine; the lockbox itself remained hidden. The pool table was heavy, but Anthony had managed to push it over onto its side.

He the guy you did the favor for?

I'm telling you it's not an issue. Fuck him, okay? I don't know what you heard, but no one knows about that money except me and you and some missing faggot named Ray Nunez.

The lockbox was gunmetal grey, about two feet by one foot and about eight inches deep. Cemented to the bottom of the table as promised, solid but not unbreakable. Anthony first tried the crowbar in the traditional way on the box, but the lid was too tight to allow him to get the edge in at all. Instead, he'd used the crowbar as a tool of simple destruction. The lid of the lockbox was only about an inch and a half wide, so it was difficult to aim accurately with enough force to be effective.

So you didn't tell anyone else about it?

I swear on my mother's life.

I'm gonna ask you one more time. You didn't tell anyone else about the money? Because someone else knows.

Fuck. *Boxes. The guy with all the boxes.*

Yeah, the Lieutenant said, *Boxes. So you want to think about your story again?*

Anthony stood up and surveyed the havoc he'd wreaked. The rage was still present but retreated, coiled. The money was not there.

I didn't tell that faggot about the money, he'd told the Lieutenant. *That fucker already knew about it.*

How? How did he know about it?

How do you think he knew about it? You think the fucking cats told him? He knows from the other one.

The Lieutenant jolted forward in a way that made Anthony think he might hit him. *What did you say?*

About what. Anthony didn't know what line he'd crossed.

Cats. About the cats.

Take it easy, man. It was a joke. About those loud fucking cats of his. Someone had put the cats in Mindy's friend's apartment in a carrying case by the door, which was the main reason Anthony had been convinced that someone was coming back to the apartment, why he'd waited there all weekend. *Look, it's obvious that Boxes and Mindy's friend know each other. I didn't fucking tell him about it. He knew.*

That was when the Lieutenant's phone had rung and his mood had turned on a dime. He'd gotten all friendly, *Hey baby, you being good?* Started talking about how he was saving the world. After he hung up, the Lieutenant had sat still for a moment, then laid down the law.

If you want to get out of this without jail time, you're going to do everything I say from now on. Regardless of how he found out, Boxes knows about the money and now this Carlo knows too.

I'm telling you. He already knew. He knows where it is.

Maybe. But we'll find out my way. No more knocking people out. You're a fucking loose cannon.

In the basement, doing the favor for Carlo almost two weeks ago, Anthony had gotten three good hits and made a good dent in the lockbox when his forth swing missed it entirely and hit the floor with a loud crack. He'd felt the floorboard give way to the iron bar. It wasn't until then that he'd even noticed that the basement floor was wood, not cement. He'd pushed the pool table to the wall and rolled back the carpet to expose the cracked board and the darkness of space beneath it. He'd used the crowbar to pry the board up as well as those around it until he opened up what was a sizable hole in the earth below the

313

basement. He'd squinted into the darkness, a bulky, black shape, a smaller, lighter square on top of it. Lying on his stomach, Anthony had reached into the hole until his hands felt the dusty leather bag.

In the apartment that Anthony had just trashed, the police radio on his belt came to life, static followed by a voice mumbling his name and a code that meant he had to call the Lieutenant ASAP. It took him a minute to locate the phone under the chaos he'd created.

"Get out now," the Lieutenant said without greeting. "Our boy's on the move, probably headed there."

"I'll wait here for him then."

"Don't even fucking think about it."

Anthony hung up. Fuck it. He was tired of waiting for permission from that fucking holier-than-thou dickhead.

On his stomach in the basement, two weeks or a lifetime ago, Anthony pulled the leather bag into the light. He watched the smaller, lighter square slip off and float back into the darkness, but not before he identified it as a yellowed cocktail napkin with two words written on it: *I'm Sorry*. The words were intriguing only until the money in the doctor's bag was revealed. After that, the aged apology was left, forgotten and facedown in the dirt.

Fifty-three

Raymond Nunez was pulled into consciousness slowly and with great effort, though not of his own, a thick milkshake through a tight straw. He'd been experiencing something from his childhood so vividly; it was shocking to be pulled from the scene straight up into the sky head first and then flipped onto his back and shown to a white night sky where unrelated images flashed consecutively but with no logical order. A cartoon mouse, his mother with a man's beard, the Eiffel Tower, a shopping cart, a beetle from three different angles, a cow eating a hamburger, Jesus Christ on a cross dipped in gold.

A distant beep accompanied each image change and Ray's first coherent thought was to wonder if the beeps caused the images or the other way around. A drawing of a tornado, a football helmet, a boy with a yoyo from a bygone era, the same beetle from a fourth angle. The beeping sounded like something he'd heard before and he knew that it somehow meant that he was alive. He became aware of his hands, the weight of them by his sides, and then the firmness of the mattress under his back. He felt a cool hand gentle on his forehead.

"Ray."

The voice wasn't one he recognized.

"Can you hear me?"

Ray's attempt to answer was thwarted by his tongue, thick and uncooperative.

"Hold still. I'm going to give you some water."

He felt a plastic cup touch his lips and then the cold liquid coat the inside of his mouth, his throat, and all of his insides, bringing new life to his body from the inside out.

"Do you want some more?"

Ray felt the hand that belonged to the voice move from his forehead around to the back of his neck without ever losing contact, allowing Ray to nod ever so slightly.

"Good," the voice said. "That's good. You can hear me. Do you know where you are?"

The vivid scene from his childhood was gone, and Ray knew for sure that it was a dream. The house was wrong. The lawn was bright blue. This was reality and he remembered where he was. He became aware that the top half his bed had been raised to an incline.

"Ma - mmm, Mm," Ray struggled to get the words out.

"Shhh. Hold on." More water. "You can whisper if you need to." The voice was closer to his face. "I can hear you."

"Mmmmmatt."

"Matt?"

Ray nodded again and got more water.

"Mmatt. Dilln's. Bbbed?"

"You wish, buddy," the voice sounded smiley. "You wish you were in Matt Dillon's bed." The hand that belonged to the voice stroked Ray's hair. "I thought you might be funny."

"Yyou. Doc?" Ray's voice was more groan than whisper this time. His eyelids fluttered a bit then stayed closed.

"No. I'm not a doctor. I'm just a friend. My name is Joey."

"Youuu. Cute?"

"Me?" the voice laughed. "Yeah I'm a real knockout."

"Mmmmm... ggood."

"You're incorrigible, Mr. Nunez."

"I'm. Fliirrt."

"You are a flirt. And quite a looker yourself."

Ray shook his head. "Blnd."

The thumb of the hand rested lightly on one of Ray's eyelids. "I know. You can't see right now, that's why you need someone to tell you how good looking you are."

Ray let his head tilt to the side and the weight of it rest into the hand.

"Ray. I need you to answer some questions for me. Can you do that? I'll try to make them easy to answer. Okay?"

Ray nodded into the hand.

316

"Did Mindy take someone's money?"

"Mm. Priss."

"Who's a priss."

"Puh-riss."

"Paris?"

"Priss. Mmedicinne."

"You and Mindy are going to Paris?"

"Mm." Another nod.

"Mmedicine. Mme."

"For medicine."

"Me."

"I know."

Ray felt the cup at his lips again and drank.

"The truth, Ray, is that Mindy is in trouble."

"Mmind?" Ray tried to stand up, but the narcotics still in his system made it impossible.

"Shhh. Don't. It's okay. I'm going to help her."

Ray let his head rest into the hand again.

"The guy she stole the money from."

"Tone."

"Right. Tony. He's really upset. Do you have the money?"

Ray shook his head once. "Nono."

"You don't have it?"

"Doe. No."

"Hm. Shit. Do you know where it is?"

"Doan. Know. Don'T. Know. Fff."

"You don't know if you have it."

"Ysss." Ray had told Mindy not to take it, but Mindy said it wasn't really Tony's anyway, that he found it. He saw the cartoon mouse again.

Still, he'd told her, *don't do it.*

"Is it in your apartment?"

But she had taken it. She'd shown up with a bag of money and left it in his apartment. When he first looked at it, Ray thought that the

317

money looked so old. It didn't even look like it was real. Every once in a while in life, one might come across an old bill that was somehow still in circulation, but this many of them? He thought of taking them to the bank with a story of a dead relative's mattress, one who had not trusted banks.

"Ray. Mindy's in trouble. Could it be in your apartment?"

"Yss. Hre too."

"It could be in here?"

If they could just get the money to France, he'd thought. He knew they couldn't spend it there, but maybe they could trade it in at a French bank where they were less familiar with American money. They just had to get it to France. And they had very little time; Ray was out of the hospital at the time but he didn't know for how long that might last.

"Box," Ray said with sudden clarity.

"What kind of box?"

Ray had never mailed anything overseas and he didn't know what kind of regulations there were. Mailing a box of money seemed questionable; mailing a box of stolen money felt felonious. He needed to mail in some way that should some nosy official notice, they'd look the other way. Hopefully.

"Porn."

"The box of porn from your house?"

"Prn." Ray relaxed, confident that he'd communicated effectively. He reached up and felt for the hand that belonged to the voice. He wanted to hold it. Once he'd thought of the idea for mailing the money, Ray just needed the tools to carry it out. He had a few videotapes of his own, but not enough to hide all the bills. He figured he could find what he needed pillaging the sidewalks of the West Village, so downtown he'd gone.

"I think I know where that box is," the voice told him.

Ray squeezed the hand in reply. Let's go to Paris then,he thought.

The sidewalks of the West Village were littered with anemic estate sales of dead men, possessions too mundane to pass along but not worthless enough to throw away. Cassette tapes, albums, books, and videotapes put out for the scavenging. Ray had found enough of what he needed to do the job: hard plastic video holders, pictures of nude, erect models on the front, lurid titles on the side. He'd packed the money into them and put these on the bottom of the box. He put three layers of actual porn movies on top, in case anyone looked.

"Wrkd," The following morning, Ray woke up with a nosebleed that wouldn't stop so he took a cab down to St. Vincent's. Sometime later he'd woken up and not been able to see.

"Yep," the voice said. "It worked."

"Mmm." Ray brought the hand to his lips and rested it there.

"Ray. Do you know what month it is?"

Yes. "Lie!"

"July?"

"Lie."

"Okay. Good man. It's time to go back to sleep, okay buddy?"

"Priss."

"Yes." Ray felt cool lips on his forehead and felt safe. "We'll go to Paris." He'd done it, it all made sense. His vision was gone but Ray could see everything his future held: the Eiffel Tower, cheese and baguettes, a glass of rich red wine. French medicine that worked, a bird at a feeder. A paved highway peppered with taillights. A strong man with an ax. A cartoon mouse. A beetle on its back, his mother's shoes. A purple chain link fence.

At last, it all made sense.

Fifty-four

"How was the show?" Collier asked as he held the plastic evidence bag open for Joey's belongings.

"Fantastic." Joey knew that Flaars had already reported back to Collier where he'd spent the last couple of hours so when Collier asked how his evening was, Joey corroborated it. Joey dropped his wallet and keys into the bag as he had done the night before. Collier had said that he'd feel better if Joey spent the night in the cell again, for protection. Joey pretended to be flattered by the concern, as he'd been the night before. He held up his cigarettes and lighter. "These too?"

"In the bag, hotshot. Your lungs will appreciate a night off."

Joey dropped them in. If Collier knew that Joey had slipped out after the opening numbers and gone to question Ray, he was acting like he didn't. It didn't much matter either way. Joey had half expected Collier to find him there in Ray's room in the hospital.

"Belt and shoelaces."

"For real?"

"Real."

"You didn't need them last night. You gonna ask for my pants too?"

Collier raised his eyebrows. "Maybe tomorrow."

Joey removed his belt and went to work on his laces. The duffel bag with his skates and disguise was hidden behind a dumpster behind the Winter Garden Theater.

"The show was fantastic, huh? I thought you hated it."

"I don't know why you would think that."

"Hm. I guess you said the other day something about it not making sense."

"It's art. It doesn't have to make sense. Plus there's a giant tire on stage." Joey dropped his shoelaces and belt into the bag with the rest of his belongings and stepped into the cell.

Collier slid the gate of bars closed. "That tire is pretty cool." The lock clicked into place, insuring Joey's 'safety.' "Speaking of cats," Collier said like it was an afterthought.

"Yes."

"How did you know Ray had them?"

Joey stretched out on the jail cell cot. He was only of average height and his body took up the entire length; a taller person's feet would dangle uncomfortably off the end. "I told you already. I don't know that he did, I said I thought he might have."

"Tell me again?"

"There's one of those cat trees in his bedroom." Joey couldn't help but think that whoever chose this particular model of cot to furnish the cells must have known they were on the small side and selected them anyway as a little way to tell those yet to be convicted, 'Your punishment starts now.' Innocent until proven guilty had a long way to go.

"Hm. So where are the cats now?" Collier said. "Let me guess. You don't know."

"That's right. And why don't I know?"

"Because you never met Ray Nunez or Mindy Shorent before any of this, you've never been in his apartment, you don't know anything about anything."

"That is right again."

"Except you somehow know everything."

"So I was right? Ray did have cats?"

"The bag of dirt from the vacuuming of his apartment, the one that was inside Mindy's purse that you paid a homeless man to bring to me? The lab called me today. There's a lot to sift through in terms of trying to locate any evidence, but they said the preliminary findings are that it's mostly cat hair. Where are the cats, Joe?"

Before slipping out of the theater, Joey had watched the first couple of numbers, wanting to be confident that Flaars had left his post outside. The opening was a rousing group number describing all sorts of cats and, as Joey had remembered correctly, assigning them many human attributes along the way. From there, the actors came out into the audience, pawing and preening while intoning the definition of a made-up word and inferring an inherent, duplicitous feline nature necessitating the use of three different names. But again, they weren't really talking about cats; cats were fairly straightforward beings. They were describing people.

"The only cats I know," Joey said, "are the ones on Broadway."

Collier the Cop.

Collier the Flirt.

Collier the Crook.

"You're fucking with me. All over the place. I know it." Joey wasn't sure which Collier was speaking to him then. "I know you killed her and I'm going to prove it."

Okay, maybe he could rule out Collier the Flirt.

"I'm going to find out tonight, and tomorrow morning, you're fucked."

Joey knew then why Collier had wanted his belt and shoelaces.

"Sleep tight." And with that, all three Colliers walked away.

———

About eight minutes after Collier left, the lights in Joey's cell went out along with the lights in the hall outside the cell. This had not happened either of the previous nights. It was a holding cell, not intended for long-term accommodations, and not designed with occupant comfort in mind. Joey had been rattled by Collier's upfront accusations and had to remind himself that instilling suspicion was part of the plan. Carlo had told Anthony he had proof that Joey killed Mindy and Joey assumed this would get back to Collier. Still, he'd expected Collier to hold his cards a little closer to his vest. The outright confrontation had been unsettling. The darkness surrounding Joey was also not part of the plan. Joey sat up on the cot, as if there were anywhere to run to.

He knew that his was the last in a row of five cells, a couple of which were occupied by passed-out drunks, which put about forty feet between him and whoever had turned out the lights. Maybe it was a blown fuse and he'd soon hear an authoritative custodial voice letting him know that it was being taken care of. He heard footsteps moving cautiously toward him and suddenly felt very stupid for allowing himself to be locked in here, a sitting duck for anyone with a key. Anthony Tandino, he imagined, could easily have a key. He smelled the familiar pipe tobacco scent that hung around Flaars and breathed a sigh of relief. Plan back on track.

"Joe?" Flaars said cautiously.

"You scared the shit out of me."

"Sorry, there are cameras." Flaars slid a key into the sliding door and pushed it open. "You better be right about this."

"Okay." Joey didn't know exactly how to respond to an ultimatum that didn't involve any consequences. He felt Flaars's hand find his shoulder and then the small of his back to guide him down the dark hall to the light in the distance. Flaars opened a door that dumped both of them onto 51st Street, down the block from the precinct's main entrance. He looked both ways for someone who might be running to stop their great escape, but no one was around. The two unlikely conspirators looked at each other. Joey spoke first.

"Did you bring -"

Flaars reached into his jacked pocket and handed Joey a pack of cigarettes and a lighter.

"Thanks."

"You have proof that Collier's in with this Tandino guy?"

"Yes." Joey lit one.

"Shit," Flaars exhaled. "Alright come on, let's go. He gestured to a row of sedans parked in diagonal symmetry.

Joey stayed in place. "There's been a slight change of plans."

"No," Flaars stopped. "No way."

323

"Yes way. It's just a detour, trust me." Joey started to walk backwards, away from the direction Flaars had been told to take him. "Just go to 6A and wait there. I swear, everything will work out. Quick errand, I'll be like a half hour. Tops."

"I never should have done this," Flaars shook his head.

Joey turned to go and heard Flaars behind him.

"Shit. Stop."

The second word was barked with enough authority to make Joey look over his shoulder. Flaars was pointing a gun at him. Joey stopped but didn't go back. "I know you wish you could shoot me, but you're the by-the-book-one."

"You think that letting you outta there is by-the-book?"

"Relax. Collier only put me in there to keep me out of his way for the night. There's no record that it even happened."

"Fuck you. I could lose my pension."

"You won't. Trust me."

"I don't trust you."

"I haven't done anything wrong." Joey meant in terms of Mindy and Ray and the money. But he thought of Henry. And Milt. Brian. Tom. The others. Could he have done more? Could he do more now somehow? Was there still time for him to do something, something to help?

"What the hell are you smiling about?"

There had to be.

"Just that if you really want to kill me," Joey took a drag of his cigarette, "you're gonna have to take a number."

Fifty-five

1958

-

Jack watched the handsome man with the square chin take a seat at the other end of Libby's bar. Libby poured him what looked like a double and the man made no move for his wallet, which made Jack wonder if the man was an officer of the law. Jack could see that the man was asking Libby questions but he couldn't hear what they were. Libby had started off smiling and nodding, but had soon switched to furrowing her brow and shaking her head, all while towel drying the same glass for five minutes. The man had dark hair, cleanly parted and slicked to the side like Clark Kent, but the way he sat hunched over his drink made him look shiftier. Maybe the man had wandered in by mistake as people did from time to time, not knowing that it wasn't Their Kind of Place. He certainly looked out of place. Maybe he was a cop. Or maybe he was in there on purpose, very much in the know. *She can't tell either*, Jack thought as he watched Libby walk to the other end of the bar. She was playing it safe. Jack didn't much care for playing it safe.

"Pardon me all over the place Mr. Libby," Jack sloshed what was left of his third martini onto the bar. "Is this seat reserved for some unnamed guest of honor or may I rest my weary bones?" Jack knew he had the gift of gab. He beveled his leg and let his hip curve out, sophisticated and sultry.

"Make yourself comfortable Jack." Libby winked and smiled as she whipped the bar rag over her shoulder.

Jack lowered himself to a delicate perch on the edge of the stool and crossed his long legs while lifting his glass for a sip only to find that it was empty. "And since you offered so politely, sir, I think I will have another, thank you very much."

"Coming right up, Jack."

Jack watched Libby's eyes dart toward the front door then back to wink at Mr. Kent beside him. Jack had only ever seen Libby wink at women, and certainly never at him. Jack knew full well that Libby didn't like him, which was not his problem. He was a paying customer too. "I do declare, Monsieur Libby, you need to expand your customer base something awful." Jack gestured generally toward the smattering of other patrons, a dozen or so women talking in hushed groups. The men wouldn't show up until later. "This bunch is a collection of grade A twats to the nth degree."

The man next to Jack chuckled. Jack didn't look at him, didn't want to initiate a formal introduction, not yet. It wouldn't be proper. Jack pulled a silver cigarette case from the 1920s out of his inside jacket pocket.

"Not one iota of elegance to be found collectively among these dykes in here." The man laughed again. Jack had found an appreciative audience. "Please tell me you're opening up the downstairs bar tonight once and for all, or I fear I might pitch myself off the nearest tall building just for a change of scenery."

Libby put a fresh martini in front of him. "Give it a rest, will ya Jack? Let the man enjoy his drink. This one's on me." She walked to the other end of the bar, taking Jack's opportunity for banter with her.

Jack pulled a cigarette from the silver case. The case had recently been part of a rich woman's estate, a woman whose children felt had surrounded herself with useless baubles and knickknacks. They'd been happy to unload them all at Jack's antique shop for a fraction of what they were worth. Most people had no appreciation for finery. Jack felt around his pockets for a lighter when Mr. Kent beside him struck a Zippo and held it up to Jack's cigarette. Jack froze for a moment, knowing the light was flattering, before leaning in to the flame. He let the smoke trickle out of his mouth before inhaling it through his nose, like the French. "Why thank you." He let his eyelids close to half-mast, à la Bette Davis. "At least someone in this hole has some manners."

"My pleasure," the handsome man said as he closed and pocketed the lighter. "My name's Carlo. And you are?"

"Enchanté, Carlo. I'm Jack," Jack offered his hand, tilted at the wrist. The handsome man named Carlo took his hand and smiled like he'd never met anyone like Jack before.

"You come here often?"

"Occasionally, if I feel like slumming it." Jack was here every night. "Someone's got to liven up this wake." Jack let his hand slide out of Carlo's to find the cigarette he'd left leaning into the ashtray. He could feel himself slipping away into the alcohol, he could feel Rose coming through. He held the cigarette elegantly between the tips of two gently curled fingers in his upturned hand. He could smell the eau de parfum he'd dabbed onto his wrist before leaving his shop for the evening.

"What do you do for a living, Jack?"

"I have a shop." Jack pulled a business card from his pocket and put it on the bar. "Collectibles. It's not far from here, you should stop in sometime."

"I just might do that." Carlo leaned in to Rose. "You seem like a fella who knows what time it is; you mind doing me a favor?"

"I could be persuaded, I suppose." Jack imagined dressing for Carlo while Carlo reclined on the burgundy chaise in his boudoir. He had never let anyone see Rose, not entirely.

"I'm going to show you a couple of pictures." Carlo glanced at Libby who was still down at the other end, stepping out from behind the bar with a tray of drinks. "You let me know if you know the people in them."

"I know everybody." Jack uncrossed and re-crossed his legs, feeling the smooth stockings worn secretly underneath his slacks.

"I thought you might." Carlo took a small stack of pictures from his shirt pocket and placed them on the bar in front of Jack while glancing once more in Libby's direction.

"Don't worry," Jack pulled the candle between them closer. "I can keep a secret."

The man in the first two pictures was far away from the camera. In the third he was closer, or the photographer had zoomed in.

327

Dark hair, stocky. In the fourth picture the same man was with a young woman, his arm around her in front of a building. The next few pictures were of the young woman by herself, walking. She was carrying a make-up case in her hand; Jack recognized it because he had a similar one at home. He recognized the young woman from the other day when she'd been huddled with Libby at the bar where Jack and Carlo were now sitting. In the third picture of her alone, she was also carrying a black bag. The same bag was with her in the fourth picture and in the fifth, the final image caught on film was her stepping into a dark sedan.

"And the mystery lady lost you once she got into the car," Jack said as he slid the pictures back toward Carlo.

Carlo smiled as he picked them up. "Something like that."

"Are you a detective, Carlo? A private investigator?"

"Something like that." Carlo produced his Zippo again for Jack's new cigarette.

"And I assume you showed Libby these same photographs and she claimed ignorance?"

"Something like that. You know different, Jack?"

"Depends. What's in it for me, Carlo?" Jack transferred his cigarette into his other hand so that he could put the hand closest to Carlo gently on Carlo's knee. He watched Carlo glance down where his hand rested and smile. He felt Carlo shift on his barstool slightly and move his knee closer so that Jack's hand moved higher up on his thigh.

Carlo opened Jack's cigarette case and helped himself. He winked at Jack then leaned in slowly like he was going to kiss him, steering his lips to Jack's ear at the last second. "The first thing that's in it for you, Jack, is that I let you keep the use of your hand. The second thing I let you keep is your home. Your shop. Next I let you keep this place. I let all of you keep this place. Otherwise, I burn it down with you inside. You understand me?"

"Hey Jack." Neither Jack nor Carlo had sensed Libby's presence before she spoke. "I thought I asked you to leave this gentleman alone. He bothering you Carlo?"

328

"Not a bit, Libby. Not a bit. We're getting along very well, aren't we, Jack."

Libby nodded and furrowed her brow. She looked as if she might say something else. A waving customer pulled her attention.

Carlo continued. "I hope you understand that this is not personal, Jack. You seem like a fun guy, and I would get no pleasure from hurting you. But I would hurt you, you understand. I would hurt all of you. There's quite a bit of money at stake here. The question you need to ask yourself is who do you care more about: the people in this bar? Or the people in the photographs."

Jack lifted his cigarette to his mouth and took a drag, not noticing that it had gone out in the ashtray. "Him I don't know." He exhaled clear air. "I overheard her name a couple of times. It's a flower."

"Where. In here?"

Jack glanced at Libby before catching himself and deliberately averting his gaze.

"It's okay, Jack, I don't want to hurt her any more than I want to hurt you. You understand that you're in control here, right?"

Jack nodded.

"You seen the girl in here?"

Jack nodded again.

"You seen her talking to Libby?"

And again.

"Good boy." Carlo crushed out the cigarette he'd taken from Jack's case. "Alright. Here's what I want you to do. You do this and you can save all your friends in here."

Jack picked up his martini and finished it.

"After I leave, you tell Libby everything we talked about. Tell her I showed you the pictures, tell her you recognized the girl, but tell her you covered for her. Then tell her I believed you. Then tell her you think the girl's in trouble."

Jack nodded again.

"Don't worry, sweetheart." Carlo stood up. "This will all be behind you soon."

Fifty-six

1985

"I don't know shit about the money."

Dr. Carolyn had opened her apartment door for Joey before walking away from him to the tiled island that separated the kitchen from the living room. She hadn't invited him in, but seemed to acknowledge that she couldn't keep him out. Joey closed the door behind him as he stepped inside and leaned against it, as welcome as an in-law.

"Not to be rude, but you're interrupting my dinner." Carolyn picked up a pot from the counter by its handle. The design of the room was intended to be light and open, perfect for entertaining. She spooned what looked like plain pasta into her mouth directly from the pot, a one-dish meal. A bowlpot. "I'm guessing that's why you're here, right? Why you've been coming around, trying to get to Ray. Since you're a friend of that girl... that Mindy person." She poured the remains of a beer from a bottle into a glass and took a sip. "You want a beer?"

"No, thanks." Joey stepped further into the living room.

"Just the money, right?" She finished the rest of the beer. "Alright, let's get this over with."

"Okay. What are we getting over with?"

"This." She pointed to Joey then back to herself. "Let's get this, *us*, over with. Whatever's going on here, I want no part of it, you understand me? I don't know where the money is. I know *of* the money, I know that girl stole it from someone who's very unhappy and wants it back. That's as much as I want to know. In fact, I'd like to know less. My job is to protect my patient, and I know he doesn't have it. That's all."

"I'm not really interested in the money. But, you're right. Someone very unhappy wants it back. I'm more interested in finding out who killed Mindy."

"Who *killed* her? Jesus. I didn't know -" Carolyn expelled a long breath through puffed cheeks as she ran her fingers through her graying hair. She clasped her hands together then folded her arms across her chest. "Shit. I didn't know."

"It's been in the papers."

"I guess I haven't been paying attention." She leaned on the island like it needed to be held in place. "My God. I thought - I don't know. I thought she was being dramatic."

Joey walked over and sat on a barstool. "What do you know about a trip to Paris?"

"Uh, well," Carolyn pushed the pasta pot away from her. "I know that they, that Mindy and Ray had some ridiculous plan to go to Paris to try to get him on an experimental anti-viral called HPA-23."

"Does it work?"

"No. Not in the long run. It would be a fool's errand for someone in Ray's advanced condition. I told them, but he was pretty intent on it."

"When was this?"

"A couple of weeks ago? I'd have to check his chart to be sure. It was before he came in this last time that they were talking about it. Before he got really bad."

"So no Paris."

"No Paris. But Mindy was, well, hysterical isn't the right word. I guess in hindsight she was probably terrified. She was adamant about seeing Ray even though he was sedated, insisting that I wake him up. I was worried that whoever Mindy was afraid of might come try to find Ray. So I sedated him."

"So you believed she was in real danger? Or that she was just being dramatic."

"Hm?"

"Did you think she was being dramatic or did you think she was in real danger?"

"I didn't know. I guess both. I guess I believed both."

Joey nodded. "What about his father?"

"Ray's father? I made that up, the abuse part. I needed a believable reason to tell the staff to make sure all of his visitors went through me. The part about Ray not wanting his parents to know about his sexuality is true. But they know. They're just very religious."

"They know?"

"They know he has AIDS. I called them myself, probably three or four times. They never called me back until you left a message. Mr. Nunez apparently thought you were some sort of collection agency and he only called me back to say that they didn't have any money."

Joey nodded again.

"So. That's all I know. Sorry, kid. I don't know about the money and I don't know about any murder." She put the empty bottle in the sink and dropped the glass into the trash bin next to the kitchen island.

"That's okay. I know kind of a lot about both."

Dr. Carolyn froze in place for a second, then turned and faced Joey and folded her arms again.

"I know that you and I have both been lying to each other, which is unnecessary since we are on the same side."

"I've told you everything I know, Joey."

"No you haven't. It's okay. I probably wouldn't tell me either. I'll go first. I don't know Mindy or Ray at all. I'm the one who discovered Mindy's body. Long story. Now the cops think I had something to do with it and, more importantly, the guy who Mindy stole money from thinks I did too."

She squinted at him.

"Here's what I do know. I know that Ray hid the money that Mindy stole. Not even Mindy knew where he hid it. I know Mindy loved Ray but she was scared and was trying to hide when the guy she stole it from caught up with her. She led him to Ray's apartment, thinking the money was in there, which it was. It was in that box." Joey pointed to a cardboard box next to Carolyn's sofa. He'd noticed it when he'd walked in. "I know she loved Ray. I know that no matter how hard she got hit, she never told where Ray was."

Carolyn's jaw clenched as her eyes welled with tears.

"I know that when Anthony, that's the guy Mindy took the money from, when he left her, Mindy was alive. He was pissed that he couldn't find the money, and he was probably going to kill her because he started getting rid of the evidence. But he didn't do it."

"Stop."

Joey ignored her. "Here's what I think happened. I think that you thought Mindy was being dramatic. At first. I think Ray convinced you, begged probably, to go to his apartment and get that box. It wasn't until you got there that you realized how serious the situation was. I believe you tried to help."

As if on cue, a medium-sized gray cat came into the living room from the hall leading to the bedroom. It paused to yawn and stretch before making its way to Carolyn to rub its face against her shin.

"I believe you tried to help Mindy, but something went wrong. I believe you sedated Ray to protect him, but also to protect yourself."

"Joey, stop."

"I believe that you meant well, that you were trying to help her. And I believe there was an accident. I believe both."

"I said *stop!*" Dr. Carolyn picked up the pot she'd been eating out of and banged it against the edge of the counter before letting it fall to the floor. The gray cat leapt two feet into the air and took off down the hall. "Stop trying to make this nice. I'm a fucking doctor. You think I wouldn't know how to help a victim of assault if I came across one? You think I don't know how to call a fucking ambulance?"

Joey thought that she did know how to call an ambulance, but her wording made him unsure whether the appropriate answer would be yes or no.

"You know what I did when I saw her there, bloody and whimpering on the couch? I hit her. I slapped," her voice caught with a hiccup, "her face. I was just so outraged. So enraged that, with everything going on, that this perfectly healthy young woman would act so irresponsibly. So recklessly."

334

It occurred to Joey that the scene Carolyn was describing should make him feel something: pity, anger, sympathy. But it didn't.

"I never, never should have moved her. I reacted like she'd gotten too drunk at a college party. I remember thinking *wake up, you stupid fuck. Wake up.* I yanked her off the couch and pulled her down the hall. I was going to put her in the tub and turn the shower on cold. And then – then I fell. I fell when I was dragging her. I fell on her and she started to seize." She stepped back until she came in contact with her kitchen sink.

Joey stepped toward her. "You were trying to help."

"No. That's bullshit." Carolyn put her finger out to stop Joey from getting any closer. "No one who knows the first thing about triage would agree with that. You never move someone if you don't know the extent of their injuries. You make sure their ambulance is clear -" she suddenly gasped as if she'd been held underwater for too long. She gulped air again, and then a third time as she slid down until she was sitting on the linoleum floor. Then she was still. "You make sure their *airway* is clear and you call an ambulance."

She was silent for a long moment. When she spoke again, her voice was high-pitched and conversational. "I'm not sure what I was trying to do. I was trying to punish her, maybe. I don't know." She laughed, a strange forced laugh. "I'm so tired. All the time I'm so tired. And I'm doing everything everything everything and it isn't enough. I'm losing. It isn't enough. I'm -" She wiped her face with her hands and looked up at Joey, her voice back to normal. "I wasn't trying to kill her. But I think I tried to hurt her. You should call the police now."

Joey stared at her. He knew that if he turned her in that everything she'd accomplished in her life would be eclipsed by one word printed in the morning paper: murderer. But she was right, it was time to call the police. He left Dr. Carolyn where she was and walked to the cardboard box that Ray had packed to ship to Paris. He opened it to find a framed picture of a tanned, handsome boy in a floppy beach hat. Ray. It was a goofy picture, the kind you would take as a joke, not imagining it might be the only picture of you someone ever sees.

Beneath that were the videotapes. Joey lifted a stack of three out and opened the fourth to find a wad of bills folded and tied with a rubber band. Next to the couch was an end table with a cordless phone. Joey picked it up and took a guess by pressing speed dial and then number one, that Carolyn most often called her work. He was right.

"Hi," Joey said to the woman who answered. "There are some visitors in Ray Nunez's... no, I know visiting hours are over, but I think they're in there. One of them is named Lieutenant Collier. Could you do me a favor and go get him? It's an emergency. Thanks." While Joey waited on hold he lifted more tapes out of the box. On the bottom were two thin, black notebooks, which could only be Carlo's ledgers. Joey wondered why Ray would have packed them. Maybe just because they were in the same bag as the money, and Ray hadn't really been thinking clearly.

"Joe?" Collier's voice came through the phone.

"You're not hurting him, are you?" Joey repacked the tapes into the box.

"Of course not. I'm not an asshole."

"Well, your friend might."

"He's not."

"The money's not there. I have it."

"Joe."

"Meet me at my apartment in a half hour. Don't be late. You have my keys." Joey hung up without waiting for a response. He put the box by the front door and walked over to where Carolyn had been sitting between her sink and kitchen island. She was no longer there. He picked the pot off the floor and paper toweled up the spilt pasta. He pulled the glass she'd dropped from the trash and put it in the sink next to the pot.

"Carolyn." Joey walked down the short hall to her bedroom. She had changed clothes into matching pants and blazer, something one might wear to a business lunch, but was barefoot. She was sitting on the edge of her bed, looking at her hands.

"I killed her."

336

"It was an accident. You're in the business of helping people. And you're good at it."

"I don't think I have anything – I just don't know if I can care anymore."

Joey stayed in the doorway. "Me neither. But we both have to."

"I'm so tired."

"I know." Joey turned off her bedroom light. "Get some sleep. We need you tomorrow."

Fifty-seven

1958

Libby waited to leave for an hour after Carlo had. Jack had told her everything. She wasn't surprised that Carlo had shown Jack the same pictures of Frankie and Iris that he'd shown to her. She was surprised that Jack had covered for her, that he'd had the sense to lie and say he didn't recognize Iris. If she'd ever been presented with this scenario hypothetically, Libby would have guessed that Jack would sell her out, especially if a handsome man was involved. But he hadn't.

It was difficult to wait, even for only an hour, after Carlo had left. The pictures he'd shown her of Iris had been disturbing for several reasons. It was troubling to think that Carlo had been watching Frankie; Libby wondered how long he'd been doing so, if he'd ever noticed her following him as well. It was troubling to think that Iris had gotten further involved with Frankie and hadn't, for whatever reason, told Libby. It was troubling to think that Iris could be, as Jack said, in trouble.

As she walked, Libby scanned the sidewalks for what she needed. She found one, and another, in the dirt around planted trees that lined the sidewalk: rocks that had the approximate size and weight of baseballs, not softballs. They felt familiar in her hand.

Libby had lied the other day, about having no idea how to find Iris were she ever to disappear, that she wouldn't even know where to start. The first day she met Iris, after Iris had left her bar where she'd learned about her dead husband, Libby had unrolled the newspaper she'd twisted while telling Iris the story of Frankie and the protection money. She'd already read about the arrests from her bar that morning. They hadn't been reported the very next day, as they'd happened too late to make the morning edition. In the paper, she'd found the police blotter page. She hadn't known Iris's last name, only her dead husbands first name. She'd had no trouble locating his arrest, his full name, his place of employment, and his address. The address, she'd

338

rightly figured, was the kind to have a doorman. A doorman that would need to be distracted. In front of that address now, Libby stood in the shadows and looked at the sentry in her way. She'd once been offered sixty-five dollars a week. She'd turned it down and ended up paying much more to live a life of fear. No more. She looked at the building across the street, large, backlit windows. She wound up and pitched, one rock, then the other.

———

Iris and Frankie were too far up and away to hear the window across the street shatter; they were startled by the loud bang on the apartment door followed by two more, even harder. Bam. Bam BAM. It was not a polite, inquiring knuckled rap. It was the insistent side of someone's fist. The locked door handle jiggled but did not turn. There was a lower sound then against the door, like a kick. Frankie threw off the covers.

Iris grabbed his arm and pointed at the bedroom window that opened onto the fire escape.

"No," Frankie said to Iris as he pulled on his pants. "There's more than one of them. Get my gun." He headed down the hall turning the lights on as he did. "Stay behind me. Don't say a fucking thing."

Iris pulled on clothes of her own. 'More than one of them'could only mean that the men that Frankie worked for or with, the men he'd stolen from, had found him. She followed Frankie's instructions and got his gun from the doctor's bag before following him.

"What the fuck?" Frankie was looking though the peephole. He yanked the door open.

"Libby?" Iris said from behind Frankie while putting the gun behind her back as if there were still a chance to come up with an innocent explanation for all this. "What are you doing here?"

"You know her?" Frankie asked Iris.

"I thought you might be in trouble," Libby said as she stepped into the apartment.

The three of them stared at each other while Frankie and Libby took some time to piece together what the other's presence meant for each of them.

"Holy shit," Frankie shook his head. "I should have known. I should have fucking known."

"Frankie, wait. Libby -" Iris wanted to explain this somehow, but there wasn't a rational motivation behind her choices. "You should have waited, Libby. Why didn't you just wait?"

"Yeah?" Libby said. "What would I have gotten by waiting?"

"Who hired you," Frankie turned to Iris. "Carlo hire you?"

"Carlo?" Iris said. "Who's Carlo?"

"Don't you fucking dare -" Frankie lurched at Iris but Libby stopped him by lifting the bat she was holding up in both her hands like she was at home plate. Neither Frankie nor Iris had noticed the bat. Frankie lifted his hands in surrender.

"Iris," Libby said. "You have to decide right now what the fuck you are doing here. If you want me to help you, you need to say it right now."

Iris didn't say anything.

"Do you want my help? Or am I wasting my time here?"

"Libby," Iris said. "Just go. Please. You don't understand. It doesn't have anything to do with you."

"Oh yeah? Since when?"

"Since I don't know when. It's just different now."

"Different?"

"It's changed. Please. Just go."

Libby looked at the floor and shook her head. "No," she said. "Nothing's changed." She lowered the bat and let it gently come to rest on Frankie's collarbone.

"Libby, stop," Iris said.

"Iris," Frankie kept his hands at his sides, but rapidly curled the fingers of one hand twice, signaling Iris to hand him his gun which was

340

still behind her back. His other hand reached up to push the bat away, but Libby had anticipated this. She lifted the bat before his hand could reach it and knocked it against the side of his head by his ear, only hard enough to distract him. Frankie didn't make a sound, but Iris gasped. Before Iris knew what had even really happened, Libby had managed to change her grip on the bat in her hand again, holding it in the middle now. She swung at Frankie's head a second time and connected hard enough to drop him to his knee.

"Libby! Stop it!" Iris pulled the gun from behind her back and pointed it at Libby. "Stop it!" Her voice choked.

"You wouldn't use that." Libby took a small step backwards, which allowed Frankie to get to his feet. Blood trickled down his neck and onto his shoulder. He wiped it away like it was an annoyance before holding his hand out for the gun.

"Give it here, Iris. Let me take care of this dyke once and for all."

"Fuck you, Frankie," Libby said, her eyes darting from him to Iris and then back to him.

"Give me the fucking gun, Iris."

Frankie stepped toward Iris and reached for the gun as Libby swung the bat at his hand. They both missed.

"Stop it!" Iris had stepped back from both of them. "Both of you, stop it."

"No," Frankie said. "There's no stopping this now."

Libby shook her head in agreement. "I told you from the start that this was none of your business. But now, you have to decide, Iris."

Iris turned the gun in her hand and slowly handed the grip of it to Frankie. Libby took two steps back.

"Good girl," Frankie said. "That's my girl." He accepted the gun and lifted to aim it at Libby.

"Frankie," Iris said, "let's just go."

"Remember the other night?" Frankie kept his eyes on Libby but was talking to Iris. "Remember when I asked you what a conundrum was?"

341

"Frankie, let's go." Iris stepped back away from him.

"There was something I didn't tell you that night."

"Frankie, come on." Iris had started crying. "Let's just go."

"I knew the whole time what conundrum meant. I've just never personally faced one." Frankie turned quickly and pointed the gun at Iris's forehead and pulled the trigger.

"No!" Libby screamed.

Frankie pulled the trigger again. Then again. Nothing happened.

Iris took her other hand from behind her back and showed Frankie the bullets in it before letting them fall to the floor. The three of them looked at the gun in Frankie's limp hand, as powerless as a hex.

"Go," Libby told Iris.

Iris looked at the front door. The black doctor's bag sat beside it, waiting for someone to run.

Libby's eyes darted to the bag, then to Iris, then back to Frankie. She tightened her grip on the bat. "Take it," she jerked her head toward the bag. "This isn't about money anymore."

Fifty-eight

1985

Aggie broke down and called Joey first. Not because she felt like she was in the wrong but because she was trapped at home with Alice and going stir crazy, flipping channels on late night television. The two women occupied either end of Aggie's white leather sofa, a distance of roughly four feet and forty years between them. Alice stared at each program with the same level of interest, which was about a negative six on a scale of one to ten, her hands politely folded in her lap. Aggie snapped her fingers twice in Alice's direction. *Jesus Christ,* she thought. *This broad doesn't have any fucking clue where she is.* Aggie hoped that if she ended up like that one day, useless and vacant, that someone would be kind enough to feed her a few Quaaludes and put a pillow over her face.

She dialed Joey's number and after three rings he picked up. Except it wasn't him.

"Joe?" the man's voice said on the other end.

It confused Aggie and she answered back, "Joey?"

There was silence on the other end.

"Hello?" Aggie said.

And then the line went dead.

That was weird. Aggie dialed again. After five rings Joey's answering machine picked up. *You've reached JB; if you're calling about modeling and you have what it takes, leave your name and number. Ciao.*

That was even weirder. It was clearly Joey's voice but in some weird affected accent. Aggie got a feeling in the pit of her stomach; something felt off. Joey always made fun of people who weren't Italian from Italy who used 'ciao' as a salutation. It was possible that she'd misdialed the first time, but she didn't think she actually had. Actually, she felt pretty certain that the man who'd answered Joey's phone had been Collier. Collier who'd said he would call her and hadn't.

343

Aggie glanced at Alice again. She'd be fine by herself for an hour, right? She'd most likely just sit on the couch. She wouldn't wander out onto the balcony, would she? Was this the lack of nurturing instinct that Diane had been concerned about? Shit.

"Come on, Alice," Aggie stood up and held out her hand. "We're going for a ride."

Down on the street, Aggie stepped out into the traffic to hail a cab. She glanced back to the sidewalk to see if Alice had fallen over or gotten plucked up by a falcon. She had not. Aggie looked back into the traffic void of taxis. "Motherfuckers, come on," she said to no one in particular.

"Aunt Aggie?"

Aggie turned to see her younger nephew standing behind her. "Brian? What are you doing here?" She looked for Diane. "Is your mom here?"

"I came by myself." Brian arms were wrapped around his thin torso, an even thinner cardigan hung from his bony frame halfway to his knees.

"Alan!" Alice came up between them. "Don't you look fantastic…"

"Alice, that's Brian," Aggie practically yelled. "That's your grandson, Brian."

Alice patted Brian's hand and winked. "You're going to be just fine, Alan. Princess Marsha said so."

"She calls me that sometimes, Alan." Brian said this more to the sidewalk than anyone.

"She literally has not said one word all night, and then that." Aggie stuck her arm out into the traffic again. "Does your mother know where you are?"

"No."

Shit. "Brian, sweetheart, we have to call her. She's probably worried sick." They would call from Joey's.

"She doesn't care about me."

A cab flashed its lights and Aggie waved her arms as it pulled over. "Don't be ridiculous, of course she does. We all care about you." Aggie opened the cab's door and grabbed Brian's shoulder. "Come on, in, in." His head hit the side of the roof as she pushed him.

"Ow!"

"You'll live," Aggie grabbed Alice next. "Princess Marsha, you're in the middle. Come on. Go, go." Aggie slid in third and closed the door. "Fifty-first between First and Second," she said to the driver. "Thank you." She sat back and looked across Alice at her nephew. "Did you run away?"

"Yeah. I hate it there."

"Well. Of course you do; it's New Jersey. Is this about the fight?"

"Yeah," Brian chewed the skin around his thumb. "They don't know what to do with me because I'm bi."

"Oooh," Aggie nodded. She wasn't surprised. "So that's what the fight was about."

"My parents are fascists."

"No they're not. They're not fascists and you're not bisexual."

"Yes I am!"

"No, sweetie, trust me." Aggie reached across and patted his knee. "You're full-on homo."

———

Joey buzzed his own apartment from the stoop outside. After a moment he heard the front door click. Propping it open with Ray's box of porn, Joey pulled a six-inch length of duct tape from a roll that Carlo the ex-mafia man had stashed between the garbage cans in front of Joey's building, as they'd planned. Joey put the tape over the latch as Carlo had described to stop the door from locking behind him. In the lobby he pressed the elevator button before carrying the box, two stairs at a time up to the fifth floor. His apartment door was ajar. He rapped twice with his knuckle and pushed it open. Joey put the box down and pushed it into the foyer with his foot.

345

From the doorway, Joey could see into his darkened apartment by the light from the hall outside; it had been rendered almost unrecognizable. Clothes, books, records, everything he hadn't unpacked or dealt with was strewn around the living room. His couch and chair had been gutted so savagely that a layer of stuffing covered everything on the floor like a light, fluffy, beige snow that might fall through the smoggy skies of Los Angeles. His television was smashed in, his stereo speakers broken, the turntable in multiple pieces. It seemed to Joey that even for a thorough apartment search, this one was fairly vindictive. He pretended to be stunned by the damage while using his thumb to gently flip the switch on this lock so that this door, like the one downstairs, would not lock behind him.

"Hiya." Joey nodded to Collier. Before the front door fully closed, he saw that Anthony was standing against the wall next to the living room window as if he were deliberately staying out of view. The first step of Joey and Carlo's plan was to throw away the ugly pull down blind that he hated. Joey's neighbors in the apartment above the one directly across from him, #6A, were an elderly couple who took little convincing to believe that Carlo was a detective following up on their previous complaint of indecent exposure on Joey's part. If everything was on track, both Carlo and Flaars were up there now. Joey nodded to Anthony. "Hello again. Nice to see you."

"Fuck you."

"Sure. Or that." Joey thought the scowl on Anthony's face, the blatant hatred, seemed extreme for a mere fifty thousand dollars. Not that fifty thousand dollars wasn't a lot of money, it was.

"What's going on, Joe?" Collier asked. His hands were on his hips; fingers tented on his belt casually, but ready to spring in any direction.

"Not much." Joey walked past Collier into the kitchen. "I'm a little thirsty." He turned on the kitchen light knowing it would spill over into the living room. The few dishes and glasses that he'd unpacked onto cupboard shelves lay shattered on the tiny kitchen's tiled floor. He turned on the faucet and cupped his hand under the cool stream before bringing it to his mouth.

He heard Anthony from the other room say something that sounded like, "Come on, man, let's just do this."

Then Collier's voice, clearer: "Relax, I'll handle it."

Joey walked back into the living room empty handed. "The money's not here," Joey said to both men. He saw Collier's eyes dart to the box on the floor, then back to him.

"Do you know where it is?" Collier asked quietly.

Joey nodded.

"Are you going to tell me where it is?"

"I haven't decided." This was on purpose. Carlo was sure that if he got dicked around enough, Anthony would do something violent. He was correct. Whether he knew how quickly Anthony would do something violent had not been discussed.

Joey was looking at Collier when he saw a flurry of confusing activity in his peripheral vision that didn't make much sense at first. It seemed as though Anthony took one step out of the shadows in Joey's direction, tripped and fell face forward onto the mess he'd created and strewn around Joey's living room floor. Joey immediately identified the two sounds that had accompanied Anthony's fall as a gunshot from the window above where Carlo and Flaars were watching, and the simultaneous sound of that bullet penetrating Joey's living room window. The gun that Anthony had drawn and aimed at Joey, prompting the sniper shot from above, tumbled out of his hand as he fell and landed at Joey's feet.

"What the fuck!" Collier shouted.

Joey picked up the gun and saw that Collier had drawn his own. Not knowing that anyone was watching from above, it had taken Collier a couple of seconds longer to piece together what must have happened and he'd spent those few seconds with his back against the front door where he'd stumbled into a crouch, unable to decide where to aim: Joey, the window, Anthony, the window, Joey again.

"What are you doing, Joe, put that down. Drop it. Right now."

347

Joey stared at the weapon in the palm of his hand. "You better hurry, they'll be here in a minute."

"What are you talking about?" Collier's feet scrambled beneath him to regain their balance as he kept his gun aimed on Joey. "Drop it. Drop it!"

"The money's in the box," Joey said. "That's what you want, right?"

Collier's eyes darted to the box then back to Joey. He wiped a bead of sweat from his forehead. "Joe. Drop the gun. Put it down. I do not want to shoot you."

"It's okay," Joey told him. "You can take it. I won't tell." Joey heard a whirring sound from the hall outside his apartment that meant the building's elevator was on the move. "Take the stairs. Go up."

Collier cocked his head at Joey as his gun relaxed just a bit. "You think I'm after the money? Oh Joey, what have you -"

Collier didn't finish his sentence. Instead he jerked his aim to the left, past Joey in reaction to something, movement or sound, from the floor where Anthony had sprawled. Joey turned in time to see Collier's bullet hit Anthony between the eyes. Joey felt a searing heat tear through his shoulder. Neither this pain, nor the sight of Anthony's head snapping back, seemed as relevant as the fact that he recognized shards of the vase Aggie had given him around Anthony's body. He turned back to Collier to point this out to him and saw that Collier had fallen back against the wall and was sliding to the floor, his capable hands holding his throat as if they might be able to do something to stop the blood flowing steadily between his clutching fingers. It was only then that Joey realized that Anthony must have had another gun, and a bullet from that gun had gone through Joey's arm and into Collier's neck.

——

Alice heard the gunshots as she climbed the stairs. The hospital must be under attack, she thought. She followed the other nurse who took the stairs two at a time and seemed to know where she was going.

348

The gunshots had caused the other nurse to scream out loud and yell at Alice to stay where she was.

"Both of you," the other nurse yelled, "stay there. Stop. Stay there!"

Alice looked behind her to see Alan couched on a landing in the corner. "Aunt Aggie," he called out. "Stop!"

"Stay there, Brian! Stay there, Alice!"

Why did the other nurse think Alan's name was Brian? She would ask later; Alice knew she was needed and didn't panic as she continued to follow the other nurse into one of the hospital rooms. Once inside, the other nurse lost it completely, which was understandable considering the scene they'd walked into. Alice knew the first step of triage: ignore the dead and the living; focus on those in between. The nearest soldier writhed on the floor, blood covering his chest and neck. Alice could hear sirens in the distance, footsteps pounding in the hall, the other nurse screaming for help into the telephone.

Alice got down and pulled the soldier's head into her lap to both calm him down and try to get a better look at his wound. His eyes were wild with fear as his hands clasped at nothing like a newborn's. The sirens were getting closer, but she didn't think they'd make it in time. Alice stroked the sailor's hair as the booted feet of soldiers and medics stomped around her. Their presence seemed to agitate the young man in her lap, so she pulled him in tighter, sliding her leg under his head like a pillow. She put her mouth to the sailor's ear and began to sing as she rocked him gently. It was a song about going home, what every soldier wants the most.

One Week Later

Carlo looked straight ahead. He recognized the scent of a specific aftershave.

"I knew I'd get you in here, one way or another. What took you so long?"

"Fuck you. I come to church all the time." The voice of his old friend Del came low and whispered from his left through the latticed circle in the wall of the confessional.

"But not to confession." Carlo smiled, knowing the response.

"I don't have anything to confess."

The two old friends laughed at their old inside joke.

"No one does," Carlo said.

"I should be asking you that question: What the fuck took you so long?"

"There were some complications."

Carlo had waited a week to hand over the ledgers. He didn't want to draw attention to himself by checking with any of his resources inside the NYPD, the situation was too hot. Instead he relied on the media coverage to determine what was known and unknown. Two cops had been shot and one was dead. Internal affairs was covering its own ass; Anthony, who'd been killed, had become the scapegoat, a bad seed and a murderer of a young, innocent woman. The other two cops emerged as heroes. One was in the hospital. *The Post* had picked up the story from the most sensational angle it could find: Soap Actress In Real Life Shootout. She'd been on the front page two days in a row. Once the coverage of the incident had dwindled to a story about the actress's many new offers from Hollywood, Carlo decided it was safe to make the exchange.

"Complications?" Del shifted on the kneeler. "Are we all good? Are we in the clear?"

"Yeah, yeah. Just sit tight for a couple of minutes." Carlo wanted to cover all his bases, just in case. "This process usually takes a few minutes."

Carlo had been thinking a lot about the money that Anthony had unearthed along with Del's ledgers. Frankie had sworn up and down, that night in '58, that the bag of money had just been carried out of the building by the woman Carlo didn't know. She'd taken the stairs down, a probably arbitrary decision that had saved her life.

If you take the stairs, you'll live to be a hundred.

"If I fall over," Del shifted again, "it ain't cause I seen the face of God. It's cause my knees gave out."

"You want to know what my nephew says about the face of God?" Carlo asked.

"Which nephew?"

"Davey."

"Davey? How old is he, nine?"

"He's twenty-six. He's a biologist."

"Well. Fuck me. What does he say?"

"He said if God truly created his most beloved creation in his own image, that he could draw the face of God. So I said okay, do it. I gave him a piece of paper and he drew a carbon atom. Said that's the only thing that lives, no matter what else happens. God is a fucking atom."

Del laughed. "When did he get to be such a smart ass?"

The woman with Frankie, that Libby had lied about knowing, had taken the stairs, and it had saved her life. It was as simple as that. It was an example of the seeming arbitrariness of life, one of many that had led Carlo to search for meaning in it all. Had Carlo met that woman in the elevator that night after he'd followed Libby, he most likely would have killed her and taken the money. He might have brought her back up to her apartment. He might have taken her back in there and together they would have discovered what Carlo discovered alone.

"My nephew thinks I'm an antique," Carlo said to Del.

351

"We are antiques."

"He thinks all this," Carlo gestured to the church around them, "is an antique."

The fight between Frankie and Libby would have been fairer if Libby hadn't had a bat, or if they'd both had bats. When Carlo found them, Libby was winning. Frankie had been resourceful, making weapons and armor out of anything he could get his hands on, a bookcase, two lamps, a radio and a chair. Libby had been bloodied but Frankie had been beaten. If Carlo hadn't broken the door down when he had, Frankie would be dead.

Don't go home, Carlo had said to Libby once he'd discovered the money wasn't there. *Don't go back to the bar.*

Where the fuck, Libby had asked, *am I supposed to go?*

Carlo reached in his pocket and handed her the card the fairy in the bar had given him, the address of his collectibles shop. *Go here. He'll help you.*

"I can't say I disagree with him," Del said. "I guess I might not ever understand why you chose this."

"I might not either," Carlo said. "I suppose I like the big questions."

"Hm." Del had never really questioned anything.

Carlo had never fully agreed with the positions and policies of the church that employed him and had long ago decided that he didn't need to in order to be effective in his position. He'd never agreed completely with his employers when he was in the business of hurting people, so he didn't see why his job as a priest should be any different. His nephew implied that science was better, somehow, in its search for the answers to life's questions because science, unlike religion, relied on examining past experiments and then improving them in the aim of better results. His nephew didn't know that Carlo had for years now been conducting an experiment of his own. The experimental question might be, "What power does someone in a position to collect money wield?" Frankie had conducted the initial research and Carlo had been conducting the follow-up. The job of counting the money collected from the congregation after mass was considered tedious in Carlo's particular church, but Carlo didn't mind doing it. Several times a week he counted up everything collected and recorded it in the church's own ledgers, put it in a small manila envelope, and handed it over to his superiors. Most of it, at least. Carlo had gotten the idea from Frankie and improved upon his system so as not to get caught. He hadn't known that he'd been participating in the scientific method. Over the years, the organizations that benefitted from Carlo's skimming included, among others, Planned Parenthood, The Peace Corps, The National Organization for Women, a variety of homeless shelters, a particular puppet theater for children in the Bronx, PBS, his nephew's university, the NAACP, and several methadone clinics throughout the city. This week he had started looking into where his money could be most effective in helping with this AIDS crisis after talking to this Joey guy. He figured those guys were going to need it.

"Alright," Del stood. "That's gotta be long enough."

"We should see each other more often, my friend."

"That would be good. I'd like that."

Carlo heard the door on the other side of the confessional open and then close again as Del left with his ledgers, leaving Carlo with his big questions.

Is there a purpose?

Is there a plan?

Even the smaller questions Del had asked felt big.

Are we all good?

Are we in the clear?

Carlo was thrilled by all the questions. He loved the questions and had yet to be satisfied by any of the proposed answers. He preferred to live in the questions.

Two Weeks Later

Iris never looked back.

It was advice that Dorothy Schiff had given her long ago, back when Dorothy had still been in a position to give advice. *Never look back,* Dolly had said. So far, Iris had not, even as she prepared to celebrate this anniversary of sorts, a day of tradition that she'd created on her own.

"Oh. I'm sorry," the two young women behind the counter at Slate eyed each other nervously. "I thought we called everyone." The first step in Iris's self-created tradition was to get her hair done. It made her feel beautiful, and feeling beautiful was a big part of the day. She'd just informed the two receptionists that she had an appointment with Joey.

"Joey…" one of them started the sentence.

"…isn't with us…" the other continued.

"Anymore." Together they answered Iris's question about Joey as well as the question of why the salon needed two people to do the job of one. Iris didn't need to know the details; she could fill in the blanks herself. She'd find out where he was and send flowers. But not today.

"That's fine," Iris said to the two young women. "Whoever is available will be fine." Ten minutes later, a stylist named Reggie reclined her head and guided it under a stream of warm water. Not looking back didn't mean Iris didn't remember. It meant that she chose not to second-guess anything she'd done.

After leaving the apartment she'd shared with Christopher that night in 1958, Iris walked straight to Libby's bar. There were only a few patrons and no one questioned her as she walked down the stairs with Frankie's bag of money to the dark basement with the wooden floor. From there she'd gone to a pay phone and called Dorothy Schiff. She'd wanted to call her mother, but that was impossible. Of all the people who'd told Iris over the years that they would take care of everything, Dorothy Schiff had been the only one to follow through.

You can imagine the tremendous strain the poor girl has endured.

A few days later, Dorothy called the police on Iris's behalf. She'd learned through one of her reporters on the police blotter that someone at Iris's former address had called the operator and requested an ambulance. When the ambulance arrived, the apartment had been empty except for an unconscious man beaten more than half to death.

I can only imagine the man must be some… associate of her late husband's. Dorothy had served the detectives coffee and cake and walked them through the fabricated but most logical sequence of events starting with Christopher's arrest in a raid on a bar catering to homosexuals and ending with a man beaten half to death in Iris's apartment. *It's the only rational explanation I can wrap my mind around,* Dorothy told them, hinting that the female mind was not quite agile enough to fully comprehend the world's complexities. The implication made the detectives feel in control and at ease.

Still, they said, they'd like to talk to Iris, when she was available. They'd like to confirm her whereabouts for the night in question, in case of any confusion.

I can have her telephone you when she's feeling a little better, when she's awake. It was a few days after the discovery of Frankie's beaten body. Iris was shaky but wide awake, listening from behind a closed door in Dorothy's large apartment. *I am certain she was here, though, for an intimate dinner party.*

One of the detectives, Dorothy told Iris later, had taken a notebook out of his pocket at that point.

Let's see, it was myself, Iris, Martha Graham…

Graham? The writing detective asked.

Yes, Dorothy peeked at his notebook. *H, A, M. Graham. Fantastic dancer. Legendary.*

The detective, Dorothy reported to Iris later, looked very skeptical. *Anyone else?*

Just the four of us, I'm afraid.

Four? The detective glanced down at his jottings.

Oh! Dorothy had been enjoying playing a scatterbrained woman. *And J. Edgar Hoover.*

J. Edgar Hoover? Even from behind the door, Iris had been able to hear the disbelief in the detective's voice.

Yes, Dorothy said sweetly. *J. Edgar Hoover. I can give you a number to call to confirm with his… well, I'm not sure exactly what his job title is. But his name is Clyde Tolson. Just make sure that you let him know that it was I who gave you the number and let him know that Iris is safe here, I'm sure he'll be very concerned once he's heard what happened.*

Iris never heard from the police again.

She never saw Libby again.

An hour and a half and three glasses of Chardonnay later, Iris left the salon, eased herself into the town car, and gave the driver the address of where they were going in Brooklyn. She leaned her head back and closed her eyes, comforted by the rhythm of the wheels spinning beneath her.

In early 1959, Iris met Walt, the man who would eventually become her husband, at one of Dorothy's dinner parties. He was older than Iris by fifteen years and not very handsome.

You can pick and choose what you want from a person, Dorothy had told her. Dorothy was very candid about her own marriages and extramarital affairs when talking with Iris. She was a modern woman with money and a career of her own and saw no reason to behave as if she needed to live under a man's thumb in any way. It wasn't the first time Dorothy had given Iris that particular piece of advice, and Iris's decision to accept a dinner invitation from Walt was not the first time she'd taken it.

Several months after the night she'd left Frankie and Libby in her apartment, and several months before she met Walt, Iris found herself on the subway, bound for Brooklyn. She'd been taking one of her walks and told herself she'd not gone intentionally, but once she did, the rest of the journey became inevitable. She'd let herself in with the key she'd never returned and climbed the stairs to the second floor

356

of the house that Frankie shared with his mother. Ignoring the voices of the neighbors or cousins or aunts from the living room, she'd found Frankie in his bed, beaten and bandaged. The way he looked at her as she closed the door to his bedroom told her that not only his body had been broken. Iris had been given permission to pick and choose what she wanted from a person. She knew that Frankie loved her, in his way. Just because he'd tried to kill her didn't mean that she should have to sacrifice the good with the bad. Going there did not make her weak, she decided. It made her strong. *I'm not giving him anything; I'm taking what I need.* And this started Iris's tradition, one day a year.

Frankie's body never worked quite right again. Any question as to why the men he'd stolen from had let him live could be answered by the continued punishment that his diminished capacity provided. Still, there were times it worked better than others. Over the years, through her visits, Iris had been able to track his progress, without having to ask, by the presence then absence of a wheelchair, a walker, then a cane, then the wheelchair again. The house Frankie shared also changed; eventually the signs of his mother faded away. One year, maybe ten years ago, the whole house appeared to have been repainted inside, bright white. But Iris never saw anything to indicate the presence of another woman.

Some years Iris stayed for an hour, sometimes she stayed the night. Sometimes they made love and sometimes they just lay together. More than once Frankie had spent her whole visit crying softly into her bare shoulder. They never talked. She never asked if he knew what happened to Libby, preferring to picture her riding off into the sunset, triumphant and whole. Perhaps it was cowardly not to inquire, but Libby had told her in no uncertain terms to leave her alone, so Iris had.

The world is full of problems, everywhere you turn, Dorothy had told her. *In order to survive, one has to be able to face them and not be moved. It's just an inevitable callus.*

Iris stepped out of the town car and let herself into the house that Frankie lived in alone. The carpeting on the stairs had been redone. As she climbed them, she took her wedding ring off and put it in her purse. She didn't care if Frankie knew that she was married, she didn't really care what he thought at all. The tradition of this day, for Iris, was about imagining that the needle on the record album of life could be lifted and brought back to some earlier point and set back down. If it was like any other record album, it would surely repeat the same songs in the same order. Iris liked to imagine that it was not, that lifting the needle and pulling it back might reveal a new tune. It was from this imagined reset place that she liked, once a year, to look forward.

Diane looked at her watch, trying not to let her agitation get the best of her. The traffic into the city had been light but she'd forked over the equivalent of a mortgage payment to put the car in a lot for the day. She didn't know how anyone lived in this city, the noise, the crowds. She looked at her younger son next to her. She thought maybe he'd dressed up for the occasion but couldn't be sure. She looked at her watch again, took a breath and reminded herself that what felt like Aggie being late was really her being early.

"Where did you get those pants?" she asked Brian as she lifted her sunglasses to get a better look.

"They're my karate pants."

"You dyed your karate pants green?" She'd been so preoccupied on the drive in that she hadn't really looked at them.

"Yeah."

Well. That was money well spent. "I thought they looked familiar."

This day had been Aggie's idea and, while she wasn't sure she was ready for it, it was clear to her that it was her son's timetable they were on, not her own. She hadn't asked Peter's opinion, she'd just told him: this is what we're doing, and he didn't react. Her husband hadn't really spoken to their younger son for the past couple of weeks; he hadn't broached an apology for his initial outburst that ended so badly. Diane knew that he was embarrassed but not ready to say that he was wrong. Diane knew that her husband's stubbornness was a facet of his strength; she didn't know how to ask him to release one and retain the other. She put her hand on her son's shoulder. "You look nice."

"Diane!"

She heard Aggie's voice and turned to see her moving down Broadway in a carefree, girlish skip. She landed next to them like a paratrooper. "Hi!" Diane hugged her sister.

"Look at you!" Aggie appraised her nephew, looking him up and down. "You look fabulous. Simply. Fabulous."

Diane's eyebrows shot up behind her sunglasses. Fabulous?

"Where's Alice?" Aggie looked around.

"She's at home."

"By herself?"

"No. We hired a nurse."

Aggie beamed. "Fabulous."

"Well. It's only three days a week."

Aggie put her arm around her nephew. "Your mother needs to learn how to sell a story."

Diane was about to argue that it wasn't the mark of a bad storyteller to stick to the facts, but the joke at her expense made Brian smile in a way that seemed to surprise him. She hadn't seen her son smile like that in a long time. "Where's Joey?"

"He's coming," Aggie gestured indistinctly over her shoulder. Diane looked up the street and saw her sister's best friend making his way toward them at his own pace.

It was nothing short of a miracle, Aggie had said when she'd called Diane's house from the hospital that night to let her know that the three of them were okay, in case she was watching the news. *And you know I don't throw that word around.* Diane had not been watching the news. She'd been pacing, waiting for Brian to come home, not having imagined that he'd go off into the city alone.

"Hi," Joey said. His left arm was in a sling; he waved a bit with his right as he either smiled or squinted into the sun. Diane offered her fingers in a tight blade that Joey took. The two of them then shared an awkward afterthought of a hug.

"Hi, Joey. I'm glad to see you're alright." Diane gestured to his arm but was picturing Henry at the Christmas party, the plastic cup of wine that she'd watched them share.

"Thanks. Went straight through." Joey pointed to his shoulder where, Diane knew from Aggie's telling, the bullet had indeed gone straight through Joey and into the police detective's neck.

He's in surgery now. The doctors said that he would have died already if Alice hadn't put his head in that position; that that was the only way he'd been able to breathe. Diane had barely been able to hear her sister's description of the injuries of a man she didn't know. Aggie had glossed over the news that Brian was in the city, with her, and had been near a shootout. *Brian's fine, Diane,* Aggie had said between sniffs. Once Brian had been returned safely to Montclair, Diane was able to endure follow-up reports on the detective's progress from her sister, which usually contained some retold version of the Alice miracle. It all seemed a little overblown to Diane, it wasn't a *miracle* that a woman who'd once been a nurse would have some instincts in a crisis. But her sister saw it differently. She claimed to be in love and so Diane was now on her way to meet the man who was still in the hospital and couldn't talk.

"Joey, you remember Brian." Aggie stepped aside so Joey and Brian could be face to face.

"Hey." Joey and Brian said at the same time as they lifted their chins at each other, suddenly so macho.

"So!" Aggie put her arm through Diane's, hooking elbows. "Shall we?"

"I guess so!" Diane tried to match her sister's carefree tone. The day had been Aggie's idea and Diane was still not sure it was a good one.

What will they do? Diane had asked.

I don't know! Walk around, eat lunch, whatever people do. It's not like Joey's going to have sex with him.

Aggie! I know that.

I just think it would be good for Brian to know someone -

Right. Diane had cut her sister off. She'd be able to say it one day.

"Should we meet back up at six, Superman?" Aggie said to her friend.

Diane might be bad at telling stories, but at least she told them. What she couldn't grasp was why there was so much that people chose simply not to discuss. The bullet that they were talking about had passed through Joey's shoulder. Joey's lover had died of AIDS. The bullet had torn through Joey and entered the neck of the policeman that her sister claimed to be in love with.

"Sure. Six. Tell him I said hi."

"I will," Aggie kissed him on the lips.

The bullet, the plastic cup, the blond boy offering his body. There was a mess that Diane did not know how to begin to clean.

"Brian, here, let me give you some money," Diane reached for her purse.

"It's okay," her son said. "I have money."

"Well. I don't want Joey to have to pay for your lunch."

"Don't worry about it," Joey said.

"No, no, I can't let you do that - " Diane overlapped.

"Mom," Brian put his hand on top of hers. "I'm good. I'll be fine."

"You will be?"

"Yeah. Dad gave me thirty dollars."

And just for a moment, Diane glimpsed an alternate version of the future she feared. Her son was grown and strong and healthy. He was not alone, not by a long shot. And he was happy.

"Fabulous," Diane said, and decided she might even be close to meaning it.

———

Brian looked at his aunt's friend after she and his mom walked away. He wasn't sure what he was supposed to do. He figured his mom wanted them to talk about stuff, running away or whatever. He hoped that they wouldn't. This idea was pretty stupid; Brian didn't need to talk to some guy he didn't really even know just 'cause he was gay. It's not like he would know what it was like to be a teenager in today's world.

"Well," his aunt's friend Joey said, "this is pretty weird."

"Yeah," Brian said.

"You smoke?" His aunt's friend reached into his back pocket with his good arm, pulled out a crumpled pack and offered it to him.

"Yeah." Brian took a cigarette and then the lighter after his Aunt's friend lit his own.

"What should we do?"

Brian shrugged and took a drag of his cigarette.

"You hungry?"

"Not really."

"Me neither. We'll eat something anyway though. Later. You like thrift stores?"

"Sure." Brian wasn't expecting that. He knew there were cool places downtown; he even knew the names of some of them. "You know good ones?"

"Yup." His aunt's friend Joey touched him gently on the back and gestured with the elbow of his injured arm down the street. "It's this way." They started to walk. "Oh, by the way, if I start crying out of the blue, just ignore it. It's something I've been doing lately."

Brian didn't know what to say so he didn't say anything.

"Apparently I'm grieving," Joey said in explanation. He rolled his eyes as he said the word 'grieving'.

"About what?" Brian still didn't really know what to say but felt like he should say something.

"Dead people."

Brian went back to not saying anything.

"Anyway," his aunt's friend continued, "I believe I'm well into the Bargaining phase, which bodes well for our afternoon of shopping."

Brian could tell by the rhythm of it that it had been a joke, but he didn't totally get it. Still, it put him at ease. He figured he'd understand it more when he was a bit older. The two of them looked ahead.

"We can start at the Salvation Army," Joey said. "They love me there."

The End

Acknowledgements

My editor, Marcy Dermansky, is a true champion and a straight-shooter. If you find yourself in need of a kickass, no-holds-barred editor, or in the mood to read some really terrific books, visit www.marcydermansky.com. Her services and novels can be found there.

I had some great sets of eyes on various drafts of this, who asked probing questions and found gentle ways of pointing out where it was not making sense. I am particularly indebted to Jeff Hiller, Dave Mowers, Michael Holland, Jenna Bruce, and Anita Slivinsky. Suszy Bernat is able to see the entirety of the big picture I am aiming for, the tiny, extra space between two words, and everything in between. For better or for worse, she has always helped me find my voice.

All mistakes are mine.

Thanks for reading,

eb

Printed in Great Britain
by Amazon